HOUSE RULES

ALSO BY JODI PICOULT

Handle with Care

Change of Heart

Nineteen Minutes

The Tenth Circle

Vanishing Acts

My Sister's Keeper

Second Glance

Perfect Match

Salem Falls

Plain Truth

Keeping Faith

The Pact

Mercy

Picture Perfect

Harvesting the Heart

Songs of the Humpback Whale

HOUSE RULES

A Novel

JODI PICOULT

**Doubleday Large Print
Home Library Edition**

ATRIA BOOKS

NEW YORK LONDON TORONTO SYDNEY

ATRIA BOOKS

A Division of Simon & Schuster, Inc.
1230 Avenue of the Americas
New York, NY 10020

First Atria Books hardcover edition March 2010

ATRIA BOOKS and colophon are trademarks of
Simon & Schuster, Inc.

Manufactured in the United States of America

ISBN 978-1-61664-130-6

For Nancy Friend Stuart (1949–2008)
and David Stuart

ACKNOWLEDGMENTS

I have so many people to thank, as always:

My brilliant legal team: Jennifer Sternick and Lise Iwon; as well as Jennifer Sargent, Rory Malone, and Seth Lipschutz.

The CSIs who let me tag along: Cpl. Claire Demarais, Betty Martin, Beth Anne Zielinski, Jim Knoll, Lt. Dennis Pincince, Lt. Arthur Kershaw, Sgt. Richard Altimari, Lt. John Blessing, Detective John Grassel, Ms. Robin Smith, Dr. Thomas Gilson, Dr. Peter Gillespie, Detective Patricia Cornell—Providence Police, Ret. Trooper Robert Hathaway—Connecticut State

Police, Ret. Lt. Ed Downing—Providence Police, Amy Duhaime, and Kim Freeland.

Katherine Yanis and her son Jacob, whose generous donation to Autism Speaks UK inspired the name of my fictional Jacob.

Jim Taylor, who provided the computer lingo for Henry, and who keeps my website the best one I've ever seen for an author.

Chief Nick Giaccone, for police procedure.

Julia Cooper, for her banking expertise.

My publishing team: Carolyn Reidy, Judith Curr, Kathleen Schmidt, Mellony Torres, Sarah Branham, Laura Stern, Gary Urda, Lisa Keim, Christine Duplessis, Michael Selleck, the sales force, and everyone else who somehow keeps finding readers who haven't heard of me and bullying them into getting on the bandwagon.

My editor, Emily Bestler, who actually makes me forget that this is supposed to be work, and not fun.

My publicist, Camille McDuffie, who still gets just as excited as I do over the good press.

My agent, Laura Gross, who may lose belts and BlackBerries (and provides excellent comic relief during stressful tours) but who has never lost sight of the fact that we make a phenomenal team.

My mom. We don't get to pick our parents, but if we did, I still would have chosen her.

My dad. Because I've never thanked him formally for being so proud of me.

I spoke with numerous people who have personal experience with Asperger's syndrome: Linda Zicko and her son Rich, Laura Bagnall and her son Alex Linden, Jan McAdams and her son Matthew, Deb Smith and her son Dylan, Mike Norbury and his son Chris, Kathleen Kirby and her son David, Kelly Meeder and her sons Brett and Derek, Catherine McMaster, Charlotte Scott and her son James, Dr. Boyd Haley, Lesley Dexter and her son Ethan, Sue Gerber and her daughter Liza, Nancy Albinini and her son Alec, Stella Chin and her son Scott Leung, Michelle Snail, Katie Lescarbeau, Stephanie Loo, Gina Crane and Bill Kolar and their son Anthony, Becky Pekar, Suzanne Harlow and her son Brad.

A special thanks to Ronna Hochbein, a mighty fine author in her own right, who works with autistic kids and not only was a font of information for me regarding vaccines and autism but also arranged for multiple face-to-face interviews with children and their parents.

Thanks aren't really enough for Jess Watsky. She needs something much larger—gratitude, humility, slavish devotion. As a teen with Asperger's, she not only allowed me to pick through her life and her mind and steal specific memories and incidents for fiction; but she also read every word of this book with lightning speed, told me what made her laugh and what needed to be fixed. She's the heart of this novel; I could not have created a character like Jacob without her.

And last (but never least): to Tim, Kyle, Jake, and Sammy. If you four were all I had to call my own, I'd be the richest woman on the planet.

HOUSE RULES

CASE 1: SLEEP TIGHT

At first glance, she looked like a saint: Dorothea Puente rented out rooms to the elderly and disabled in Sacramento, California, in the 1980s. But then, her boarders started to vanish. Seven bodies were found buried in the garden, and traces of prescription sleeping pills were found in the remains, through forensic toxicology analysis. Puente was charged with killing her boarders so that she could take their pension checks and get herself plastic surgery and expensive clothing, in order to maintain her image as a doyenne of Sacramento society. She was charged with nine murders and convicted of three.

In 1998, while serving two consecutive life sentences, Puente began corresponding with a writer named Shane Bugbee and sending him recipes, which were subsequently published in a book called Cooking with a Serial Killer.

Call me crazy, but I wouldn't touch that food with a ten-foot pole.

1

Emma

Everywhere I look, there are signs of a struggle. The mail has been scattered all over the kitchen floor; the stools are overturned. The phone has been knocked off its pedestal, its battery pack hanging loose from an umbilicus of wires. There's one single faint footprint at the threshold of the living room, pointing toward the dead body of my son, Jacob.

He is sprawled like a starfish in front of the fireplace. Blood covers his temple and his hands. For a moment, I can't move, can't breathe.

Suddenly, he sits up. "Mom," Jacob says, "you're not even *trying*."

This is not real, I remind myself, and I watch him lie back down in the exact same position—on his back, his legs twisted to the left.

"Um, there was a fight," I say.

Jacob's mouth barely moves. "And . . . ?"

"You were hit in the head." I get down on my knees, like he's told me to do a hundred times, and notice the crystal clock that usually sits on the mantel now peeking out from beneath the couch. I gingerly pick it up and see blood on the corner. With my pinkie, I touch the liquid and then taste it. "Oh, Jacob, don't tell me you used up all my corn syrup again—"

"Mom! Focus!"

I sink down on the couch, cradling the clock in my hands. "Robbers came in, and you fought them off."

Jacob sits up and sighs. The food dye and corn syrup mixture has matted his dark hair; his eyes are shining, even though they won't meet mine. "Do you honestly believe I'd execute the same crime scene twice?" He unfolds a fist, and for the first time I see a tuft of corn silk hair. Jacob's father is a tow-head—or at least he *was* when he walked out on us fifteen years ago, leaving me with Jacob and Theo, his brand-new, blond baby brother.

"*Theo* killed you?"

"Seriously, Mom, a kindergartner could have solved this case," Jacob says, jumping to his feet. Fake blood drips down the side of his face, but he doesn't notice; when he is intensely focused on crime scene analysis, I think a nuclear bomb could detonate beside him and he'd never flinch. He walks toward the footprint at the edge of the carpet and points. Now, at second glance, I notice the waffle tread of the Vans skateboarding sneakers that Theo saved up to buy for months, and the latter half of the company logo—NS—burned into the rubber sole. "There was a confrontation in the kitchen," Jacob explains. "It ended with the phone being thrown in defense, and me being chased into the living room, where Theo clocked me."

At that, I have to smile a little. "Where did you hear that term?"

"*CrimeBusters*, episode forty-three."

"Well, just so you know—it means to punch someone. Not hit them with an actual clock."

Jacob blinks at me, expressionless. He lives in a literal world; it's one of the hallmarks of his diagnosis. Years ago, when we were moving to Vermont, he asked what it was like. *Lots of green*, I said, *and rolling hills.* At that, he burst into tears. *Won't they hurt us?* he said.

"But what's the motive?" I ask, and on cue, Theo thunders down the stairs.

"Where's the freak?" he yells.

"Theo, you will *not* call your brother—"

"How about I stop calling him a freak when he stops stealing things out of my room?" I have instinctively stepped between him and his brother, although Jacob is a head taller than both of us.

"I didn't steal anything from your room," Jacob says.

"Oh, really? What about my sneakers?"

"They were in the *mudroom*," Jacob qualifies.

"Retard," Theo says under his breath, and I see a flash of fire in Jacob's eyes.

"I am *not* retarded," he growls, and he lunges for his brother.

I hold him off with an outstretched arm. "Jacob," I say, "you shouldn't take anything that belongs to Theo without asking for his permission. And Theo, I don't want to hear that word come out of your mouth again, or *I'm* going to take your sneakers and throw them out with the trash. Do I make myself clear?"

"I'm outta here," Theo mutters, and he stomps toward the mudroom. A moment later I hear the door slam.

I follow Jacob into the kitchen and watch him back into a corner. *"What we got here,"* Jacob mutters, his voice a sudden drawl, *"is . . . failure to communicate."* He crouches down, hugging his knees.

When he cannot find the words for how he feels, he borrows someone else's. These come from *Cool Hand Luke;* Jacob remembers the dialogue from every movie he's ever seen.

I've met so many parents of kids who are on the low end of the autism spectrum, kids who are diametrically opposed to Jacob, with his Asperger's. They tell me I'm lucky to have a son who's so verbal, who is blisteringly intelligent, who can take apart the broken microwave and have it working again an hour later. They think there is no greater hell than having a son who is locked in his own world, unaware that there's a wider one to explore. But try having a son who is locked in his own world and still *wants* to make a connection. A son who tries to be like everyone else but truly doesn't know how.

I reach out to comfort him but stop myself—a light touch can set Jacob off. He doesn't like handshakes or pats on the back or someone ruffling his hair. "Jacob," I begin, and then I realize that he isn't sulking at all. He holds up the telephone receiver he's been hunched over, so that I can see the smudge of black on the side. "You missed a fingerprint, too," Jacob says cheerfully. "No offense, but you would make a lousy crime scene investigator." He rips a sheet of paper towel off the roll, dampens it in the sink. "Don't worry, I'll clean up all the blood."

"You never did tell me Theo's motive for killing you."

"Oh." Jacob glances over his shoulder, a wicked grin spreading across his face. "I stole his sneakers."

In my mind, Asperger's is a label to describe not the traits Jacob *has* but rather the ones he lost. It was sometime around two years old when he began to drop words, to stop making eye contact, to avoid connections with people. He couldn't hear us, or he didn't want to. One day I looked at him, lying on the floor beside a Tonka truck. He was spinning its wheels, his face only inches away, and I thought, *Where have you gone?*

I made excuses for his behavior: the reason he huddled in the bottom of the grocery cart every time we went shopping was that it was cold in the supermarket. The tags I had to cut out of his clothing were unusually scratchy. When he could not seem to connect with any children at his preschool, I organized a no-holds-barred birthday party for him, complete with water balloons and Pin the Tail on the Donkey. About a half hour into the celebration, I suddenly realized that Jacob was missing. I was six months pregnant and hysterical—other parents began to search the yard, the street, the house. I was the one who found him, sitting in the basement, repeatedly inserting and ejecting a VCR tape.

When he was diagnosed, I burst into tears. Remember, this was back in 1995; the only experience I'd had with autism was Dustin Hoffman in *Rain Man*. According to the psychiatrist we first met, Jacob suffered from an impairment in social communication and behavior, without the language deficit that was a hallmark of other forms of autism. It wasn't until years later that we even *heard* the word *Asperger's*—it just wasn't on anyone's diagnostic radar yet. But by then, I'd had Theo, and Henry—my ex—had moved out. He was a computer programmer who worked at home and couldn't stand the tantrums Jacob would throw when the slightest thing set him off: a bright light in the bathroom, the sound of the UPS truck coming down the gravel driveway, the texture of his breakfast cereal. By then, I'd completely devoted myself to Jacob's early intervention therapists—a parade of people who would come to our house intent on dragging him out of his own little world. *I want my house back*, Henry told me. *I want you back.*

But I had already noticed how, with the behavioral therapy and speech therapy, Jacob had begun to communicate again. I could see the improvement. Given that, there wasn't even a choice to make.

The night Henry left, Jacob and I sat at the kitchen table and played a game. I made a face, and he tried to guess which emotion went with it. I smiled, even though I was crying, and waited for Jacob to tell me I was happy.

Henry lives with his new family in the Silicon Valley. He works for Apple and he rarely speaks to the boys, although he sends a check faithfully every month for child support. But then again, Henry was always good with organization. And numbers. His ability to memorize a *New York Times* article and quote it verbatim—which had seemed so academically sexy when we were dating—wasn't all that different from the way Jacob could memorize the entire TV schedule by the time he was six. It wasn't until years after Henry was gone that I diagnosed him with a dash of Asperger's, too.

There's a lot of fuss about whether or not Asperger's is on the autism spectrum, but to be honest, it doesn't matter. It's a term we use to get Jacob the accommodations he needs in school, not a label to explain who he is. If you met him now, the first thing you'd notice is that he might have forgotten to change his shirt from yesterday or to brush his hair. If you talk to him, you'll have to be the one to start the conversation. He won't look you in the eye. And if you pause to speak to someone else for a brief moment, you might turn back to find that Jacob's left the room.

Saturdays, Jacob and I go food shopping.

It's part of his routine, which means we rarely stray from it. Anything new has to be introduced early on and prepared for— whether that's a dentist appointment or a vacation or a transfer student joining his math class midyear. I knew that he'd have his faux crime scene completely cleaned up before eleven o'clock, because that's when the Free Sample Lady sets up her table in the front of the Townsend Food Co-op. She recognizes Jacob by sight now and usually gives him two mini egg rolls or bruschetta rounds or whatever else she's plying that week.

Theo's not back, so I've left him a note— although he knows the schedule as well as I do. By the time I grab my coat and purse, Jacob is already sitting in the backseat. He likes it there, because he can spread out. He doesn't have a driver's license, although we argue about it regularly, since he's eighteen and was eligible to get his license two years ago. He knows all the mechanical workings of a traffic light, and could probably take one apart and put it back together, but I am not entirely convinced that in a situation where there were several other cars zooming by in different directions, he'd be able to remember whether to stop or go at any given intersection.

"What do you have left for homework?" I ask, as we pull out of the driveway.

"Stupid English."

"English isn't stupid," I say.

"Well, my English *teacher* is." He makes a face. "Mr. Franklin assigned an essay about our favorite subject, and I wanted to write about lunch, but he won't let me."

"Why not?"

"He says lunch isn't a subject."

I glance at him. "It *isn't*."

"Well," Jacob says, "it's not a predicate, either. Shouldn't he *know* that?"

I stifle a smile. Jacob's literal reading of the world can be, depending on the circumstances, either very funny or very frustrating. In the rearview mirror, I see him press his thumb against the car window. "It's too cold for fingerprints," I say offhandedly—a fact he's taught me.

"But do you know *why*?"

"Um." I look at him. "Evidence breaks down when it's below freezing?"

"Cold constricts the sweat pores," Jacob says, "so excretions are reduced, and that means matter won't stick to the surface and leave a latent print on the glass."

"That was my second guess," I joke.

I used to call him my little genius, because even when he was small he'd spew forth an explanation like that one. I remember once, when he was four, he was reading the sign for a doctor's office when the postman walked by. The guy couldn't stop staring, but then again, it's not every day you hear a preschooler pronounce the word *gastroenterology*, clear as a bell.

I pull into the parking lot. I ignore a perfectly good parking spot because it happens to be next to a shiny orange car, and Jacob doesn't like the color orange. I can feel him draw in his breath and hold it until we drive past. We get out of the car, and Jacob runs for a cart; then we walk inside.

The spot that the Free Sample Lady usually occupies is empty.

"Jacob," I say immediately, "it's not a big deal."

He looks at his watch. "It's eleven-fifteen. She comes at eleven and leaves at twelve."

"Something must have happened."

"Bunion surgery," calls an employee, who is stacking packages of carrots within earshot. "She'll be back in four weeks."

Jacob's hand begins to flap against his leg. I glance around the store, mentally calculating whether it would cause more of a scene to try to get Jacob out of here before the stimming turns into a full-blown breakdown or whether I can talk him through this. "You know how Mrs. Pinham had to leave school for three weeks when she got shingles, and she couldn't tell you beforehand? This is the same thing."

"But it's eleven-fifteen," Jacob says.

"Mrs. Pinham got better, right? And everything went back to normal."

By now, the carrot man is staring at us. And why shouldn't he? Jacob *looks* like a totally normal young man. He's clearly intelligent. But having his day disrupted probably makes him feel the same way I would if I was suddenly told to bungee off the top of the Sears Tower.

When a low growl rips through Jacob's

throat, I know we are past the point of no return. He backs away from me, into a shelf full of pickle jars and relishes. A few bottles fall to the floor, and the breaking glass sends him over the edge. Suddenly Jacob is screaming—one high, keening note that is the soundtrack of my life. He moves blindly, striking out at me when I reach for him.

It is only thirty seconds, but thirty seconds can last forever when you are the center of everyone's scrutiny; when you are wrestling your six-foot-tall son down to the linoleum floor and pinning him with your full body weight, the only kind of pressure that can soothe him. I press my lips close to his ear. *"I shot the sheriff,"* I sing. *"But I didn't shoot no deputy . . ."*

Since he was little, those Bob Marley lyrics have soothed him. There were times I played that song twenty-four hours a day just to keep him calm; even Theo knew all the verses before he was three. Sure enough, the tension seeps out of Jacob's muscles, and his arms go limp at his sides. A single tear streaks from the corner of his eye. *"I shot the sheriff,"* he whispers, *"but I swear it was in self-defense."*

I put my hands on either side of his face and force him to meet my eyes. "Okay now?"

He hesitates, as if he is taking a serious inventory. "Yes."

I sit up, inadvertently kneeling in the puddle of pickle juice. Jacob sits up, too, and hugs his knees to his chest.

A crowd has gathered around us. In addition to the carrot man, the manager of the store, several shoppers, and twin girls with matching constellations of freckles on their cheeks are all staring down at Jacob with that curious mix of horror and pity that follows us like a dog nipping at our heels. Jacob wouldn't hurt a fly, literally or figuratively— I've seen him cup his hands around a spider during a three-hour car ride so that, at our destination, he could set it free outside. But if you are a stranger and you see a tall, muscular man knocking over displays, you don't look at him and assume he's frustrated. You think he's violent.

"He's autistic," I snap. "Do you have any questions?"

I've found that anger works best. It's the electric shock they need to tear their gaze away from the train wreck. As if nothing's happened, the shoppers go back to sifting through the navel oranges and bagging their bell peppers. The two little girls dart down the dairy aisle. The carrot man and the manager do not make eye contact, and that suits me just fine. I know how to handle their morbid curiosity; it's their kindness that might break me.

Jacob shuffles along behind me as I push the cart. His hand is still twitching faintly at his side, but he's holding it together.

My biggest hope for Jacob is that moments like this won't happen.

My biggest fear: that they *will*, and I won't always be there to keep people from thinking the worst of him.

Theo

I've had to get twenty-four stitches on my face, thanks to my brother. Ten of them left a scar cutting through my left eyebrow, after the time that Jacob knocked over my high chair when I was eight months old. The other fourteen stitches were on my chin, Christmas 2003, when I got so excited about some stupid gift that I crumpled the wrapping paper, and Jacob went ballistic at the sound. The reason I'm telling you this has nothing to do with my brother, though. It's because my mother will tell you Jacob's not violent, but I am living proof that she's kidding herself.

I am supposed to make exceptions for Jacob; it's one of our unwritten house rules. So when we need to take a detour away from a detour sign (how ironic is *that*?) since it's orange and freaks Jacob out, that trumps the fact that I'm ten minutes late for school. And he *always* gets the shower first, because a hundred billion years ago when I was still a baby Jacob took the first shower, and he can't handle having his routine messed up. And when I turned fifteen and made an appointment to get my learner's permit at the DMV—an appointment that got canceled when Jacob had a melt-down over buying a pair of new sneakers—I was expected to understand that these things happen. The problem is, something happened the next three times I tried to get my mom to take me to the DMV and, finally, I just stopped asking. At this rate, I'll be riding my skateboard till I'm thirty.

Once, when Jacob and I were little, we were playing in a pond near our house with an inflatable boat. It was my job to watch Jacob, even though he was three years older than I am and has had just as many swimming lessons as I have. We overturned the boat and swam up underneath it, where the air was heavy and wet. Jacob started talking about dinosaurs, which he was into at the time, and he wouldn't shut up. Suddenly I began to panic. He was sucking up all the oxygen in that tiny space. I pushed at the boat, trying to lift it off us, but the plastic had created some kind of seal on the surface of the water—which only made me panic even more. And sure, with twenty-twenty hindsight, I know I could have swum out from underneath the boat, but at that moment it didn't occur to me. All I knew, at the time, was that I couldn't breathe. When people ask me what it's like growing up with a brother who has Asperger's, that's what I always think of, even though the answer I give out loud is that I've never known anything different.

I'm no saint. There are times I'll do things to drive Jacob crazy, because it's just so damn easy. Like when I went into his closet and mixed up all his clothes. Or when I hid the toothpaste cap so that he couldn't put it back on when he was done brushing his teeth. But then I wind up feeling bad for my mom, who usually bears the brunt of one of Jacob's meltdowns. There are times I hear her crying, when she thinks Jacob and I are asleep. That's when I remember that she didn't sign up for this kind of life, either.

So I run interference. I'm the one who physically drags Jacob away from a conversation when he's starting to freak people out by being too intense. I'm the one who tells him to stop flapping when he's nervous on the bus, because it makes him look like a total nutcase. I'm the one who goes to his classes before I go to my own, just to let the teachers know that Jacob had a rough morning because we unexpectedly ran out of soy milk. In other words, I act like the big brother, even though I'm not. And during the times when I think it's not fair, when my blood feels like lava, I step away. If my room isn't far enough, I get on my skateboard and tool somewhere—anywhere that isn't the place I am supposed to call home.

That's what I do this afternoon, after my brother decides to cast me as the perp in his fake crime scene. I'll be honest with you—it wasn't the fact that he took my sneakers without asking or even that he stole hair out of my brush (which is, frankly, *Silence of the Lambs* creepy). It was that when I saw Jacob in the kitchen with his corn-syrup blood and his fake head injury and all the evidence pointing to me, for a half a second, I thought: *I wish*.

But I'm not allowed to say my life would be easier without Jacob around. I'm not even allowed to think it. It's another one of those unwritten house rules. So I grab my coat and head south, although it is twenty degrees outside and the wind feels like knives on my face. I stop briefly at the skateboarding park, the only place in this stupid town where the cops even let you skate anymore, although it's totally useless during the winter, which is like nine months of the year in Townsend, Vermont.

It snowed last night, about two inches, but there's a guy with a snow-skate trying to Ollie off the stairs when I get there. His friend is holding a cell phone, recording the trick. I recognize them from school, but they're not in my classes. I'm sort of the antiskater personality. I take AP everything, and I have a 3.98 average. Of course, that makes me a freak to the skating crowd, just like the way I dress and the fact that I like to skate make me a freak to the honors crowd.

The kid who's skating falls down on his ass. "I'm putting that on YouTube, bro," his friend says.

I bypass the skate park and head through town, to this one street that curls like a snail. In the very center is a gingerbread house—I guess you call them Victorians. It's painted purple and there's a turret on one side. I think that's what made me stop the first time—I mean, who the hell has a *turret* on their house, besides Rapunzel? But the person who lives in that turret is a girl who's probably ten or eleven, and she has a brother who's about half her age. Their mom drives a green Toyota van, and their dad must be some kind of doctor, because twice now I've seen him come home from work wearing scrubs.

I've been going there a lot, lately. Usually I crouch down in front of the bay window that looks into the living room. I can see pretty much everything from there—the dining room table, where the kids do their homework. The kitchen, where the mom cooks dinner. Sometimes she opens the window a crack and I can almost taste what they're eating.

This afternoon, though, nobody is home. That makes me feel cocky. Even though it's broad daylight, even though there are cars going up and down the street, I walk behind the house and sit down on the swing set. I twist the chains around and then let them untangle, even though I am way too old for this kind of stuff. Then I walk up to the back porch and try the door.

It opens.

It's wrong, I know that. But all the same, I go inside.

I take off my shoes because it's the polite thing to do. I leave them on a mat in the mudroom and walk into the kitchen. There are cereal bowls in the sink. I open the fridge and look at the stacked Tupperware. There's leftover lasagna.

I take out a jar of peanut butter and sniff inside. Is it just my imagination, or does it smell better than the Jif we have at *our* house?

I stick my finger in and take a taste. Then, with my heart pounding, I carry the jar to the counter—plus another jar of Smucker's. I take two slices of bread from the loaf on the counter and rummage in the drawers till I find the silverware. I make myself a PB&J sandwich as if it's something I do in this kitchen all the time.

In the dining room, I sit down in the chair that the girl always sits in for meals. I eat my sandwich and picture my mother coming out of the kitchen, carrying a big roast turkey on a platter. "Hey, Dad," I say out loud to the empty seat on my left, pretending that I have a real father instead of just a guilty sperm donor who sends a check every month.

How's school? he would ask.

"I got a hundred on my bio test."

That's incredible. Wouldn't be surprised if you wind up in med school, like I did.

I shake my head, clearing it. Either I've imagined myself into a TV sitcom or I have some kind of Goldilocks complex.

Jacob used to read to me at night. Well, not really. He read to himself, and he wasn't reading as much as he was reciting what he'd memorized, and I just happened to be in the same general geographic location, so I couldn't help but listen. I liked it, though. When Jacob talks, his voice rolls up and down as if every sentence is a song, which sounds really strange in normal conversation but somehow works when it's a fairy tale. I remember hearing the story about Goldilocks and the Three Bears and thinking she was such a loser. If she'd played her cards right, she might have been able to stay.

Last year, when I was a freshman at the regional high school, I got to start over. There were kids from other towns who knew nothing about me. I hung out the first week with these two guys, Chad and Andrew. They were in my Methods class and seemed pretty cool, plus they lived in Swanzey instead of Townsend and had never met my brother. We laughed about the way our science teacher's pants were hemmed two inches too short and sat together in the caf at lunch. We even made plans to check out a movie if a good one was playing on the weekend. But then Jacob showed up in the caf one day because he'd finished his physics packet in some freakishly short amount of time and his teacher had dismissed him, and of course he made a beeline for me. I introduced him and said he was an upperclassman. Well, that was my first mistake—Chad and Andrew were so psyched at the thought of hanging out with an upperclassman that they started asking Jacob questions, like what grade he was in and if he was on a sports team. "Eleventh," Jacob said, and then he told them he didn't really like sports. "I like forensics," he said. "Have you ever heard of Dr. Henry Lee?" He then yapped for ten straight minutes about the Connecticut pathologist who'd worked on major cases like O. J. Simpson and Scott Peterson and Elizabeth Smart. I think he lost Chad and Andrew somewhere around the tutorial on blood spatter patterns. Needless to say, the next day when we picked lab partners in Methods, they ditched me fast.

I've finished my sandwich, so I get up from the dining room table and head upstairs. The first room at the top is the boy's, and there are dinosaur posters all over the walls. The sheets are covered with fluorescent pterodactyls, and a remote-control *T. rex* lies on its side on the floor. For a moment, I stop dead. There was a time when Jacob was as crazy about dinosaurs as he is now about forensic science. Could this little boy tell you about the therizinosaurid found in Utah, with fifteen-inch claws that look like something out of a teen slasher flick? Or that the first nearly complete dinosaur skeleton—a hadrosaur—was found in 1858 in New Jersey?

No, he's just a kid—not a kid with Asperger's. I can tell, just by looking into the windows at night and watching the family. I know, because that kitchen with its warm yellow walls is a place I want to be, not somewhere I'd run away from.

I suddenly remember something. That day when Jacob and I were playing in the pond underneath the inflatable boat, when I started to freak out because I couldn't breathe and the boat was stuck on top of us? He somehow broke the suction-cup seal of the boat on the surface of the water and wrapped his arms around my chest, holding me up high so that I could swallow huge gulps of air. He dragged me to the shore, and he sat beside me shivering until I could figure out how to speak again. It's the last time I remember Jacob watching out for *me,* instead of the other way around.

In the bedroom where I'm standing, there's a whole wall of shelves filled with electronic games. Wii and Xbox, mostly, with a few Nintendo DS tossed in for good measure. We don't have any gaming systems; we can't afford them. The crap Jacob has to take at breakfast—a whole extra meal of pills and shots and supplements—costs a fortune, and I know that my mother stays up nights sometimes doing freelance editing jobs just so that she can pay Jess, Jacob's social skills tutor.

I hear the hum of a car on the quiet street, and when I peek out the window I see it: the green van turning in to the driveway. I fly down the stairs and through the kitchen, out the back door. I dive into the bushes, where I hold my breath and watch the boy spill out of the van first, wearing hockey gear. Then his sister gets out, and finally his parents. His father grabs a bag of equipment from the hatch, and then they all disappear into the house.

I walk to the road and skate away from the gingerbread house. Underneath my coat is the Wii game I grabbed at the last minute—some Super Mario challenge. I can feel my heart pounding against it.

I can't play it. I don't even really want it. The only reason I took it is because I know they'll never even know it's missing. How *could* they, when they've got so much?

Jacob

I may be autistic, but I can't tell you what day of the week your mother's thirty-second birthday fell on. I can't do logarithms in my head. I can't look at a patch of sod and tell you it has 6,446 individual blades of grass. On the other hand, I *could* tell you anything you ever wanted to know about lightning, polymerase chain reactions, famous movie quotes, and Lower Cretaceous sauropods. I memorized the periodic table without even trying; I taught myself how to read Middle Egyptian; and I helped my calculus teacher fix his computer. I could talk forever about friction ridge detail in fingerprint analysis and whether said analysis is an art or a science. (For example, DNA of identical twins is identical; we know that based on scientific analysis. But the fingerprints of identical twins differ in their Galton details—which evidence would *you* rather have if you were a prosecutor? But I digress.)

I suppose these talents would make me a hit at a cocktail party if (a) I drank, which I don't, or (b) I had any friends to invite me to a party, cocktail or not. My mother has explained it to me this way: imagine what it's like to have someone with an intense stare come up to you and start talking about medium-velocity-impact blood spatter patterns caused by objects moving between 1.5 and 7.5 meters per second and how they differ from high-velocity-impact spatter from gunshots or explosives. Or even worse, imagine *being* the person talking, and not getting the hint when the victim of your conversation is desperately trying to escape.

I was diagnosed with Asperger's syndrome long before it became the mental health disorder du jour, overused by parents to describe their bratty kids so that people think they're supergeniuses instead of simply antisocial. To be honest, most kids in my school know what Asperger's is now, thanks to some candidate on *America's Next Top Model.* So many people have mentioned her to me that they must think we're related. As for myself, I try not to say the word out loud. *Asperger's.* I mean, doesn't it sound like a Grade Z cut of meat? Donkey on the barbecue?

I live with my mother and my brother, Theo. The fact that we emerged from the same gene pool is mind-boggling to me, because we could not be more different from each other if we actively attempted it. We look like polar opposites—his hair is fine and so blond it could pass for silver; mine is dark and gets bushy if I do not have it cut religiously every three weeks (actually, part of the reason I get it cut every three weeks is that three is a good, safe number, unlike four, for example, and the only way I can handle someone touching my hair is if I know it's coming in advance). Theo is always caught up in what other people think of him, while I already *know* what people think of me—that I'm the weird kid who stands too close and doesn't shut up. Theo listens to rap almost exclusively, which gives me a headache. He skateboards as if the wheels are attached to the bottoms of his feet, and I do mean that as a compliment, since I can barely walk and chew gum simultaneously. He puts up with a lot, I suppose. I get upset if plans don't work out or if something in my schedule changes, and sometimes I just can't control what happens. I go all Hulk—screaming, swearing, hitting things. I haven't ever hit Theo, but I've thrown things at him and have wrecked some of his things, most notably a guitar that my mother then made me pay for in increments for the next three years of my life. Theo also is the one who suffers the brunt of my honesty:

CASE IN POINT 1

Theo walks into the kitchen wearing jeans so low that his underwear is showing, an oversize sweatshirt, and some weird medal around his neck.

Theo: 'Sup?

Me: Yo, homey, maybe you didn't get the memo, but we live in suburbia, not the 'hood. Is it Tupac Appreciation Day or something?

I tell my mother we have nothing in common, but my mother insists that will change. I think she's crazy.

I don't have any friends. The bullying started in kindergarten, when I got my glasses. The teacher made a popular boy wear fake glasses so I'd have someone to connect with, but as it turned out, he didn't really want to talk about whether archaeopteryx should be categorized as a prehistoric bird or a dinosaur. Needless to say, that friendship lasted less than a day. By now, I have gotten used to kids telling me to leave, to sit somewhere else. I never get called on the weekends. I just don't get the social hints that other people do. So if I'm talking to someone in class and he says, "Man, is it one o'clock already?" I look at the clock and tell him that yes, it *is* one o'clock already, when in reality he is trying to find a polite way to get away from me. I don't understand why people never say what they mean. It's like immigrants who come to a country and learn the language but are completely baffled by idioms. (Seriously, how could anyone who isn't a native English speaker "get the picture," so to speak, and not assume it has something to do with a photo or a painting?) For me, being in social situations—whether that's school, or Thanksgiving dinner, or the line at the movies—is like moving to Lithuania when you haven't studied Lithuanian.

If someone asks me what I'm doing for the weekend, I can't respond as easily as Theo would, for example. I'll stumble over how much information is too much, and so instead of giving a blow-by-blow description of my future plans, I'll rely on someone else's words. Doing my best De Niro *Taxi Driver* impression, I'll say, *"You talkin' to me?"* Mind you, it's not just my peers that I misunderstand. Once, my health teacher had to take a phone call in the main office, and she told the class, "Don't move—don't even breathe." Normal kids ignored the statement; a few Goody Two-shoes worked quietly at their desks. And me? I sat like a statue with my lungs on fire, until I was on the verge of passing out.

I used to have a friend. Her name was Alexa, and she moved away in seventh grade. After that, I decided to treat school like an anthropological study. I tried to cultivate an interest in topics that normal kids talked about. But it was so boring:

CASE IN POINT 2

Girl: Hey, Jacob, isn't this the coolest MP3 player?
Me: It was probably made by Chinese kids.

Girl: You want a sip of my Slushee?

Me: Sharing drinks can give you mono. So can kissing.

Girl: I'm going to go sit somewhere else . . .

Can you blame me for trying to jazz up conversations with my peers a little, by talking about topics like Dr. Henry Lee's take on the Laci Peterson murder? Eventually I gave up engaging in mundane chats; following a discussion about who was going out with whom was as hard for me as cataloging the mating rituals of a nomadic tribe in Papua New Guinea. My mother says sometimes I don't even *try*. I say I try all the time, and I keep getting rejected. I'm not even sad about it, really. Why would I want to be friends with kids who are nasty to people like me, anyway?

There are some things I really can't stand.

1. The sound of paper being crumpled. I can't tell you why, but it makes me feel like someone's doing that to all my internal organs.

2. Too much noise or flashing lights.

3. Having plans change.

4. Missing *CrimeBusters,* which is on the USA Network at 4:30 every day, thanks to the wonders of syndication. Even though 1 know all 114 of the episodes by heart, watching them daily is as important to me as taking insulin would be to a diabetic. My whole day is planned around it, and if 1 can't have my fix, 1 get shaky.

5. When my mother puts my clothes away. 1 keep them in rainbow order, ROYGBIV, and the colors can't touch. She does her best, but the last time, she completely forgot about indigo.

6. If someone else takes a bite of my food, 1 have to cut off the part that his/her saliva has touched before 1 can eat any more of it.

7. Loose hair. It freaks me out, which is why mine is military short.

8. Being touched by someone 1 don't know.

9. Foods with membranes, like custards; or foods that explode in your mouth, like peas.

10. Even numbers.

11. When people call me retarded, which 1 am not.

12. The color orange. It means danger, and there's no rhyme for it in English, which makes it suspicious. (Theo wants to know why I can tolerate things that are silver, then, but I won't even rise to the argument.)

I have spent much of my eighteen years learning how to exist in a world that is occasionally orange, chaotic, and too loud. In between classes, for example, I wear headphones. I used to wear this great pair that made me look like an air traffic controller, but Theo said everyone made fun of me when they saw me in the halls, so my mother convinced me to use earbuds instead. I hardly ever go to the cafeteria, because (a) there's no one for me to sit with and (b) all those conversations crossing each other feel like knives on my skin. Instead, I hang out in the teachers' room, where if I happen to mention that Pythagoras did not really discover the Pythagorean theorem (the Babylonians used it thousands of years before Pythagoras was even a seductive gleam in his Grecian parents' eyes), they do not look at me as if I have grown a second head. If things get really bad, pressure helps—like lying under a pile of laundry or a weighted blanket (a blanket with little poly pellets inside that make it heavier)—because the deep touch sensory stimulation calms me down. One of my therapists, a Skinner aficionado, got me to relax to Bob Marley songs. When I get upset, I repeat words over and over and talk in a flat voice. I close my eyes and ask myself, *What would Dr. Henry Lee do?*

I don't get into trouble because rules are what keep me sane. Rules mean that the day is going to go exactly the way I am predicting it to be. I do what I'm told; I just wish everyone else would do it, too.

We have rules in our house:

1. Clean up your own messes.

2. Tell the truth.

3. Brush your teeth twice a day.

4. Don't be late for school.

5. Take care of your brother; he's the only one you've got.

The majority of these rules come naturally to me—well, except for brushing my teeth, which I hate doing, and taking care of Theo. Let's just say my interpretation of rule number 5 doesn't always synchronize with Theo's interpretation. Take today, for example. I included him in a starring role in my crime scene, and he got furious. He was cast as the perpetrator ... how could he not see that as the highest form of flattery?

My psychiatrist, Dr. Moon Murano, often asks me to rate anxiety-producing situations on a scale of one to ten.

CASE IN POINT 3

Me: My mom went out to the bank and said she was going to be back in fifteen minutes and when it got to seventeen minutes, I started to panic. And then when I called her, she didn't pick up on her cell, and I was sure she was lying dead in a ditch somewhere.

Dr. Moon: On a scale of one to ten, how did that make you feel?

Me: A nine.

(Note: It was really a ten, but that's an even number, and saying it out loud would make my anxiety level blow off the chart.)

> Dr. Moon: Can you think of a solution that might have worked better than calling 911?
> Me *(doing my best Cher from* Moonstruck *impression): Snap out of it!*

I rate my days, too, although I haven't told this to Dr. Moon yet. High numbers are good days; low numbers are bad days. And today is a one, between my fight with Theo and then the absence of the Free Sample Lady at the grocery store. (In my defense, I have worked out an algorithm to predict what she's going to serve, and maybe I wouldn't have been upset if it was the first Saturday of the month, when she hands out vegetarian items. But today was a *dessert* day, for God's sake.) I have been in my room since we got home. I bury myself under my covers, and put a weighted blanket on top of that. I cue "I Shot the Sheriff" on my iPod on repeat and listen to that one song until 4:30, when it is time to watch *CrimeBusters* and I have to go into the living room, where the TV is.

The episode is number 82, one of my top five ever. It involves a case where one of the CSI investigators, Rhianna, doesn't show up for work. It turns out she is taken hostage by a man racked with grief over his wife's recent death. Rhianna leaves behind clues for the rest of the team to solve, to lead them to where she is being kept.

Naturally, I figure out the conclusion long before the rest of the CSI team does.

The reason I like the episode so much is that they actually got something wrong. Rhianna gets dragged to a diner by her kidnapper and leaves a coupon for her favorite clothing store underneath her finished plate. Her colleagues find it, and need to prove it's actually hers. They process it for prints, using a small-particle reagent followed by ninhydrin, when in reality, you're supposed to use ninhydrin first. It reacts to the amino acid and then is followed by the small-particle reagent, which reacts with fats. If you used the small-particle reagent first, like they did in the episode, it would ruin the porous surface for the ninhydrin procedure. When I spotted the error, I wrote to the producers of *Crime-Busters.* They sent me back a letter and an officially licensed T-shirt. The T-shirt doesn't fit me anymore, but I still keep it in my drawer.

After watching the episode, my day definitely improves from a one to a three.

"Hey," my mother says, poking her head into the living room. "How are you doing?"

"Okay," I reply.

She sits down beside me on the couch. Our legs are touching. She is the only person I can stand having close to me. If it were anyone else, I would have moved away a few inches by now. "So, Jacob," she says, "I just want to point out that you did in fact survive the day without the free food sample."

It's times like this I am glad I don't look people in the eye. If I did, surely they would die on the spot from the contempt shooting out of mine. Of *course* I survived. But at what cost?

"Teachable moment," my mother explains, and she pats my hand. "I'm just saying."

"Frankly my dear," I murmur, *"I don't give a damn."*

My mother sighs. "Dinner at six, Rhett," she says, even though it's always at six, and even though my name is Jacob.

At different times, the media have posthumously diagnosed certain famous people with Asperger's. Here is just a sampling:

1. Wolfgang Amadeus Mozart

2. Albert Einstein

3. Andy Warhol

4. Jane Austen

5. Thomas Jefferson

I am 99 percent sure not a single one of them had a meltdown in a grocery store and wound up breaking a whole shelf of relish and pickle jars.

Dinner proves to be a painful affair. My mother seems driven to start a conversation, although neither Theo nor I is inclined to hold up the other end of it. She has just gotten another packet of letters from the *Burlington Free Press,* and sometimes she reads them out loud at dinner and we make up politically incorrect responses that my mother would never in a million years write in her advice column.

CASE IN POINT 4

Dear Auntie Em,
My mother-in-law insists on cooking roast beef every time my husband and I

come to visit, even though she knows that I am a lifelong vegetarian. What should I do next time it happens?

Steamed in South Royalton

Dear Steamed,
Turnip your nose at her and walk away.

Sometimes the questions she gets are really sad, like the woman whose husband had left her and who didn't know how to tell her kids. Or the mom dying of breast cancer who wrote a letter for her baby daughter to read when she grew up, about how she wished she could have been there for her daughter's high school graduation, her engagement, her first child. Mostly, though, the questions come from a bunch of idiots who made bad choices. *How do I get my husband back, now that I realize I shouldn't have cheated on him?* Try being faithful, lady. *What's the best way to win back a friend you've hurt with a nasty remark?* Don't say it in the first place. I swear, sometimes I can't believe my mother gets *paid* to state the obvious.

Tonight she holds up a note from a teenage girl. I can tell, because the ink of the pen is purple and because the *i* in *Auntie Em* has a heart over it where the dot should be. *"Dear Auntie Em,"* she reads, and just like always, I picture a little old lady wearing a bun and sensible shoes, not my own mother. *"I like a guy who already has a girlfriend. I know he likes me cuz*—God, don't they teach you how to spell these days?"

"No," I answer. "They teach us to use spell-check."

Theo looks up from his plate long enough to grunt in the direction of the grape juice.

"I know he likes me because," my mother edits, *"he walks me home from school and we talk for hours on the phone and yesterday I couldn't take it anymore and I kissed him and he kissed me back* . . . Oh, please, someone get this girl a comma." Then she frowns at the loose-leaf paper. *"He says we can't go out but we can be friends with benefits. Do you think I should say yes? Sincerely, Burlington Buddy."* My mother glances at me. "Don't *all* friends have benefits?"

I stare at her blankly.

"Theo?" she asks.

"It's a saying," he mutters.

"A saying that means what, exactly?"

Theo's face turns bright red. "Just Google it."

"Just *tell* me."

"It's when a guy and a girl who aren't going out hook up, all right?"

My mother considers this. "You mean like . . . have sex?"

"Among other things . . ."

"And then what happens?"

"I don't know!" Theo says. "They go back to ignoring each other, I guess."

My mother's jaw drops. "That is the most demeaning thing I've ever heard. This poor girl shouldn't just tell that guy to go jump in a lake, she ought to slash all four of his car tires, and—" Suddenly she pins her gaze on Theo. "You haven't treated a girl like that, have you?"

Theo rolls his eyes. "Can't you be like other mothers and just ask me if I'm smoking weed?"

"Are you smoking weed?" she says.

"No!"

"Do you have friends with benefits?"

Theo pushes back from the table and stands up in one smooth move. "Yeah. I have thousands. They line up outside the front door, or haven't you noticed them lately?" He dumps his plate in the sink and runs upstairs.

My mother reaches for a pen she's tucked into her ponytail (she always wears a ponytail, because she knows how I feel about loose hair swishing around her shoulders) and begins to scrawl a response. "Jacob," she says, "be a sweetheart and clear the table for me, will you?"

And off goes my mother, champion of the confused, doyenne of the dense. Saving the world one letter at a time. I wonder what all those devoted readers would think if they knew that the real Auntie Em had one son who was practically a sociopath and another one who was socially impractical.

I'd like a friend with benefits, although I'd never admit that to my mother.

I'd like a friend, period.

For my birthday last year my mother bought me the most incredible gift ever: a police scanner radio. It operates by receiving frequencies that regular radios cannot—ones assigned by the federal government in the VHF and UHF range above the FM stations, and which are used by police, fire, and rescue crews. I always know when the highway patrol is sending out the sanding trucks before they arrive; I get the special weather alerts when a nor'easter is coming. But mostly I listen to the police and emergency calls, because even in a place as small as Townsend you get a crime scene every now and then.

Since Thanksgiving alone, I have gone to two crime scenes. The first was a break-in at a jewelry store. I rode my bike to the address I heard on the scanner and found several officers swarming the storefront for evidence. It was the first time I got to see spray wax being used on snow to cast a footprint, a definite highlight. The second crime scene was not really a crime scene. It was the house of a kid who goes to my school, who is a real jerk to me. His mother had called 911, but by the time they got there she was standing at the front door, her nose still bleeding, saying that she didn't want to press charges against her husband.

Tonight I have just gotten into my pajamas when I hear a code on the scanner that is different from any I've ever heard, and I've heard plenty:

10–52 AMBULANCE NEEDED.
10–50 MOTOR VEHICLE ACCIDENT.
10–13 CIVILIANS PRESENT AND LISTENING.
10–40 FALSE ALARM, PREMISES SECURE.
10–54 LIVESTOCK ON HIGHWAY.

Right now, though, I hear this:

10–100

Which means, *Dead body.*

I don't think I've ever gotten dressed so quickly in my life. I grab a composition note-book, even though it's a used one, because I don't want to waste any time; and I scrawl down the address that keeps getting men-tioned on the scanner. Then I tiptoe down-stairs. With any luck my mother is already asleep and won't even know I'm gone.

It's bitterly cold out, and there are about two inches of snow on the ground. I'm so excited about the crime scene that I am wear-ing sneakers instead of boots. The wheels of my mountain bike skid every time I go around a turn.

The address is a state highway, and I know I have reached the right spot because there are four police cars with their flashing blues on. There is a wooden stake with police tape (yellow, not orange) fluttering in the wind, and a visible trail of footprints. An abandoned car, a Pontiac, sits on the side of the road cov-ered in ice and snow.

I take out my notebook and write: *Vehicle has been abandoned for at least twelve hours, prestorm.*

I duck into the edge of the woods as another police car arrives. This one is unmarked and ordinary, except for the domed police light magnetically affixed to the top. The man who gets out of it is tall and has red hair. He is wearing a black overcoat and heavy boots. On one of his hands, he has a Dora the Explorer Band-Aid.

I write this in my notebook, too.

"Captain," an officer says, coming out from between the trees. He's dressed in a uniform, with heavy gloves and boots, too. "Sorry to call you in."

The captain shakes his head. "What have you got?"

"A jogger found a body in the woods. Guy's half naked and there's blood all over him."

"Who the hell goes jogging at night in the dead of winter?"

I follow them into the woods, careful to stay in the shadows. There are searchlights illuminating the area around the body, so that the evidence can be fully recorded.

The dead man is lying on his back. His eyes are open. His pants are gathered around his ankles, but he is still wearing his underwear. The knuckles of his hands are bright red with blood, as are the bottoms of his palms, and his knees and calves. His jacket is unzipped, and he's missing one shoe and one sock. All around him, the snow is pink.

"Holy crap," the captain says. He kneels down and snaps on a pair of rubber gloves that he takes from his pocket. He examines the body up close.

I hear two more sets of footsteps, and another man steps into the pool of light, escorted by a uniformed officer. The uniformed officer takes one look at the dead guy, goes totally pale, and throws up. "Jesus H.," the other man says.

"Hey, Chief," the captain replies.

"Suicide or homicide?"

"I don't know yet. Sexual assault seems like a given, though."

"Rich, the guy's covered in blood from head to toe and he's lying here in his tighty whites. You think he got sexually assaulted and then committed hara-kiri?" The police chief snorts. "I know I don't have the vast detective experience you do after fifteen years on the job in the metropolis of Townsend but—"

I look down at the list in my notebook.

What would Dr. Henry Lee do? Well, he'd examine the wounds up close. He'd analyze why there was only superficial blood—that pink transfer on the snow, without any dripping or spatter. He'd note the footprints in the snow—one set that matches the lone sneaker on the victim's foot, and the other set that has been matched to the jogger who found the body. He'd ask why, after a sexual assault, the victim would still be wearing his underwear if other items of clothing were still removed.

I am so cold I'm shaking. I stomp my frozen feet in their sneakers. Then I look down at the ground, and suddenly everything's crystal clear.

"Actually," I say, stepping out of my hiding place, "you're both wrong."

Rich

I don't know why I kid myself into thinking that I'll get anything done on the weekends. I have the best intentions, but something always gets in the way. Today, for example, I was determined to build an ice rink in the backyard for Sasha, my seven-year-old. She lives with my ex, Hannah, but she's with me from Friday night to Sunday, and she is currently planning on joining the U.S. Figure Skating team (if she doesn't become a singing veterinarian). I figured she'd get a kick out of helping me flood the tarp I set up in the back, bordered by two-by-fours that I hammered into place all week long after work, just to get ready. I promised her that when she woke up on Sunday morning, she'd be able to skate.

What I hadn't counted on was the fact that it would be so freaking cold outside. Sasha started to whine as soon as the wind picked up, so I nixed the plan and drove her to dinner in Burlington instead— she's a big fan of one place, where you can draw on the tablecloths. She falls asleep on the car ride home while I am still singing along to Hannah Montana songs on her CD, and I carry her upstairs to her bedroom. It's a haven of pink in a bachelor pad. During the settlement, I got the house, but Hannah got nearly everything inside it. It's weird to pick Sasha up from her other home and see her new stepdad sprawled on my old couch.

She stirs a little while I get her undressed and into her nightgown, but then she sighs and curls on her side beneath the covers. For a minute, I just stare at her. Most of the time, being the only detective in a one-horse town is a losing battle. I get paid crap; I investigate cases that are too dull to even make the police log in the local paper. But I'm making sure that Sasha's world, or at least this tiny corner of it, is a little bit safer.

It keeps me going.

Well . . . that and my twenty-year retirement bonus.

Downstairs, I grab a flashlight and head out to the aborted ice rink. I turn on the hose. If I stay up for a few more hours, maybe there will be enough water in the tarp to freeze overnight.

I don't like breaking promises; I leave that to my ex.

I'm not a bitter guy; I'm not. It's just that, in my profession, it's a lot easier to see actions as either right or wrong, without shades of explanation between them. I didn't really *need* to know how Hannah realized her soul mate was not the guy she'd married but instead the one who serviced the coffee machines in the teachers' room. "He started bringing hazelnut for me," she said, and somehow I was supposed to be able to understand that meant *I don't love you anymore.*

Back inside, I open the fridge and grab a bottle of Sam Adams. I settle down on the couch, turn on a Bruins game on NESN, and pick up the newspaper. Although most guys turn to the stocks or sports page, I always go for the entertainment section, because of the column in the back. I'm hooked on an agony aunt—that's the old-fashioned term for an advice column. She calls herself Auntie Em, and she's my guilty pleasure.

> **I've fallen in love with my best friend, and I know I'll never be with him . . . so how do I get over him?**

> **My partner just walked out and left me with a four-month-old baby. Help!**

> **Can you be depressed if you're only fourteen?**

There are two things I like about this column: that the letters are a constant reminder my life doesn't suck as much as someone else's, and that there is at least one person on this planet who seems to have all the answers. Auntie Em is forever coming up with the most practical solutions, as if the key to the great riddles of existence involves surgically cutting away the emotional component and looking at just the facts.

She's probably eighty years old and living with a horde of cats, but I kind of think Auntie Em would make a great cop.

The last letter takes me by surprise.

I'm married to a great guy, but I can't stop thinking about my ex, and wondering if I made a mistake. Should I tell him?

My eyes widen, and I can't keep myself from checking the byline. The letter writer doesn't live in Strafford, like Hannah, but instead hails from Stowe. *Get a grip, Rich,* I tell myself silently.

I reach for the beer bottle, and I'm just about to take that first indescribable sip when my cell phone rings. "Matson," I answer.

"Captain? Sorry to bug you on your night off . . ."

It's Joey Urqhart, a rookie patrolman. I'm sure it's my imagination, but the new officers get younger every year; this one's probably still wearing a Pull-Up at night. No doubt, he's calling to ask me where we keep the extra Kleenex down at the station or something equally inane. The new kids know better than to bother the chief, and I'm the second in command.

". . . it's just that we got a report of a dead body and I figured you'd want to know."

Immediately, I'm on alert. I know better than to ask him questions—like if there are signs of foul play, or if we're talking suicide. I'll figure that out myself.

"Where?"

He gives me the address of a state highway, near a stretch of conservation land. It's a popular place for cross-country skiers and snowshoers this time of year. "I'm on my way," I say, and I hang up.

I take one last, longing look at the beer I didn't drink and spill it down the drain. Then I grab Sasha's coat from the front hallway and rummage through the mudroom for her boots. They're not there; they're not on the floor of her bedroom, either. I sit down on the edge of her bed and gently shake her out of sleep. "Hey, baby," I whisper. "Daddy's got to go to work."

She blinks up at me. "It's the middle of the night."

Technically, it's only 9:30 P.M., but time is relative when you're seven years old. "I know. I'm going to take you over to Mrs. Whitbury's."

Mrs. Whitbury probably has a first name, but I haven't ever used it. She lives across the street and is the widow of a guy who'd been on the job for thirty-five years, so she understands that emergencies happen. She babysat Sasha back when Hannah and I were together, and nowadays when Sasha is staying with me and I get an unexpected call.

"Mrs. Whitbury smells like feet."

She does, actually. "Come on, Sash. I need you to get moving." She sits up, yawning, as I pull on her coat, tie her fleece hat under her chin. "Where are your boots?"

"I don't know."

"Well, they're not downstairs. You'd better find them, because I can't."

She smirks. "Wow, and *you're* a detective?"

"Thanks for the vote of confidence." I lift her into my arms. "Wear your slippers," I say. "I'll carry you to the car."

I buckle her into her car seat even though we're only going twenty yards, and that's when I see them—the boots, lying on the rubber mats in the backseat. She must have kicked them off on the way home from Hanover, and I didn't notice, since I'd carried her into the house.

If only all mysteries were that easy to solve.

Mrs. Whitbury opens the door as if she's been expecting us. "I'm so sorry to bother you," I begin, but she waves me off.

"Not at all," she says. "I was just hoping for a little company anyway. Sasha, I can't remember, are you a fan of chocolate ice cream or cookie dough?"

I set Sasha down inside the threshold. "Thanks," I mouth to Mrs. Whitbury, and I turn to leave, already mentally mapping out the fastest route to the crime scene.

"Daddy!"

I turn back to find Sasha with her arms outstretched.

For a long time after the divorce, Sasha couldn't stand to have anyone leave her. We came up with a ritual that somehow, along the way, turned into a good-luck charm. "Kiss, hug, high five," I say, kneeling down and putting the motions to the words. Then we press our thumbs together. "Bag of peanuts."

Sasha leans her forehead against mine. "Don't worry," we say in unison.

She waves to me as Mrs. Whitbury closes the door.

I stick a magnetic light on top of my car and drive twenty miles over the speed limit before realizing that the dead guy won't be getting any deader if I'm five minutes late, and that there's black ice all over the roads.

Which reminds me.

I never turned off the hose, and by the time I get home, Sasha's rink might well have spread to the entirety of my back lawn.

Dear Auntie Em, I think.

I had to second-mortgage my house to pay my water bill. What should I do?
Troubled in Townsend

Dear Troubled,
Drink less.

I'm still smiling when I pull up to the spot where police tape is marking a crime scene. Urqhart meets me as I am checking out the abandoned vehicle, a Pontiac. I brush off a bit of snow from the window and peer inside with a flashlight to see a backseat full of empty gin bottles.

"Captain. Sorry to call you in," he says.

"What have you got?"

"A jogger found a body in the woods. Guy's half naked and there's blood all over him."

I start to follow him along a marked trail. "Who the hell goes jogging at night in the dead of winter?"

The victim is half dressed and frozen. His pants are pooled around his ankles. I do a quick canvass of the other officers to see what evidence they've found—which is minimal. Except for all the blood on the man's extremities, there's no hint of an altercation. There are footprints that match the victim's one remaining sneaker, and another set that apparently were made by the jogger (whose alibi already eliminated him as a suspect)—but the perp either brushed his own footprints away or flew in for the kill. I crouch down and am examining the crosshatch abrasions on the victim's lower left palm when the chief arrives. "Jesus H.," he says. "Suicide or homicide?"

I'm not sure. If it's homicide, where are the signs of a struggle? Or the defense wounds on the hands? It's almost as if the skin's been rubbed off raw instead of scratched, and there's no trauma to the forearms. If it's suicide, why is the guy in his underwear, and how did he kill himself? The blood is on his knuckles and knees, not his wrists. The truth is, we just don't see this often enough in Townsend, Vermont, to make a quick judgment call.

"I don't know yet," I hedge. "Sexual assault seems like a given, though."

Suddenly a teenager steps out of the edge of the woods. "Actually, you're both wrong," he says.

"Who the hell are you?" the chief asks, and two of the patrolmen take a step forward to flank the boy.

"Not you again," Urqhart says. "He showed up at a robbery about a month ago. He's some kind of crime scene groupie. Get lost, kid. You don't belong here."

"Wait," I say, vaguely remembering the

teenager from that robbery scene. Right now, I'm laying odds that this kid's the perp, and I don't want him to bolt.

"It's really very simple," the boy continues, staring at the body. "On episode twenty-six of Season Two, the whole *CrimeBusters* team got hauled up to Mount Washington to investigate a naked guy who was found at the summit. No one could figure out what a naked guy was doing on top of a mountain, but it turned out to be hypothermia. The same thing happened to this man. He became disoriented and fell down. As his core body temperature rose, he took off his own clothes because he felt hot . . . but in reality, that's what made him freeze to death." He grins. "I can't believe you guys didn't know that."

The chief narrows his eyes. "What's your name?"

"Jacob."

Urqhart frowns. "People who freeze to death don't usually bleed all over the place—"

"Urqhart!" the chief snaps.

"He *didn't* bleed all over the place," Jacob says. "Blood spatter would show up in the snow, but instead, there's just transfer. Look at the wounds. They're abrasions on the knuckles, the knees, and the lower hands. He fell down and he scraped himself up. The blood on the snow came from him crawling around before he lost consciousness."

I look at Jacob carefully. One major flaw with his theory, of course, is that you don't spontaneously start bleeding when you crawl around on the snow. If that were the case, there would be hundreds of elementary school children exsanguinating at recess during the winters in Vermont.

There's something just the tiniest bit . . . well . . . *off* about him. His voice is too flat and high; he won't make eye contact. He's bouncing on the balls of his feet and I don't even think he realizes it.

On the spot where he's been bouncing, the snow has melted, revealing a patch of briars. I kick at the ground beneath my boots and shake my head. That poor, drunk, dead bastard had the misfortune to fall down in a field of brambles.

Before I can say anything else, the regional medical examiner arrives. Wayne

Nussbaum went to clown college before getting his medical degree, although I haven't seen the guy crack a smile in the fifteen years I've been on the job. "Greetings, all," he says, coming into the clearing of artificial light. "I hear you have a murder mystery on your hands?"

"You think it could be hypothermia?" I ask.

He considers this, carefully rolling the victim forward and examining the back of his head. "I've never seen it firsthand . . . but I've read about it. It certainly would fit the bill." Wayne glances up at me. "Nice work—but you didn't need to pull me away from the Bruins in overtime for death by natural causes."

I glance to the spot where Jacob was standing moments before, but he's disappeared.

Jacob

I run all the way home, even though I hate running. I can't wait to transcribe my notes from the crime scene into a fresh notebook. I plan to draw pictures, using colored pencils and scaled maps. I slip into the house through the garage, and I am just taking off my boots when the door opens behind me again.

Immediately, I freeze.

It's Theo.

What if he asks me what I've been doing?

I have never been a very good liar. If he asks, I'm going to have to tell him about the scanner and the dead body and the hypothermia. And that makes me angry because right now I want to keep it all to myself instead of sharing it. I tuck my notebook into the back of my pants and pull my sweater down over it and then cross my hands behind my back to hide it.

"What, now you're going to spy on me?" Theo says, kicking off his boots. "Why don't you get your own life?"

It isn't until he's halfway up the stairs that I look at him and see how red his cheeks are, how his hair is windblown. I wonder where he's been, and if Mom knows, and then the thought is gone, replaced by the vision of the dead man's bare skin, blue underneath the floodlights, and the pink, stained snow all around him. I will have to remember all that, the next time I set up a crime scene. I could use food coloring in water, and spray it on the snow outside. And I'll draw with red Sharpie on my knuckles and my knees. Although I am not too keen on lying in the snow in my underwear, I am willing to make the sacrifice for a scenario that will totally stump my mother.

I am still humming under my breath when I get to my room. I take off my clothes and put on my pajamas. Then I sit down at my desk and carefully cut the page out of the old, used notebook so that I don't have to hear the sound of paper being crumpled or torn. I take out a fresh spiral notebook and begin to sketch the crime scene.

Go figure. On a scale of one to ten, this day's turned out to be an eleven.

CASE 2: IRONY 101

Imette St. Guillen was an honors student pursuing a degree in criminal justice in New York. One winter night in 2006, she went out drinking with her friends, eventually splitting from them and heading to SoHo, where she called a friend to say she was at a bar. She never returned home. Instead, her naked body was found fourteen miles away, in a deserted area off the Belt Parkway in Brooklyn, wrapped in a flowered bedspread. Her hair had been cut off on one side, her hands and feet were secured with plastic ties, she'd been gagged with a sock, and her face was wrapped in packaging tape. She had been raped, sodomized, and suffocated.

Blood was found on one of those

plastic ties, but DNA evidence revealed that it didn't belong to the
victim. Instead, it was matched to
Darryl Littlejohn, a bouncer who had
been asked to remove the drunk
young woman from the bar at around
4:00 A.M. Witnesses said they argued
before leaving the bar.

Fibers were also found in Littlejohn's residence that matched those
on the packing tape on the victim's
body.

Littlejohn was also arraigned for a
second kidnapping and assault of another college student who managed
to get away from him after he impersonated a police officer, handcuffed
her, and threw her into his van.

And Imette St. Guillen, tragically,
went from being a student of criminal
justice to being the lesson taught by
professors of forensic DNA analysis.

2

Emma

I used to have friends. Back before I had children, when I was working at a textbook publishing company outside of Boston, I'd hang out with some of the other editors after hours. We'd go for sushi, or to see a movie. When I met Henry—he was a technical consultant on a computer programming textbook—my friends were the ones who encouraged me to ask him on a date, since he seemed too shy to ask me. They leaned over my cubicle, laughing, asking if he had a Superman side underneath all that Clark Kent. And when Henry and I got married, they were bridesmaids.

Then I got pregnant, and suddenly the people I could relate to were enrolled in my birthing class, practicing their breathing and talking about the best deals on Diaper Genies. After we had our babies, three of the other mothers and I formed a casual playgroup. We rotated hosting duties. The adults would sit on the couch and gossip while the babies rolled around on the floor with a collection of toys.

Our children got older and started to play *with* each other instead of *beside* each other. All of them, that is, except Jacob. My friends' boys zoomed Matchbox cars all over the carpet, but Jacob lined them up with military precision, bumper to bumper. While the other kids colored outside the lines, Jacob drew neat little blocks in a perfect rainbow spectrum.

I didn't notice, at first, when my friends forgot to mention at whose house the next playgroup was taking place. I didn't read between the lines when I hosted and two of the mothers begged off because of previous engagements. But that afternoon, Jacob got frustrated when my friend's daughter reached for the truck whose wheels he was spinning, and he hit her so hard that she fell against the edge of the coffee table. "I can't do this anymore," my friend said, gathering up her shrieking child. "I'm sorry, Emma."

"But it was an accident! Jacob didn't understand what he was doing!"

She stared at me. "Do *you*?"

After that, I didn't really have friends anymore. Who had time, with all the early intervention specialists that were occupying every minute of Jacob's life? I spent the entire day on the carpet with him, forcing him to interact, and at night I stayed up reading the latest books about autism research—as if I might find a solution that even the experts couldn't. Eventually, I met families at Theo's preschool—who were welcoming at first but distanced themselves when they met Theo's older brother; when they invited us for dinner and all I could talk about was how a cream of transdermal glutathione had helped some autistic kids, who couldn't produce enough of the substance themselves to bind to and remove toxins from the body.

Isolation. A fixation on one particular subject. An inability to connect socially.

Jacob was the one diagnosed, but I might as well have Asperger's, too.

* * *

When I come downstairs at seven in the morning, Jacob is already sitting at the kitchen table, showered and dressed. An ordinary teenager would sleep in till noon on a Sunday—Theo will, certainly—but then again, Jacob isn't ordinary. His routine of getting up for school trumps the fact that it's a weekend and there's no urgency to leave the house. Even when it is a snow day and school is canceled, Jacob will get dressed instead of going back to bed.

He is poring over the Sunday paper. "Since when do you read the paper?" I ask.

"What kind of mother doesn't want her son to be aware of current events?"

"Yeah, I'm not falling for that one. Let me guess—you're clipping Staples coupons for Krazy Glue?" Jacob goes through that stuff like water; it's part of the process used to get fingerprints off objects, and it's a common occurrence in this household for something to go missing—my car keys, Theo's toothbrush—and then to resurface beneath the overturned fish tank Jacob uses to fume for prints.

I measure out enough coffee into the automatic drip to make me human and then get started on breakfast for Jacob. It's a challenge: he doesn't eat glutens and he doesn't eat caseins—basically, that means no wheat, oat, rye, barley, or dairy. Since there's no cure yet for Asperger's, we treat the symptoms, and for some reason, if I regulate his diet his behavior improves. When he cheats, like he did at Christmas, I can see him slipping backward—stimming or having meltdowns. Frankly, with 1 in 100 kids in the United States being diagnosed on the spectrum, I bet I could have a top-rated show on the Food Network: *Alimentary Autism.* Jacob doesn't share my culinary enthusiasm. He says that I'm what you'd get if you crossed Jenny Craig with Josef Mengele.

Five days of the week, in addition to having a limited diet, Jacob eats by color. I don't really remember how this started, but it's a routine: all Monday food is green, all Tuesday food is red, all Wednesday food is yellow, and so on. For some reason this helped with his sense of structure. Weekends, though, are free-for-alls, so this morning my breakfast spread includes defrosted homemade tapioca rice muffins, and EnviroKidz Koala Crisp cereal with soy milk. I fry up some Applegate Farms turkey bacon and set out Skippy peanut butter and gluten-free bread. I have a three-inch binder full of food labels and toll-free numbers that is my chef's Bible. I also have grape juice, because Jacob mixes it with his liposome-enclosed glutathione— one teaspoon, plus a quarter teaspoon of vitamin C powder. It still tastes like sulfur, but it's better than the previous alternative—a cream he rubbed on his feet and covered with socks because it smelled so bad. The downside of the glutathione, though, pales in comparison to its upside: binding and removing toxins that Jacob's body can't do itself, and leaving him with better mental acuity.

The food is only part of the buffet.

I take out the tiny silicone bowls we use for Jacob's supplements. Every day he takes a multivitamin, a taurine capsule, and an omega-3 tablet. The taurine prevents meltdowns; the fatty acids help with mental flexibility. He lifts the newspaper up in front of his face as I set down the two treatments he hates the most: the oxytocin nasal spray and the B12 shot he injects himself, both of which help with anxiety.

"You can hide but you can't run," I say, tugging down the edge of the newspaper.

You would think that the shot is the worst for him, but he actually lifts up his shirt and pinches his stomach to inject himself without much fanfare. However, for a kid who's got sensory issues, using a nasal spray is like waterboarding. Every day I watch Jacob stare down that bottle and finally convince himself he will be able to handle the feeling of the liquid dripping down his throat. And every day, it breaks my heart.

It goes without saying that none of these supplements—which cost hundreds of dollars each month—are covered by medical insurance.

I put a plate of muffins in front of him as he turns another page in the paper. "Did you brush your teeth?"

"Yes," Jacob mutters.

I put my hand down on the paper so that it blocks his view. "Really?"

The few times Jacob lies, it's so obvious to me that all I have to do is raise an eyebrow and he caves. The only times I've ever even seen him attempt dishonesty are when he's asked to do something he doesn't want to do—like take his supplements or brush his teeth—or to avoid conflict. In those cases, he'll say what he thinks I want to hear. "I'll do it after I eat," he promises, and I know he will. "Yes!" he crows suddenly. "It's in here!"

"What?"

Jacob leans over, reading aloud. "Police in Townsend recovered the body of fifty-three-year-old Wade Deakins in a wooded area off Route 140. Deakins succumbed to hypothermia. No foul play was indicated." He scoffs, shaking his head. "Can you believe that got buried on page A fourteen?"

"Yes," I say. "It's gruesome. Why would anyone want to read about a man who froze to death?" I suddenly pause in the act of stirring half-and-half into my coffee. "How did you *know* that article was going to be in the paper this morning?"

He hesitates, aware he's been caught in the act. "It was a lucky guess."

I fold my arms and stare at him. Even if he won't look me in the eye, he can feel the heat of my gaze.

"Okay!" he confesses. "I heard about it on the scanner last night."

I consider the way he's rocking in his seat and the blush that has continued to work its way up his face. "And?"

"I went there."

"You *what?*"

"It was last night. I took my bike—"

"You rode your bike in the freezing cold to Route 140—"

"Do you want to hear the story or not?" Jacob says, and I stop interrupting. "The police found a body in the woods and the detective was leaning toward sexual assault and homicide—"

"Oh my God."

"—but the evidence didn't support that." He beams. "I solved their case for them."

My jaw drops. "And they were *okay* with that?"

"Well . . . no. But they needed help. They were totally going in the wrong direction given the wounds to the body—"

"Jacob, you can't just crash a crime scene! You're a civilian!"

"I'm a civilian with a better understanding of forensic science than the local police," he argues. "I even let the detective take the credit."

I have visions of the Townsend Police showing up at my house today to berate me (at best) and arrest Jacob (at worst). Isn't it a misdemeanor to tamper with a police investigation? I imagine the fallout if it becomes public knowledge that Auntie Em, the advice expert, doesn't even know where her own son is at night.

"Listen to me," I say. "You are absolutely *not* to do that again. Ever. What if it *was* a homicide, Jacob? What if the killer had come after *you*?"

I watch him consider this. "Well," he says, entirely literal, "I guess I would have run really fast."

"Consider it a new house rule. You are not to sneak out of here unless you tell me first."

"Technically, that wouldn't be *sneaking*," he points out.

"Jacob, so help me—"

He bobs his head. "Don't sneak out to go to a crime scene. Got it." Then he looks directly at me, something that happens so infrequently I find myself catching my breath. "But, Mom, seriously, I wish you could have seen it. The crosshatch marks on the guy's shins and—"

"Jacob, that *guy* died a horrible, lonely death and deserves a little respect." But even as I say it, I know he can't understand. Two years ago, at my father's funeral, Jacob asked if the casket could be opened before the burial. I thought it was to say good-bye to a relative he'd loved, but instead, Jacob had put his hand against my father's cold, rice-paper cheek. *I just want to know what dead feels like,* he had said.

I take the newspaper and fold it up. "You'll write a note to the detective today apologizing for getting in his way—"

"I don't know his name!"

"Google it," I say. "Oh, and you can consider yourself grounded until otherwise notified."

"Grounded? You mean, like I can't leave the house?"

"Not unless you're going to school."

To my surprise, Jacob shrugs. "I guess you'll have to call Jess, then."

Dammit. I've forgotten about his social skills tutor. Twice a week, Jacob meets with her to practice social interaction skills. A graduate student at UVM who plans to teach autistic kids, Jess Ogilvy is terrific with Jacob. He adores her, just as much as he dreads what she makes him do: look cashiers in the eye, initiate conversation with strangers on the bus, ask bystanders for directions. Today they have planned to visit a local pizza parlor so that Jacob can practice small talk.

But in order to do that, he'll have to be allowed out of the house.

"Muffin?" he asks innocently, handing me the platter.

I hate it when he knows he's right.

Ask the mom of one autistic kid if vaccines had anything to do with her child's condition, and she will vehemently tell you yes.

Ask another, and she'll just as vehemently tell you no.

The jury's still out, literally. Even though a handful of parents have sued the government—alleging that vaccinations caused their children's autism—I haven't gotten my class action suit check in the mail, and I'm not banking on it.

Here are the facts:

1. In 1988, the Centers for Disease Control recommended a change to infant immunizations schedules in America, adding three hepatitis B shots (including one at birth) and three haemophilis B shots, all given before the baby is six months old.

2. Drug companies stepped up to the challenge by providing multiple-dose containers of

vaccines preserved with thimerosal, an anti-bacterial made up of 49 percent ethyl mercury.

3. Although the effects of mercury poisoning had been identified in the 1940s, the Food and Drug Administration and the CDC didn't consider the effects of the dosage that newborns would receive because of these shots. The drug companies didn't raise a red flag, either, even though the new regimen meant an average two-month-old at a well-baby checkup got a single-day dose of mercury one hundred times greater than the government's long-term safe exposure level.

4. The symptomology of autism looks an awful lot like the symptomology of mercury poisoning. To give you an example: when scientists studied the migration of mercury into primate brains, they noticed that the primates began to avoid eye contact.

5. Between 1999 and 2002, thimerosal was quietly removed from the majority of childhood vaccines.

There's the opposing argument, too. That ethyl mercury—the kind in the vaccines—leaves the body faster than methyl mercury, the kind that is a poison. That in spite of the fact that most vaccines are now mercury-free, autism is still on the rise. That the CDC, the World Health Organization, and the Institute of Medicine completed five large studies, none of which have found a link between vaccines and autism. Those facts are compelling, but the next one is all I needed to convince me there's some sort of connection:

1. My son looked like any other two-year-old until he had a round of shots that included DTaP, Hib, and hepatitis B.

I don't think it's a causal link. After all, out of 100 children receiving the same vaccine schedule, 99 will never become autistic. But just like we probably all have markers for cancer in our genes, if you smoke two packs a day you're more likely to develop it than if you don't. Kids with a certain predisposition in their genes can't get rid of mercury as easily as most of us can and, as a result, wind up on the spectrum.

I'm not one of these parents who swings so far to the other side that she eschews immunization. When Theo was born, he had his shots. In my opinion, the benefits of vaccination still outweigh the risks.

I believe in vaccines, I do. I just believe in spreading them out.

It is because of Jess Ogilvy that Jacob went to his junior prom.

It was not something I ever expected him to do, to be honest. There are a lot of moments I used to consider "definites" for a child of mine that, after Jacob's diagnosis, became "wishes" instead. Going to college. Holding down a job. Finding someone to love him. I suppose Theo bears the brunt of all my dreams. I hope for Jacob to blend into the world more seamlessly, but I hope for his brother to leave his mark.

Which is why, when Jacob announced last spring that he planned to go to his Spring Fling, I was surprised. "With whom?" I asked.

"Well," Jacob said. "Jess and I haven't quite worked that out yet."

I could see why Jess had suggested it: the photographs, the dancing, the table conversation—all of these were skills he needed to know. I agreed with her, but I also didn't want to see Jacob hurt. What if no one he asked would go with him?

Don't think I'm a bad mother; I'm just a realistic one. I knew that Jacob was handsome, funny, and so smart it sometimes left me reeling. It was hard, though, for others to see him in that light. To them, he just seemed odd.

That night, I went into Jacob's room. The pleasure of seeing him excited for once about initiating a social interaction was tempered by the thought of a string of girls laughing in his face. "So," I said, sitting down on the edge of his bed. I waited for him to put down his reading material—the *Journal of Forensic Sciences*. "The prom, huh?"

"Yes," he said. "Jess thinks it's a good idea."

"How about you? Do you think it's a good idea?"

Jacob shrugged. "I guess. But I'm a little worried . . ."

I seized on this. "About what?"

"My date's dress," Jacob said. "If it's orange, I don't think I could deal with it."

A smile tugged at my mouth. "Trust me. No girl wears orange to a prom." I picked at a thread on his blanket. "Is there any particular girl you're thinking of asking?"

"No."

"No?"

"That way I won't be disappointed," he said, matter-of-fact.

I hesitated. "I think it's terrific that you're trying this. And even if it doesn't work out—"

"Mom," Jacob interrupted, "of *course* it will work out. There are 402 girls in my school. Assuming that one of them finds me remotely attractive, the probability of getting one of them to say yes is statistically in my favor."

As it was, he had to ask only 83. One finally said yes—Amanda Hillerstein, who had a younger brother with Down syndrome and was kindhearted enough to see past Jacob's Asperger's, at least for one night.

What ensued was a two-week crash course in prom etiquette. Jess worked with Jacob to make small talk during dinner. (*Appropriate: Are you visiting colleges this summer? Inappropriate: Did you know there's a place in Tennessee called the Body Farm where you can study how corpses decay?*) Me, I worked with him on everything else. We practiced how to walk close to a girl instead of keeping a full foot of space between you. We practiced how to look at the camera when someone takes your photograph. We practiced how to ask your date if she'd like to dance, although Jacob drew the line at slow dancing ("Do I really have to *touch* her?").

The day leading up to the prom, a thousand pitfalls raced through my head. Jacob had never worn a tuxedo; what if the bow tie aggravated him and he refused to put it on? He hated to bowl because he disliked the thought of putting his feet in shoes that had housed someone else's feet moments before. What if he pitched a fit about his rented patent leather loafers for the same reason? What if the prom decorating committee had not gone with an under the sea theme, like they'd planned, but a disco party instead—with flashing lights and mirrored balls that would overstimulate Jacob's senses? What if Amanda wore her hair loose, and Jacob took one look at her and ran back up to his room?

Amanda, bless her heart, had offered to drive since Jacob couldn't. She pulled up in her Jeep Cherokee at 7:00 on the dot. Jacob was waiting for her with a wrist corsage he'd picked out at the florist that afternoon. He'd been standing at the window, watching, since 6:00.

Jess had come over with a video camera to record the event for posterity. We all held our breath as Amanda stepped out of her car in a long peach gown.

"You said she wouldn't wear orange," Jacob whispered.

"It's peach," I corrected.

"It's in the orange *family*," he said, all he had time for before she knocked. Jacob yanked the door open. "You look beautiful," he announced, just like we'd practiced.

When I took their picture on the front lawn, Jacob even looked at the camera. It remains, to this day, the only photo I have of him where he's doing that. I admit, I cried a little as I watched him extend his crooked elbow to escort his date to her car. Could I have asked for a better outcome? Could Jacob have done a finer job of remembering every lesson we'd worked on so diligently?

Jacob opened Amanda's door and then walked around to the passenger side.

Oh no, I thought.

"We totally forgot about that," Jess said.

And sure enough, Jess and I watched Jacob slide into his usual position in a car, the backseat.

Theo

"This is it," I say, and my mother pulls the car over in front of some random house I've never seen before.

"When do you want me to come get you?" she asks.

"I don't know. I'm not sure how long it's going to take us to write up the lab report," I say.

"Well, you have your cell phone. Call me." I nod and get out of the car. "Theo!" she yells. "Aren't you forgetting something?"

A backpack. If I'm doing schoolwork with an imaginary lab partner, I should at least be smart enough to carry a freaking notebook.

"Leon's got everything," I say. "It's on his computer."

She peers over my shoulder to the front door of the house. "Are you sure he's expecting you? It doesn't look like anyone's home."

"Mom, I told you. I talked to Leon ten minutes before we left the house. I'm supposed to go in the back door. Relax, okay?"

"Make sure you're polite," she says, as I shut the car door. "Please and thank—"

You, I mutter under my breath.

I start up the driveway and along a path that leads around the house. I have just turned the corner when I hear my mother pull away.

Of course it looks like there's no one here. I planned it that way.

I don't have a lab report to do. I don't even know anyone named Leon.

This is a new neighborhood for me. A lot of professors who work at UVM live here. The houses are old and have little brass plaques on them with the years they were built. The really cool thing about old houses is that they have crappy locks. You can jimmy them open most of the time with a credit card slipped in the right way. I don't have a credit card, but my school ID works just as well.

I know that no one's home because there aren't any footprints on the driveway after last night's snow—something my mother didn't notice. On the porch, I kick the snow off my sneakers and walk inside. The house smells like old people—oatmeal and mothballs. There's a cane propped inside the entryway, too. But—weird—there's also a Gap hoodie hanging up. Maybe their granddaughter left it behind.

Like last time, I go to the kitchen first.

The first thing I see is a bottle of red wine on the counter. It's about half full. I pop the cork and take a swig, and nearly spit the shit out all over the countertop. How come people drink if it tastes like this? Wiping my mouth, I rummage through the pantry for something to make me forget the taste of the wine, and find a box of crackers. I rip it open and eat a few. Then I check out the contents of the fridge and make myself a Black Forest ham and sage-cheddar sandwich on a baguette. No ham and cheese for this house. It's even too fancy for good ol' yellow mustard—I have to use champagne mustard instead, whatever that is. For a second I worry it will taste like the wine, but if there's alcohol in it, you could have fooled me.

Trailing crumbs, I walk into the living room. I haven't taken my sneakers off, so I'm leaving behind a trail of melting snow, too. I pretend I'm superhuman. I can see through walls; I can hear a pin drop. Nobody could ever take me by surprise.

The living room is exactly what you'd be expecting. Couches with crackly leather and stacks of paper every-where, so many dusty books that even though I don't have asthma I feel it coming on.

A woman and a man live here. I can tell because there are books on gardening and little glass bottles lined up on the mantel. I wonder if they sit in this room and talk about their kids, way back when. I bet they finish each other's sentences.

Remember when Louis found a piece of felt on the driveway after Christmas . . .
. . . and he took it to show-and-tell as proof of Santa Claus?

I sit down on the couch. The television remote is on the coffee table, so I pick it up. I put my sandwich down beside me on the couch and turn on the entertainment system, which is much nicer than you'd think for ol' Grandpa and Grandma. They have shelves of CDs, with every kind of music you can imagine. And a state-of-the-art, flat-screen HDTV.

They have TiVo, too. I punch buttons until I reach the screen to show what they've recorded.

Antiques Roadshow.

The Three Tenors on Vermont Public TV.

And, like, everything on the History Channel.

They've also taped a hockey game on NESN and a movie that aired last weekend—*Mission Impossible III.*

I double-click that one—because it's hard to believe Mr. and Mrs. Professor watching Tom Cruise kick ass, but sure enough, there it is.

So I decide to let them have that one. The rest, I delete.

Then I start adding programs to tape.

The Girls Next Door
My Super Sweet 16
South Park

And for good measure, I go to HBO and add a dollop of *Borat.*

When that movie came out, it was playing at the same theater as *Pirates of the Caribbean 3.* I wanted to see *Borat,* but my mother said I had to wait a decade or so. She bought us tickets to *Pirates* and said she would meet us in the parking lot after the film, because she had to go grocery shopping. I knew that Jacob would never have suggested it, so I told him that I wanted to let him in on a secret—but he had to promise not to tell Mom. He was so psyched about the secret he didn't even care that we were breaking the rules, and when I sneaked into the other theater after the opening credits, he came along. And in a way, I guess he did keep his promise—he never actually told my mother that we'd gone to see *Borat*.

She figured it out when he started quoting lines from the film, like he always does. *Very nice, very nice, how much? I like to make sexy time!*

I think I was grounded for three months.

I have a fleeting vision of Mrs. Professor turning on her TiVoed programs and seeing the Playboy bunnies and having a heart attack. Of her husband having a stroke when he finds her.

Immediately, I feel like shit.

I erase all the programming and put back in the original shows. *This is it. This is the last time I'm breaking in somewhere,* I tell myself, even though there's another part of me that knows this won't be true. I'm an addict, but instead of the rush some people get from shooting up or snorting, I need a fix that feels like home.

I pick up the telephone, intending to call my mother and ask her to come pick me up, but then on second thought I put down the receiver. I don't want there to be any trace of me. I want it to feel like I was never here.

So I leave the house cleaner than it was when I first entered. And then I start walking home. It's eight miles, but I can try to hitch once I reach the state highway.

After all, Leon's got the kind of parents who wouldn't mind dropping me off.

Oliver

I'm feeling pretty good, because this Friday, I won my case against the pig.

Okay, so technically, the pig was not the one who filed the lawsuit. That honor belongs to Buff (short for Buffalo, and I swear I am not making this up) Wings, a three-hundred-pound motorcyclist who was riding his vintage Harley down a road in Shelburne when a gigantic rogue pig wandered off the side of the road and directly into his path. As a result of the accident, Mr. Wings lost an eye—something he showed the jury at one point, by lifting up his black satin patch, which of course I objected to.

Anyway, when Wings got out of the hospital,

he sued the owner of the land from which the pig wandered. But it turned out to be more complicated than that. Elmer Hodgekiss, the owner of the pig, was only renting the property from a landlord who lived down in Brattleboro—an eighty-year-old lady named Selma Frack. In Elmer's lease was a direct clause that said no pets, no animals. But Elmer defended his forbidden pig keeping (and his equally subversive chicken keeping for that matter) on the grounds that Selma was in a nursing home and never visited the property and what she didn't know wouldn't hurt her.

I was representing Selma Frack. Her caretaker at the Green Willow Assisted Living Facility told me that Selma picked me out of the phone book because of my Yellow Pages ad:

Oliver O. Bond, Esquire, it read, with a graphic that looked like 007's gun—except it was OOB, my initials. *When you need an attorney who won't be shaken OR stirred.*

"Thanks," I said. "I came up with that myself."

The caretaker just stared at me blankly. "She liked the fact that she could read the font. Most of them lawyers, their print is too tiny."

In spite of the fact that Buff Wings wanted Selma's insurance to cover his medical bills, I had two strikes in my favor.

1. Buff Wings's convoluted argument was that Selma should be held responsible even though she (a) didn't know about the pig, (b) had expressly banned the pig, and (c) had evicted Elmer Hodgekiss as soon as she learned that he had loosed his killer pig on the general populace.

2. Buff Wings had chosen to represent himself.

I had trotted out experts to refute Wings's claims about damages—both emotional and physical. For example, did you know that there is a guy from Ohio who actually is an expert on driving with one eye? And that in almost all states you can continue to drive—even a motorcycle—as long as your other eye has 20/20 vision? And that in certain circumstances, the term *blind* spot can be politically incorrect?

After the judge had ruled in our favor, I followed Selma and her caretaker to the elevator at the courthouse. "Well," the caretaker said, "all's well that ends well."

I glanced down at Selma, who'd been asleep for most of the proceedings. "It's all fun and games till somebody loses an eye," I replied. "Please extend my congratulations to Mrs. Frack on her victory in court."

Then I ran down the stairs to the parking lot, punching my fist in the air.

I have a hundred percent success rate in my litigation.

So what if I've only had one case?

Contrary to popular belief, the ink is not still drying on my bar certificate.

That's pizza sauce.

But it was an honest accident. I mean, since my office is above the town pizza joint, and Mama Spatakopoulous routinely blocks my ascension on the staircase to thrust a plate of spaghetti or a mushroom-and-onion pie into my hands, it would be downright rude to turn her down. Coupled with that is the fact that I can't really afford to eat, and turning away free food would be stupid. Granted, it was dumb of me to grab a makeshift napkin from a stack of papers on my desk, but the odds of it being my bar certificate (as opposed to my recent Chinese take-out order) had been pretty slim.

If any new clients ask to see my bar certificate, I'm just going to tell them it's being framed.

Sure enough, as I am headed back inside, Mama S. meets me with a calzone. "You gotta wear a hat, Oliver."

My hair is still dripping wet from my shower

at the high school locker room. Ice has started to form. "You'll take care of me when I have pneumonia, won't you?" I tease.

She laughs and pushes the box at me. As I jog up the stairs, Thor starts barking his head off. I open the door just a crack, so that he doesn't come flying out. "Relax," I say. "I was only gone for fifteen minutes."

He launches all twelve pounds of himself at me.

Thor's a miniature poodle. He doesn't like to be called a poodle within hearing distance— he'll growl, and can you blame him? What guy dog wants to be a *poodle*? They should only come in female denominations, if you ask me.

I do the best I can for him. I gave him the name of a mighty warrior. I let his hair grow out, but instead of making him look less ef- feminate, it only makes him look more like a mop head.

I pick him up and tuck him into my arm like a football, and then I notice that there are feathers all over my office. "Oh, crap," I say. "What'd you do, Thor?"

Setting him down, I survey the damage. "Great. Thank you, mighty guard dog, for pro- tecting me from my own damn pillow." I drag the vacuum out of the closet and start to suck up the debris. It's my own fault, I know, for not putting away my bedding before running my errand. My office is currently also doubling as my living quarters. Not permanently, of course, but do you know how expensive it is to pay rent on a law office *and* an apartment? Plus, being in town, I can walk to the high school every day—and the janitor there has been very cool about letting me use the locker room as my own personal shower. I gave him some free advice about his divorce, and this is his thanks.

Usually, I fold up my blanket and tuck it with my pillow in the closet. I hide my little thirteen-inch TV inside a cavernously empty filing cabinet. That way, if a client comes in to retain my services, they won't get the vibe that I'm hideously unsuccessful.

I'm just new in town, that's all. Which is why I spend more time organizing the paper clips on my desk than actually doing any legal work.

I graduated with honors from the University of Vermont seven years ago with a degree in English. Here's a little nugget of wisdom for you, just in case you're interested: You can't practice English in the real world. What skills did I have, honestly? I could outread anyone in a quick draw? I could write a totally smoking analytical essay about the homoerotic overtones of Shakespeare's sonnets?

Yeah, that and $1.50 will get you a cup of coffee.

So I decided that I needed to stop living in the theoretical and start experiencing the physical. I answered a classified ad I'd found in the *Burlington Free Press* to be a farrier's apprentice. I traveled around the countryside and learned to spot what was normal gait for a horse and what wasn't. I studied how to trim a donkey's hoof and how to shape a horseshoe around an anvil, nail it into place, file it down, and watch the animal take off again.

I liked being a farrier. I liked the feel of fifteen hundred pounds of horse pressed up against my shoulder as I bent the leg to examine the hoof. But after four years I got restless. I decided to go to law school, for the same reason everyone else goes to law school: because I had no idea what else to do.

I'll be a good lawyer. Maybe even a great one. But here I am, at twenty-eight, and my secret fear is that I'm going to be just another guy who spends his whole life making money by doing something he's never really loved to do.

* * *

I have just put the vacuum back in the closet when there is a tentative knock at the door. A man stands there in Carhartt coveralls, feeding the seam of a black wool cap through his hands. He reeks of smoke.

"Can I help you?" I ask.

"I'm looking for the lawyer?"

"That's me." On the couch, Thor begins to growl. I shoot him a dirty glance. If he starts scaring away my potential clients, he'll be homeless.

"Really?" the man says, peering at me. "You don't look old enough to be a lawyer."

"I'm twenty-eight," I say. "Wanna see my driver's license?"

"No, no," the man says. "I, uh, I got a problem."

I usher him into the office, closing the door behind him. "Why don't you have a seat, Mr. . . ."

"Esch," he says, settling down. "Homer Esch. I was out in my backyard this morning burning brush and the fire got out of control." He looks up at me as I sit down at my desk. "It kind of burned down my neighbor's house."

"Kind of? Or did?"

"Did." He juts out his jaw. "I had a burn permit, though."

"Great." I write that down on a legal pad: LICENSED TO BURN. "Were there any casualties?"

"No. They don't live there no more. They built another house across the field. This was just a shed, pretty much. My neighbor swears he's suing me for every penny he put into that place. That's why I came to you. You're the first lawyer I found who's open on a Sunday."

"Right. Well. I may have to do a little research before I can take your case," I say, but I'm thinking: *He burned the guy's house down. There's no way to win this one.*

Esch takes a photograph out of the inner pocket of his coveralls and pushes it across the table. "You can see the place in the background here, behind my wife. My neighbor says it's twenty-five thousand dollars I'll have to pay out."

I glance at the photo. Calling this place a shed is generous. Me, I'd have said shack. "Mr. Esch," I say, "I think we can definitely get that down to fifteen."

Jacob

Here are all the reasons I hate Mark, the boy-friend Jess has had since last September.

1. He makes her cry sometimes.

2. Once, I saw bruises on her side, and I think he's the one who gave them to her.

3. He always wears a big orange Bengals sweatshirt.

4. He calls me Chief, when I have explained multiple times that my name is Jacob.

5. He thinks I am retarded, even though the diagnosis of mental retardation is reserved

for people who score lower than 70 on an IQ test, and I myself have scored 162. In my opinion, the very fact that Mark doesn't know this diagnostic criterion suggests that he's a lot closer to actual retardation than I am.

6. Last month I saw Mark in CVS with some other guys when Jess was not around. I said hello, but he pretended that he did not know me. When I told Jess and she confronted him, he denied it. Which means that he is both a hypocrite *and* a liar.

I was not expecting him to be at today's lesson, and for that reason I start to feel out of control right away, even though being with Jess usually calms me down. The best way I can describe it is like being in the path of a flash flood. You might be able to sense that a catastrophe is imminent; you might feel the faintest mist on your face. But even when you see that wall of water rushing toward you, you know you are powerless to budge an inch.

"Jacob!" Jess says, as soon as I walk in, but I see Mark across the room sitting in a booth, and just like that, I can hardly even hear her voice.

"What's *he* doing here?"

"You know he's my boyfriend, Jacob. And he wanted to come today. To help."

Right. And I want to be drawn and quartered, just for giggles.

Jess links her arm through mine. It took me a while to get used to that, and to the perfume she wears, which isn't very strong but to me smelled like an overdose of flowers. "It's going to be fine," she says. "Besides, we said we're going to work on being friendly to people we don't know, right?"

"I know Mark," I reply. "And I don't like him."

"But I do. And part of being social means being civil to someone you don't like."

"That's stupid. It's a huge world. Why not get up and walk away?"

"Because that's rude," Jess explains.

"I think it's rude to stick a smile on your face and pretend you like talking to someone when in reality you'd rather be sticking bamboo slivers under your fingernails."

Jess laughs. "Jacob, one day, when we wake up in the world of the Painfully Honest, *you* can be *my* tutor."

A man comes down the stairs that lead up from the entryway of the pizza place. He has a dog on a leash, a miniature poodle. I step into his path and start patting the dog.

"Thor! Down!" he says, but the dog doesn't listen.

"Did you know poodles aren't French? In fact the name *poodle* comes from the German word *Pudel,* which is short for *Pudelhund,* or splashing dog. The breed used to be a water dog."

"I didn't know that," the man says.

I do, because before I used to study forensics, I studied dogs. "A poodle took Best in Show at Westminster in 2002," I add.

"Right. Well, this poodle's going to take a whiz if I don't get him outside," the man says, and he pushes past me.

"Jacob," Jess says, "you don't just accost someone and start rattling off facts."

"He was interested in poodles! He *has* one!"

"Right, but you *could* have started off by saying, 'Hey, that's a really cute dog.'"

I snort. "That's not informative at all."

"No, but it's *polite* . . ."

At first, when Jess and I started working together, I used to call her a few days before our lesson just to make sure it was still on—that she wasn't sick, or expecting to have some kind of emergency. I'd call whenever I was obsessing about it, and sometimes that was three in the morning. If she didn't pick up her cell phone, I'd freak out. Once, I called the police to report her missing, and it turned out that she was just at some party. Eventually, we agreed that I would call her at 10:00 P.M. on Thursdays. Since I meet with her on Sundays and Tuesdays, that means I don't have to spend four days out of touch and worrying.

This week she moved out of her dorm room and into a professor's house. She is babysitting for the house, which sounds like an immense waste of time, because it's not as if the house is going to touch the stove if it's hot or eat something poisonous or fall down its own stairs. She will be there for the semester, so next week we are going to meet there for our lesson. In my wallet I have the address, and the phone number, and a special map she's drawn, but I'm a little nervous about it. It will probably smell like someone else, instead of Jess and flowers. Plus I have no idea what it looks like yet, and I hate surprises.

Jess is beautiful, although she says this was not always the case. She lost a lot of weight two years ago after she had an operation. I've seen pictures of her before, when she was obese. She says that's why she wants to work with kids whose disabilities make them targets—because she remembers being one, too. In the pictures, she looks like Jess, but hidden inside someone larger and puffier. Now, she is curvy, but only in the right places. She has blond hair that is always straight, although she has to work hard to make that happen. I have watched her use this contraption called a flat iron that looks like a sandwich press but actually sizzles her curly, wet hair and turns it smooth and silky. When she walks into a room, people look right at her, which I really like, because it means they are not looking at me.

Lately I have been thinking that maybe she should be my girlfriend.

It makes sense:

1. She has seen me wear the same shirt twice in a row and doesn't make a big deal about it.

2. She is getting a master's degree in education, and is writing an enormous paper about Asperger's syndrome, so I am hands-on research for her.

3. She is the only girl, other than my mother, who can put her hand on my arm to get my attention without making me want to jump out of my skin.

4. She ties her hair back into a ponytail without me even having to ask.

5. She is allergic to mangoes and I don't like
them.

6. I could call her whenever I want, not just
Thursdays.

7. I would treat her so much better than
Mark.

And of course, the most important reason of
all:

8. If I had a girlfriend, I'd appear to be more
normal.

"Come on," Jess says, tapping me on the
shoulder. "You and I have work to do. Your
mom says this place has a gluten-free pizza.
They make it on some kind of special crust."

I know what love is. When you find the
person you are supposed to love, bells ring
and fireworks go off in your head and you
can't find words to speak and you think about
her all the time. When you find the person
you are supposed to love, you will know by
staring deeply into her eyes.

Well, that's a deal breaker for me.

It is hard for me to explain why it is so difficult to look into people's eyes. Imagine what it would be like if someone sliced your chest with a scalpel and rummaged around inside you, squeezing your heart and lungs and kidneys. That level of complete invasion is what it feels like when I make eye contact. The reason *I* choose not to look at people is that I don't think it's polite to rifle through someone's thoughts, and the eyes might as well be glass windows, they're that transparent.

I know what love is, but only theoretically. I don't feel it the way other people do. Instead, I dissect it: *Oh, my mother is putting her arms around me and telling me how proud she is of me. She is offering me her last French fry even though I know she wants it. If* p *then* q. *If she acts this way, then she must love me.*

Jess spends time with me that she could otherwise spend with Mark. She doesn't get angry with me, except for the time when I took all the clothes out of her closet in her dorm room and tried to organize them like mine. She watches *CrimeBusters* when we are together, although the sight of blood makes her faint.

If *p* then *q*.

Maybe I'll tell Jess my idea today. And she will say yes to being my girlfriend and I will never have to see Mark again.

In psychoanalytic theory there is a phenomenon called transference. The therapist becomes a blank screen, onto which the patient projects some incident or feeling that began in childhood. For example, a patient who spends sessions silent might be asked by the therapist if there is a reason she doesn't feel comfortable making free associations. Is it because she is afraid the therapist will find her comments stupid? And then, lo and behold, the patient breaks down. *That's what my father used to call me. Stupid.* Suddenly, with the dam broken, the patient will begin to recall all sorts of repressed childhood memories.

My mother never called me stupid; however, it would not be a far reach for someone to look at my feelings for Jess and assume that, in the context of our relationship as tutor and pupil, I am not in love.

I'm just in transference.

"A medium gluten-free pizza," I say to the mountainous woman at the cash register, who is Greek. If she's Greek, why does she have an Italian restaurant?

Jess nudges me.

"Please," I add.

"Eye contact," Jess murmurs.

I force myself to look at the woman. She has hair growing on her upper lip. "Please," I repeat, and I hand her the money.

She gives me back my change. "I'll bring it over when it's ready," the woman says, and she turns back to the wide mouth of the oven. She sticks an enormous paddle inside, like a tongue, and pulls out a calzone.

"So how's school going?" Jess asks.

"It's okay."

"Did you do your homework?"

She doesn't mean my academic homework, which I *always* do. She means my social skills homework. I grimace, thinking about our last lesson. "Not quite."

"Jacob, you promised."

"I didn't promise. I *said* I would try to strike up a conversation with someone my own age, and I did."

"Well, that's great!" Jess says. "What happened?"

I had been in the library at the bank of

computers, and there was a kid sitting next to me. Owen is in my Advanced Placement physics class. He is really quiet and very smart, and if you ask me, he has a little bit of Asperger's in him. It's like gaydar; I can tell.

For fun, I had been on a search engine researching fracture pattern interpretation in the skull, and how you can differentiate between blunt-force trauma and ballistic trauma using concentric fractures, and that factoid seemed to be the perfect opening salvo for a conversation. But I remembered Jess saying that not everyone is wowed by someone who's the human equivalent of a Snapple cap. So instead, I said this:

Me: Are you going to take the AP test in May?

Owen: I don't know. I guess.

Me (snickering): Well, I sure hope they don't find semen!

Owen: What the hell?

Me: An AP test—acid phosphatase test—it's used with a forensic light source to test for presumptive semen. It's not as conclusive as DNA, but then again, when you get a rapist who's had a vasectomy, there won't be any sperm, and if an AP test and a 530-nanometer trispot is all you've got—

Owen: Get the fuck away from me, freak.

Jess has gone all red in the face. "The good news," she says evenly, "is that you tried to initiate a conversation. That's a really big step. The fact that you chose to discuss semen is unfortunate, but still."

By now we have reached the table in the back where Mark is waiting for us. He is chewing gum with his mouth wide open, and wearing that stupid orange sweatshirt. "Hey, Chief," he says.

I shake my head and take a step backward. That sweatshirt, he wasn't wearing it when I first saw him. I bet he put it on on purpose, because he knows I don't like it.

"Mark," Jess says, after glancing at me, "the sweatshirt. Take it off."

He grins at her. "But it's more fun when you do it, baby," he says, and he grabs Jess and tugs her into the booth, practically onto his lap.

Let me just come out and say I don't get the sex thing. I don't understand why someone like Mark, who seems completely hellbent on exchanging bodily fluids with Jess, isn't equally excited to talk about the fact that snot, bleach, and horseradish can all give you false positives for blood during presumptive tests. And I don't understand why neurotypical guys are obsessed with girl breasts. I think it would be an enormous pain to have those sticking out in front of you all the time.

Fortunately, Mark does take off the orange sweatshirt, and Jess folds it up and puts it on the seat where I can't see it. It's bad enough just knowing it's *there,* frankly. "You get me mushroom?" Mark asks.

"You know Jacob isn't a fan of mushroom . . ."

There is a lot I'd do for Jess, but not mushrooms. Even if they're touching the crust on the far side of the pizza, I might have to vomit.

She pulls her cell phone out of her pocket and sets it on the table. It is pink and has my name and number programmed into it. It might be the only cell phone that has my name in it. Even my mother's cell phone lists our number as HOME.

I stare down at the table, still thinking about Mark's sweatshirt.

"Mark," Jess says, sliding his hand out of the back of her shirt. "Come *on.* We're in public." Then she addresses me. "Jacob, while we're waiting for the food, let's practice."

Practice waiting? I don't really need to. I'm fairly proficient at it.

"When there's a lull in the conversation, you can toss out a topic that gets people talking again."

"Yeah," Mark says. "Like: Chicken nuggets are neither chicken nor nuggets. Discuss."

"You're not helping," Jess mutters. "Are you looking forward to anything this week in school, Jacob?"

Sure. Rampant dismissal and abject humiliation. In other words, the usual.

"In physics I have to explain gravity to the rest of the class," I say. "The grade's half on content and half on creativity, and I think I've found the perfect solution."

It took me a while to think of this, and then when I did I couldn't believe I hadn't thought of it before.

"I'm going to drop my pants," I tell her.

Mark bursts out laughing, and for a second, I think maybe I've misjudged him.

"Jacob," Jess says, "you will *not* drop your pants."

"It completely explains Newton's law—"

"I don't care if it explains the meaning of life! Think about how inappropriate that would be. Not only would you embarrass your teacher and make him angry but you'd be teased by other students for doing it."

"I don't know, Jess . . . you know what they say about guys with long IEPs . . . ," Mark says.

"Well, *you* don't have an IEP," Jess answers, smiling. "So there goes that theory."

"You know it, baby."

I have no idea what they're talking about.

When Jess is my girlfriend, we will eat pizza without mushrooms every Sunday. I'll show her how to enhance the contrast of fingerprints on packing tape, and I will let her read my *CrimeBusters* journals. She'll confide that she has quirks, too, like the fact that she has a tail that she keeps hidden under her jeans.

Okay, maybe not a tail. No one really wants a girlfriend with a tail.

"I have something to talk about," I say. My heart starts pounding, and my palms are sweaty. I analyze this the way Dr. Henry Lee would analyze any other piece of forensic evidence and store it away for the future: *Asking girls out can cause changes to the cardiovascular system.* "I would like to know, Jess, if you would like to accompany me to a movie this Friday night."

"Oh, Jacob—well done! We haven't practiced that in a whole month!"

"On Thursday I'll know what's playing. I

can look it up on Moviefone.com." I fold my napkin into eighths. "I could go out on Saturday instead if it's better for you." There is a *CrimeBusters* marathon, but I am willing to make a sacrifice. Surely that will show her how serious I am about this relationship.

"Holy shit," Mark says, grinning. I can feel his eyes on me. (That's the other thing about eyes; they can be hot as lasers, and how would you ever know when they're about to be turned on full force? Better not to risk it, and to avoid eye contact.) "He isn't showing you some communication skill, Jess. The retard is actually asking you out."

"Mark! For God's sake, don't call him—"

"I'm not a retard," I interrupt.

"You're wrong. Jacob knows we're just friends," Jess says.

Mark snorts. "You fucking get *paid* to be his friend!"

I stand up abruptly. "Is that true?"

I guess I have never thought about it. My mother arranged for me to meet with Jess. I assumed Jess wanted to do it because she (a) is writing that paper and (b) likes my company. But now I can picture my mother ripping another check out of the checkbook and complaining like always that we don't have enough to cover our expenses. 1 can picture Jess opening the envelope in her dorm room and tucking that check into the back pocket of her jeans.

1 can picture her taking Mark out for pizza, using cash that came from my mother's bank account.

Gluten-rich mushroom pizza.

"It's not true," Jess says. "1 *am* your friend, Jacob—"

"But you wouldn't be hanging out with Forrest Gump if you didn't get that sweet check every month," Mark says.

She turns on him. "Mark, go away."

"Did you say what 1 think you said? Are you taking *his* side?"

1 start rocking back and forth. *"Nobody puts Baby in a corner,"* 1 quote under my breath.

"This isn't about sides," Jess says.

"Right," Mark snaps. "It's about priorities. 1 want to take you skiing for the afternoon and you blow me off—"

"1 didn't blow you off. 1 invited you along to a standing appointment 1 had, one that 1 couldn't just change at the last minute. 1 already explained to you how important plans are to someone with Asperger's."

Jess grabs Mark's arm, but he shakes her

off. "This is bullshit. I might as well be fucking Mother Teresa."

He storms out of the pizza place. I don't understand what Jess likes about him. He is in the graduate school of business and he plays a lot of hockey. But whenever he's around, the conversation always has to be about him, and I don't know why that's okay if it's Mark talking but not if it's me.

Jess rests her head on her folded arms. Her hair is spread out over her shoulders like a cape. From the way her shoulders are moving, she is probably crying.

"Annie Sullivan," I say.

"What?" Jess looks up. Her eyes are red.

"Mother Teresa saved the poor and the sick, and I'm not poor or sick. Annie Sullivan would have been a better example to use, because she's a famous teacher."

"Oh, God." Jess buries her face in her hands. "I can't handle this."

There is a lull in the conversation, so I fill it. "Are you free on Friday now?"

"You can't be serious."

I consider this. Actually, I am serious all the time. Usually I get accused of not having a sense of humor, although I am capable of that, too.

"Does it matter to you that Mark is the first guy who's ever told me I'm pretty? Or that I actually *love* him?" Her voice is climbing, each word another step on a ladder. "Do you even care if I'm happy?"

"No . . . no . . . and yes." I am getting flustered. Why is she asking me all these things? Mark's gone now; and we can get back to business. "So I made a list of the things people sometimes say that really mean they're tired of listening to you, but I don't know if they're right. Can you check it?"

"Jesus Christ, Jacob!" Jess cries. "Just get lost!"

Her words are huge and fill the entire pizza place. Everyone is watching.

"I have to go talk to him." She stands up.

"But what about my lesson?"

"Why don't you think about what you've learned," Jess says, "and get back to me?"

Then she stomps out of the restaurant, leaving me alone at the table.

The pizza lady brings out the pie, which I will have to eat by myself now. "Hope you're hungry," she says.

I'm not. But I lift up a slice anyway and take a bite and swallow. It tastes like cardboard.

Something pink winks at me from the other side of the napkin dispenser. Jess has left behind her cell phone. I would call her to tell her I have it, but obviously, that won't work.

I tuck it into my pocket and make a mental note. I will just bring it to her when we meet on Tuesday, when I have figured out what it is that I am supposed to have learned.

For over a decade now, we have received a Christmas card from a family I do not know. They address it to the Jenningses, who lived in the house before we did. There is usually a snowy scene on the front, and then inside there is printed gold lettering: HAPPY HOLIDAYS. FONDLY, THE STEINBERGS.

The Steinbergs also include a photocopied note that chronicles everything they have been doing over the years. I've read about their daughter, Sarah, who went from taking gymnastics lessons to being accepted at Vassar to joining a consulting firm to moving to an ashram in India and adopting a baby. I've come to know Marty Steinberg's big career breaks at Lehman Brothers and his shock at being out of a job in 2008, when the company folded; and how he went on to teach business at a community college in upstate New York. I've seen Vicky, his wife, go from being a stay-at-home mom to an entrepreneur selling cookies with the faces of pedigreed dogs on them. (One year there were samples!) This year, Marty took a leave of absence, and he and Vicky went on a cruise to Antarctica—apparently a lifelong dream that was now possible since Eukanuba had bought out Vicky's company. Sarah and her partner, Inez, got married in California, and there was a picture of Raita, now three, as the flower girl.

Each Christmas season, I try to get to the Steinbergs' letter before my mother does. She tosses them into the trash, saying things like *Don't these people ever get the message when the Jenningses don't send a card back?* I fish the card out and put it in a shoe box I have reserved specially for the Steinbergs in my closet.

I don't know why reading their holiday cards makes me feel good, the same way a warm load of laundry does when I'm lying underneath it, or when I take the thesaurus and read through an entire letter's words in one sitting. But today, after I come home from my meeting with Jess, I suffer through the obligatory conversation with my mother *(Mom: How did it go? Me: Fine.*) and then go straight up to my room. Like an addict who needs a fix, I go right for the Steinberg letters and I reread them, from the oldest to the most recent.

It gets a little easier to breathe again, and when I close my eyes I don't see Jess's face on the backs of my lids, grainy like a drawing on an Etch A Sketch. It's like some kind of cryptogram, and *A* really means *Q* and *Z* really means *S* and so on, so the twist of her mouth and the funny note that jumped in her voice are what she really wanted to say, instead of the words she used.

I lie down and imagine showing up on the doorstep of Sarah and Inez.

It is so good to see you, I'd say. *You look exactly like I thought you would.*

I pretend that Vicky and Marty are sitting on the deck of their ship. Marty is sipping a martini while Vicky writes out a postcard with a picture of Valletta, Malta, on the front.

She scrawls, *Wish you were here.* And this time, she addresses it directly to me.

Emma

Nobody dreams of being an agony aunt when they grow up.

Secretly, we all read advice columns—who hasn't scanned *Dear Abby*? But sifting through the problems of other people for a living? No thanks.

I thought that, by now, I'd be a real writer. I'd have books on the *New York Times* list and I'd be feted by the literati for my ability to combine important issues with books that the masses could relate to. Like many other writer wannabes, I'd gone the back route through editing—textbooks, in my case. I liked editing. There was always a right and a wrong answer. And I had assumed that I'd go back to work when Jacob was in school full-time—but that was before I learned that being an advocate for your autistic child's education is a forty-hour-a-week profession in and of itself. All sorts of adaptations had to be argued for and vigilantly monitored: a cool-off pass that would allow Jacob to leave a classroom that got too overwhelming for him; a sensory break room; a paraprofessional who could help him, as an elementary school student, put his thoughts into writing; an individualized education plan; a school counselor who didn't roll her eyes every time Jacob had a meltdown.

I did some freelance editing at night—texts referred to me by a sympathetic former boss—but it wasn't enough to support us. So when the *Burlington Free Press* ran a contest for a new column, I wrote one. I didn't know about photography or chess or gardening, so I picked something I knew: parenting. My first column asked why, no matter how hard we were trying as moms, we always felt like we weren't doing enough.

The paper got over three hundred letters in response to that test column, and suddenly, I was the parenting advice expert.

This blossomed into advice for those without kids, for those who wanted kids, for those who didn't. Subscriptions increased when my column bumped from once a week to twice a week. And here's the really remarkable thing: all these people who trust me to sort out their own sorry lives assume that I have a clue when it comes to sorting out my own.

Today's question comes from Warren, Vermont.

> **Help! My wonderful, polite, sweet twelve-year-old boy has turned into a monster. I've tried punishing him, but nothing works. Why is he acting up?**

I lean over my keyboard and start to type.

> **Whenever a child misbehaves, there's some deeper issue driving the action. Sure, you can take away privileges, but that's putting a Band-Aid over a gaping wound. You need to be a detective and figure out what's really upsetting him.**

I reread what I've written, then delete the whole paragraph. Who am I kidding?

Well, the greater Burlington area, apparently.

My son sneaks out at night to crime scenes, and do I heed my own advice? No.

I am saved from my hypocrisy by the sound of the telephone ringing. It's Monday night, just after eight, so I assume it's for Theo. He picks up on an extension upstairs and a moment later appears in the kitchen. "It's for you," Theo says. He waits till I pick up and disappears into the sanctuary of his bedroom again.

"This is Emma," I say into the receiver.

"Ms. Hunt? This is Jack Thornton . . . Jacob's math teacher?"

Inwardly, I cringe. There are some teachers who see the greater good in Jacob, in spite of all his quirks—and there are others who just don't get him and don't bother to try. Jack Thornton expected Jacob to be a math savant when that's not always part of Asperger's—in spite of what Hollywood seems to think. Instead, he's been frustrated by a student whose handwriting is messy, who transposes numbers when doing calculations, and who is far too literal to understand some of the theoretical concepts of math, like imaginary numbers and matrices.

If Jack Thornton is calling me, it can't be good news.

"Did Jacob tell you what happened today?"

Had Jacob mentioned anything? No, I would remember. But then again, he probably wouldn't confess unless he was directly asked. More likely, I would have read the clues through his behavior, which would have seemed a little off. Usually when Jacob's even more withdrawn, or stimming, or conversely too talkative or manic, I know something's wrong. In this way, I am a better forensic scientist than Jacob would ever guess.

"I asked Jacob to come up to the board to write out his homework answer," Thornton explains, "and when I told him that his work was sloppy, he shoved me."

"*Shoved* you?"

"Yes," the teacher says. "You can imagine the reaction of the rest of the class."

Well, that explains why I didn't see a deterioration in Jacob's behavior. When the class started laughing, he would have assumed he'd done something good.

"I'm sorry," I say. "I'll talk to him."

No sooner have I hung up the phone than Jacob appears in the kitchen and takes the carton of milk out of the fridge.

"Did something happen in math class today?" I ask.

Jacob's eyes widen. *"You can't handle the truth,"* he says, in a dead-on imitation of Jack Nicholson, as sure a sign as any that he's squirming.

"I already talked to Mr. Thornton. Jacob, you cannot go around shoving teachers."

"He started it."

"He did not shove you!"

"No, but he said, 'Jacob, my three-year-old could write more neatly than that.' And *you're* always saying that when someone makes fun of me I should stick up for myself."

The truth is, I *have* said that to Jacob. And there's a piece of me rejoicing in the fact that *he* initiated an interaction with another human, instead of the other way around—even if the interaction wasn't socially appropriate.

The world, for Jacob, is truly black and white. Once, when he was younger, his gym teacher called because Jacob had a meltdown during kickball when a kid threw the big red ball at him to tag him out. *You don't throw things at people,* Jacob tearfully explained. *It's a rule!*

Why should a rule that works in one situation not work in another? If a bully taunts him and I tell him it's all right to reciprocate—because sometimes that's the only way to get these kids to leave him alone—why shouldn't he do the same with a teacher who humiliates him in public?

"Teachers deserve respect," I explain.

"Why do they get it for free, when everyone else has to earn it?"

I blink at him, speechless. *Because the world isn't fair,* I think, but Jacob already knows that better than most of us.

"Are you mad at me?" Unfazed, he reaches for a glass and pours himself some soy milk.

I think that's the attribute I miss seeing the most in my son: empathy. He worries about hurting my feelings, or making me upset, but that's not the same as viscerally feeling someone else's pain. Over the years, he's learned empathy the way I might learn Greek—translating an image or situation in the clearinghouse of his mind and trying to attach the appropriate sentiment to it, but never really fluent in the language.

Last spring, we were filling one of his prescriptions at the pharmacy and I noticed a rack of Mother's Day cards. "Just once I'd like you to buy one of those for me," I said.

"Why?" Jacob asked.

"So I know you love me."

He shrugged. "You already know that."

"But it would be nice," I said, "to wake up on Mother's Day and, like every other mother in this country, to get a card from her son."

Jacob thought about this. "What day is Mother's Day?" he asked.

I told him, and then I forgot about the conversation, until May 10. When I went downstairs and started my Sunday morning coffee-making routine, I found an envelope propped up against the glass carafe. In it was a Mother's Day card.

It didn't say *Dear Mom*. It wasn't signed. In fact, it wasn't written on at all—because Jacob had only done what I'd told him to do, and nothing more.

That day, I sat down at the kitchen table and laughed. I laughed until I started to cry.

Now, I look up at my son, who isn't looking at me. "No, Jacob," I say. "I'm not mad at you."

* * *

Once, when Jacob was ten, we were walking the aisles of a Toys "R" Us in Williston when a little boy jumped out from an endcap wearing a Darth Vader mask and brandishing a light saber. "Bang, you're dead!" the boy cried, and Jacob believed him. He started shrieking and rocking, and then he swept his arm through the display on the shelves. He was doing it to make sure he was not a ghost, to make sure he still could leave an impact in this world. He spun and flailed, trampling boxes as he ran away from me.

By the time I tackled him in the doll section, he was completely out of control. I tried singing Marley to him. I shouted at him to make him respond to my voice. But Jacob was in his own little world, and finally the only way I could make him calm was to become a human blanket, to pin him down on the industrial tile with his arms and legs flung wide.

By then, the police had been called on suspicion of child abuse.

It took fifteen minutes to explain to the officers that my son was autistic, and that I wasn't trying to hurt him—I was trying to help him.

I've often thought, since then, about what would happen if Jacob was stopped by the police while he was on his own—like on Sundays, when he bikes into town to meet Jess. Like the parents of many autistic kids, I've done what the message boards suggest: In Jacob's wallet is a card that says he's autistic, and that explains to the officer that all the behaviors Jacob is exhibiting—flat affect, an inability to look him in the eye, even a flight response—are the hallmarks of Asperger's syndrome. And yet, I've wondered what would happen if the police came in contact with a six-foot, 185-pound, out-of-control boy who reached into his back pocket. Would they wait for him to show his ID card, or would they shoot first?

This is in part why Jacob isn't allowed to drive. He has had the state drivers' manual memorized since he was fifteen, and I know he'd follow traffic rules as if his life depended on it. But what if he got pulled over by a state trooper? *Do you know what you were doing?* the trooper would say, and Jacob would reply: *Driving.* Immediately, he'd be tagged as a wise guy when, in fact, he was only answering the question literally.

If the trooper asked him if he ran a red

light, Jacob would say yes—even if it had happened six months earlier, when the trooper was nowhere nearby.

I know better than to ask him whether my butt looks fat in a particular pair of jeans, because he'll tell me the truth. A police officer would not have that history to help color Jacob's answer.

Well, at any rate, they are not likely to stop him while he's riding into town on his bicycle—unless they take pity on him because it's so cold. I learned a long time ago to stop asking Jacob if he wants a ride. The temperature matters less to him than his independence, in this one small thing.

Hauling the laundry basket into Jacob's room, I place his folded clothes on the bed. When he comes home from school, he'll put them away on his own, with the collars all lined up precisely and the boxer shorts arranged by pattern (stripes, solids, polka dots). On his desk is an overturned fish tank with a small coffee cup warmer, a tinfoil dish, and one of my lipstick containers beneath it. Sighing, I lift the fingerprint fuming chamber and reclaim my makeup, careful not to disturb the rest of the precisely ordered items.

Jacob's room has the nuclear precision of an *Architectural Digest* feature: everything has its place; the bed is made neatly; the pencils on the desk sit at perfect right angles to the wood grain. Jacob's room is the place entropy goes to die.

On the other hand, Theo is messy enough to make up for both of them. I can barely kick my way through the field of dirty clothes tangled on his carpet, and when I set the basket down on Theo's bed, something squeaks. I don't put away Theo's laundry, either—but that's because I can't bear to see the drawers haphazardly stuffed with clothes that I distinctly remember folding on the laundry counter.

I glance around and spy a glass with something green festering inside it, beside a half-eaten container of yogurt. I place these into the empty basket to go back downstairs and then, in a fit of kindness, try to pull the bedding into some semblance of order. It's when I am shaking the pillowcase into position around Theo's pillow that the plastic case falls down and hits my ankle.

It's a game—something called Naruto, with a manga cartoon character brandishing a sword.

It's played on the Wii, a gaming system we've never owned.

I could ask Theo why he has this, but something tells me I do not want to hear the answer. Not after this weekend, when I learned that Jacob's been running away at night. Not after last night, when his math teacher called to tell me he's acting out in class.

Sometimes I think the human heart is just a simple shelf. There's only so much you can pile onto it before something falls off an edge and you are left to pick up the pieces.

I stare at the video game for a moment, and then I slip it back into the pillowcase again before leaving Theo's room.

Theo

I taught my brother how to stick up for himself.

It happened when we were younger—I was eleven and he was fourteen. I was on a jungle gym on the playground and he was sitting on the grass, reading a biography that the librarian had purchased just for him about Edmond Locard, the father of fingerprint analysis. Mom was inside, having one of a bazillion IEP meetings to make sure that Jacob's school could be as safe a place for him as his home.

Apparently, that didn't include the playground.

Two boys on incredibly sweet skateboards were doing tricks on the stairs when they spotted Jacob. They walked over, and one of them grabbed his book.

"That's mine," Jacob said.

"Then come and get it," the kid said. He tossed the book to his buddy, who tossed it back, playing monkey in the middle with Jacob, who kept grabbing at it. But Jacob isn't exactly a natural athlete, and he never caught it.

"It's a *library* book, you cretins," Jacob said, as if that might make a difference. "It's going to get ruined!"

"That would suck." The boy tossed the book into a huge mud puddle.

"Better rescue it," his friend added, and Jacob dove for the book.

I called out to him, but it was too late. One of the boys knocked Jacob's feet out from underneath him, so that he landed facefirst in the puddle. He sat up, soaking wet, spitting dirt.

"Happy reading, 'tard," the first boy

said, and they both laughed and skated away.

Jacob didn't move. He sat in the puddle, holding the book to his chest. "Get up," I said, and I held out my hand to help him.

With a grunt, Jacob stood. He tried to turn the pages in the book, but they were glued together with mud. "It'll dry," I said. "You want me to get Mom?"

He shook his head. "She'll be mad at me."

"No, she won't," I said, even though he was probably right. His clothes were totally destroyed. "Jacob, you've got to learn to fight back. Do whatever they do, only ten times worse."

"Push them into a puddle?"

"Well, no. You can just . . . I don't know. Call them names."

"Their names are Sean and Amahl," Jacob said.

"Not *those* names. Try *You dickhead.* Or *Cut it out, prick.*"

"That's swearing . . ."

"Yeah. But it will get them to think twice before they cream you again."

Jacob started rocking. "During the Vietnam War, the BBC was worried about how to pronounce the name of a bombed village—Phuoc Me—without offending their listeners. They decided to use the name of a nearby village instead. Unfortunately, it was called Ban Me Tuat."

"Well, maybe the next time a bully is holding your face down in a mud puddle you can shout out the names of Vietnamese villages."

"I'll get you, my pretty, and your little dog too!" Jacob quoted.

"You might want to go a little more hard-core," I suggested.

He thought for a moment. *"Yippee kay yay, motherfucker!"*

"Nice. So next time a kid like that grabs your book, what do you say?"

"Pussbucket asshole, give it back!"

I burst out laughing. "Jacob," I said. "You just might be gifted at this."

I honestly do not have any intention of going into another house. But then on Tuesday I have an absolutely crappy day at school. First, I get a 79 on a math test, and I never get Cs; second, I am the only kid whose yeast doesn't manage to grow in the lab we're doing in bio; and third, I think I am getting a cold. I cut last period, because I just want to huddle in bed with a cup of tea. In fact, it's the craving for tea which makes me think about that professor's house I was in last week, and as luck would have it, I am only three blocks away when the thought enters my mind.

There's still no one in the house, and I don't even have to jimmy the back door; it's been left unlocked. The cane is still leaning against the entryway wall, and that same hoodie is hanging, but now there's a wool coat, too, and a pair of work boots. Someone's finished the bottle of red wine. There's a Bose stereo on the counter that wasn't there last week, and a hot pink iPod Nano is charging in its dock.

I push the power button and see that Ne-Yo is cued up.

Either these are the hippest professors ever or their grandkids need to stop leaving their shit lying around.

The teakettle is sitting on the stove, so I fill it up and turn on the burner while I rummage around the cabinets for a tea bag. They are hiding on a shelf behind a roll of tinfoil. I choose Mango Madness, and while my water is heating, I scroll through the iPod. I am impressed. My mom can barely figure out how to use iTunes, and yet here is some elderly professor couple whizzing through technology.

I suppose they might not be that *old.* I've imagined them that way, but maybe the cane is for arthroscopic surgery, because the professor plays hockey on the weekends and blew out his knee as a goalie. Maybe they're my mom's age and the hoodie belongs to their daughter, who's my age. Maybe she goes to my school. Or even sits next to me in biology.

I slip the iPod into my pocket and pour the water from the whistling kettle, and that's when I realize that I can hear a shower running above me.

Forgetting my tea, I creep into the

living room, past the monster enter-tainment system, and up the stairs.

The water sound is coming from the master bathroom suite.

The bed's unmade. It's a quilt with roses embroidered all over it, and there is a pile of clothes on a chair. I pick up a lacy bra and run my hand over the straps.

That's when I realize that the bath-room door's ajar, and that I can sort of see the shower reflected in the mirror.

My day has gotten considerably better in the past thirty seconds.

There's steam, so I can only make out the curves when she turns and the fact that her hair reaches her shoulders. She's humming, and she's wicked off-key. *Turn,* I silently beg. *Full frontal.*

"Oh, crap," the woman says, and suddenly she opens the door of the shower. I see her arm emerge as she blindly feels around for her towel, which is hanging on a rack beside the shower door, and wipes her eyes. I hold my breath, staring at her shoulder. Her boob.

Still blinking, she lets go of the towel and turns.

In that second, our eyes meet.

Jacob

People say things all the time they don't mean, and neurotypical folks manage to figure out the message all the same. Take, for example, Mimi Scheck in school. She said she'd die if Paul McGrath didn't ask her to the Winter Formal, but in reality, she would not have died—she would just have been really sad. Or the way Theo sometimes smacks another kid's shoulder and says "Get out!" when that really means he wants his friend to keep talking. Or that time my mom muttered "Oh, that's just *great*" when we got a flat tire on the highway although it clearly was not great; it was a co-lossal hassle.

So maybe when Jess told me to get lost on Sunday, she really meant something else.

I think I might be dying of spinal meningitis. Headaches, dementia, stiffness of the neck, high fever. I have two out of the four. I don't know if I should ask my mother to take me for a lumbar puncture or just ride it out until I die. I have already prepared a note explaining how I'd like to be dressed at my funeral, just in case.

It is equally possible, I suppose, that the reason I have a severe headache and stiff neck is I have gotten no sleep since Sunday, when I last saw Jess.

She didn't send me pictures of her new house in advance, like she promised. I sent her forty-eight emails yesterday to remind her, and she didn't respond to any of them. I can't call to remind her to send the pictures because I still have her cell phone.

Last night at about four in the morning, I asked myself what Dr. Henry Lee would do, if confronted with the evidence that:

1. No photos ever arrived by email.

2. None of my forty-eight messages were acknowledged.

Hypothesis One would be that Jess's email account is not functional, which seems unlikely because it is connected with the entirety of UVM. Hypothesis Two would be that she is actively choosing to not communicate with me, which would indicate anger or frustration (see above: *Just get lost*). But that doesn't make sense, since she specifically told me at our last meeting that I should tell her what I'd learned . . . which implies another meeting.

Incidentally, I have made a list of what I learned at our last meeting:

1. Gluten-free pizza tastes disgusting.

2. Jess is not available to go to a movie this Friday night.

3. Her cell phone sounds like a bird chirping when you power it down.

4. Mark is a dim-witted moron. (Although, in fairness, this is (a) redundant and (b) something I already knew.)

The only reason I went to school today, feeling as awful as I do, is that if I stayed home I know my mother would insist I miss my lesson with Jess, and I can't do that. I have to give her back her phone, after all. And if I see her face-to-face, I can ask her why she didn't answer my emails.

Usually it is Theo's job to walk me to the UVM campus, which is only a half mile from school. He drops me off at Jess's dorm room, which she has always left unlocked for me, so that I can wait for her until she gets out of her anthropology class. Sometimes I do my homework while I'm waiting, and sometimes I look through the papers on her desk. Once I sprayed her perfume on my clothes and went around smelling like her for the rest of the day. Then Jess shows up and we go to the library to work, or sometimes to the student union or a café on Church Street.

I could probably get to Jess's dorm while comatose, but today—when I really do need Theo's help to find my way to a new location—he leaves school because he's sick. He searches me out after sixth period and tells me he feels like crap and is going home to die.

Don't, I tell him. *That would really upset Mom.*

My immediate first instinct is to ask him how I am supposed to get to Jess's if he goes home sick, but then I remember Jess telling me that not everything is about me, and that putting yourself in someone else's shoes is part of social interactions. (Not literally. I would not fit in Theo's shoes. He wears a ten and a half, while I wear a twelve.) So I tell Theo to feel better and then I go to the guidance counselor, Mrs. Grenville. We examine the map Jess has given me and decide that I should take Bus H-5 and get off at the third stop. She even draws a route in highlighter pen from the bus stop to the house.

As it turns out, the map is a very good one, even if it's not drawn to scale. After I get off the bus, I turn right at the fire hydrant and then count six houses on the left. Jess's new temporary home is an old brick house with ivy growing up the sides. I wonder if she knows that the tendrils of ivy can break apart mortar and brick. I wonder if I should tell her. If someone told *me,* I would lie in bed at night wondering if the whole house was going to crumble around me.

I am still very nervous when I ring the front doorbell, because I have never seen the inside of this house before and that makes me feel like my bones have gone to jelly.

No one answers, so I go around the back.

I glance down at the snow and make a mental note of what I see, but it isn't really important because The Door Is Unlocked, and that must mean Jess is expecting me. I feel myself relaxing already: it's just like her dorm room; I will go in and wait, and when she returns, everything will be back to normal.

There are only two times that Jess has gotten angry with me, and both occurred while I was waiting for her to show up. The first was when I took all her clothes out of her closet and arranged them according to the electromagnetic color spectrum, like mine. The second time was when I sat down at her desk and noticed the calculus problem set she was working on. She'd done half the problems wrong, so I fixed them for her.

Theo is the person who made me understand that the rules of violence are based on threat. If there is an actual problem, there are only two options:

1. Retaliation

2. Confrontation

It's gotten me into trouble.

I have been sent to the principal's office for smacking a boy who threw a paper airplane at me during English class. When Theo ruined one of my forensic experiments-in-progress, I went into his bedroom with a pair of scissors and systematically hacked his comic book collection to bits. Once in eighth grade, I found out that a group of kids were making fun of me, and as if someone had flipped an electrical switch inside me, I went into a frantic rage. I huddled in a cubicle in the school library, crafting a hit list of the people I hated and how I would like their lives to end: knife wound in the locker room at gym, bomb in their locker, cyanide in their Diet Coke. As is the Aspergian nature, I'm fanatically organized about some things and disorganized about others, and as luck would have it I lost that piece of paper. I figured someone (maybe me) had thrown it out, but my history teacher found it and gave it to the principal, who called my mother.

She yelled at me for seventy-nine straight minutes, mostly about how violated she felt by my actions, and then she got even more angry because I couldn't really understand why something *I* did had upset *her.* So she took ten of my *CrimeBusters* notebooks and ran them through her bill shredder page by page, and suddenly, her point was crystal clear. I was so furious that, that night, I dumped the bin of shredded paper over her head while she was asleep.

Luckily, I didn't get suspended—most of the administration of the school knew me well enough to know I was not a threat to public safety—but my mother's lesson was enough to make me see why I could never do anything like that again.

I say all this by way of explanation: Impulsiveness is part of what it means to have Asperger's.

And it never ends well.

Emma

I am allowed to work at home on my column, but every Tuesday afternoon I have to trot downtown to meet with my editor. Mostly it's a therapy session—she tells me what's wrong with her life and expects me to dole her out advice, the way I do for the masses in the paper.

I don't mind, because I think that one hour a week of counseling is a pretty fair trade for a paycheck and health insurance. But it also means that on Tuesdays, when Jacob meets with Jess, she is responsible for getting him back to our house.

Tonight, as soon as I walk through the

door, I find Theo in the kitchen. "How do you feel?" I ask, pressing my palm against his forehead. "Do you have a fever?"

I'd called home from Burlington, like I usually do before I leave the office, only to find out that Theo was sick and frantic because he'd left school without remembering that today is the day he walks Jacob to his appointment with Jess. A second call to the guidance department kept me from panicking: Mrs. Grenville had talked to Jacob about taking a bus to Jess's new house and said he felt confident about doing it on his own.

"It's just a cold," Theo says, ducking away. "But Jacob's not home yet and it's past four-thirty."

He doesn't really need to say any more: Jacob would rather saw off his arm with a butter knife than miss an episode of *Crime-Busters*. But Jacob's only fifteen minutes later than normal. "Well, he was meeting Jess somewhere new today. Maybe it's a little farther away than her dorm was."

"But what if he never got there?" Theo says, visibly upset. "I should have just stayed in school and walked him there like usual—"

"Honey, you were sick. Besides, Mrs. Grenville thought this might be a good opportunity for Jacob to be independent. And I think I've got Jess's new phone number on my email; I can call if it makes you feel better." I wrap my arms around Theo. It's been too long since I hugged him; at fifteen, he ducks away from physical affection. But it's sweet to see him worried about Jacob. There might be friction between them, but at heart, Theo loves his brother. "I'm sure Jacob's fine, but I'm glad he's got you looking out for him," I say, and in that instant, I make a snap decision to capitalize on the goodwill Theo's feeling for Jacob. "Let's go out for Chinese tonight," I suggest, even though eating out is a luxury we can't afford; plus, it's harder to find food Jacob can eat if I don't make it myself.

An unreadable expression crosses Theo's face, but then he nods. "That would be cool," he says gruffly, and he slides away from my grasp.

The door to the mudroom opens. "Jacob?" I call, and I go to meet him.

For a moment, I can't speak. His eyes are wild and his nose is running. His hands flap at his sides as he shoves me into the wall and runs up to his room. "Jacob!"

He has no lock on his bedroom door; I

removed it years ago. Now, I push the door open and find Jacob inside his closet, underneath the tendrils of shirt cuffs and sweatpants, rocking back and forth and emitting a high, reedy note from his throat.

"What's the matter, baby?" I say, getting down on my hands and knees and crawling into the closet, too. I wrap my arms tight around him and start singing:

"I shot the sheriff . . . but I didn't shoot the deputy."

Jacob's hands are flapping so hard that he is bruising me. "Talk to me," I say. "Did something happen with Jess?"

At the sound of her name, he arches backward, as if he's been pierced by a bullet. He starts smacking his head against the wall so hard that it dents the plaster.

"Don't," I beg, using every bit of strength I have to drag him forward, so that he cannot hurt himself.

Dealing with an autistic meltdown is like dealing with a tornado. Once you are close enough to see it coming, there's nothing to do but weather the storm. Unlike a child having a temper tantrum, Jacob doesn't care if his behavior is making me react. He doesn't make sure he's not hurting himself.

He isn't doing it in order to get something. In fact, he's not in control of himself at all. And unlike when he was four or five, I am not big enough to control him anymore.

I get up and turn off all the lights in the room and pull down the blackout shades so that it is dark. I put on his Marley CD. Then I start pulling clothes off the hangers in his closet and pile them on his body— which at first makes him scream harder and then, as the weight builds, calms him down. By the time he falls asleep in my arms, I have ripped my blouse and my stockings. The CD has repeated four times in its entirety. The LED display on his alarm clock reads 8:35 P.M.

"What set you off?" I whisper. It could have been anything—an argument with Jess, or the fact that he didn't like the layout of the kitchen in her new accommodations, or the realization too late that he was missing his favorite TV show. I kiss Jacob on the forehead. Then, gently, I disengage myself from the knot of his arms and leave him curled on the floor with a pillow under his head. I cover him with the rainbow postage-stamp summertime quilt that's been folded up for the season in his closet.

Muscles stiff, I walk downstairs again. The lights have all been turned off, except for one in the kitchen.

Let's go out for Chinese tonight.

But that was before I knew that I would be sucked into the black hole that Jacob can become at any given moment.

There is a cereal bowl on the counter, with a puddle of soy milk still in the bottom. The Rice Chex box stands beside it like an accusation.

Motherhood is a Sisyphean task. You finish sewing one seam shut, and another rips open. I have come to believe that this life I'm wearing will never really fit.

I carry the bowl to the sink and swallow the tears that spring to the back of my throat. *Oh, Theo. I'm so sorry.*

Again.

CASE 3: BRAGGED, TAUNTED, "KAUGHT"

Dennis Rader was a married man with two grown children, a former Cub Scout leader, and president of his Lutheran church. He also—after a thirty-one-year investigation—was revealed to be the serial killer known as BTK, short for Bind, Torture, and Kill—his method for murdering ten people in the Wichita, Kansas, area between 1974 and 1991. After the killings, letters were sent to the police bragging of the killings and offering grisly details. Following a twenty-five-year silence, those letters and packages resumed in 2004, claiming responsibility for a murder for which he had not been suspected. DNA was taken from beneath the fingernails of a victim, and authorities gathered

eleven hundred DNA samples, attempting to find the serial killer.

In one of BTK's communications—a computer disk mailed to KSAS-TV—metadata from the Microsoft Word document revealed that the author was someone named Dennis, as well as a link to the Lutheran Church. Searching on the Internet, police were able to find a suspect: Dennis Rader. By obtaining his daughter's DNA and comparing it with DNA samples found on the victims, the police were able to make a familial match—giving them enough probable cause for arrest. He has been sentenced to 175 years to life.

So to all of you who surf for Internet porn or spend your free time writing anarchist manifestos: Beware. You can't ever really get rid of something on your computer.

3

Rich

I've faced down a lot of harrowing situations in my twenty years on the job: suicides in progress, felons on the run after an armed robbery, rape victims too traumatized to tell me their story. None of these, however, compare to having to work an audience made up of seven-year-olds.

"Can you show us your gun again?" one kid asks.

"Not a great idea," I say, glancing at the teacher, who already asked me to remove my holster and weapon before coming into the class for Job Day—a request I had to refuse, since technically, I was still on the clock.

"Do you get to shoot it?"

I look over the ammo-obsessed boy's head at the rest of the class. "Any other questions?"

A little girl raises her hand. I recognize her; she might have come to one of Sasha's birthday parties. "Do you always get the bad guys?" she asks.

There's no way to explain to a child that the line between good and evil isn't nearly as black and white as a fairy tale would lead you to believe. That an ordinary person can turn into a villain, under the right circumstances. That sometimes we dragon slayers do things we aren't proud of.

I look her in the eye. "We sure try," I say.

On my hip, my cell phone starts to vibrate. I flip it open, see the number of the station, and stand up. "I'm going to have to cut this short . . . So one more time— what's the number one rule of crime scenes?"

The class sings the answer back to me: "Don't touch something wet if it's not from you!"

As the teacher asks them all to thank me with a round of applause, I crouch down near Sasha's desk. "What do you think? Did I embarrass you beyond repair?"

"You did okay," she says.

"I can't stay to have lunch with you," I apologize. "I have to go down to the station."

"That's all right, Daddy." Sasha shrugs. "I'm used to it."

The hell with a bullet. What kills me is disappointing my kid.

I kiss her on the crown of her head and let the teacher walk me to the door. Then I drive right to the station and get a quick briefing from the sergeant who took the original complaint.

Mark Maguire, a UVM graduate student, is slouched in the waiting room. He's wearing a baseball cap pulled low over his face and is bouncing his leg up and down nervously. I watch him for a second through the window before I head out to meet him.

"Mr. Maguire?" I say. "I'm Detective Matson. What can I do for you?"

He stands up. "My girlfriend's missing."

"Missing," I repeat.

"Yeah. I called her last night, and there was no answer. And this morning, when I went to her place, she was gone."

"When was the last time you saw her?"

"Tuesday morning," Mark says.

"Could there have been some emergency? Or an appointment she didn't tell you about?"

"No. She never goes anywhere without her purse, and it was still in the house . . . along with her coat. It's freezing out. Why would she have gone somewhere without her coat?" His voice is wild, worried.

"You two have a fight?"

"She was kind of pissed off at me this weekend," he admits. "But we'd talked it out. We were good again."

I bet, I think. "Have you tried calling her friends?"

"No one's seen her. Not her friends, not her teachers. And she's not the kind of person who cuts classes."

We do not usually open up a missing person's case until thirty-six hours have passed—although that's not a hard-and-fast rule. The extent of the net to be cast is determined by the missing person's status: at risk, or at no apparent risk. And right now, there's something about this guy—some hunch—that makes me think he's not telling me everything. "Mr. Maguire," I say, "why don't you and I take a ride?"

Jess Ogilvy is doing pretty damn well for a grad student. She lives in a tony neighborhood full of brick houses and BMWs. "How long has she lived here?" I ask.

"Only a week—she's house-sitting for one of her professors, who's in Italy for the semester."

We park on the street, and Maguire leads me to the back door, which isn't locked. That's not an uncommon occurrence around here; in spite of all my warnings about being safe instead of sorry, a lot of folks make the incorrect assumption that crime could not and does not happen in this town.

In the mudroom, there's a mélange of items—from the coat that must belong to the girl to a walking stick to a pair of men's boots. The kitchen is tidy, and there is a mug in the sink with a tea bag in it. "I didn't touch anything," Maguire says. "This was all here when I showed up this morning." The mail is stacked neatly in a pile on the table. A purse lies on its side, and I open it to find a wallet with $213 still in it.

"Did you notice anything missing?" I ask.

"Yeah," Maguire says. "Upstairs." He leads me to a guest bedroom where the drawers of a single dresser are half open, clothes spilling out of them. "She's a neat freak," he says. "She'd never leave the bed unmade, or have clothes lying around the floor like this. But this box with the gift wrap on it? It had a backpack inside that's gone now. It still had the tags on it. Her aunt got it for her for Christmas, and she hated it."

I walk to the closet. Inside are several dresses, as well as a few button-down men's shirts and pairs of jeans. "Those are mine," Maguire says.

"You live here, too?"

"Not officially, as far as the professor goes. But yeah, I've been staying over most nights. Until she kicked me out, anyway."

"She kicked you out?"

"I told you, we kind of had a fight. She didn't want to talk to me on Sunday night. But Monday, we'd worked things out."

"Define that," I say.

"We had sex," Maguire replies.

"Consensual?"

"Jesus, dude. What kind of guy do you think I am?" He seems truly affronted.

"What about her makeup? Her toiletries?"

"Her toothbrush is missing," Maguire says. "But her makeup's still here. Look, shouldn't you be calling in backup or something? Or posting an AMBER Alert?"

I ignore him. "Did you try contacting her parents? Where do they live?"

"I called them—they're in Bennington, and they haven't heard from her, and now they're in a panic, too."

Great, I think. "Has she ever disappeared like this before?"

"I don't know. I've only been going out with her for a few months."

"Look," I say. "If you stick around, she'll probably call, or just come back home. Sounds to me like she needed to cool off for a while."

"You gotta be kidding me," Maguire says. "If she left on purpose, why would she forget to take her wallet but remember her cell phone? Why would she use a backpack she couldn't wait to return for store credit?"

"I don't know. To throw you off her trail, maybe?"

Maguire's eyes flash, and I know the moment before he springs that he is going to come after me. I throw him off with one quick move that twists his arm behind his back. "Careful," I mutter. "I could arrest you for that."

Maguire tenses in my hold. "My girlfriend's gone missing. I pay your salary, and you won't even do your job and investigate?"

Technically, if Maguire is a student, he's not paying my salary, but I am not about to press the point. "Tell you what," I say, releasing him. "I'll take one more look around."

I wander into the master bedroom, but clearly Jess Ogilvy hasn't been sleeping there; it is pristine. The master bathroom reveals slightly damp towels, but the shower floor is already dry. Downstairs, there's no sign of disorder in the living room. I walk around the perimeter of the house and then check the mailbox. Inside is a note, printed from a computer, asking the postman to hold the mail until further notified.

Who the hell types a note to the postman?

Snapping on a pair of gloves, I slip the note into an evidence bag. I'll have the lab run a ninhydrin test for prints.

Right now, my hunch is that if they don't match Jess Ogilvy's, they're going to match Mark Maguire's.

Emma

I don't know what to expect when I go into Jacob's room the next morning. He slept through the night—I checked on him every hour—but I know from past experience that he won't be expressive until those neurotransmitters aren't raging through his bloodstream anymore.

I called Jess twice—on her cell, and at her new residence—but only got voice mail. I've sent her an email, asking her to tell me what happened at yesterday's session, if there was anything out of the ordinary. But until I hear back from her, I have to deal with Jacob.

When I peek in at 6:00 A.M., he's not

sleeping anymore. He's sitting on his bed with his hands in his lap, staring at the wall across from him.

"Jacob?" I say tentatively. "Honey?" I walk closer and gently shake him.

Jacob continues to stare at the wall in silence. I wave a hand in front of his face, but he doesn't respond.

"Jacob!" I grab his shoulders and pull on them. He topples to the side and just lies where he has fallen.

Panic climbs the ladder of my throat. "Speak to me," I demand. I am thinking catatonia. I am thinking schizophrenia. I am thinking of all the lost places Jacob could slip to in his own mind, and not return.

Straddling his big body, I strike him hard enough across the face to leave a red handprint, and still he doesn't react.

"Don't," I say, starting to cry. "Don't do this to me."

There is a voice at the door. "What's going on?" Theo asks, his face still hazy with sleep and his hair sticking up in hedgehog spikes.

In that instant, I realize that Theo might be my savior. "Say something that would upset your brother," I order.

He looks at me as if I'm crazy.

"There's something wrong with him," I explain, my voice breaking. "I just want him to come back. I *need* to make him come back."

Theo glances down at Jacob's slack body, his vacant eyes, and I can tell he's scared. "But—"

"Do it, Theo," I say.

I think it's the quiver in my voice, not the command, which makes him agree. Tentatively, Theo leans close to Jacob. "Wake up!"

"Theo," I sigh. We both know he's holding back.

"You're going to be late for school," Theo says. I watch closely, but there's no recognition in Jacob's eyes.

"I'm getting in the shower first," Theo adds. "And then I'm gonna mess up your closet." When Jacob just stays silent, the anger Theo usually keeps hidden rolls over him like a tsunami. "You freak," he shouts, so loud that Jacob's hair stirs with the force of his breath. "You stupid goddamn freak!"

Jacob doesn't even flinch.

"Why can't you be normal?" Theo yells, punching his brother in the chest. He hits him again, harder this time. "Just be fucking normal!" he cries, and I realize tears are streaming down Theo's face. For a moment, we are caught in this hell, with Jacob unresponsive between us.

"Get me a phone," I say, and Theo turns and flies out the door.

As I sink down beside Jacob, the bulk of his weight sways toward me. Theo reappears with the telephone, and I punch in the page number for Jacob's psychiatrist, Dr. Murano. She calls me back thirty seconds later, her voice still rough with sleep. "Emma," she says. "What's going on?"

I explain Jacob's meltdown last night, and his catatonia this morning. "And you don't know what triggered it?" she asks.

"No. He had a meeting with his tutor yesterday." I look at Jacob. A line of drool snakes from the corner of his mouth. "I called her, but she hasn't phoned me back yet."

"Does he look like he's in physical distress?"

No, I think. *That would be me.* "I don't know . . . I don't think so."

"Is he breathing?"

"Yes."

"Does he know who you are?"

"No," I admit, and this is what really scares me. If he doesn't know who I am, how can I help him remember who *he* is?

"Tell me his vitals."

I put the phone down and look at my wrist-watch, make a count. "His pulse is ninety and his respirations are twenty."

"Look, Emma," the doctor says, "I'm an hour away from where you are. I think you need to take him to the ER."

I know what will happen then. If Jacob is unable to snap out of this, he'll be a candidate for a 302 involuntary commitment in the hospital psych ward.

After I hang up, I kneel down in front of Jacob. "Baby, just give me a sign. Just show me you're on the other side."

Jacob doesn't even blink.

Wiping my eyes, I head to Theo's room. He's barricaded himself inside; I have to bang heavily on the door to be heard over the beat of his music. When he finally opens it, his eyes are red-rimmed and his jaw is set. "I need your help moving him," I say flatly, and for once Theo doesn't fight me. Together we try to haul Jacob's big frame out of his bed and downstairs, into the car. I take his arms; Theo takes his legs. We drag, we push, we shove. By the time we reach the mudroom door, I am bathed in sweat and Theo's legs are bruised from where he twice stumbled under Jacob's weight.

"I'll get the car door," Theo says, and he runs into the driveway, his socks crunching lightly on the old snow.

Together, we manage to get Jacob to the car. He doesn't even make a sound when his bare feet touch the icy driveway. We put him into the backseat headfirst, and then I struggle to pull him to a sitting position, practically crawling into his lap to fasten his seat belt. With my head pressed up against Jacob's heart, I listen for the click of metal to metal.

"Heeeeere's Johnny."

The words aren't his. They're Jack Nicholson's, in *The Shining*. But it's his voice, his beautiful, tattered, sandpaper voice.

"Jacob?" I cup my hands around his face.

He is not looking at me, but then again, he never looks at me. "Mom," Jacob says, "my feet are really cold."

I burst into tears and gather him tight in my arms. "Oh, baby," I reply, "let's do something about that."

Jacob

This is where I go, when I go:

It's a room with no windows and no doors, and walls that are thin enough for me to see and hear everything but too thick to break through.

I'm there, but I'm not there.

I am pounding to be let out, but nobody can hear me.

This is where I go, when I go:

To a country where everyone's face looks different from mine, and the language is the act of not speaking, and noise is everywhere in the air we breathe. I am doing what the Romans do in Rome; I am trying to communicate, but no one has bothered to tell me that these people cannot hear.

This is where I go, when I go:

Somewhere completely, unutterably orange.

This is where I go, when I go:

To the place where my body becomes a piano, full of black keys only—the sharps and the flats, when everyone knows that to play a song other people want to hear, you need some white keys.

This is why I come back:

To find those white keys.

I am not exaggerating when I say that my mother has been staring at me for fifteen minutes. "Shouldn't you be doing something else?" I finally ask.

"Right. You're right," she says, flustered, but she doesn't actually leave.

"Mom," I groan. "There has got to be something more fascinating than watching me eat." There's watching paint dry, for example. Or watching the laundry cycle.

I know that I've given her a scare today, because of what happened this morning. It's apparent in (a) her inability to leave my side for more than three seconds and (b) her willingness to cook me Ore-Ida Crinkles fries for breakfast. She even forced Theo to take the bus today, instead of being driven into school like usual, because she didn't want to leave me at home alone and had already decided that I was going to have a sick day.

Frankly, I don't understand why she's so upset, when I am the one who went missing.

Frankly, I wonder who Frank was, and why he has an adverb all to himself.

"I'm going to take a shower," I announce. "Are you coming, too?"

That, finally, shocks her into moving. "You're sure you feel all right?"

"Yes."

"I'll come up and check on you in a few minutes, then."

As soon as she is gone, I put the plate with the French fries on the nightstand. I am going to take a shower; I just have something to do first.

I have my own fuming chamber. It used to be the home of my pet fish, Arlo, before he died. The empty fish tank sits on the top of my dresser now, inverted. Underneath the fish tank is a coffee cup warmer. I used to use a Sterno, but my mother wasn't very enthusiastic about fire (even one burning at low level) in my room, hence the electric warmer. On top of this I make a little boat out of aluminum foil, and then I squeeze in a small nickel-size dollop of Krazy Glue. I take the mug of cocoa (nondairy, of course) my mother brought me and stick it in the chamber, too—it will provide humidity in the air, even though I won't want to drink it after the fuming, when white scum is floating around on its surface. Finally, I place inside the drinking glass that has a known sample on it—my test fingerprint—to make sure everything is working.

There's only one thing left to do, but it makes my stomach clench.

I have to force myself to sort through the clothes I was wearing yesterday to find the item I want to fume, the one I took home from her house. And that of course makes me think of everything else, which means the corners of my mind go black.

I have to actively work to not be sucked into that hole again.

Even through the latex glove I've slipped on I can feel how cold the metal is. How cold everything was, last night.

In the shower, I scrub really hard, until my skin is too pink and my eyes are raw from staring into the stream of water. I remember everything.

Even when I don't want to.

Once, when I was in third grade, a boy made fun of the way I talked. I didn't understand why his impression of me, with words falling flat as pancakes, would be funny to anyone. I didn't understand why he kept saying things like *Take me to your leader.* All I knew was that he followed me around on the playground, and everywhere he went, people would laugh at me. *What is your problem?* I finally asked, turning around to find him right on my heels.

What is your problem? he parroted.

I'd really prefer it if you could find something else to do, I said.

I'd really prefer it if you could find something else to do.

And before I knew what I was really planning, my fingers closed into a fist and punched him square in the face.

There was blood everywhere. I didn't like having his blood on my hand. I didn't like having it on my shirt, which was supposed to be yellow.

The boy, meanwhile, was knocked unconscious, and I was dragged to the principal's office and suspended for a week.

I don't like to talk about that day, because it makes me feel like I am full of broken glass.

I never thought I'd see that much blood again on my hands, but I was wrong.

It only takes ten minutes for the cyanoacrylate—the Krazy Glue—to properly work. The monomers in its vapors polymerize in the presence of water, amines, amides, hydroxyl, and carboxylic acid—all of which happen to be found in the oils left by fingerprints. They stick to those oils, creating a latent image, which can be made more visible by dusting with powder. Then, the image can be photographed and resized and compared to the known sample.

There's a knock on my door. "You okay in there?"

"No, I'm hanging from a closet rod," I say.

This is not the truth.

"That's not funny, Jacob," my mother replies.

"Fine, I'm getting dressed."

This is not the truth, either. I am actually wearing my underwear and a T-shirt right now.

"Okay," she says. "Well, give a holler when you're done."

I wait until her footsteps fade down the hall, and then I remove the glass from beneath the fish tank. Sure enough, there are several prints. I dust them with a dual-use powder, which has contrast on both white and black surfaces. Then I dust the prints on the second item, too.

I photograph them at close range with the digital camera I got for Christmas two years ago and load the images into my computer. It's always a good idea to photograph your latent prints prior to lifting them, just in case you destroy them during the process. Later, in Adobe Photoshop, I can invert the colors of the ridges and resize the prints. I can begin an analysis.

I carefully tape over the print to preserve it, intending to hide what I took away from her house in a place where no one will ever find it.

My mother, by then, is tired of waiting. She opens the door. "Jacob, put on a pair of pants!"

She holds her hand over her eyes but enters my bedroom all the same.

"No one told you to come in," I say.

She sniffs. "You've been using Krazy Glue again, haven't you? I told you I don't want you fuming while you're in the room—that can't be good for you." She pauses. "Then again, if you're fuming, you must be feeling better."

I don't say anything.

"Is that your cocoa in there?"

"Yes," I say.

She shakes her head. "Come on downstairs," my mother sighs. "I'll make you a fresh cup."

Here are some facts about forensics:

1. Forensics is defined as the scientific methods and techniques used in connection with the detection of crime.

2. The word *forensic* comes from the Latin *forensis,* which means "before the forum." In Roman times, a criminal charge was presented in front of a public group in the forum. The accused and the victim would give testimony, and the one who had the best argument would win.

3. The first written account of forensics to solve cases was during the Song Dynasty in China in 1248. After a person was killed with a sickle, an investigator told everyone to

bring their sickles to a specified location, and when the flies were drawn to one by the smell of blood, the murderer confessed.

4. The earliest incidence of fingerprint use to determine identity was in the seventh century, when a debtor's fingerprints were attached to a bill, as proof of the debt for the lender.

5. Forensic science is a lot easier to perform when you aren't personally involved.

The tips of your fingers, the palms of your hands, and the soles of your feet aren't smooth. They are friction-ridged skin, series of lines with contours and shapes, like a topographical map. Along those lines are sweat pores, and if they become contaminated with sweat, ink, blood, or dirt, they'll leave a reproduction of those lines on the object that's been touched. Or, in less fancy terms, a fingerprint.

If the print can be seen, it can be photographed. If it can be photographed, it can be preserved and compared to a known sample. It's an art as much as it's a science: since I don't have an AFIS terminal in my house to scan the latent print and spit out fifty candidates with matching similarities, I have to rely on the naked eye. The goal is to find ten to twelve similarities between the known sample and the latent print—that's what most examiners would conclude to be a match.

On my computer screen, I set images of the two prints. I place my cursor on the core, the centermost part of the print. I mark a delta—a small triangular formation to the left of the core. I note ending ridges and bifurcations and a circular whorl. A bifurcation, then two ridges, then another bifurcation downward.

Just like I assumed: This is a match.

That makes me feel like I am going to throw up, but I swallow and force myself to do what needs to be done.

Like yesterday.

Shaking my head clear, I take a small Tupperware container that I've filched from the kitchen and place the evidence inside. Then I rummage around in my closet until I find Jemima Puddle-Duck. She's a stuffed animal that I used to sleep with when I was a kid, and because she is white, she is up on a shelf above the rest of my clothes that have actual pigmentation. I place her facedown in my lap and, using a box cutter, make an incision in the place where she might have had a heart.

The Tupperware has to be jammed inside, and it makes Jemima look like she has an unsightly rib cage, but it works. I suture her with the same thread I used last week to fix a hole in my sock. I'm not very good at it—I stick myself nearly every stitch—but I get the job done.

Then I take out a notebook and start writing.

When I am done, I lie down on my bed. I wish I were at school. It's harder, when I'm not working at something.

"I shot the sheriff," I whisper. *"But I swear it was in self-defense."*

I've often thought about how a person could commit the perfect crime.

Everyone always talks about the proverbial icicle—stab someone and the murder weapon will melt—but it's a long shot (a) that you will be able to grip that icicle long enough to inflict a wound and (b) that it won't break off when it hits the skin before puncturing it. Mescaline sprinkled over someone's salad would be subtler—the brown powder would be virtually indistinguishable mixed with vinaigrette, and you wouldn't taste the bitter flavor, especially if there was chicory or arugula in the mix. But what if you only made your victim have a bad trip instead of die, and plus, where would you get your stash? You could take someone sailing and shove him overboard, preferably after getting him drunk, and say he fell accidentally—but then, you would need to have a boat. A mix of Vicodin and alcohol would slow the heart excessively, but your victim would have to pretty much be a party animal for a detective to not find that suspicious. I've heard of people who try to burn down a house after committing murder, but that never really works. The arson inspectors can trace where the fire started. Plus, a body has to be charred beyond recognition—and dental work—to not point a finger back at you. I wouldn't recommend anything that leaves blood, either. It's messy; you'll need lots of bleach to clean it, and there's bound to still be a drop left behind.

The conundrum of the perfect crime is complicated, because getting away with murder has very little to do with the mechanism of the killing and everything to do with what you do before and after. The only way to really cover a crime is to not tell a soul. Not your wife, not your mother, not your priest. And, of course, you have to have killed the right kind of person—someone who isn't going to be looked for. Someone who nobody wants to see again.

Theo

Once, a girl came up to me in the cafeteria and asked me if I wanted to go to Jesus Camp. *You will be saved,* she told me, and man, I was tempted. I mean, it's been pretty clear to me for a while that I'm going to hell, because of all the secret thoughts I'm not supposed to have about Jacob.

You always read these books about kids who have autistic siblings and who are constantly looking out for them, who love them to death, who do a better job defusing their tantrums than the adults. Well, I'm not one of those people. Sure, when Jacob used to wander off I'd feel sick in the pit of my stomach, but it wasn't because I was worried about him. It was because I had to be an awful brother to be thinking what I was: *Maybe he'll never be found, and I can get on with my life.*

I used to have dreams that my brother was normal. You know, that we could fight about ordinary things, like whose turn it was to control the television remote, or who got to ride shotgun in the car. But I was never allowed to fight with Jacob. Not when I'd forget to lock my bedroom door and he came in and stole my CDs for some forensics project; not when we were little and he'd walk around the table at *my* birthday party, eating cake off the plates of my friends. My mother said it was a house rule, and she explained it like this: *Jacob's different from the rest of us.* Gee, you think? And by the way, since when does being different net you a free pass in life?

The problem is, Jacob's difference

doesn't confine itself to Jacob. It's like the time my mother's red shirt bled in the wash and turned all my clothes pink: my brother's Asperger's has made *me* different, too. I could never have friends over, because what if Jacob had a meltdown? If I thought it was weird to see my brother peeing on the heater to watch steam rise, what the hell would someone from school think? That I was a freak, no doubt, by association.

True confession number one: When I'm walking down the hall in school and I see Jacob at the other end of the corridor, I intentionally divert my path to avoid him.

True confession number two: Once, when a bunch of kids from another school started making fun of Jacob as he attempted to play kickball—a hot mess if ever there was one—I pretended that I didn't know him; I laughed along, too.

True confession number three: I truly believe that I have it worse than Jacob, because he's oblivious most of the time to the fact that people want nothing to do with him; but I am one hundred percent aware that they're all looking at me and thinking, *Oh, that's the bizarre kid's brother.*

True confession number four: I don't sit around thinking about having kids, normally, but when I do it scares the shit out of me. What if my own son winds up being like Jacob? I've already spent my whole childhood dealing with autism; I don't know if I can handle doing it for the rest of my life.

Any time I think of one of these things, I feel like crap. I'm pretty much useless: not Jacob's parent, and not one of his teachers. I'm just here as the benchmark alternative, so that my mother can look from Jacob to me and measure the distance between an AS kid and a so-called normal one.

When that girl asked me to go to Jesus Camp, I asked her if Jesus was going to be there. She looked confused, and then said no. *Well,* I said, *isn't that a little like going to hockey camp and not playing hockey?* As I walked away, the girl told me Jesus loved me.

How do you know? I asked.

Once, after Jacob had raged through my room like a tropical storm and destroyed most of what was important to me, my mother came in to commiserate. *Deep down, he loves you,* she told me.

How do you know? I asked.

I don't, she admitted. *But it's what I have to believe to keep going.*

I've looked in my jacket, my pants. I've scoured the driveway. But I can't find the iPod, and that means it's lost somewhere between here and her house.

What if she knows I tried to take it?

What if she tells someone?

By the time I get home from school, life is back to normal. My mother is typing away on her laptop at the kitchen table, and Jacob is in his room with the door closed. I make myself ramen noodles and eat them in my room with Coldplay blasting as I do my French homework.

My mother's always telling me I can't listen to music when I do my homework. Once, she barged in and accused me of not working on my English paper when it was what I'd been doing all along. *How good could it possibly be,* she said, *if you're not concentrating?*

I told her to sit down and read the stupid paper on my computer.

She did, and shut up pretty quickly. I got an A on that project, as I recall.

I guess that somehow the gene pool in our family got all mixed up, and as a result, Jacob can only focus on one thing, an extreme obsession, while I can do sixteen thousand things at a time.

When I finish my homework I'm still hungry, so I go downstairs. My mother is nowhere to be found—and there's no freaking food in the house, for a change (not)—but I notice Jacob sitting in the living room. I look up at the clock, but I hardly have to—if it's 4:30 in our house, it must be *CrimeBusters.*

I hesitate at the doorway, watching him pore over his notebooks. Half of me is ready to slink away without being seen by Jacob, but the other half remembers what he looked like this morning. In spite of all I've said about wishing he was never born, seeing him like that—like the light had gone out inside him, sort of—made me feel like I'd been punched over and over in the gut.

What if I'd been born first, and was the one who wound up with Asperger's? Would he be standing here wishing I wouldn't notice him, too?

Before I can even let myself get good and guilty, Jacob starts talking. He doesn't look at me—he never does—but that probably means all his other senses are more finely tuned. "It's episode twenty-two today," he says, as if we have been in the middle of a conversation. "An oldie but a goodie."

"How many times have you seen this one?" I ask.

He glances down at his notebook. "Thirty-eight."

I'm not a huge fan of *CrimeBusters*. In the first place, I think the acting is bad. In the second place, this has to be the richest CSI lab ever, with all its bells and whistles. Something tells me that the fuming chamber at the state lab in Vermont looks a lot more like Jacob's duct-taped old fish tank than the *CrimeBusters* version, which is jazzed up with blue neon lights and lots of chrome. Plus, the investigators seem to spend a lot more time figuring out who's going to jump into bed with whom than they do solving crimes.

All the same, I sit down next to my brother on the couch. There's a good foot of space between us, because Jacob isn't crazy about being touched. I know better than to talk when the show is on—instead, I limit my editorial comments to the moments when there are commercials for erectile dysfunction drugs and OxiClean.

The story line involves a girl who's found dead after a hit-and-run. There's a paint scrape on her scooter, so the sexy CSI takes it to the lab. Meanwhile, the dude who does the autopsies finds a bruise on the girl's body that looks like a fingerprint. The crusty old CSI photographs it and takes it to the lab and gets a hit—some retired government employee who's drinking his prune juice and using a Clapper when Crusty and Sexy show up. They ask him if he's had a car accident lately, and he says that his car was stolen. Unfortunately for him, the CSIs find it parked in the attached garage. Caught red-handed, he admits that he was driving and that his foot hit the accelerator instead of the brake. When Sexy examines the car, though, she finds the driver's seat pushed back too far for the old man's height, and the stereo set to hip-hop. Sexy asks if anyone else drives Grandpa's car just as a teenage boy enters. Gramps admits that after hitting the girl on her scooter, he banged his head, so his grandson drove him home. Needless to say, no one believes him, but it's his word against theirs until Crusty finds a piece of tooth lodged in the steering wheel, which gets matched to the grandson. The kid's arrested, and his grandfather gets released.

The whole time I am watching this, Jacob is scribbling away in his notebooks. He has shelves full of them, all filled with crime scenarios that aired on this TV show. "What do you write down in there?" I ask.

Jacob shrugs. "The evidence. Then I try to deduce what will happen."

"But you've seen this one thirty-eight times," I say. "You already know how it's going to turn out."

Jacob's pen keeps scratching across the page. "But maybe it'll end differently this time," he says. "Maybe today, the kid won't get caught."

Rich

On Thursday morning my phone rings.

"Matson," I say, answering.

"The CDs are in alphabetical order."

I frown at the unfamiliar voice. Sounds like some kind of speakeasy password. *The CDs are in alphabetical order. And the bluebird wears fishnet stockings.* And just like that, you get entry to the inner sanctum.

"I beg your pardon?" I say.

"Whoever took Jess hung around long enough to alphabetize the CDs."

Now I recognize the voice—Mark

Maguire. "I assume your girlfriend hasn't returned yet," I say.

"Would I be calling you if she had?"

I clear my throat. "Tell me what you noticed."

"I dropped a handful of change on the carpet this morning, and when I picked it up, I realized that the tower that holds the CDs had been moved. There was a little sunken spot in the carpet, you know?"

"Right," I say.

"So these professors—they've got hundreds of CDs. And they keep them in this four-sided tower that spins. Anyway, I noticed that all the *W*s were organized together. Richard Wagner, Dionne Warwick, Dinah Washington, the Who, John Williams, Mary Lou Williams. And then Lester Young, Johann Zumsteeg—"

"They listen to the Who?"

"I looked on all four sides—and every single CD is in order."

"Is it possible they always were, and you didn't notice?" I ask.

"No, because last weekend, when Jess and I were looking for some decent music to listen to, they sure as hell didn't look that way."

"Mr. Maguire," I say. "Let me call you right back."

"Wait—it's been two days now—"

I hang up and pinch the bridge of my nose. Then I dial the state lab and talk to Iris, a grandmother type who has a little crush on me, which I milk when I need my evidence processed fast. "Iris," I say, "how's the prettiest girl in the lab?"

"I'm the only girl in the lab." She laughs. "You calling about your mailbox note?"

"Yeah."

"Came up clean. No prints at all."

I thank her and hang up the phone. It figures that a perp who alphabetizes CDs is smart enough to wear gloves while leaving a note. We probably won't get any prints off the computer keyboard, either.

On the other hand, the spices might be organized by indigenous regions.

If Mark Maguire is involved with his girlfriend's disappearance, and wants to lead us on a very different profiling track, he might conceivably alphabetize CDs— the least likely thing I'd ever expect of Mark Maguire.

Which could also explain why it took him twenty-four more hours to do it.

In any case, I am going to take a look at those CDs myself. And the contents of Jess Ogilvy's purse. And anything else that might indicate where she is, and why she's there.

I stand up and grab my jacket, heading past dispatch to tell them where I am going, when one of the desk sergeants pulls at my sleeve. "This here's Detective Matson," he says.

"Good," another man barks. "Now I know who to get the chief to fire."

Behind him, a woman in tears twists the leather straps of her handbag.

"I'm sorry," I say, smiling politely. "I didn't catch your name?"

"Claude Ogilvy," he replies. "*State Senator* Claude Ogilvy."

"Senator, we're doing everything we can to find your daughter."

"I find that hard to believe," he says, "when you haven't even had anyone in this department investigating it."

"As a matter of fact, Senator, I was just on my way to your daughter's residence."

"I assume, of course, that you're meeting the rest of the police force there. Because I certainly wouldn't want to find out that two whole days had gone by without this police department taking my daughter's disappearance seriously—"

I cut him off midsentence by taking his arm and propelling him toward my office. "With all due respect, Senator, I'd prefer it if you didn't tell me how to do my own job—"

"I damn well will tell you whatever I want *whenever* I want until my daughter is brought back safe and sound!"

I ignore him and offer a chair to his wife. "Mrs. Ogilvy," I say, "has Jess tried to contact you at all?"

She shakes her head. "And I can't call her. Her voice-mail box is full."

The senator shakes his head. "That's because that idiot Maguire kept leaving messages—"

"Has she ever run away before?" I ask.

"No, she'd never do that."

"Has she been upset lately? Worried about anything?"

Mrs. Ogilvy shakes her head. "She was so excited about moving into that house. Said it beat out the dorms any day . . ."

"How about her relationship with her boyfriend?"

At that, Senator Ogilvy stays blissfully, stonily silent. His wife spares him a quick glance. "There's no accounting for love," she says.

"If he hurt her," Ogilvy mutters. "If he laid a finger on her—"

"Then we will find out about it, and we will take care of it," I smoothly interject. "The first priority, though, is locating Jess."

Mrs. Ogilvy leans forward. Her eyes are red-rimmed. "Do you have a daughter, Detective?" she asks.

Once, at a fairground, Sasha and I were walking through the midway when a rowdy group of teenagers barreled between us, breaking the bond between our hands. I tried to keep my eye on her, but she was tiny, and when the group was gone, so was Sasha. I found myself standing in the middle of the fairground, turning in circles and screaming her name, while all around me rides spun in circles and wisps of cotton candy flew from their metal wheels onto a spool and the roar of chain saws spitting through wood announced the lumberjack contest. When I finally found her, petting the nose of a Jersey calf in a 4-H barn, I was so relieved that my legs gave out; I literally fell to my knees.

I haven't even responded, but Mrs. Ogilvy puts her hand on her husband's arm. "See, I told you, Claude," she murmurs. "He understands."

Jacob

The sensory break room at school has a swing hanging from the ceiling. It's made of rope and stretchy blue material, and when you sit inside it, it wraps you like a cocoon. You can pull the sides close so that you can't see out and no one can see in, and spin in circles. There are also mats with different textures, wind chimes, a fan. There's a fiber-optic lamp that has hundreds of points of light that change from green to purple to pink. There are sponges and Koosh balls and brushes and Bubble Wrap and weighted blankets. There's a noise machine that only an aide is allowed to turn on, and you can choose to listen to waves or rain or white noise or a jungle. There's a bubble tube, about three feet tall, with plastic fish that move in lazy circles.

In school, part of my IEP is a cool-off pass— a COP. If I need to, at any time, even during an exam, my teachers will allow me to leave the classroom. Sometimes, the outside world gets a little too tight for me, and I need a place to relax. I can come to the sensory break room, but the truth is, I hardly ever do. The only kids who use the sensory break room are special needs, and walking through the door, I might as well just slap a big fat label on myself that says I'm not normal.

So most of the time when I need a break, I wander around the hallways. Sometimes I go to the cafeteria to get a bottle of Vitaminwater. (The best flavor? Focus, kiwi-strawberry, with vitamin A and lutein for clarity. The worst? Essential. Orange-orange. Need I say more?) Sometimes I hang out in the teachers' room, playing chess with Mr. Pakeeri or helping Mrs. Leatherwood, the school secretary, stuff envelopes. But these past two days, when I leave my classroom I head right for that sensory break room.

The aide who staffs the room, Ms. Agworth, is also the Quiz Bowl teacher. Every day at

11:45 she leaves to make photocopies of whatever it is she's using in Quiz Bowl later that day. For this very reason, I've made it a point to use my COP pass at 11:30 for the past two days. It gets me out of English, which is a blessing in disguise, since we are reading *Flowers for Algernon* and just last week a girl asked (not in a mean way but truly curious) whether there were any experiments under way that might cure people like me.

Today, I enter the sensory break room and make a beeline for the Koosh balls. Holding one in each hand, I wrestle my way into the swing and pull the material closed around me. "Morning, Jacob," Ms. Agworth says. "You need anything?"

"Not right now," I murmur.

I don't know why people with AS are so sensitive to things like texture and color and sound and light. When I don't look someone in the eye, and when other people very pointedly look away from me so they don't appear to be staring, I sometimes wonder if I even really exist. The items in this room are the sensory equivalent of the game Battleship. Instead of calling out coordinates—B-4, D-7—I call for another physical sensation. Each time

I feel the weight of a blanket on my arm, or the pop of Bubble Wrap under my body when I roll on it, it's a direct hit. And at the end of my sensory break, instead of sinking my battleship, I've just found a way to locate myself in the grid of this world.

I close my eyes and slowly spin inside this dark, close ball. *"Pay no attention to the man behind the curtain,"* I murmur.

"What's that, Jacob?" Ms. Agworth says.

"Nothing," I shout. I wait until I've swung in three more slow pivots, and then I emerge.

"How are you doing today?" she asks.

It seems like a pretty gratuitous question, given the fact that I wouldn't be in this room if I were able to tolerate sitting in class like neurotypical people. But when I don't answer, she doesn't pry. She just keeps reading her trivia books and jotting down notes.

The largest fish in the world is a whale shark, at fifty feet.

Four million marshmallow Peeps are made each day.

(That sort of makes me wonder who on earth is buying them when it's *not* Easter.)

It takes the average adult man thirteen minutes to eat his dinner.

"I've got one for you, Ms. Agworth," I say. "The word *ass* is in the Bible 170 times."

"Thanks for that, Jacob, but it's not really appropriate." She shuffles her papers and looks down at her watch. "You think you'd be okay for a few minutes, if I ran down to the office to make some copies?"

Technically, she is not supposed to leave me alone. And I know there are certain other autistic kids who use the sensory room that she'd never stop watching like a hawk—Mathilda, for example, would probably fashion a noose out of the rope on the swing; Charlie would start tearing the shelves off the walls. But me, I'm a pretty safe bet. "No problem, Ms. A," I say.

In fact, I am counting on it. And the moment the door closes behind her again, I pull the cell phone out of my pocket. As soon as I flip it open and press the power button, it lights up: little blue squares around each number, and a picture of Jess and Mark on the screen saver.

I cover Mark's face with my thumb.

It's Thursday, and today I'm allowed to call her. I already broke the rules and called her twice before from this phone—dialing her own cell number, even though I knew I would be automatically dumped into voice mail. *Hey, so, this is Jess, and you know what to do.*

I am already starting to forget the notes in the song of her voice.

Today, though, instead of hearing her message, I heard a tinny voice telling me that this wireless customer's mailbox is full.

I'm prepared for this. I have memorized the phone number she gave me a week ago, the one that belongs to the new house. I dial it, even though I have to do it twice because it's unfamiliar and the numbers get tangled in my head.

A machine picks up. *Hey, this is Jess at the Robertsons' house. They're out of town, but you can leave a message for me!*

I hang up and dial it again.

Hey, this is Jess at the Robertsons' house.

I wait till the beep, and then I hang up. I turn off the power button on the cell phone, too. Then I speak my message, the same words I say to her every Thursday: *See you in three days.*

Emma

By Thursday, Jacob looks like the old Jacob, but he still isn't back to normal. I can tell by the way he's distracted—I'll set a full dinner plate down in front of him and he won't eat until I remind him that it's time to pick up his fork and dig in—and by the moments I catch him rocking or bouncing on the balls of his feet. His meds don't seem to be helping. And I've heard from teachers at his school that he's been spending nearly half the day in the sensory break room.

I've called Jess Ogilvy twice, but her voice-mail box is full. I'm afraid to bring her name up to Jacob, but I don't know what else to do. So after dinner on Thursday, I knock on the door of his bedroom and let myself inside. "Hi," I say.

He looks up from a book he is reading. "Hey."

It took me two years to realize that Jacob had not learned to read along with the rest of his kindergarten class. His teacher said he was among the most gifted language arts students, and sure enough, every night, he would pick out a book from a big basket in his room and read it aloud. But one day I realized that what everyone assumed was reading was actually just Jacob's photographic memory. If he'd heard the book once; he could spit it back. *Read this*, I had said, handing him a Dr. Seuss book, and he'd opened it up and started the story. I'd stopped him, pointing to a letter.

What's that?

A B.

And what sound does a B make?

He hesitated. *Buzz*, he said.

Now, I sink down beside him on the bed. "How are you feeling?"

"Interrupted," Jacob says.

I take the book out of his hands. "Can we talk?" He nods. "Did you and Jess have a fight on Tuesday?"

"No."

"When you went to her house, she didn't say anything to upset you?"

He shakes his head. "No, she didn't say anything."

"Well, I'm a little lost here, Jacob, since you came home from your tutoring session very upset . . . and I think there's still something bothering you."

Here is the thing about Asperger's syndrome: Jacob won't lie. So when he says he didn't have an argument with Jess, I believe him. But that doesn't mean he wasn't traumatized by something else that relates to her. Maybe he walked in on her having sex with her boyfriend. Maybe he got freaked out by her new residence.

Or maybe it has nothing to do with Jess, and he ran across an orange construction zone sign on the way home that required him to take a detour.

I sigh. "You know that I'm here when you're ready to talk about it. And Jess, too. She's there if you need her."

"I'm going to see her again on Sunday."

"Same bat-time," I say. *"Same bat-channel."*

I hand him back his book and realize that tucked beneath his arm is the old Jemima Puddle-Duck toy he used to carry as a child. Jacob carried her so fiercely that I had to sew a leopard cape onto her back because her fur kept rubbing bald. It was a ritual piece, according to Dr. Murano— something Jacob could hold to calm himself down. She described it as a way to reboot, to remind him that he's all right. Over the years, Jemima was retired to make room for more discreet objects that could be tucked in his pockets: a photo-booth strip of the two of us, so folded and faded you could barely see our faces; a small green pebble a teacher brought him back from Montana; a piece of sea glass Theo gave him for Christmas one year. In fact, I haven't seen this stuffed animal in ages; she's been buried in his closet.

It is hard to see your eighteen-year-old son clutching a stuffed toy. But that's what autism is, a slippery slope. One minute, you convince yourself that you are so far up that hill you can't see the bottom anymore, and the next, it's covered with black ice, and you are falling fast.

* * *

Auntie Em's column, Thursday, January 14, Teen Edition:

The best parenting advice I ever got was from a labor nurse who told me the following:

1. After your baby gets here, the dog will just be a dog.

2. The terrible twos last through age three.

3. Never ask your child an open-ended question, such as "Do you want to go to bed now?" You won't want to hear the answer, believe me. "Do you want me to carry you upstairs, or do you want to walk upstairs to go to bed?" That way, you get the outcome you want and they feel empowered.

Now that my children are older, not much has changed.

Except we do not have a dog.

The terrible twos last through age eighteen.

And questions still shouldn't be open-ended, because you won't get an answer to "Where were you last night till two A.M.?" or "How did you get a D on your math test?"

There are two deductions you can glean from this. That *parenting* isn't a noun but a verb—an ongoing process instead of an accomplishment. And that no matter how many years you put into the job, the learning curve is, well, fairly flat.

I leave Jacob's room, intending to watch the evening news. But when I reach the living room, Theo is tuned to some god-awful MTV show about spoiled girls who are shipped off to third-world countries by their parents to learn humility. "Don't you have homework to do?" I ask.

"Done."

"I want to watch the news."

"I was here first."

I stare as a girl shovels elephant dung into a large plastic bag in Burma. "Eeew," she squeals, and I glance at Theo. "Please tell me you'd rather open your mind to current affairs than watch this."

"But I'm supposed to tell the truth," Theo says, grinning. "House rules."

"Okay, let's try this: if I watch this program with you, I might be suitably moved to send *you* to Burma to broaden your horizons by cleaning up elephant dung."

He tosses me the remote control. "That is such blackmail."

"And yet it worked," I say, flipping the channel to a local broadcast. A man is shouting into a microphone. "All I know," he cries, "is that it's a crime for a local police department to sit on the disappearance of a young girl, instead of actively pursuing an investigation."

A white banner flashes beneath the face: STATE SENATOR CLAUDE OGILVY.

"Hey," Theo says. "Isn't that the name—"

"Ssh . . ."

The reporter's face fills the screen. "Townsend Police Chief Fred Huckins says that the disappearance of Jess Ogilvy is a priority and urges anyone with information to contact the department at 802-555-4490."

Then a picture of Jacob's social skills tutor appears, with the phone number below it.

Theo

"Live from Townsend," the reporter wraps up, "I'm Lucy McNeil."

I look at my mother. "That's Jess," I say, the obvious.

"Oh my God," she murmurs. "That poor girl."

I don't understand. I totally don't understand.

My mother grabs my arm. "This information doesn't leave this room," she says.

"You think Jacob isn't going to find out? He reads the papers. He's online."

She pinches the bridge of her nose.

"He's so fragile right now, Theo. I can't throw this at him yet. Just give me a little while so I can figure out how."

I take the remote out of her hand and turn the TV off. Then, muttering some excuse about an essay, I run upstairs to my room and lock the door.

I walk in circles, my arms braced behind my head, like I'm cooling off after running a marathon. I run through everything I heard that senator say, and the reporter. The police chief, for God's sake, who said the disappearance is a *priority*.

Whatever the fuck that means.

I wonder if it will turn out to be a big hoax, like that college girl who vanished and later said she was abducted and it turned out that she was making the whole story up to get attention. I kind of hope that's what happens, because the alternative is something I don't want to think about.

Here's all I really need to know:

Jess Ogilvy is missing, and I was one of the last people to see her.

Rich

On the answering machine at the Robert-sons' house, there are six messages. One is from Mark Maguire, asking Jess to call him when she gets back. One is from a dry cleaner, letting her know that her skirt is ready. One is identified by caller ID as E. Hunt. The message says, "Hi, Jess, this is Jacob's mom. Can you give me a call?" The other three messages are hang-ups, and all three came from the number registered to Jess Ogilvy's mobile phone.

That tells me either she's a battered woman in hiding, trying to get the nerve to call her boyfriend and failing, or her boyfriend is covering his ass after accidentally killing her.

I spend Friday crossing off the names in Jess Ogilvy's Day-Timer. My first call is to the two girls whose names pop up the most often in the history of months past. Alicia and Cara are grad students, like Jess. Alicia has cornrowed hair that hangs to her waist, and Cara is a tiny blonde wearing camouflage cargo pants and black work boots. Over coffee at the student center, they admit they haven't seen Jess since Tuesday.

"She missed an exam with the Gorgon," Cara says. "Nobody misses an exam with the Gorgon."

"The Gorgon?"

"Professor Gorgona," she explains. "It's a seminar course on special education."

GORGONA, I write in my notes. "Has Jess ever gone away for a few days before?"

"Yeah—once," Alicia says. "She went to Cape Cod for a long weekend and didn't tell us beforehand."

"She went with Mark, though," Cara adds, and she wrinkles her nose.

"I take it you aren't a fan of Mark Maguire?"

"Is anyone?" Alicia says. "He doesn't treat her right."

"What do you mean by that?"

"If he says jump, she doesn't even ask 'How high?' She goes out and buys a pogo stick."

"We haven't seen a lot of her since they started hooking up," Cara says. "Mark likes to keep her all to himself."

So do most abusive partners, I think.

"Detective Matson?" Alicia asks. "She's going to be okay, right?"

A week ago, Jess Ogilvy was probably sitting here where I am, drinking coffee with her friends and freaking out about the Gorgon's upcoming exam.

"I hope so," I say.

People don't just disappear. There's always a reason, or an enemy with a grudge. There's always a loose thread that starts to unravel.

The problem is that Jess Ogilvy is, apparently, a saint.

"I was surprised when she missed the exam," Professor Gorgona says. A slight woman with a white bun and a trace of a foreign accent, she doesn't seem nearly as threatening as Alicia and Cara made her out to be. "She's my star student, really. She's getting her master's and writing an honors thesis at the same time. Graduated with a 4.0 from Bates and worked with Teach for America for two years before she decided to make a career out of it."

"Is there anyone who might be jealous of the fact that she does so well in class?" I ask.

"Not that I've noticed," the professor says.

"Did she confide in you about any personal problems?"

"I'm not exactly the warm and fuzzy type," the professor says wryly. "Our communication was strictly adviser-advisee in an academic sense. The only extracurricular activities I even know she participated in are education-related: she organizes the Special Olympics here in town, and she tutors an autistic boy." Suddenly the professor frowns. "Has anyone contacted him? He'll have a hard time coping if Jess doesn't show up for her scheduled appointment. Changes in routine are very traumatic for kids like Jacob."

"Jacob?" I repeat, and I open the Day-Timer.

This is the boy whose mother left a message on the answering machine at the professor's house. The boy whose name is entered into Jess's schedule on the day she disappeared.

"Professor," I say, "you wouldn't happen to know where he lives?"

Jacob Hunt and his family reside in a part of Townsend that's a little more run-down than the rest of it—the part you have to work harder to find behind the picture-postcard town green and the stately New England antique homes. Their house is just beyond the condos that are filled with the recently separated and newly divorced, past the train tracks for an Amtrak route that's long defunct.

The woman who opens the door has a blue stain on her shirt and dark hair wound into a messy knot and the most beautiful eyes I have ever seen. They're pale, like a lioness's, nearly golden, but they also look like they've done their share of crying, and we all know that a sky with clouds in it is much more interesting than one that doesn't have any. I'd place her in her early forties. She's holding a spoon, which is dribbling its contents onto the floor. "I don't want any," she says, starting to close the door.

"I'm not selling anything," I say. "You're, um, dripping."

She glances down, and then sticks the spoon into her mouth.

That's when I remember why I'm here. I hold up my badge. "I'm Detective Rich Matson. Are you Jacob's mother?"

"Oh, God," she says. "I thought he'd already called you to apologize."

"Apologize?"

"It's really not his fault," she interjects. "Granted, I should have known that he was sneaking out, but with him, this hobby is almost a pathology. And if there's any way I can convince you to keep this quiet— not a bribe, of course, just maybe a hand-shake agreement . . . You see, if it becomes public knowledge, then my career could really take a hit, and I'm a single mom who's barely scraping by as is . . ."

She is babbling, and I have no idea what the hell she is talking about. Although I did hear the word *single.* "I'm sorry, Ms. Hunt—"

"Emma."

"Emma, then. I . . . have no idea what you're talking about. I came because your son is tutored by Jess Ogilvy—"

"Oh," she says, sobering. "I heard about Jess on the news. Her poor parents must be frantic. Are there any leads yet?"

"That's why I'm here to speak to your son."

Those eyes of hers darken. "You can't possibly think Jacob had anything to do with her disappearance?"

"No, but he was the last appointment in her date book before she disappeared."

She folds her arms. "Detective Matson, my son has Asperger's syndrome."

"Okay." And I'm red-green color-blind. Whatever.

"It's high-functioning autism. He doesn't even know Jess is missing yet. He's had a hard time lately, and the news could be devastating to him."

"I can be sensitive about the subject."

She measures me for a moment with her gaze. Then, turning, she heads into the house, expecting me to follow. "Jacob," she calls as we reach the kitchen.

I stand in the entryway, waiting for a child to appear. After all, Jess Ogilvy is a teacher and Professor Gorgona referred to a boy she worked with. Instead, a behemoth teenager who's taller than I am, and probably stronger, shuffles into the room. *This* is who Jess Ogilvy tutored? I stare at him for a second, trying to place the reason he looks so familiar out of context, and suddenly it comes to me: hypothermic man. This kid identified the cause of death before the medical examiner did.

"You?" I say. *"You're* Jacob Hunt?"

Now his mother's rushed apologies make sense. She probably thought I'd come to slap a fine on the kid, or arrest him for interfering with a crime scene.

"Jacob," she says drily, "I think you're already acquainted with Detective Matson."

"Hi, Jacob." I hold out a hand. "Nice to officially meet you."

He doesn't shake it. He doesn't even look me in the eye. "I saw the article in the paper," he says, his voice flat and robotic. "It was buried in the back. If you ask me, someone dying of hypothermia is worthy of at least page two." He takes a step forward. "Did the full autopsy results come back? It would be interesting to know if the alcohol lowered the freezing point for the body, or if there's not a significant change."

"So, Jake," I say.

"Jacob. My name is Jacob, not Jake."

"Right, Jacob. I was hoping to ask you a few questions?"

"If they're about forensics," he says, growing animated, "then I am more than happy to help. Have you heard about the research coming out of Purdue, on desorption electrospray ionization? They found that the sweat from finger pores slightly corrodes metal surfaces—anything from a bullet to a piece of a bomb. If you spray the fingerprints with positively charged water, the droplets dissolve chemicals in the fingerprints and transfer minute amounts that can be analyzed by mass spectrometer. Can you imagine how handy it would be to not only get fingerprint images but also identify the chemicals in them? You could not only place a suspect at a crime scene but also get proof that he handled explosives."

I look at Emma Hunt, begging for help. "Jacob, Detective Matson needs to talk to you about something else. You want to sit down for a minute?"

"A minute. Because it's almost four-thirty."

And what, I wonder, *happens at 4:30?* His mother doesn't react at all to his comment. I feel a little like Alice in Wonderland, in the Disney video that Sasha likes to watch on her weekends with me, and everyone is in on the Unbirthday routine but me. Last time we'd watched it, I realized that being a parent wasn't all that different. We're always bluffing, pretending we know best, when most of the time we're just praying we won't screw up too badly.

"Well, then," I say to Jacob. "I guess I'd better start."

Emma

The only reason I let Rich Matson into my house is because I'm still not entirely sure that he doesn't want to punish Jacob for showing up at his crime scene last weekend, and I will do whatever I have to do to make that whole nightmare go away.

"Jacob," I say, "Detective Matson needs to talk to you about something else. You want to sit down for a minute?"

We are racing against a clock, not that Matson would understand. "A minute. Because it's almost four-thirty," Jacob tells me.

I don't know how anyone could look at Jacob and think he'd be a viable witness.

Sure, his mind is a steel trap. But half the time, there's no lock to get inside it.

The detective sits at the kitchen table. I turn down the flame on the stove and then join him. Jacob is struggling to look in Matson's direction, but his eyelids keep fluttering, as if he's staring into the sun, and finally he gives up and lets his gaze slide away.

"You have a friend named Jess, right?" the detective asks.

"Yes."

"What do you and Jess do together?"

"We practice social skills. Conversations. Good-byes. Things like that." He hesitates. "She's my best friend."

This doesn't surprise me. Jacob's definition of a friend isn't legitimate. To him, a friend might be the kid whose locker is next to his in school, who therefore has an interaction at least once a day to say, *Could you move over?* A friend is someone who he's never met but who doesn't actively taunt him in school. Jess may be paid by me to meet with Jacob, but that doesn't take away from the fact that she honestly cares about him and connects with him.

The detective looks at Jacob, who, of course, is not looking at him. I watch people falter over that normal courtesy of communication all the time—after a while, it feels like staring, so they look away from Jacob, mirroring his behavior. Sure enough, after a moment, Matson stares down at the table as if there's something fascinating in the wood grain. "Right now, Jacob, Jess is missing. And it's my job to find her."

I suck in my breath. "*That's* what you call sensitive?"

But Jacob doesn't seem to be surprised, which makes me wonder if he's seen the news, or read about the disappearance in the papers or online. "Jess is gone," he repeats.

The detective leans forward. "Were you supposed to meet with her last Tuesday?"

"Yes," Jacob says. "At two thirty-five."

"And did you?"

"No."

Suddenly, Jacob's breakdown makes perfect sense. To travel to Jess's unfamiliar new residence—which already would have set off his alarm bells—and then to never have Jess show up . . . Well, talk about a perfect storm for an AS kid. "Oh, Jacob. Was that why you had a meltdown?"

"Meltdown?" Matson echoes.

I glance at him briefly. "When Jacob's

routine is disrupted, he gets very agitated. This was a double whammy, and by the time he came home—" I break off, suddenly remembering something else. "You walked home from Jess's place? Alone?"

It isn't that he wouldn't know the way— Jacob is a veritable human GPS; he can take one look at a map and have it memorized. But knowing geography and knowing how to follow directions are two very different things. Getting from point A to point B to point C inevitably trips him up.

"Yes," Jacob says. "It wasn't so bad."

It was nearly eight miles. In the freezing cold. I suppose I should consider us lucky: on top of everything else, Jacob could have wound up with pneumonia.

"How long did you wait for her?"

Jacob looks up at the clock. He starts rubbing the tips of his fingers against his thumbs, back and forth. "I have to go now."

I notice the detective staring at Jacob as he fidgets, and I know damn well what he's thinking. "I bet when you see someone who doesn't make eye contact and who can't sit still, you immediately assume guilt," I say. "Me, I assume he's on the spectrum."

"It's four-thirty." Jacob's voice is louder, more urgent.

"You can go watch *CrimeBusters*," I tell him, and he bolts into the living room.

The detective stares at me, dumbfounded. "Excuse me, I was in the middle of an interrogation."

"I thought this *wasn't* an interrogation."

"A young girl's life might be at stake, and you think it's more important for your son to watch a television show?"

"Yes," I snap.

"It doesn't strike you as odd that your son isn't upset by his tutor's disappearance?"

"My son didn't even get upset when his grandfather died," I reply. "It was a forensics adventure for him. His feelings about Jess going missing will be determined only by how it affects him—which is the way he measures everything. When he realizes that his Sunday session with Jess might not take place, *then* he'll get upset."

The detective looks at me for a long moment. I think he's going to give me a lecture about obstruction of justice, but instead, he tilts his head to one side, thoughtful. "That must be really hard on you."

I don't remember the last time anyone has said those words to me. I would not trade Jacob for the world—for his tenderness, his incredible brain, his devotion to following rules—but that doesn't mean it's been an easy ride. An ordinary mother doesn't worry about whether her son being shunned at a school concert hurts him as much as it hurts me. An ordinary mother doesn't call Green Mountain Power when the electricity goes out to say that one of the residents has a disability that requires immediate intervention—because missing *CrimeBusters* actually qualifies, when it comes to Jacob. An ordinary mother doesn't lie awake at night wondering if Theo will ever accept his brother enough to watch over him when I'm gone.

"It's my life," I say, shrugging.

"Do you work outside the home?"

"Are you interviewing me, too?"

"Just making conversation until the commercial break," he says, smiling.

Ignoring him, I stand up and stir the blueberries I am cooking down for tonight's pie filling.

"Your son, he took us by surprise the other night," Matson continues. "We're not used to minors crashing our crime scenes."

"Technically, he's not a minor. He's eighteen."

"Well, he's got more forensic scientific knowledge than guys I know who are four times his age."

"Tell me something I don't know."

"You've got pretty eyes," the detective says.

Fumbling, I drop the spoon into the pot. "What did you just say?"

"You heard me," Matson replies, and he walks into the living room to wait for the opening credits of *CrimeBusters* to finish.

Jacob

I have never been a big fan of *I Love Lucy*. That said, every time I see the episode when Lucy and Ethel are working at the candy factory and get behind on the packaging, it makes me laugh. The way they stuff the candy into their mouths and inside their uniforms—well, you know it's going to end with Lucy wailing her famous wail.

Having Detective Matson ask me these questions makes me feel like Lucy at the candy factory. At first, I can keep up—especially after I realize that he is not angry at me for coming to the hypothermic man's crime scene. But then it begins to get more complicated.

The questions stack up like that candy, and I am still trying to wrap the last one when he sends the next one my way. All I want to do is take his words and stuff them somewhere where I don't have to hear them anymore.

Detective Matson is standing in front of me as soon as the first commercial airs. It's for Pedi Paws, a new incredible pet nail trimmer. That makes me think of the miniature poodle at the pizza place that we saw, and that makes me think of Jess, and that makes me feel like there's a bird caught inside my rib cage.

What would he say if he knew that right now, in my pocket, is Jess's pink cell phone?

"Just a couple more questions, Jacob," he promises. "I'll make sure I'm done in ninety seconds."

He smiles, but it's not because he's happy. I had a biology teacher like that once. When I corrected Mr. Hubbard's mistakes in class, he smiled with the left side of his mouth. I assumed that meant he was grateful. But that weird half smile apparently meant he was annoyed with me, even though if someone's smiling it is supposed to signify that they're cheerful. So I got sent to the principal's office for my bad attitude when, really, it was just because the expressions on people's faces are not always reflections of how they feel inside.

He glances at my notebook. "What's that for?"

"I take notes on the episodes," I tell him. "I have over a hundred."

"Episodes?"

"Notebooks."

He nods. "Was Mark at Jess's place when you got there?"

"No." Now, the commercial on television is for denture cream. Secretly I am very scared of losing all my teeth. Sometimes I dream about waking up and finding them rolling around on my tongue like marbles. I close my eyes so I don't have to watch. "You know Mark?"

"We've met," the detective says. "Did you and Jess ever talk about him?"

My eyes are still closed, so maybe that's why I see what I do: Mark with his hand sliding up Jessica's shirt at the pizza place. His hideous orange sweatshirt. The earring in his left ear. The bruises I saw once on Jessica's side when she reached for a book on a high shelf, two uneven purple ovals like quality stamps on a cut of beef. She told me she'd fallen off a stepladder, but she looked away when she said it. And unlike me, who looks away out of comfort, *she* does it in moments of discomfort.

I see Mark smiling with only half his mouth, too.

Now the commercial is for *Law & Order: SVU,* a promo, which means that the next image on the screen will be *CrimeBusters* again. I pick up my pen and turn the page in my notebook.

"Did Jess and Mark fight?" the detective asks again.

On the TV, Rhianna is in the woods with Kurt, and they're investigating a dead dog with a human finger found undigested in its stomach.

"Jacob?"

"Hasta la vista, baby," I murmur, and I make up my mind that, no matter what this detective says to me, I'm not speaking again until my show is over.

Theo

So I'm headed downstairs to get something to eat when I hear a voice in the kitchen I do not recognize. This is pretty extraordinary—I'm not the only one who doesn't have friends as a result of Jacob's Asperger's; I can probably count on one hand the number of people my mother has ever trusted enough to invite over. The fact that the voice is *male* is even more bizarre. And then I hear my mom refer to him as Detective Matson.

Holy crap.

I run back upstairs and lock myself

in my room. He's here because of Jess Ogilvy, and I'm officially freaked out.

And, for the record, still hungry.

Here's what I know for sure: Jess was alive and well at about 1:00 P.M. on Tuesday. I know this because I saw her—*all* of her. Her tits, let me just say, rank right up there as masterworks of art.

I'd say we were equally surprised when she reached for her towel, wiped her eyes, and looked in the mirror. She certainly didn't expect to find some random guy in her house, watching her naked. And I sure as hell didn't expect the object of my momentary lust to be my brother's tutor.

"Hey!" she yelled, and in one smooth move she grabbed the towel and wrapped it around herself. Me, meanwhile, I was totally paralyzed. I stood there like an idiot until I realized she was pissed and she was coming after me.

The only reason I got away is that the floor of the bathroom was wet. When she stumbled, I flew out of the master bedroom, where I'd been standing, down the stairs. In my hurry, I crashed into some of the furniture and knocked a whole mess of papers off the kitchen counter, but I didn't care. All I wanted to do was get the hell out of that house and join a monastery or hop on a plane to Micronesia—anything that would put me far away by the time Jess Ogilvy asked my brother and my mom whether they were aware that Theo Hunt was a Peeping Tom, a total perv.

But sometime between now and then, Jess Ogilvy got dressed, left her house, and vanished. Is she wandering around with amnesia? Or hiding out and plotting some kind of revenge scheme against me?

I don't know.

I can't tell the cops, though, without incriminating myself.

It's just past five-thirty when I get the nerve to leave my bedroom. I can smell blueberry pie cooking (the only good thing about Blue Food Fridays, if you ask me) and know it will be ready at six—like everything else, we eat on a schedule to keep Jacob calm.

The door to his room is open, and he's standing on his desk chair, slipping one of his *CrimeBusters* journals back into its predetermined spot on a shelf.

"Hey," I say to him.

He doesn't answer. Instead, he sits down on the bed with his back to the wall and picks up a book on his nightstand.

"I saw that the cops were here."

"Cop," Jacob murmurs. "Singular."

"What did he want to talk to you about?"

"Jess."

"What did you tell him?"

Jacob draws his knees up to his chest. *"If you build it, he will come."*

My brother may not communicate the way the rest of us do, but after all this time, I've learned to read him loud and clear. When he doesn't feel like talking, he hides behind someone else's words.

I sit beside him, just staring at the wall while he reads. I want to tell him that I saw Jess alive on Tuesday. I want to ask him if he did as well, and if that's part of the reason he doesn't want to talk to the police, either.

I wonder if he's got something to hide, too.

For the first time in my life, Jacob and I just might have something in common.

Emma

It all starts with a mouse.

After our weekly Saturday shopping excursion (thank goodness, the Free Sample Lady had been replaced temporarily by a sullen teenager handing out vegetarian cocktail wieners at the door of the grocery store), I leave Jacob sitting at the kitchen table with the remainders of his lunch while I do a cursory cleaning of his room. He forgets to bring glasses and bowls of cereal downstairs to the kitchen, and if I don't play middleman, we wind up with thriving colonies of mold that have bonded to my dishes like concrete. I pick up a bevy of mugs from his desk and spot the tiny face of a field mouse struggling to survive this winter by taking up residence behind Jacob's computer.

I am embarrassed to admit I have a very typical female reaction and go completely ballistic. Unfortunately, I am holding a half-full glass of chocolate soy milk at the time, and most of it spills over Jacob's comforter.

Well, it has to be washed. Although it's the weekend, and that's problematic. Jacob doesn't like seeing his bed stripped; it has to be made at all times unless he happens to be in it. Usually I wash his sheets while he's at school. Sighing, I pull fresh sheets out of the linen closet and tug the winter comforter off his bed. He can make do for a night with his summertime quilt, an old postage-stamp design in all the rainbow colors—ROYGBIV—in correct order, which my mother sewed for him before she died.

The summer quilt is kept in a black trash bag on the upper shelf of his closet. I pull it down and shake out the blanket inside.

A backpack rolled into its center tumbles to the floor.

It's clearly not one that belongs to the boys. Flesh-colored with red and black stripes, it seems to be trying to be a Burberry knock-off, but the stripes are too wide and the colors too bright. There is still a Marshalls' tag on the strap, with the price ripped off.

Inside is a toothbrush, a satin blouse, a pair of shorts, and a yellow T-shirt. The blouse and shorts are both plus-size. The T-shirt is much smaller and says SPECIAL OLYMPICS on the front and STAFF on the back.

At the very bottom of the backpack is a notecard still inside its torn envelope. There's a picture of a snowy landscape, and the inside reads, in spidery handwriting: *Merry Christmas Jess, Love Aunt Ruth.*

"My God," I murmur. "What did you do?" I close my eyes for a moment, and then I bellow Jacob's name. He comes running into his room, stopping abruptly when he sees me holding the backpack in my arms.

"Oh," he says.

He sounds as if I've caught him in a white lie: *Jacob, did you wash your hands before dinner?*

Yes, Mom.

Then how come the bar of soap's still dry?

Oh.

But this isn't a white lie. This is a girl

who's missing. A girl who could be dead by now. A girl whose backpack and clothes my son inexplicably has.

Jacob starts to flee downstairs, but I grab his arm to stop him. "Where did this come from?"

"A box at Jess's place," he grinds out, shutting his eyes tight until I let go.

"Tell me why you have this. Because a lot of people are searching for Jess, and this does not look good."

His hand starts twitching at his side. "I told you I went to her house Tuesday, like I was supposed to. And things weren't right."

"What do you mean?"

"There were stools knocked over in the kitchen, and papers all over the floor, and all the CDs were thrown on the carpet. It wasn't right, it wasn't right . . ."

"Jacob," I say. "Focus. How did you get this backpack? Does Jess know you have it?"

There are tears in his eyes. "No. She was already gone." He starts to walk in a small circle, his hand still flapping. "I went in, and the mess . . . and I was scared. I didn't know what happened. I called out her name and she wouldn't answer and I saw the backpack and the other things and I took them."

His voice is a roller coaster, reeling off-track. *"Houston, we have a problem."*

"It's okay," I say, wrapping my arms around him and holding him with the deepest pressure, the way a potter would center the clay on her wheel.

But it isn't okay. It won't be, until Jacob gives Detective Matson this new information.

Rich

I am *not* in a good mood.

It's Saturday, and although I am supposed to have Sasha for the weekend, I had to cancel as soon as it became apparent that we had an ongoing investigation that demanded my full resources. Basically, I'm going to eat, sleep, and breathe Jess Ogilvy until I find her, dead or alive. Not that that seemed to sway my ex, who made sure to give me a fifteen-minute tongue-lashing about parental responsibility and how on earth was she supposed to carry on with her life when my emergencies kept interrupting? It wasn't worth pointing out that this was not my emergency, technically, or that the disappearance of a young woman might take precedence over rescheduling a date night with her new spouse, Mr. Coffee. I tell myself that missing one weekend with Sasha is worth it if I can make sure that Claude Ogilvy gets to have another weekend with *his* daughter.

En route to Jess's home, where a team of CSIs is entrenched, I get a call from the local FBI field agent, who has been trying to ping the girl's cell phone. "You're not getting a signal," I repeat. "So what does that mean?"

"Several things," the agent explains. "The GPS locator only works when the phone's active. So it could be at the bottom of a lake right now. Or she could be alive and well and just have run out of juice."

"Well, how am I supposed to know which of those it is?"

"Guess once you find a body, it'll be pretty clear," he says, and then I drive through one of Vermont's notorious dead zones and the call is dropped.

When the phone rings again, I am still cursing out the FBI (which is good for one thing and one thing only: screwing up a perfectly sound local investigation), so you can imagine how surprised I am to hear Emma Hunt on the end of the line. I had left her my card yesterday, just in case. "I was hoping you might be able to come back to my house," she says. "Jacob has something he needs to tell you."

I have a team of investigators waiting for me on-site. I have a surly boyfriend who might be a murderer and a state senator breathing down my boss's neck, demanding my job if I don't find his missing kid. But I put on my flashing blues and do an illegal U-turn. "Give me ten minutes," I tell her.

I'm in a slightly better mood now.

I have, fortunately, three whole hours before *CrimeBusters* airs. We are sitting in the living room—Emma and Jacob on one couch, me on a side chair. "Tell the detective everything you told me, Jacob," Emma says.

His eyes roll upward, as if he is reading something printed on the ceiling. "I went to her house that day, like I was supposed to. Things weren't right. There were stools knocked over in the kitchen, and papers all over the floor, and all the CDs were thrown on the carpet. It wasn't right, it wasn't right." His voice seems almost computerized, it's that mechanical. "She was already gone. I went in, and the mess . . . and I was scared. I didn't know what happened. I called out her name and she wouldn't answer and I saw the backpack and the other things and I took them. *Houston, we have a problem.*" He nods, satisfied. "That's it."

"Why did you lie to me about going to Jess's?" I ask.

"I didn't lie," he says. "I told you I didn't have my session with her."

"You didn't tell me about the backpack, either," I point out. It sits between us, on a coffee table.

Jacob nods. "You didn't ask."

Wiseass, I think, just as Emma jumps in. "A kid with Asperger's, like Jacob, is going to be painfully literal," she says.

"So if I question him directly, he'll answer directly?"

"*He,*" Jacob interjects testily, "is sitting within earshot."

That makes me grin. "Sorry," I say,

addressing him. "How did you get into Jess's house?"

"She used to leave her dorm room open for me, and when I got to her house, that door was left open, too. So I went in to wait."

"What did you see when you went inside?"

"The kitchen was a mess. Stools were knocked over; and the mail was all over the floor."

"How about Jess? Was she there?"

"No. I called her name, and she didn't answer."

"What did you do?"

He shrugs. "I cleaned up."

I sink back into the cushions of the chair. "You . . . cleaned up."

"Yes, that's correct."

My mind is racing through all the tampered evidence sacrificed to Jacob Hunt's obsessive-compulsive tendencies. "You know all about preserving evidence at crime scenes," I say. "What on earth would make you destroy it?"

Just like that, Emma bristles. "My son's doing you a favor by speaking with you,

Detective. We didn't *have* to call and give you this information."

I tamp down my frustration. "So you cleaned up the mess you saw downstairs?"

"Right," Jacob says. "I picked up the stools and I set the mail back onto the kitchen counter. And I put all the CDs that had been knocked over in alphabetical order."

"Alphabetical order," I repeat, remembering Mark Maguire's call, and my theory about an anal-retentive kidnapper. "You're kidding me."

"That's what his room's like," Emma says. "Jacob's a big fan of everything being in its right place. For him, it's the spatial equivalent of knowing what's coming next."

"So when did you take the backpack?"

"After I cleaned up."

The backpack still has its tags on, just like Maguire said. "Would you mind if I hang on to it, for the case?"

Suddenly, Jacob lights up. "You *have* to take it. You're going to need to run DNA tests on the straps and you can do an AP on the underwear inside. It might be worth spraying the whole thing with Luminol, to be honest. And you can probably get prints off the card inside with ninhydrin, but you'll want to compare them against my mother's since she handled the card when she first found the backpack. Which reminds me, you can look through it now if you want. I have latex gloves upstairs in my room. You don't have a latex allergy, do you?" He is halfway out of the room when he turns back. "We have a grocery bag somewhere, don't we? That way Detective Matson can carry this back to the lab."

He runs upstairs, and I turn to Emma. "Is he always like that?"

"And then some." She looks up at me. "Is anything Jacob said helpful?"

"It's all food for thought," I say.

"Everything changes if there are signs of a struggle," she points out.

I raise a brow. "You're a closet CSI, too?"

"No, in spite of Jacob's best efforts to teach me." She glances out the window for a moment. "I've been thinking about Jess's mother," she says. "The last time she talked to her daughter, was it about stupid things, you know? Did they have a fight about how she never called, or how she had forgotten to send a thank-you card to her aunt?" She faces me. "I used to say *I love you* every time I tucked my boys in at night. But now, they go to bed after I do."

"My dad used to say that living with regrets was like driving a car that only moved in reverse." I smile faintly. "He had a stroke a few years ago. Before that, I used to screen his calls because I didn't have time to talk about whether the Sox would make it into the playoffs. But afterward, I started to call *him*. Every time, I'd finish by saying I loved him. We both knew why; and it didn't sit right after all the time I *hadn't* said it. It was like trying to bail out an ocean of water with a teaspoon. He died eight months ago."

"I'm sorry."

I laugh tightly. "And I don't know why the hell I'm telling you this."

At that moment, Jacob reappears, clutching a pair of latex gloves. I snap them on and carefully lift the backpack just as my cell rings. "Matson," I say.

It's one of the lieutenants in the department, asking how much longer I'm going to be.

"I have to run." I lift the grocery bag into my arms.

Jacob ducks his head. "I'd be interested in hearing the test results, naturally."

"Naturally," I reply, although I have no intent of sharing them. "So what's on *CrimeBusters* today?"

"Episode sixty-seven. The one where a mutilated woman is found in a shopping cart outside a box store."

"I remember that one. Keep an eye on—"

"—the store manager," Jacob finishes. "I've seen it already, too."

He walks me to the door, his mother trailing behind. "Thanks, Jacob. And Emma?" I wait until she glances up. "Say it when you wake them up in the morning, instead."

When I reach Jess Ogilvy's place, the two CSIs who have been processing the house are standing outside in the freezing cold, staring at a cut window screen.

"No prints?" I say, my breath fogging in the cold.

But I already know the answer. So

would Jacob, for that matter. The chances of prints being preserved in temperatures as low as these are pretty slim.

"No," the first investigator says. Marcy's a bombshell with a knockout figure, a 155 IQ, and a girlfriend who could probably knock my teeth out. "But we did find the window jimmied to break the lock, too, and a screwdriver in the bushes."

"Nice. So the question is, was this a B and E gone bad? Or was the screen cut to make us think that?"

Basil, the second investigator, shakes his head. "Nothing inside screams breaking and entering."

"Yeah, well, that's not necessarily true. I just interviewed a witness who says otherwise and who, um, cleaned up."

Marcy looks at Basil. "So he's a suspect, not a witness."

"No. He's an autistic kid. Long story." I look at the edge of the screen. "What kind of knife was used?"

"Probably one from the kitchen. We've got a bunch to take back to the lab to see if any of them have traces of metal on the blade."

"You get any prints inside?"

"Yeah, in the bathroom and off the computer, plus a few partials around the kitchen."

But in this case, Mark Maguire's prints won't raise a red flag; he's admitted to living here part-time with Jess.

"We also got a partial boot print," Basil says. "The silver lining to it being crap weather for prints on the sill is that it's perfect for footwear impressions." Underneath the overhang of the gutter I can see the red splotch of spray wax he's used to make a cast. He's lucky to have found a protected ledge; there's been a dusting of fresh snow since Tuesday. It's the heel, and there's a star in the center, surrounded by what look like the spokes of a compass. Once Basil photographs it, we can enter it into a database to see what kind of boot it is.

The sound of a car driving down the street is punctuated by the slam of a door. Then footsteps approach, crunching on the snow. "If that's the press," I say to Marcy, "shoot first."

But it's not the press. It's Mark Maguire, looking like he hasn't slept since I last saw him. "It's about fucking time you got around to looking for my girlfriend," he shouts, and even from a few feet away, the fumes of alcohol on his breath reach me.

"Mr. Maguire," I say, moving slowly toward him. "You happen to know if this screen's always been cut?"

I watch him carefully to see his reaction. But the truth is, I can amass all the evidence I want against Mark Maguire and I still have nothing to arrest him for unless a body is recovered.

He squints at the window, but the sun is in his eyes, as well as the brilliant reflection of snow on the ground. As he moves a little closer, Basil steps behind him and shoots a jet of spray wax on the boot print he left behind.

Even from this far away I can make out the star, and the spokes of a compass.

"Mr. Maguire," I say, "we're going to have to take your boots."

Jacob

The first time I saw a dead person was at my grandfather's funeral.

It was after the service, where the minister had read aloud from the Bible, even though my grandfather did not routinely go to church or consider himself religious. Strangers got up and talked about my grandfather, calling him Joseph and telling stories about parts of his life that were news to me: his service during the Korean War, his childhood on the Lower East Side, his courtship of my grandmother at a high school carnival kissing booth. All of their words landed on me like hornets, and I couldn't make them go away until I could see the grandfather 1 knew and remembered, instead of this impostor they were all discussing.

My mother was not crying so much as dissolving; that is the one way 1 can describe the fact that tears had become so normal for her it looked strange to see her face smooth and dry.

It should be noted that 1 do not always understand body language. That's quite normal, for someone with Asperger's. It's pointless to expect me to look at someone and know how she is feeling simply because her smile is too tight and she is hunched over and hugging her arms to herself, just as it would be pointless to expect a deaf person to hear a voice. Which means that when 1 asked to have my grandfather's coffin opened, 1 shouldn't be blamed for not realizing it would upset my mother even more.

1 just wanted to see if the body inside was still my grandfather, or maybe the man all those speakers had known, or something entirely different. 1 am skeptical about lights and tunnels and afterlives, and this seemed the most logical way to test my theories.

Here is what 1 learned: Dead isn't angels or ghosts. It's a physical state of breakdown, a change in all those carbon atoms that create the temporary house of a body so that they can return to their most elemental stage.

I don't really see why that freaks people out, since it's the most natural cycle in the world.

The body in the coffin still looked like my grandfather. When I touched his cheek, though, with its crosshatched wrinkles, the skin no longer felt like human skin. It was cold, and slightly firm, like pudding that's been left too long in the refrigerator and has developed a virtual hide as a surface crust.

I may not understand emotion, but I can feel guilt about not understanding it. So when I finally cornered my mother, hours after she ran sobbing from the sight of me poking The-Thing-That-Used-to-Be-My-Grandfather's cheek, I tried to explain why she shouldn't be crying. "He's not Grandpa," I told her. "I checked."

Remarkably, this did not make her feel better at all. "That doesn't mean I miss him any less," my mother said.

Pure logic suggests that if the entity in the coffin is not fundamentally the person you used to know, you cannot miss him. Because that's not a loss; that's a change.

My mother had shaken her head. "Here's

what I miss, Jacob. I miss the fact that I won't get to ever hear his voice again. And that I can't talk to him anymore."

This wasn't really true. We had Grandpa's voice immortalized on old family videos that I sometimes liked to watch when I couldn't sleep at night. And it wasn't that she couldn't talk to him that was hard for her to accept; it was that he could no longer talk back.

My mother had sighed. "You'll get it, one day. I hope."

I would like to be able to tell her that, yes, now I get it. When someone dies, it feels like the hole in your gum when a tooth falls out. You can chew, you can eat, you have plenty of other teeth, but your tongue keeps going back to that empty place, where all the nerves are still a little raw.

I am headed to my meeting with Jess.

I'm late. It's 3:00 A.M., which is really Monday, not Sunday. But there's no other time for me to go, with my mother watching over me. And although she will probably argue that I broke a house rule, technically, I didn't. This isn't sneaking out to a crime scene. The crime scene is three hundred yards away from where I'm headed.

My backpack is full of necessities; my bike whispers on the pavement as I pedal fast. It's easier not being on foot this time, not having to support more than my own weight.

Directly behind the yard of the house into which Jess had moved is a small, scraggly forest. And directly behind that is Route 115. It runs across a bridge over the culvert that siphons the runoff from the woods in the spring, when the water level is high. I noticed it last Tuesday when I took the bus from school to Jess's new residence.

My mind is full of maps—from social flowcharts (*Person is frowning → Person keeps trying to interrupt → Person takes step backward = Person wants to leave this conversation, desperately*) to grids of relativity, like an interpersonal version of Google Earth. (*Kid says to me, "You play baseball? What position? Left out?" and gets a big laugh from the rest of the class. Kid is one person out of 6.792 billion humans on this planet. This planet is only one-eighth of the solar system, whose sun is one of two billion stars in the Milky Way galaxy. Put that way, the comment loses its importance.*)

But my mind also functions geographically and topographically, so that at any given moment I can locate myself (this shower stall is on the upper level of the house at 132 Birdseye Lane, Townsend, Vermont, United States, North America, Western Hemisphere, Planet Earth). So by the time I got to Jess's new house last Tuesday, I completely understood where it lay in relation to everywhere else I'd ever been.

Jess is just where I left her five days ago, propped against the damp stone wall.

I lean my bike against the far end of the culvert and squat down, shining a flashlight into her face.

Jess is dead.

When I touch her cheek with the backs of my knuckles, it feels like marble. That reminds me, and so I open up my backpack and pull out the blanket. It is a silly thing, I know, but so is leaving flowers on a grave, and this seems to make more sense. I tuck it around Jess's shoulders and make sure it covers her feet.

Then I sit down beside her. I put on a pair of latex gloves and I hold Jess's hand for a moment before taking out my notebook. In it, I begin to write down the physical evidence.

The bruises underneath her eyes.

The missing tooth.

The contusions on her upper arms, which

are, of course, covered up by her sweatshirt right now.

The leathery yellow scrapes on her lower back, which are also covered by that sweat-shirt.

To be honest, I'm a little disappointed. I would have expected the police to be able to read the clues I left behind. But they haven't found Jess, and so I have to take the next step.

Her phone is still in my pocket. I have carried it everywhere with me, although I've only turned it on five times. Detective Matson would have subpoenaed Jess's cell phone records by now; they'll see the instances when I called her residence to listen to her voice on the answering machine, but they will assume it was Jess herself who made the call.

He's probably tried to locate her by GPS, too, which nearly all phones have now and which can be accessed by the FBI using a computer program that will pinpoint an active phone within a range of a few feet. This was first piloted in emergency response programs, namely, the 911 call. As soon as dispatch picks up on the other end, they begin to track, just in case an officer or an ambulance has to be sent out.

I decide to make it easy for them. I sit down next to Jess again, so that our shoulders are touching. "You are the best friend I ever had," I tell her. "I wish this had never happened."

Jess, of course, does not respond. I cannot say whether she has ceased to be or if this is just her body and the thing that makes Jess Jess has gone somewhere else. It makes me think of my meltdown—of the room with no windows, no doors, the country where nobody speaks to each other, the piano with only black keys. Maybe this is why funeral dirges are always in a minor key; being on the other side of dead isn't that different from having Asperger's.

It would be incredible to stay and watch. There is nothing I would like more than to see the police swarm in to rescue Jess. But that would be too risky; and so I know I'll just get on my bike and be safe and sound in my bed before the sun or my mother rises for the day.

First, though, I power up her pink Motorola. It feels like I should recite something, a tribute or a prayer. *"E.T., phone home,"* I finally say, and then I press 911 and place the little receiver on the stone beside her.

Through the speakers I can hear the voice

of the dispatcher. *What is your emergency?* she says. *Hello? Is anybody there?*

I am halfway through the woods when I see the flashing lights in the distance on Route 115, and I smile to myself the whole rest of the way home.

CASE 4: SOMETHING'S FISHY

Something Stella Nickell loved: tropical fish. She dreamed of opening her own store.

Something Stella Nickell did not love: her husband, whom she poisoned in 1986 with Excedrin capsules she'd laced with cyanide in order to collect on his life insurance policies.

She first attempted to poison Bruce Nickell with hemlock and foxglove, but neither worked on him. So instead she contaminated Excedrin capsules. In order to cover her tracks, she also placed several packages of poisoned Excedrin in three different stores—leading to the death of Sue Snow, who had the bad luck to have been shopping at one of them. The drug manufacturers released the batch numbers of the pills to warn consumers, which was when Stella Nickell came forward and told authorities she had two bottles of contaminated pills that had been purchased from two different stores. This seemed unlikely, since out of thousands of bottles that had been checked in that region, only five were found to have tainted capsules. What were the odds of Stella having two of those?

While examining the Excedrin capsules, the FBI lab found an essential clue: green crystals were mixed in with the cyanide. These turned out to be Algae Destroyer—a product used in fish tanks. Stella Nickell had an aquarium and had bought Algae Destroyer at a local fish store. According to the police, Stella had crushed some algae tablets for her beloved fish in a bowl and then, later, used the same bowl to mix the cyanide. Stella's estranged daughter subsequently went to the police and testified that her mother had planned to kill Bruce Nickell for years.

Talk about the mother of all headaches.

4

Rich

Sometimes I'm just too damn late.

Last year, the day after Christmas, a thirteen-year-old girl named Gracie Cheever never came downstairs. She was found hanging from a closet rack. When I arrived with the CSIs who were photographing the scene, the first thing I noticed was what a mess Gracie's room was—cereal bowls stacked high and papers and dirty laundry thrown on the floor—no one ever asked this kid to clean up. I looked through her journals and learned that Gracie was a cutter; Gracie hated her life and herself;

Gracie hated her face and thought she was fat, and wrote down every morsel she ate and every time she cheated on her diet. And then, on one page: *I miss my mom.* I asked one of the patrol officers if the mother was dead, and he shook his head. "She's in the kitchen," he said.

Gracie was the older child of two. She had a younger sister with Down syndrome, and boy, did her mom live for that kid. She home-schooled her; she did the girl's physical therapy on mats in the family room. And while her mother was busy being a saint, Gracie's dad was molesting her.

I took Gracie's journal back to the station, and I Xeroxed it twice. It was covered with blood, because while she was writing, she was cutting herself. One copy I gave to the medical examiner. The second I brought to the chief. *Someone in this family needs to know what was going on,* I told him.

After Gracie was buried, I called her mother and asked to meet with her. We sat down in the living room, in front of a blazing fire. At that appointment, I gave her a copy of the journal and told her I'd marked the pages that she really needed to read. She stared at me with glassy eyes and told me the family was starting fresh. She thanked me, and then, while I was watching, she threw the journal into the flames.

I am thinking of Gracie Cheever now as I move gingerly around the culvert where Jess Ogilvy's body has been located. She is wrapped in a quilt, and fully dressed. There's a fine sheen of frost on her clothes and her skin. Wayne Nussbaum snaps off the latex gloves he's been using to examine the body and instructs his assistants to wait for the CSIs to finish their photographs of the scene before moving the victim back to the hospital for an autopsy.

"First impression?" I ask.

"She's been dead awhile. Days, I'm thinking, although it's hard to say. The cold weather made a nice makeshift morgue." He tucked his bare hands under his armpits. "I doubt she was killed here. The scrapes on her back look like they were caused by being dragged postmortem." As an afterthought, he asks, "Did any of your guys find a tooth?"

"Why?"

"Because she's missing one."

I make a mental note to tell my investigators to search for that. "Knocked out with a punch? Or taken as a trophy after death?"

He shakes his head. "Rich, you know I'm not playing a guessing game with you at four in the morning. I'll call you with my report."

As he walks off, the flash of a CSI photographer illuminates the night.

In that instant, we all look like ghosts.

Mark Maguire swallows when he sees the backpack that has been returned from the lab. "That's the one her aunt gave her," he murmurs.

He is shell-shocked. Not only has he been told his girlfriend is dead but, seconds afterward, he was arrested for her murder. It was 7:00 A.M. when the officers went to his apartment to pick him up. Now, during the interrogation, he is still wearing the clothes he wore to bed last night: sweatpants and a faded UVM tee. From time to time he's shivered in the drafty conference room, but that only makes me think of Jess Ogilvy's blue-cast skin.

My time line is shaping up. The way I see it, Maguire was fighting with Jess, punched her—knocking out her tooth and inadvertently killing her. Panicking, he cleaned up the evidence and then tried to cover his tracks by making it look like a kidnapping: the cut screen, the overturned CD rack and kitchen stools, the mailbox note, the backpack full of Jess's clothes.

I take the clothes out of the backpack— mostly plus-sizes far too big for Jess's tiny frame. "A smarter criminal who was leaving a red herring would have picked clothes that actually still fit her," I muse. "But then again, Mark, you aren't very smart, are you?"

"I already told you, I had nothing to do with—"

"Did you knock out her tooth when you were fighting with her?" I ask. "Is that the way a guy like you gets off? By beating up his girlfriend?"

"I didn't beat her up—"

"Mark, you can't win here. We've got

her body, and there are bruises clear as day on her arms and her neck. How long do you think it's going to take us to tie them to you?"

He winces. "I told you—we were having a fight, and I did grab her arms. I pinned her up against the wall. I wanted . . . I wanted to teach her a lesson."

"And this lesson went a little too far, didn't it?"

"I never killed her. I swear to God."

"Why did you bring her body out into the woods?"

He looks up at me. "Please. You have to believe me."

I rise to my feet and loom over him. "I don't have to believe anything you say, you little prick. You already lied to me once about fighting with her on the weekend, when it turns out you fought with her on Tuesday, too. I've got your boots outside the window with a cut screen, your handprints on her throat, and a dead girl who was cleaned up and moved. You ask any jury in this country, and that looks a hell of a lot like a guy who killed his girlfriend and wanted to conceal it."

"I never cut that screen. I don't know

who did. And I didn't beat her up. I got mad, and I shoved her . . . and I left."

"Right. And then you came back, and you killed her."

Maguire's eyes fill with tears. I wonder if he really is sorry about Jess Ogilvy's death, or just sorry that he's been caught. "No," he says, his voice thick. "No, I loved her."

"Did you cry this much when you were cleaning up her blood in the bathroom? How about when you had to wipe all the blood off her face?"

"I want to see her," Maguire begs. "Let me see Jess."

"You should have thought of that before you murdered her," I say.

As I walk away from him, intending to let him stew in his own guilt for a few minutes before I come back in to break his confession, Maguire buries his face in his hands. That's when I realize that they are completely uninjured—no bruising, no cuts, which you'd expect if you hit someone hard enough to make her lose a tooth.

Theo

By the time I was five, I knew that there were differences between Jacob and me.

I had to eat everything on my plate, but Jacob was allowed to leave behind things like peas and tomatoes because he didn't like the way they felt inside his mouth.

Whatever kids' tape I was listening to in the car while we drove took a backseat to anything by Bob Marley.

I had to pick up all my toys after I was done playing, but the six-foot line of Matchbox cars that Jacob had spent the day arranging perfectly straight was allowed to snake down the hallway for a month until he got tired of it.

Mostly, though, I was aware of being the odd guy out. Because the minute Jacob had any kind of crisis—and that happened constantly—my mom would drop everything and run to him. And usually the thing she dropped was me.

Once, when I was about seven, my mother had promised me she'd take us to see *Spy Kids 3-D* on a Saturday afternoon. I had been excited all week, because we didn't often see movies, much less 3-D ones. We didn't have the extra money for it, but I had gotten a free pair of glasses in our cereal box and begged and begged until my mother said yes. However—big surprise—it turned out to be a non-issue. Jacob had read all of his dinosaur books and started flapping and rocking at the thought of not having something new to read for bedtime, and my mother made an executive decision to take us to the library instead of the theater.

Maybe I would have been okay with this, but at the library, there was a big honking display case taking advantage of the movie tie-in with reading in general. *BE A SPY KID!* it said, and it was full of books like *Harriet the Spy* and stories about the Hardy Boys and Nancy Drew. I watched my mother take Jacob to the nonfiction section—567 in the world of Dewey decimals, which even *I* knew meant dinosaurs. They sat down right in the aisle, as if dragging me to the library and ruining my day didn't matter at all. They started to read a book about ornithopods.

Suddenly, I realized what I had to do.

If my mother only noticed Jacob, then that's what I would become.

It was probably seven years of frustration that boiled over just then, because I can't really explain why else I did what I did. I mean, I knew better.

Libraries are places where you are supposed to be quiet.

Library books are sacred, and don't belong to you.

One minute I had been sitting in the

children's room, in the comfy green chair that looked like a giant's fist, and the next, I was screaming my head off and yanking books off the shelves and ripping out the pages, and when the librarian said *Whose child is this?* I kicked her in the shins.

I was gifted at throwing a fit. I'd been watching a master, after all, my whole life.

A crowd gathered. Other librarians ran in to see what was going on. I only hesitated once during my tantrum, and that was when I saw my mother's face hovering at the edge of the group that was staring at me. She had gone white, like a statue.

Obviously, she had to get me out of there. And obviously, that meant Jacob couldn't check out the books he wanted to bring home. She grabbed him by the wrist as he started to have his own meltdown, and lifted me with her free arm. My brother and I both kicked and screamed the whole way into the parking lot.

When we reached the car, she set me down. I did what I'd seen Jacob do a thousand times; I went boneless as spaghetti and collapsed on the pavement.

All of a sudden, I heard something I'd never heard before. It was louder than both my yelling and Jacob's combined, and it was coming out of my mother's mouth.

She screamed. She stamped her feet. *Aaaaaauuuurrrrrggggh*, she cried. She flopped her arms and kicked and tossed her head back and forth. People stared at her from all the way across the parking lot.

I stopped right away. The only thing worse than having the whole world looking at *me* going crazy was having the whole world look at my *mother* going crazy. I closed my eyes, feverishly wishing that the ground would open up and just swallow me.

Jacob, on the other hand, kept shrieking and throwing his fit.

"Do you think *I* don't want to lose it every now and then?" my mother shouted, and then she pulled herself together and buckled a squirming Jacob into his seat in the car. She dragged me up from the asphalt and did the same with me.

But none of that is the reason I'm telling you this story. It's because that day was the first day my mother cried in front of me, instead of bravely trying to hold it all inside.

Emma

From Auntie Em's column:
When did they stop putting toys in cereal boxes?

When I was little, I remember wandering the cereal aisle (which surely is as American a phenomenon as fireworks on the Fourth of July) and picking my breakfast food based on what the reward was: a Frisbee with the Trix rabbit's face emblazoned on the front. Holographic stickers with the Lucky Charms leprechaun. A mystery decoder wheel. I could suffer through raisin bran for a month if it meant I got a magic ring at the end.

I cannot admit this out loud. In the first place, we are expected to be supermoms these days, instead of admitting that we have flaws. It is tempting to believe that all mothers wake up feeling fresh every morning, never raise their voices, only cook with organic food, and are equally at ease with the CEO and the PTA.

Here's a secret: Those mothers don't exist. Most of us—even if we'd never confess—are suffering through the raisin bran in the hopes of a glimpse of that magic ring.

I look very good on paper. I have a family, and I write a newspaper column. In real life, I have to pick superglue out of the carpet, rarely remember to defrost for dinner, and plan to have BECAUSE I SAID SO engraved on my tombstone.

Real mothers wonder why experts who write for *Parents* and *Good Housekeeping*—and, dare I say it, the *Burlington Free Press*—seem to have their acts together all the time when they themselves can barely keep their heads above the stormy seas of parenthood.

Real mothers don't just listen with humble embarrassment to the elderly lady who offers unsolicited advice in the checkout line when a child is throwing a tantrum. We take the child, dump him in the lady's cart, and say, "Great. Maybe *you* can do a better job."

Real mothers know that it's okay to eat cold pizza for breakfast.

Real mothers admit it is easier to fail at this job than to succeed.

If parenting is the box of raisin bran, then real mothers know the ratio of flakes to fun is severely imbalanced. For every moment that your child confides in you, or tells you he loves you, or does something unprompted to protect his brother that you happen to witness, there are many more moments of chaos, error, and self-doubt.

Real mothers may not speak the heresy, but they sometimes secretly wish they'd chosen something for breakfast other than this endless cereal.

Real mothers worry that other mothers will find that magic ring, whereas *they'll* be looking and looking for ages.

Rest easy, real mothers. The very fact that you worry about being a good mom means that you already *are* one.

During a short fit of writer's block, I make myself a tuna sandwich and listen to the midday news. The local station is so awful that I like to watch it for the entertainment value. If I were still in college, I'd play a drinking game and take a swig of beer every time the anchors mispronounced a word or dropped their notes. My favorite recent mistake was when the anchor reported on a Vermont senator's proposed overhaul of Medicaid. Instead of cutting to the video of his speech, they showed a clip of a polar bear plunge by a bunch of local octogenarians.

Today's top story, however, is not funny at all.

"Early Monday morning," the anchor reads, "the body of Jessica Ogilvy was found in the woods behind her residence. The twenty-three-year-old UVM student had gone missing last Tuesday."

The plate on my lap falls to the floor as I stand up, tears in my eyes. Although I'd known this was a possibility—a probability, really, as days went by and she wasn't found—that doesn't make her death any easier.

I had often wondered what the world would have looked like if there were more people like Jess around, young men and women who could see someone like Jacob and not laugh at his quirks and flaws but instead celebrate the ways they made him interesting and worthy. I imagined the boys who would one day be in a class Jess taught and who would not have to struggle with the self-esteem and bullying issues that Jacob had struggled with in grade school. And now, none of that would happen.

The story cuts to a reporter, whose segment has been filmed close to the spot where Jess's body was found. "In this very sad turn of events," she says soberly, "investigators responded to a 911 call placed from Ogilvy's cell phone and traced the call here, to a culvert behind Ogilvy's home."

This was taped near dawn; the sky is striped with pink. In the background are the crime scene investigators, setting up markers and taking measurements and photos. "Shortly afterward," the reporter continues, "authorities took Ogilvy's boyfriend, twenty-four-year-old Mark Maguire, into custody. An autopsy report is still pending . . ."

If I had blinked, I probably would never have seen it. If the reporter had not shifted her feet, I would never have seen it. The image was *that* quick—the tiniest flash on the side of the screen before it was gone.

A quilt with rainbow patchwork, ROYGBIV over and over.

I freeze the frame—a newfangled feature of the satellite system we use—and run the clip backward before letting it play again. This time maybe I will see that it was only a trick of the eye, a flutter of the reporter's scarf that I mistook for something else.

It is still there, so I run the tape backward a second time.

I once saw madness defined as doing the same thing over and over and expecting different results. My heart is pounding so fiercely now that I can feel it beating at the base of my throat. I race upstairs to Jacob's closet, where I'd found Jess's backpack a few days earlier, wrapped in the rainbow quilt.

Which is missing.

I sink down on his bed and smooth my hand over his pillow. Right now, at 12:45, Jacob is in physics class. He told me this morning that they are doing a lab on Archimedes' principle, trying to determine the density of two unknown materials. What mass, when inserted into a medium, causes it to displace? What floats, and what sinks?

I will go to the school and pick the boys up, making up an excuse—a dentist's visit, a haircut appointment. But instead of coming home we will drive and drive until we cross

the border into Canada. I will pack suit-
cases for them, and we will never come back
here.

Even as I am thinking this, I know it
could never happen. Jacob would not understand the concept of never coming back
home. And somewhere, in a police station,
Jess's boyfriend is being blamed when he
might be innocent.

Downstairs, with numb fingers, I pick
through the stack of bills that I haven't sorted.
I know it's in here somewhere . . . and then I
find it, beneath the second notice from the
phone company. Rich Matson's business card,
with his cell phone number scrawled on the
back.

Just in case, he had said.

Just in case you happen to think that your
son might be involved in a murder. Just in
case you are confronted with the glaring evidence that you have failed as a mother. Just in
case you are caught between what you want
and what you should do.

Detective Matson has been honest with
me; I will be honest with him.

His voice mail picks up immediately after
I dial the number. The first time, I hang
up, because all of my intended words have

become jammed together like putty. The second time, I clear my throat. "This is Emma Hunt," I say. "I . . . I really need to speak with you."

Still holding the phone like an amulet, I wander into the living room again. The news program is over; now there is a soap opera on. I rewind the action until the segment about Jess Ogilvy plays again. I deliberately keep my eyes trained to the other side of the screen, but it's still there: a flag on the field, a nanosecond of truth in all the shades of the color spectrum.

No matter how hard I try, I can't unsee that damn quilt.

Jacob

Jess is dead.

My mother tells me after school. She stares at me when she says it, as if she's trying to find clues in my expression, the same way I scrutinize the tilt of someone's eyebrows and the position of their mouth and the size of their pupils and try to connect them with an emotion. For a moment I think, *Does* she *have Asperger's, too?* But then, just when it seems that she is analyzing my features, hers change, and I can't tell what she's feeling. Her eyes look tight at the edges, and her mouth is pinched. Is she mad at me, or is she just upset about

Jess being dead? Does she want me to react to news I already know? I could act like I'm shocked (jaw dropped, eyes round), but that would also mean I'm lying, and then my lying face (eyes looking up at ceiling, teeth biting down on bottom lip) would do a hostile takeover of my shocked face. Besides, lying is right up there on the House Rules list. To recap:

1. Clean up your own messes.

2. Tell the truth.

Regarding Jess's death: I have done both.

Imagine what it would be like if you were suddenly dropped from America into England. Suddenly *bloody* would be a swear word, not a description of a crime scene. *Pissed* would be not angry but drunk. *Dear* would mean expensive, not beloved. *Potty* isn't a toilet but a state of mind; *public school* is private school, and *fancy* is a verb.

If you were dropped into the UK and you happened to be Korean or Portuguese, your confusion would be expected. After all, you don't speak the language. But if you're American, technically, you do. So you're stuck in conversations that make no sense to you, in which you ask people to repeat themselves over and over, in the hope that eventually the unfamiliar words will fall into place.

This is what Asperger's feels like. I have to work so hard at the things that come naturally to others, because I'm just a tourist here.

And it's a trip with a one-way ticket.

Here are the things I will remember about Jess:

1. For Christmas she gave me a piece of malachite the exact size and shape of a chicken egg.

2. She is the only person I've ever met who was born in Ohio.

3. Her hair looked different indoors than it did outdoors. When the sun was shining, it was less yellow and more like fire.

4. She introduced me to *The Princess Bride,* which is possibly one of the greatest movies in the history of filmmaking.

5. Her mailbox at UVM was number 5995.

6. She fainted at the sight of blood, but she still came to my presentation this fall in physics about spatter patterns, and she listened with her back to the PowerPoint presentation.

7. Even though there were times when she probably was sick of hearing me talk, she never, ever told me to shut up.

I am the first person to tell you that I do not really understand love. How can you love your new haircut, love your job, and love your girlfriend all at once? Clearly the word doesn't mean the same thing in different situations, which is why I have never been able to figure it out with logic.

The physical side of love terrifies me, to be honest. When you are already hypersensitive to the feeling of anything against your skin or to people standing close enough to touch you, there is absolutely nothing about a sexual relationship that makes it an experience you look forward to attempting.

I mention all this as a disclaimer to the last thing I will remember about Jess:

8. I could have loved her. Maybe I already did.

* * *

If I were going to create a science fiction series on television, it would be about an empath—a person who can naturally read the auras of people's emotions and, with a single touch, can take on their feelings, too. It would be so easy if I could look at someone who was happy, touch him on the arm, and suddenly fill with the same bubbles of joy that he's feeling, instead of anguishing over whether I'd misinterpreted his actions and reactions.

Anyone who cries at a movie is a closet empath. What's happening on that screen bleeds through the celluloid, real enough to evoke emotion. Why else would you find yourself laughing at the hijinks of two actors who, offscreen, can't stand each other? Or crying over the death of an actor who, when the camera is turned off, will dust himself off and grab a burger for dinner?

When I watch movies, it's a little different. Each scene becomes a catalog card of possible social scenarios in my mind. *If you ever find yourself arguing with a woman, try kissing her to throw her off guard. If you are in the middle of a battle and your buddy is shot,*

*friendship means you have to go back under
fire to rescue him. If you want to be the life
of the party, say, "Toga!"*

Later, if I find myself in that particular
situation, I can shuffle through my file cards
of movie interactions and mimic the behavior
and know, for once, that I will be getting it
right.

Incidentally, I have never cried at a movie.

Once, I was telling Jess everything I knew
about dogs.

1. They evolved from a small mammal called
miacis, a tree dweller that lived 40 million
years ago.

2. They were first domesticated by Paleo-
lithic cavemen.

3. No matter the breed, a dog has 321 bones
and 42 permanent teeth.

4. Dalmatians are born all white.

5. The reason they turn in a circle before lying down is because when they were wild
animals, this helped mat the long grass into
a bed.

6. Approximately one million dogs have been named the primary beneficiaries in their owners' wills.

7. They sweat through the pads of their feet.

8. Scientists have found that dogs can smell the presence of autism in kids.

You're making that up, she said.
No. Really.
How come you don't have a dog?
There were so many answers to that question, I didn't really know where to begin. My mother, for one, who said that anyone who could not remember to brush his teeth twice daily did not have the fortitude to take care of another living creature. My brother, who was allergic to nearly anything with hair on it. The fact that dogs, which had been my passion after dinosaurs but before crime scene analysis, had fallen out of favor.

The truth is that I would probably never want a dog. Dogs are like the kids in school I cannot stand: the ones who hang around and then leave when they realize they are not getting what they want or need from the conversation. They travel in packs. They lick you and you think it's because they like you, but it's really just because your fingers still smell like your turkey sandwich.

On the other hand, I think cats have Asperger's.

Like me, they're very smart.

And like me, sometimes they simply need to be left alone.

Rich

Once I leave Mark Maguire to steep in his own conscience for a few minutes, I grab a cup of coffee in the break room and check my voice mail. I have three new messages. The first is from my ex, reminding me that tomorrow is Open School Night for Sasha—an event that, by the looks of things, I'm going to have to miss yet again. The second is from my dentist, confirming an appointment. And the third is from Emma Hunt.

"Emma," I say, returning her call. "What can I do for you?"

"I . . . I saw that you found Jess." Her voice is husky, full of tears.

"Yes. I'm sorry. I know you were close to her."

There are sobs on the other end of the line.

"Are you okay?" I ask. "Do you need me to call someone for you?"

"She was wrapped in a quilt," Emma chokes out.

Sometimes, when you do what I do for work, it gets easy to forget that, after you close the file on a case, there are people who suffer with the fallout for the rest of their lives. They'll remember one little detail about the victim: a single shoe lying in the middle of the road, a hand still clutching a Bible, or—in this case— the juxtaposition between being tenderly tucked into a quilt and being murdered. But there's nothing I can do for Jess Ogilvy now except bring the person who killed her to justice.

"That quilt," Emma sobs, "belongs to my son."

I freeze in the act of stirring cream into my coffee. "Jacob?"

"I don't know ... I don't understand what that means ..."

"Emma, listen. It might not mean anything at all, and if it does, Jacob will have an explanation."

"What do I do?" she cries.

"Nothing," I tell her. "Let *me*. Can you bring him down here?"

"He's in school—"

"Then after school," I say. "And, Emma? Relax. We'll get to the bottom of this."

As soon as I hang up, I take my full mug of coffee and empty it in the sink; that's how distracted I am. Jacob Hunt admitted to being at the house. He had a backpack full of Jess Ogilvy's clothes. He was the last person known to see her alive.

Jacob may have Asperger's syndrome, but that doesn't preclude his being a murderer.

I think of Mark Maguire's flat-out denials about hurting his girlfriend, his unscarred hands, his crying. Then I think of Jacob Hunt, who cleaned up Jess's house when it looked like it had been vandalized. Had he left out the intrinsic detail that *he* was the one who'd wrecked it?

On the one hand, I have a boyfriend

who's a jackass but who's grief-stricken. I have his boot prints outside a cut screen.

On the other hand, I have a kid who's obsessed with crime scene analysis. A kid who doesn't like Mark Maguire. A kid who'd know how to take a murder and make it look like Mark Maguire did it and then attempted to cover his tracks.

I have a kid who's been known to hang out at crime scenes in the past.

I have a homicide, and I have a blanket that links Jacob Hunt to it.

The division between an observer and a participant is nearly invisible; you can cross it before you even know you've stepped over the line.

Emma

On the way home from school, I am gripping the steering wheel so hard that my hands are shaking. I keep looking in the rearview mirror at Jacob. He looks like he did this morning—wearing a faded green T-shirt, his seat belt snugly fastened over his chest, his dark hair falling into his eyes. He is not stimming or withdrawn or exhibiting any of the other hallmarks of behavior that flag the fact something is upsetting him. Does that mean he didn't have anything to do with Jess's death? Or he did, and it simply doesn't affect him the way it would affect someone else?

Theo has been talking about math—a problem he did that no one else in the class understood. I am not absorbing a single word. "Jacob and I have to swing by the police station," I say, training my voice to be as level as possible. "So Theo, I'm just going to drop you off at home first."

"What for?" Jacob asks. "Did he get back the results on the backpack?"

"He didn't say."

Theo looks at me. "Mom? Is something going on?"

For a moment I want to laugh: I have one child who cannot read me at all, and another who reads me too well. I don't answer but pull up to our mailbox instead. "Theo, hop out and get the mail, and you can let yourself into the house. I'll be back as soon as I can." I leave him standing in the middle of the road and drive off with Jacob.

But instead of heading to the police station, I stop off at a strip mall and park. "Are we getting a snack?" Jacob asks. "Because I'm actually quite hungry."

"Maybe later." I get out of the driver's seat and sit beside him in the back of the car. "I have something to tell you. Some very bad news."

"Like when Grandpa died."

"Yes, a lot like that. You know how Jess has been gone for a while, so you couldn't have your meeting on Sunday? The police found her body. She's dead." I watch him carefully as I speak, ready to mark a flicker of his eye or a twitch of his hand that I might read as a clue. But Jacob, completely impassive, just looks at the headrest in front of him.

"Okay," he says after a moment.

"Do you have any questions?"

Jacob nods. "Can we get a snack now?"

I look at my son, and I see a monster. I'm just not sure if that's his real face or if it's a mask made of Asperger's.

Honestly, I'm not even sure it matters.

By the time I reach the police station with Jacob, my nerves are strung as tight as the strings on a violin. I feel like a traitor, bringing my own son to Detective Matson, but is there an alternative? A girl is already dead. I couldn't live with myself, with this secret, if I didn't acknowledge Jacob's involvement.

Before I can even ask for him to be paged by dispatch, the detective walks into the station lobby. "Jacob," he says, and then he turns to me. "Emma. Thanks for bringing him in."

I don't have any words left to say. Instead, I look away.

Just like Jacob.

The detective puts a hand on my shoulder. "I know this isn't easy . . . but you did the right thing."

"Then why doesn't it feel that way?" I murmur.

"Trust me," Matson says, and because I want to—because I *need* someone else to take the wheel for just a moment while I struggle to breathe—I nod.

He turns back to Jacob. "The reason I asked your mom to bring you here," Matson says, "is because I want to talk to you. I could really use your help with some cases."

My jaw drops open. That is a blatant lie.

Predictably, Jacob swells with pride. "I suppose I have time for that."

"That's great," Matson replies, "because we're stumped. We've got some cold cases— and a few active ones—that have us scratching our heads. And after seeing you draw conclusions about the hypothermic guy, I know that you're incredibly well-versed in forensic criminology."

"I try to keep up-to-date," Jacob says. "I subscribe to three journals."

"Yeah? Impressive." Matson opens up the door that leads into the bowels of the police station. "Why don't we go somewhere a little more private?"

Using his love of CSI to entrap Jacob into giving a statement about Jess's death is like holding out a syringe of heroin to an addict. I am furious at Matson for being so underhanded; I am furious at myself for not realizing that he would have his priorities, just like I had mine.

Flushed with anger, I start to follow them through the doorway but am stopped by the detective. "Actually, Emma," he says, "you'll have to wait here."

"I have to go with him. He won't understand what you're asking him."

"Legally, he's an adult." Matson smiles, but it doesn't reach his eyes.

"Really, Mom," Jacob adds, his voice brimming with self-importance. "It's fine."

The detective looks at me. "Are you his legal guardian?"

"I'm his *mother*."

"That's not the same thing," Matson says. "I'm sorry."

For what? I wonder. For seducing Jacob into believing he's on his side? Or for doing the same to me?

"Then we're leaving," I insist.

Matson nods. "Jacob, it's your decision. Do you want to stay with me, or do you want to go home with your mom?"

"Are you *kidding*?" Jacob beams. "I want to talk to you, one hundred percent."

Before the door closes behind them, I have already taken off at a dead run toward the parking lot.

Rich

All is fair in love, war, and interrogation. By that I mean that if I can convince a suspect I'm the second coming of his long-dead grandma and the only way to salvation is to confess to me, so be it. None of which accounts for the fact that I cannot get Emma Hunt's face out of my mind, the minute she realized that I had betrayed her and was not going to allow her to sit in on my little chat with her son.

I can't bring Jacob into the interrogation room, because Mark Maguire is still there cooling his heels. I've left him with a sergeant who's currently doing a six-month stint with me to figure out whether or not he wants to take the test to make detective. I can't unarrest Mark until I know for sure I've got the right suspect in my sights.

So instead, I lead Jacob to my office. It's not much bigger than a closet, but it has boxes of case files all over the place and a few crime scene photos tacked up on the corkboard behind my head—all of which should get his adrenaline flowing. "You want a Coke or something?" I ask, motioning to the only other spare seat in the room.

"I'm not thirsty," Jacob says. "I wouldn't mind something to eat, though."

I rummage through my desk drawers for emergency candy—if I've learned anything on the job it's that when everything seems to be going to hell in a handbasket, a pack of Twizzlers can help you gain some perspective. I toss him some from my stash of last year's leftover Halloween candy, and he frowns.

"They're not gluten-free," Jacob says.

"Is that a bad thing?"

"Do you have any Skittles?"

I cannot believe we're negotiating candy,

but I rummage through the bowl and come up with a packet of Skittles.

"Sweet!" Jacob says. He tears a corner and tips the edge right into his mouth.

I lean back in my chair. "You mind if I tape this? That way, I can have it typed up just in case we come up with any terrific insights."

"Oh, sure. If that's helpful."

"It will be," I say, and I hit the button on the tape recorder. "So how'd you know that guy died of hypothermia, anyway?"

"Easy. There weren't any defense wounds to his arms; there was blood but no overt trauma . . . and of course the fact that he was in his underwear was a dead giveaway."

I shake my head. "You made me look like a genius in front of the medical examiner," I say.

"What's the most bizarre case you've ever heard about?"

I think for a moment. "A young guy jumps off the top of a building, intending to commit suicide, but sails past an open window at the exact moment a gunshot is fired through it."

Jacob grins. "That's an urban legend. It

was debunked by the *Washington Post* in 1996 as part of a speech given by a former president of the American Academy of Forensic Sciences, to show the legal complications of forensic analysis. But it's a good one, all the same."

"How about you?"

"The Texas Eyeball Killer. Charles Albright—who taught science—killed prostitutes and surgically removed their eyeballs as trophies." He grimaces. "Obviously that's the reason I never really liked my bio teacher."

"There are a lot of people in this world you'd never suspect as murderers," I say, watching Jacob carefully. "Don't you think?"

For just the tiniest flicker of a moment, a shadow crosses over his face. "You'd know better than me," he says.

"Jacob, I'm sort of in a predicament. I'd like to pick your brain about a current case."

"Jess's," he states.

"Yes. But that's tricky, because you knew her. So if we're going to talk openly, you'll have to waive your rights to *not* discuss it. You get what I'm saying?"

He nods and begins to recite Miranda. "I have the right to remain silent. Anything I say can and will be used against me in a court of law. I have the right to have an attorney present during questioning. If I cannot afford an attorney, one will be appointed for me . . ."

"Exactly," I murmur. "I actually have a copy of that here. If you can initial it here, and sign at the bottom, then I can prove to my chief that you didn't just memorize it—you understood what it meant."

Jacob takes a pen from me and quickly scrawls his name across the paper I've prepared. "Now can we talk about it?" he asks. "What have you got?"

"Well, the backpack was a disappointment."

"No prints?"

"Only ones we could match to Jess herself," I say. "Something else interesting turned up at the house—a screen was cut and the window jimmied open."

"You think that's how the perp got inside?"

"No, because the door wasn't locked. We did, however, find boot prints under the window that matched footwear Jess's boyfriend owns."

"There was a great *CrimeBusters* episode once where the exterior footprints didn't show up until it snowed—" Jacob breaks off, editing himself. "So Mark kills Jess and then tries to make it look like something else—a break-in—by cutting the screen and knocking over the stools and the mail and the CDs?"

"Something like that." I glance down at his hands—like Maguire's, they are injury-free. "What's your take? How hard would it be to reorganize a crime scene to mislead the investigators?"

Before he can answer, my cell phone rings. I recognize the number; it's Basil, who's accompanied the medical examiner back to the hospital. "Could you excuse me for a minute?" I ask Jacob, and I step into the hall and close the door behind me before answering the phone. "What have you got?"

"In addition to the scrapes on her back and contusions on the throat and upper arms, there are some more in the periorbital region—"

"English, Basil."

"Raccoon eyes," he says. "She's got a broken nose and a skull fracture. Cause of death is subdural hematoma."

I try to imagine Jacob Hunt throwing a right hook to Jess Ogilvy's face, hard enough to crack her skull. "Great. Thanks."

"That's not all," Basil answers. "Her underwear was on backward, but there's no evidence of sexual assault. Her face was washed clean—there were traces of blood in the hairline. And that missing tooth? We found it."

"Where?"

"Wrapped up in toilet paper, and tucked into the front pocket of her sweatpants," Basil says. "Whoever did this didn't just dump Jess Ogilvy. He cared about her."

I hang up the phone and immediately think of Sasha, who lost a tooth just a month ago when she was staying at my place. We wrapped it in tissue paper and put it in an envelope with the Tooth Fairy's name on it, for good measure. Naturally, I had to call my ex to ask her what the going rate was—$5, if you can believe it, which means my whole mouth is worth

$160. After Sasha was asleep and I swapped the envelope for a nice crisp Lincoln, I held it, wondering what the hell I was supposed to do with a baby tooth. I imagined the Tooth Fairy to have those empty glass jar lamps that hold seashells, only hers would hold thousands of tiny cuspids. Since I didn't subscribe to that kind of décor, I figured I'd just toss the damn thing, but at the last minute, I couldn't do it. This was my daughter's childhood, sealed in an envelope. How many chances would I have to hold on to a piece of her life?

Had Jacob Hunt felt the same way when he held Jess's tooth?

With a deep breath, I walk back into my office. The gloves are off. "You ever been to an autopsy, Jacob?"

"No."

I settle back down behind my desk. "The first thing the ME does is take a huge needle and stick it into the jelly of the eye so he can draw out the vitreous humor. If you run a tox screen on it, you can see what was in the victim's system at the moment of death."

"What kind of toxicity test?" Jacob

asks, not fazed at all by the gruesome image I just presented. "Alcohol? Prescription meds? Or illegal drugs?"

"Then the medical examiner cuts the torso open with a Y incision and peels back the skin. He'll saw through the ribs to make a little dome that he can lift up like the top of a jar, and then he starts pulling out the organs, one by one . . . weighing them . . . cutting slices he can look at under a microscope."

"A census taker once tried to test me. I ate his liver with some fava beans and a nice Chianti."

"Then the medical examiner takes his saw and cuts off the whole top of the skull and pops it open with a chisel. He reaches in, and he pulls her brain out. You know the sound a brain makes when it's being pried out of a skull, Jacob?" I imitate it, like a seal breaking.

"Then it gets weighed, right?" Jacob asks. "The average human brain weighs three pounds, but the biggest one on record was five pounds, one-point-one ounces."

"All that stuff I just described," I say, leaning forward. "All of that just happened to your friend Jess. What do you think about that?"

Jacob sinks deeper in his chair. "I *don't* want to think about that."

"I want to tell you some of the things that were found at Jess's autopsy. Maybe you can tell me how they might have happened."

He brightens considerably, ready to play the game.

"There were bruises that showed someone had grabbed her by the arms, and choked her around the neck."

"Well," Jacob muses, "were they fingertip bruises or handprints?"

"You tell me, Jacob. You're the one who grabbed Jess by the arms, aren't you?"

His face, when he realizes he is trapped, looks a great deal like his mother's. Jacob's hands curl over the arms of his chair, and he shakes his head. "No."

"What about choking her? You're not going to lie to me about doing that, are you?"

He closes his eyes and winces, as if he's in pain. "No . . ."

"So what made you choke her?"

"Nothing!"

"Was it a fight? Did she say something you didn't like?" I press.

Jacob moves to the edge of his chair and starts rocking. He won't look me in the eye, no matter how loud my voice gets. I wish I'd had the foresight to video-tape this conversation instead of audio-taping it. If this kid's demeanor isn't a Hallmark card for guilt, frankly, I don't know what is. "Nothing made me choke Jess," Jacob says.

I ignore this completely. "Did you choke her till she stopped breathing?"

"No—"

"Did you hit her in the face?"

"What? No!"

"Then how did her tooth get knocked out?"

He looks at me, and that takes me by surprise. His stare is direct, open, with emotion so raw that I feel compelled to turn away, like he usually does. "That was an accident," Jacob confesses softly, and only then do I realize I have been holding my breath.

Oliver

This morning, I managed to teach Thor to balance a paper clip on top of his nose. "All right," I say, "let's give it another whirl." The way I figure it, if I can get him to balance *and* multitask—roll over, maybe, or bark to the tune of "Dixie"—we can get on Letterman.

I have just placed the paper clip on top of his nose again when a crazy woman bursts in. "I need a lawyer," she announces, breathless.

She's probably in her late thirties or early forties—there are some lines around her mouth and her dark hair has a few strands of gray in it—but her eyes make her look younger. They're like caramel, or butterscotch, and why the hell am I looking at a potential client and channeling ice cream toppings? "Come right in!" I stand up, offering her a chair. "Sit down and tell me what the problem is."

"We don't have time for that. You have to come with me right now."

"But I—"

"My son is being interrogated at the police station, and you have to stop it. I'm retaining you on his behalf."

"Awesome," I say, and Thor drops the paper clip. I pick it up so he doesn't swallow it in my absence and grab my coat.

I know it's totally mercenary of me, but I'm hoping that she's going to lead me to the BMW parked outside the pizza place. Instead, she veers to the right, to the battered Volvo that probably has 300,000 miles on it. So much for asking for my retainer in cash. I slide into the passenger seat and stick out my hand. "I'm Oliver Bond."

She doesn't shake it. Instead, she slips the key into the ignition and peels out of the parking spot with a recklessness that makes my jaw drop. "Emma Hunt," she says.

She takes a corner, and the back wheels spin. "You, um, should probably tell me a little more about what's going on . . ." I gasp as she runs a red light.

"Do you watch the news, Mr. Bond?"

"Oliver, please." I tighten my seat belt. The police station is only a mile or two away, but I'd like to be alive when we reach it.

"Have you followed the story about the UVM student who went missing?"

"The one whose body was just found?"

The car screeches to a stop in front of the police station. "I think my son might be responsible," she says.

Alan Dershowitz, the famous Jewish lawyer, was once asked if he'd defend Adolf Hitler. "Yes," he said. "And I'd win."

When I fell asleep during my torts class, the professor—who spoke in a monotone and made law slightly less exciting than watching paint dry—poured a bottle of water over my head. "Mr. Bond," he intoned, "you strike me as the kind of student on whom admission should not have been wasted."

I sat up, sputtering and soaked. "Then with all due respect, sir, you should be struck harder," I suggested, and I got a standing ovation from my classmates.

I offer these anecdotes to the proverbial jury as examples of the fact that I have never lived my life by shirking a challenge, and I'm not about to start right now.

"Let's go." Emma Hunt turns off the ignition.

I put my hand on her arm. "Maybe you should start by telling me your son's name."

"Jacob."

"How old is he?"

"Eighteen," she says. "He has Asperger's syndrome."

I've heard the term, but I'm not about to pretend I'm an expert. "So he's autistic?"

"Technically, yes, but not in a *Rain Man* kind of way. He's very high-functioning." She looks longingly at the police station. "Can't we discuss this later?"

"Not if you want me to represent Jacob. How did he get here?"

"I drove him." She takes a long, shaky breath. "When I was watching the news today, and they were reporting from the crime scene, I saw a quilt that belongs to Jacob."

"Is it possible that other people have it, too? Like, anyone who happened to shop at Kohl's last season?"

"No. It's handmade. It was upstairs in his

closet, or so I thought. And then I heard the reporter say that they'd arrested Jess's boyfriend for the murder."

"Was Jacob her boyfriend?"

"No. That's someone named Mark. I don't know him, but I couldn't stand the thought of him going to jail for something he didn't do. I called the detective in charge of the case, and he said if I brought Jacob down here, he'd talk to him and take care of everything." She buries her face in her hands. "I didn't realize that meant he'd ambush Jacob. Or tell me I couldn't sit in on the interview."

"If he's eighteen, that's true," I point out. "Did Jacob agree to talk to him?"

"He practically raced into the police station, once he was told he could help analyze a crime scene."

"Why?"

"It would be like you getting a high-profile celebrity murder case after years of practicing property law."

Oh. Well, *that* I could understand. "Did the police tell you Jacob was under arrest?"

"No."

"So you just brought him down here voluntarily?"

She crumples in front of me. "I thought they

were going to talk to him. I didn't know he would be considered a suspect right away." Emma Hunt is crying now, and I know less about what to do with a crying woman than I would with a greased piglet on a New York City subway. "I was just trying to do the right thing," she sobs.

When I was a farrier, I worked with a mare that had a fracture in the pedal bone. Weeks of rest hadn't helped her; the owners were talking about putting her down. I convinced them to let me hot-fit a straight bar shoe to the hoof, and I wrapped it instead of nailing it. At first, the mare didn't want to walk, and who could blame her? It took a week of coaxing to get her to take a step from her stall, and then I worked with her for thirty minutes a day, until a year later, I led her out to a field and watched her fly across the open space, fast as a rumor.

Sometimes, you need someone else to help you take the first step.

I put my hand on her shoulder; she jumps at the contact and stares up at me with those crazy molten eyes of hers. "Let's see what we can do," I say, and I hope like hell she cannot tell that my knees are shaking.

At the dispatch desk, I clear my throat. "I'm looking for an officer . . ."

"Which one?" the bored sergeant asks.

My face floods with heat. "The one who's doing the interview with Jacob Hunt," I say. Why hadn't I thought to ask her the guy's name?

"You mean Detective Matson?"

"Yes. I'd like you to interrupt that interview he's doing."

The sergeant shrugs. "I'm not interrupting anything. You can wait. I'll let him know you're here when he's done."

Emma isn't listening. She's edged away from me, toward a door that leads down the hallway of the police department. It's on a locked mechanism controlled by dispatch. "He's down there," she murmurs.

"Well, I think right now the best course of action is to play by their rules until—"

Suddenly the door buzzes and opens. A secretary wanders into the waiting area carrying a FedEx box for pickup.

"Now," Emma says. She grabs my wrist and pulls me through the windfall of that open doorway, and in tandem, we start to run.

Jacob

I am here as living proof to tell you that dreams really do come true.

1. I am sitting with Detective Matson, shooting the shit.

2. He's sharing details of an open investigation with me.

3. Not once has he yawned or checked his watch or in any way indicated that he is not enjoying speaking to me at length about crime scene investigation.

4. He wants to talk to me about the crime

scene surrounding Jess's disappearance—a crime scene that I orchestrated.

Seriously, it doesn't get much better than this.

Or so I think until he begins firing questions at me that feel like bullets. And his mouth is smiling halfway, and I cannot remember if that means he's happy or not. And the conversation moves from the practical—the weight of the human brain, the nature of postmortem toxicity tests—to the personal.

The fascination of creating a liver slide to look at microscopically loses some of its entertainment value when Detective Matson forces me to remember that the liver in question belonged to someone I actually knew, someone I laughed with and looked forward to seeing, which is far from how I feel about most social interactions. As theoretical as I would like death to be, it turns out there is a significant difference when it's corn syrup and food coloring instead of the real McCoy. Although I can logically understand that Jess is gone, which therefore means there's no point wishing she weren't since she's not able to reverse the situation, it doesn't account for the fact that I feel like a helium balloon is caught inside me, and that it keeps inflating, and that it might actually tear me apart.

Just when I think things cannot get any worse, Detective Matson accuses me of being the one to hurt Jess.

You're the one who grabbed Jess by the arms, aren't you?

I wasn't. And I tell him so.

What about choking her? You're not going to lie to me about doing that, are you?

I know the answer, of course, but it's bogged down in the syntax. It's like when someone asks you at dinner, *You don't want that last piece of steak, do you?* when of course you *do.* If you say *yes,* are you saying that you want the last piece of steak? Or that you *don't* want it?

So what made you choke her?

Was it a fight? Did she say something you didn't like?

If Jess were here, she'd tell me to take a deep breath. *Tell the person you need him to speak more slowly,* she'd say. *Tell him you don't understand.*

Except Jess isn't here.

"Nothing made me choke Jess," I finally manage to say, which is the absolute truth.

But my face is red, and my breath feels like sawdust spilling out of me.

Once, when we were little and Theo called me a mental midget, 1 threw a couch pillow at him and, instead, it knocked over a lamp my mother had gotten from her grandmother. *How did this happen?* my mother asked, when she retained the power of speech again.

A pillow knocked it off the table.

It was unequivocally the truth, but my mother's hand came down and swatted me. 1 don't remember it hurting. 1 remember being so embarrassed that 1 thought my skin might melt off. And even though she apologized later, there was always a disconnect for me: telling the truth was supposed to set you free, wasn't it? So how come it got me in trouble when 1 told a new mother that her baby looked like a monkey? Or when 1 read another kid's paper in class during a peer edit and said it was abysmal? Or when 1 told my mother that 1 felt like an alien who'd been sent down to analyze families, since 1 never really seemed to be a part of ours?

Or now?

Did you choke her until she stopped breathing? Did you hit her in the face?

I think of Lucy and Ethel at that candy factory. Of one time when I went into the ocean and could not get out of the oncoming waves before the previous one drove me to my knees. On *CrimeBusters,* at the end, the CSIs interrogate the suspects and the suspects always crack in the face of cold, hard evidence.

None of this is happening the way I planned it to.

Or maybe it's just that my plan is working a little too well.

I never meant to hurt Jess, and that's why the next question spears me like a javelin. "Then how did her tooth get knocked out?" Detective Matson asks.

I watch it unfolding in front of me, an instant invisible replay. Lugging Jess down the stairs, dropping her on the final riser. *I'm sorry!* I had cried, even though that was not necessary; she could not hear me anymore.

Whatever words I am using, though, are falling short, since Detective Matson doesn't understand me. So I decide to take a drastic step, to show him the inside of my mind right here and right now. I take a deep breath, and then I stare directly into his eyes.

It's like having strips of my skin pulled off

from the inside. Like needles in every nerve center of the brain.

God, it hurts.

"That was an accident," I whisper. "But I saved it. I put it in her pocket."

Another truth, but one that makes him jump in his seat. I'm sure he can hear my pulse as loudly as I can. That's a sign of arrhythmia. I hope I do not die right here in Detective Matson's office.

My eyes slide to his left, his right, and then up—anywhere so that I don't have to see him directly again. That's when I notice the clock, and realize that it's 4:17.

Without any traffic it takes sixteen minutes to get from the police station to my house. That means we will not get home till 4:33, and *CrimeBusters* begins at 4:30. I stand up, both of my hands fluttering in front of my chest like hummingbirds, but I don't even care anymore about trying to stop them. It feels like the moment on the TV show when the perp finally caves in and falls to the metal table, sobbing with guilt. I want to be watching that TV show, instead of living it. "Are we done now?" I ask. "Because I really have to go."

Detective Matson gets up, and I think he

might open the door for me, but instead he blocks my exit and leans closer, until he is too close for me to breathe, because what if I wind up with some of the air that he exhaled? "Did you know you fractured her skull?" he says. "Did that happen at the same time you knocked out her tooth?"

I close my eyes. "I don't know."

"What about her underwear? You put it on backward, didn't you?"

At that, my head whips up. "It was on *backward*?" How was I supposed to know? There were no labels, like there are in my boxer shorts. Shouldn't the graphic of the butterfly have gone on the front, rather than back?

"Did you take her underwear *off* her, too?"

"No, you just said it was *on* her . . ."

"Did you try to have sex with her, Jacob?" the detective asks.

I am utterly silent. Just thinking about that makes my tongue swell up like a monkey's fist knot.

"Answer me, goddammit!" he yells.

I scramble for words, any words, because I do not want him to yell at me again. I will tell him that I had sex with Jess eighty times that night if that's what he needs to hear, if that makes him open the door.

"You moved her after she died, Jacob, didn't you?"

"Yes! Of course I moved her!" Isn't that obvious?

"Why?"

"I needed to set up the crime scene, and that's where she had to be." He, of all people, should understand.

Detective Matson tilts his head. "Is that why you did this? You wanted to commit a crime and see if you could get away with it?"

"No, that's not why—"

"Then what is?" he interrupts.

I try to find a way to put into words all the reasons I have done what I did. But if there is one subject I do not understand—not internally, much less externally—it's the ties that bind us to each other. *"Love means never having to say you're sorry,"* I mutter.

"Is this a joke to you? Some big joke? Because I don't see it that way. A girl's dead, and there's nothing funny about that." He comes closer, until his arm is brushing mine, and I can barely concentrate because of the buzzing in my head. "Tell me, Jacob," he says. "Tell me why you killed Jess."

Suddenly the door slams open, striking him in the shoulder. "Don't answer that," a strange man yells. Behind him stands my mother, and behind her are two uniformed officers, who have just raced down the hall, too.

"Who the hell are you?" Detective Matson asks.

"I'm Jacob's attorney."

"Oh, really," he says. "Jacob, is this your lawyer?"

I glance at the man. He's wearing khaki pants and a dress shirt but no tie. He has sandy hair that reminds me of Theo's and looks too young to be a real lawyer. "No," I reply.

The detective smiles triumphantly. "He's eighteen years old, Counselor. He says you're not his lawyer, and he hasn't asked for one."

I am not stupid. I've watched enough *Crime-Busters* to know where this is headed. "I want a lawyer," I announce.

Detective Matson throws up his hands.

"We're leaving now." My mother elbows her way closer. I reach for my coat, which is still draped over the back of the chair.

"Mr. . . . what's your name?" the detective asks.

"Bond," my new lawyer says. "Oliver Bond." He grins at me.

"Mr. Bond, your client is being charged with the murder of Jessica Ogilvy," Detective Matson says. "He's not going anywhere."

CASE 5: THE NOT-SO-GOOD DOCTOR

Kay Sybers was fifty-two years old and, by anyone's standards, unhealthy. She'd been a smoker years ago; she was overweight. But she didn't show signs of medical problems until one evening in 1991, when (after a dinner of prime rib and Chardonnay) she had trouble breathing and developed shooting pain down her left arm. Those are classic signs of a heart attack—something her husband, Bill, should have recognized. After all, he was a Florida physician who doubled as the county coroner. Instead of calling an ambulance or whisking her to the ER, though, he attempted to draw blood from her arm. He wanted to run a few tests that day at work, he said. Yet hours later, Kay was dead. Concluding that she had died from a coronary, Bill Sybers decided against an autopsy.

A day later, based on an anonymous tip of suspicious activity, Kay Sybers was scheduled for autopsy. The toxicology reports came back inconclusive, and Kay was buried. However, suspicions arose again when rumors circulated that Bill Sybers was sleeping with a lab technician at his workplace. Kay's body was exhumed, and forensic toxicologist Kevin Ballard screened for succinylcholine, a drug that increases the release of potassium and paralyzes the muscles, including the diaphragm. In the tissues, he discovered succinylmonocholine, a by-product of succinylcholine and proof of the poison's presence in Kay's body.

Ironically, although Bill Sybers seemed in a hurry to bury his wife and hide the evidence, the embalming process helped preserve the succinylmonocholine and made it easier to detect.

5

Rich

The minute after I arrest Jacob Hunt, all hell breaks loose. His mother cries out and starts shouting at the same moment that I put my hand on Jacob's shoulder to lead him back to the room where we do our fingerprints and mug shots—but from his reaction, you would have thought I'd just run him through with a sword. He takes a swing at me, which sets off his lawyer, who—being a lawyer—is no doubt already wondering how to keep his client from being charged for assault on an officer as well. "Jacob!" his mother shrieks, and then she grabs my arm. "Don't touch him. He doesn't like to be touched."

I gingerly test my jaw where he's decked me. "Yeah, well, I don't like to be punched," I mutter, and I twist Jacob's arms behind his back and handcuff him. "I need to type up some paperwork for your son. Then we'll drive him down to the courthouse for his arraignment."

"He can't handle all this," Emma argues. "At least let me stay with him, so that he knows it's going to be all right—"

"You can't," I say flatly.

"You wouldn't interrogate someone deaf without an interpreter!"

"With all due respect, ma'am, your son isn't deaf." I meet her gaze. "If you don't leave, I'm going to arrest you as well."

"Emma," the lawyer murmurs, taking her arm.

"Let go of me," she says, shaking him off. She takes a step toward her flailing son, but one of the other officers stops her.

"Get them out of here," I order as I start to drag Jacob down the hall to the processing room.

It's like trying to wrestle a bull into the backseat of a car. "Look," I say, "you just have to relax." But he is still struggling against my hold when I finally shove him into the small space. There's a fingerprinting machine in there, plus the camera we use for mug shots, expensive equipment that in my mind's eye I'm seeing shattered by Jacob's tantrum. "Stand here," I say, pointing to a white line on the floor. "Look at the camera."

Jacob lifts up his face and closes his eyes.

"Open them," I say.

He does—and rolls them toward the ceiling. After a minute, I take the damn picture anyway, and then his profile shots.

It's when he's turned to his right that he notices the fingerprint machine and goes very still. "Is that a LiveScan?" Jacob murmurs, the first coherent words he's said since I placed him under arrest.

"Yup." I stand at the keypad and suddenly realize that there is a much easier way to go about processing Jacob. "You want to see how it works?"

It's like a switch has been flipped; the crazed tornado has morphed into a curious kid. He takes a step closer. "They're digital files, right?"

"Yeah." I type Jacob's name onto the keypad. "What's your middle initial?"

"B."

"Date of birth?"

"December twenty-first, 1991," he says.

"You wouldn't happen to know your social security—"

He rattles off a string of numbers, looking over my shoulder at the next entry. "Weight: 185 pounds," Jacob says, growing more animated. "Occupation: Student. Place of Birth: Burlington, Vermont."

I reach for a bottle of Corn Huskers lotion that we use to make sure the ridges are slightly damp and all friction skin is captured and realize Jacob's hands are still cuffed behind him. "I'd like to show you how this machine operates," I say slowly, "but I can't do it if you're in handcuffs."

"Right. I understand," Jacob says, but he's staring at the screen on the LiveScan machine, and I think if I'd told him that he'd have to give up one of his limbs in return for seeing the scan in action, he would have eagerly agreed. I unlock the cuffs and wipe his fingertips down with the lotion before taking his right hand in mine.

"First we do the thumb flats," I say, pressing Jacob's down one at a time. "Then we do flats of the fingers." It's a simultaneous impression, the four fingers of each hand pressed on the glass surface at once. "Once the computer's got these loaded, the other images are matched up against them. You roll side to side, thumbs inward, fingers outward," I say, illustrating with the first of his fingers and following through with the rest.

When the machine rejects one of the rolled fingers, Jacob's eyebrows shoot up. "That is remarkable," he says. "It won't enter a shoddy print?"

"Nope. It lets me know when I've lifted the finger too soon or if the print is too dark, so I can redo the scan." When I finish with his fingers, I press his palm flat on the surface—it's the type of print we find most often on windows, if a criminal's been peeking inside—and then I scan a writer's palm print, the curved edge of the hand along the pinkie finger down to the wrist. By the time I switch to

Jacob's left hand, he's practically doing it himself. "It's that easy," I say, as the images line up on the screen.

"So you'll send out searches to AFIS right from here?" Jacob asks.

"That's the plan." Having a digital Live-Scan that connects to the Automated Fingerprint Identification System is a godsend; I am old enough to remember when it was far more complicated than it is now. The prints are sent to the state central depository, which documents the arrest and sends it along to the FBI. After I lock Jacob up, I will come back to see if there are any other crimes in his past for which he has a record.

I'm guessing there will not be any other hits, but that doesn't mean this is the first time Jacob's acted out. It only means it's the first time he's been caught.

The printer spits out a card that I'll put in his arrest folder, along with his mug shots. At the top, all of Jacob's biographical information is listed. Below are ten small squares, each with a rolled print. Under those are the ten fingertip digits, lined up like an army of soldiers.

In that instant, I happen to notice Jacob's

face. His eyes are shining; his mouth is bent into a smile. He's been arrested for murder, yet he's on cloud nine, because he's gotten to see a LiveScan system up close and personal.

I hit a button, and a second card is printed. "Here." I hand it to him.

He starts to bounce on the balls of his feet. "You mean . . . I can keep it?"

"Why the hell not," I say. While he's entranced by the printout, I grasp his elbow to lead him to the lockup. This time, he doesn't go ballistic when I touch him. He doesn't even notice.

Once, I was called in to a suicide. The guy had OD'd on sleeping pills when he was supposed to be babysitting for his sister's twins. The kids were ten-year-old boys, holy terrors. When they couldn't wake up their uncle, they decided to horse around with him. They covered his face with whipped cream and put a cherry on his nose, which is the first thing I saw when I took a look at the body stretched out on the living room couch.

Those kids never realized the guy was dead.

Eventually, of course, they would have been told. And even though my work was done at that point, I thought about the twins a lot. You just know that after they found out, they were never quite the same. I was probably one of the last people to see those boys when they were still just two kids, when death was the farthest thing from their minds.

That's what haunts me at night. Not the dead bodies I find, but the live ones I leave in my wake.

When I lock Jacob inside our holding cell, he doesn't react—and that scares me more than his earlier outburst. "I'm coming back for you," I say. "I just have to finish doing a little paperwork, and then we'll go to the courthouse. Okay?"

He doesn't answer. In his right hand, he clutches the fingerprint card. His left hand is flapping against his thigh.

"Why don't you sit down?" I say.

Instead of taking a seat on the bunk, Jacob immediately sinks down onto the concrete floor.

We have a video camera pointed into the cell, so that someone is always watching over a perp. I should be going through the paperwork, which takes forever, but instead, I swing into dispatch to stare at the monitor. For ten whole minutes, Jacob Hunt doesn't move, unless you count the way his hand is fluttering. Then, very slowly, he scoots backward until he is leaning against the wall, pressed against the corner of the cell. His mouth is moving.

"What the hell is he saying?" I ask the dispatcher.

"Beats me."

I walk out of dispatch and crack the door that leads to the holding cell. Jacob's voice is faint:

All around in my hometown,
They're trying to track me down.
They say they want to bring me in guilty
For the killing of a deputy.

I swing open the door and walk up to the cell. Jacob is still singing, his voice rising and falling. My footsteps echo on the concrete, but he doesn't stop, not even when I am standing on the other side of the bars, directly in front of him, with my arms crossed.

He sings through the chorus two more times before he stops. He doesn't look at me, but I can tell from the way his shoulders square that he knows I'm here.

With a sigh, I realize that I'm not going to leave this kid alone again. And I'm not going to get my paperwork done unless I can convince him it's another lesson in police procedure. "So," I say, unlocking the cell door, "have you ever filled out an intake form?"

Oliver

As soon as I hear the detective say that he'll arrest Emma Hunt if she doesn't shut up, I snap out of the panic I am in, a panic induced by the sentence he spoke just slightly before that: *Then we'll drive him down to the courthouse for his arraignment.*

What the hell do I know about arraignments?

I have won a couple of civil suits. But a criminal arraignment is a whole different animal.

We are in Emma's car, driving to the courthouse, but that was a struggle. She didn't want to leave the police station without Jacob; the only way I managed to convince her to leave was by pointing her in the direction of where her son would be heading. "I ought to be with him," she says, running a red light. "I'm his mother, for God's sake." As if that triggers something else in her mind, she grimaces. "Theo. Oh my God, Theo . . . He doesn't even know we're here . . ."

I don't know who Theo is, and to be honest, I don't have time to care. I am busy wondering where I am supposed to stand in the court-room.

What do I say?

Do I speak first, or does the prosecutor?

"This is a total misunderstanding," Emma insists. "Jacob's never hurt anyone. This couldn't be his fault."

Actually, I don't even know which court-room to go to.

"Are you even *listening*?" Emma asks, and I realize at that moment she must have asked me a question.

"Yes," I say, figuring I have a 50 percent chance of being right.

She narrows her eyes. "Left or right," she repeats.

We are sitting at a stop sign. "Left," I murmur.

"What happens at the arraignment?" she asks. "Jacob won't have to talk, will he?"

"No. The lawyer does. I mean, *I* do. The whole point of an arraignment is just to read the charges and set bail." This much I remember from law school, anyway.

But it's not the right thing to say to Emma. *"Bail?"* she repeats. "They're going to lock Jacob up?"

"I don't know," I say, totally honest. "Let's cross that bridge when we come to it."

Emma parks in the courthouse lot. "When will he get here?"

I don't know the answer to that. What I *do* know is that it's nearly the end of the business day, and if Detective Matson doesn't get his ass in gear, Jacob's going to be spending the night at the county jail—but there's no way I'm going to tell Emma *that.*

It's quiet inside the courthouse; most of the cases are through for the day. However, mine is just beginning, and I need a crash course in criminal law before my client figures out I'm a total fraud. "Why don't you wait here?" I suggest, pointing to a chair in the lobby.

"Where are you going?"

"To do, um, some paperwork that needs to be filed before Jacob arrives," I say, trying to look as confident as possible, and then I make a beeline for the office of the clerk.

It's just like nurses in a hospital tend to know more than the doctors most of the time; if you really want to get the answer to a question about court, you should spend more time buttering up the clerks than the judges. "Hello," I say to the small, dark-haired woman peering into a computer screen. "I'm here for a criminal arraignment."

She flicks a glance upward. "How nice for you," she says flatly.

My gaze falls on a nameplate on her desk. "I wonder, Dorothy, if you could tell me in which courtroom that might take place?"

"The criminal courtroom would be a safe bet . . ."

"Right." I smile, as if I knew this all along. "And the judge . . . ?"

"If it's Monday, it's Judge Cuttings," she says.

"Thanks. Thanks very much," I reply. "Really nice to meet you."

"The highlight of my day," Dorothy intones.

I am about to walk out the door when I turn back at the last moment. "One more thing . . ."

"Yes?"

"Am I, um, supposed to say anything?"

She looks up from her computer. "The judge

will ask you whether your client pleads guilty or not guilty," Dorothy answers.

"Great," I say. "I really appreciate that."

In the lobby, I find Emma hanging up her cell phone. "So?" she asks.

I sink into the empty seat beside her. "Piece of cake," I tell her, and I hope I can convince myself.

Emma and I sit through three drug possession charges, one B and E, and an indecent exposure charge before Jacob is brought into the courtroom. From my vantage point in the gallery, I can tell the moment Emma notices he's here: she sits up a little straighter, and her breath catches in her throat.

If you have spent any time in a courtroom, you'll know that high school football players—the mean ones with no necks—grow up and become bailiffs. Two of these behemoths are manhandling Jacob, who's doing his damnedest to get the hell away from them. He keeps craning his neck, looking at the people in the courtroom, and as soon as he spots Emma, his entire body sags with relief.

I stand up, heading down from the gallery, because it's showtime, and realize too late that

Emma's following me. "You have to stay here," I whisper over my shoulder as I take my place at the defendant's table beside my client.

"Hi," I say to Jacob under my breath. "My name's Oliver. Your mom hired me to be your lawyer, and I've got it all under control. Don't say anything to the judge. Just let me do the talking."

The whole time I'm speaking, Jacob is looking at his lap. The minute I finish, he twists in his seat. "Mom," he calls out, "what's going on?"

"Counselor," the bigger bailiff says, "either shut your client up or he's going back in the holding cell."

"I just told you not to talk to anybody," I tell Jacob.

"You told me not to say anything to the judge."

"You can't talk to *anybody,*" I clarify. "Do you understand?"

Jacob glances down at the table.

"Jacob? *Hello?*"

"You told me not to talk to anybody," he mutters. "Will you make up your mind already?"

Judge Cuttings is a hard-boiled New Englander who, in his time off, runs a llama farm and who, in my opinion, looks a little like a llama himself. He has just announced Jacob's name when Dorothy the clerk enters through a side door and passes him a note. Looking down his long nose at it, he sighs. "I have two arraignments for Mr. Robichaud that need to be done in another courtroom. Since he's currently here with his clients, I'll do those first, and then we'll take the prisoner's case."

The minute he says the word *prisoner,* Jacob jumps to his feet. "I need a sensory break," he announces.

"Shut *up,*" I murmur.

"I need a sensory break!"

Dozens of thoughts are running through my mind: *How do I get the kid to stop talking? How do I get the judge to forget everything that's unfolding before his eyes? How would a seasoned lawyer handle a situation like this, when a client becomes a loose cannon? How long before I am seasoned enough to stop second-guessing myself?*

The minute Jacob takes a step, the two bailiffs are on top of him. He starts screaming, a high, keening sound. "Let go of him!" Emma shrieks behind me. "He doesn't understand! He's allowed to get up in school when things are overwhelming—"

"This isn't school," the judge thunders. "This

is my courtroom, and you, madam, will be leaving it."

The second bailiff releases Jacob and steps into the gallery to pull Emma outside. "I can explain," she cries, but her voice gets fainter as she's forced down the aisle.

I look from her to my client, who has gone boneless and is being dragged out a different door. *"Take your stinking paws off me, you damned dirty ape!"* Jacob yells.

The judge narrows his eyes at me.

"It's from *Planet of the Apes*," I mutter.

"I'm mad as hell, and I'm not going to take this anymore," he replies. "That's from *Network.* I highly recommend you watch the movie after you get your client under control."

I duck my head and hurry down the aisle. Emma stands outside the courtroom door, flushed and angry, her eyes shooting daggers at the bailiff. "Your kid can wait till the courtroom's empty," he says to me. "That's when we'll arraign him. And the mother can't come back inside until then."

He enters the courtroom again; the door opens with a gasp. That leaves me standing alone in the hallway with Emma, who grabs my hand and pulls me toward the staircase. "What . . . what are you doing?"

"He's down there, isn't he? Come on."

"Hold it." I dig in my heels and fold my arms. "What was that all about?"

"I hate to say I told you so, but I told you so. That's Asperger's. Sometimes Jacob seems totally normal—brilliant, even—and sometimes the tiniest thing can set him off into a full-fledged fit."

"Well, he can't behave like that in a courtroom. I thought he knew all about crime scenes and cops and the law. He has to be respectful and quiet or this will be disastrous."

"He's trying," Emma insists. "That's why he asked for a sensory break."

"A what?"

"A place he can go to away from all the noise and confusion, so that he can calm himself down. At school, that's one of the special accommodations he gets . . . Look, can we talk about this later and just go see him?"

Jacob was getting his sensory break . . . in a holding cell. "You aren't allowed down there."

She flinches, as if I've struck her. "Well," Emma says, "are *you*?"

To be honest, I am not sure. I poke my head inside the courtroom. The bailiff stands just inside the door, arms folded. "Can I go talk to my client?" I whisper.

"Yeah," he says. "Go ahead."

I wait for him to take me to Jacob, but he doesn't budge. "Thanks," I say, and I duck out the door again and head past Emma, down the stairs.

I hope that's where the holding cells are.

After five minutes of detours through the custodial closet and the boiler room, I find what I'm looking for. Jacob is sitting in the corner of this cell, one hand flapping like a bird, his shoulders hunched, his voice thready and singing Bob Marley.

"How come you sing that song?" I ask, coming to stand in front of the bars.

He pauses in the middle of the chorus. "It makes me feel better."

I consider this. "You know any Dylan?" When he doesn't answer, I step forward. "Look, Jacob. I know you don't know what's going on. And to be honest, neither do I. I've never done this before. But we're going to figure it out together. All you have to do is promise me one thing: Let me do the talking." I wait for Jacob to nod, to acknowledge me, but it doesn't happen. "Do you trust me?"

"No," he says. "I don't." Then he gets to his feet. "Will you give a message to my mom?"

"Sure."

He curls his hands around the bars. His fingers are long, elegant. *"Life is like a box of chocolates,"* he whispers. *"You never know what you're gonna get."*

I laugh, thinking the boy can't be all that bad off if he's able to joke around. But then I realize that he's not kidding. "I'll tell her," I say.

When I return, Emma is pacing. "Is he okay?" she asks, the minute I turn the corner. "Was he responsive?"

"Yes and yes," I assure her. "Maybe Jacob's stronger than you think he is."

"You're basing this insight on the five minutes you've spent with him?" She rolls her eyes. "He has to eat by six. If he doesn't—"

"I'll get him a snack from the vending machines."

"It can't have caseins or glutens—"

I have no freaking idea what that means. "Emma, you have to relax."

She rounds on me. "My older son, who's autistic, has just been arrested for murder. He's stuck in a jail cell somewhere in the basement, for God's sake. Don't you *dare* tell me to relax."

"Well, it won't do Jacob any good if you lose it in the courtroom again." When she doesn't respond, I sit down on a bench across the hall. "He wanted me to tell you something."

The hope on her face is so naked that I have to look away.

"Life is like a box of chocolates," I quote.

With a sigh, Emma sinks down beside me. "*Forrest Gump.* That's one of his favorites."

"Movie buff?"

"An intense one. It's almost like he's studying for a test he'll have to take later." She glances at me. "When he feels something overwhelming, he doesn't always have the words for it, so he quotes someone else's."

I think about Jacob spouting Charlton Heston when the bailiff grabbed him and smile broadly.

"He sets up crime scenes for me," Emma says softly. "So that I can look at the forensic evidence and work backward. But I should have been working forward. We never really talked about what happens after. What happens *now.*"

"I know you're upset, but we have a lot of time to figure it out. Today's arraignment is just a rubber stamp."

She stares at me. When I was in college, the girls that I always found myself drooling over were the ones who had dabs of toothpaste on their chins, or who stuck pencils through their messy hair to keep it away from their faces. The ones who slayed me were so far removed from caring how they looked that they circled back to a natural, artless beauty. Emma Hunt might be a decade older than me, but she's still a knockout. "How old are you?" she asks after a moment.

"I don't really think that chronological age is a decent measure of—"

"Twenty-four," she guesses.

"Twenty-eight."

She closes her eyes and shakes her head. "I was twenty-eight a thousand years ago."

"Then you look great for your age," I say.

Blinking, she focuses fiercely on me. "Promise," she demands. "Promise me that you're going to get my son out of here."

I nod at her, and for a moment I want to be a white knight; I want to be able to tell her I know law as well as I know how to shoe a skittish mare, and I don't want it to be a lie. Just then the bailiff peers around the corner. "We're ready," he says.

I only wish I could say the same.

The courtroom is different when it's empty. Dust motes hang in the air, and my footsteps sound like gunshots on the parquet flooring.

Emma and I walk to the front of the gallery, where I leave her sitting just behind the bar as I cross through to sit at the defense table.

It's déjà vu.

Jacob is led out by the bailiffs. He's hand-cuffed, and I hear Emma suck in her breath behind me when she notices. But then again, he left the courtroom violent; there's no reason to assume he wouldn't pull the same trick twice. When he sits down beside me, the handcuffs jingle in his lap. He presses his lips together in a flat line, as if he's trying to show me he remembers my instructions.

"All rise," the bailiff says, and when I stand up, I grab Jacob's sleeve so he will, too.

Judge Cuttings enters and sits down heavily in his chair, his robes billowing around him like a storm. "I trust you've talked to your client about his behavior in the courtroom, Counselor?"

"Yes, Your Honor," I answer. "I'm sorry about the outburst. Jacob's autistic."

The judge frowns. "Are you concerned about competency?"

"Yes," I reply.

"All right. Mr. Bond, your client is here to be arraigned on a charge of first-degree murder pursuant to 13 VSA, section 2301. Do you waive the reading of the rights on his behalf at this time?"

"Yes, Your Honor."

He nods. "I'm going to enter a not guilty plea on his behalf, because of the competency issue."

For a moment, I hesitate. If the judge enters the plea, does that mean I don't have to?

"Are there any other issues with the charge as it stands today, Counselor?"

"I don't think so, Your Honor . . ."

"Excellent. This is bound over for a competency hearing fourteen days from today at nine A.M. I'll see you then, Mr. Bond."

The larger bailiff approaches the defense table and hauls Jacob to his feet. He lets loose a squeak, and then, remembering the rules of the courtroom, squelches it. "Hang on a minute," I interrupt. "Judge, didn't you just say we could go?"

"I said *you* could go, Counselor. Your client, on the other hand, is charged with murder and being held pending his competency hearing at your own request."

As he leaves the bench to return to chambers, as Jacob is pulled out of the courtroom again—silent, this time—headed to a two-week stay in jail, I gather the courage to turn around and confess to Emma Hunt that I've just done everything I told her I wouldn't.

Theo

My mother doesn't cry very often. The first time, like I said, was at the library when I had a tantrum instead of Jacob. The second time was when I was ten years old and Jacob was thirteen and he had homework for his life skills class—an extracurricular he hated because he was one of only two autistic kids, and the other boy didn't have AS but was lower on the spectrum and spent most of the class lining up crayons end to end. The other three kids in the class had Down syndrome or developmental disabilities. Because of this, a lot of time was spent on things like hygiene—stuff Jacob already knew how to do—with a little bit of social skills tossed in. And one day, his teacher assigned the class to make a friend before the next time they all met.

"You don't *make* a friend," Jacob said with a scowl. "It's not like they come with directions like you'd find on a box of macaroni and cheese."

"All you have to do is remember the steps that Mrs. LaFoye gave you," my mother said. "Look someone in the eye, tell them your name, ask them if they'd like to play."

Even at ten, I knew that this protocol would surely lead to getting your ass kicked, but I wasn't going to tell Jacob that.

So the three of us trekked to the local playground, and I sat down next to my mother on a bench while Jacob set out to make a friend. The problem was, there was no one his age there. The oldest kid I could see was about my age, and he was hanging upside down from the monkey bars. Jacob walked up to him and twisted sideways so that he could look the kid in the eye. "My name is Jacob," he said in his voice, which I'm used to but which is weird to everyone else—flat as a sheet of aluminum, even in places where there should be exclamation points. "Do you want to play?"

The kid did a neat flip onto the ground. "Are you, like, some kind of retard?"

Jacob considered this. "No."

"News flash," the boy said. "You are."

The kid ran off, leaving Jacob standing alone under the monkey bars. I almost got up to rescue him, but then he started to turn in a slow circle. I couldn't figure out what he was doing, and then I realized he liked the sound his sneaker made when it crunched a dry leaf underneath the sole.

He walked on his tiptoes, very precisely crushing the leaves, until he reached the sandbox. A pair of tiny kids—one blond and one with red pigtails—were busy making pizzas out of sand. "Here's another one," the first girl said, and she slapped a glob of sand onto the wooden railing so that the other girl could decorate it with pepperoni rocks and mozzarella grass.

"Hi, I'm Jacob," my brother said.

"I'm Annika, and I'm going to be a unicorn when I grow up," the blonde said.

Pigtails didn't look up from the pizza assembly line. "My little brother threw up in the bathroom and slipped in it and landed on his butt."

"Do you want to play?" Jacob asked. "We could dig for dinosaurs."

"There aren't any dinosaurs in the sandbox, just pizza," Annika said. "Maggie's the one who gets to put on the cheese and stuff, but you can be the waiter."

Jacob looked like a giant in the sandbox beside those two girls. A woman was staring daggers at him, and I would have bet fifty bucks it was either Annika's or Maggie's mom, wondering if the thirteen-year-old playing with her precious little daughter was a perv. Jacob picked up a stick and began to outline a skeleton in the sand. "The allosaurus had a wishbone, like other meat-eating dinosaurs," he said. "Just like you'd find on a chicken."

"Here's another one," Annika said, and she dumped a pile of sand in front of Maggie. You could practically draw a line between the little girls and Jacob. They weren't playing together as much as they were playing next to each other.

Jacob looked up at that moment and grinned at me. He tipped his head toward the girls as if to say, *Hey, check it out, I made two friends.*

I glanced at my mother, and that's when I saw her crying. Tears were rolling down her cheeks and she wasn't doing anything to try to wipe them away. It was almost as if she didn't know it was happening.

There were plenty of other times in my life that it would have made more sense for my mother to cry: when she had to go to the school to talk to the principal about something Jacob had done to get himself into trouble, for example. Or when he had one of his tantrums in the middle of a crowded space—like last year, in front of the Santa Claus pavilion at the mall while a bazillion kids and parents watched the nuclear meltdown ensue. But then, my mother had been dry-eyed, her face wiped clean of expression. In fact, during those moments, my mother looked a little like Jacob did.

I don't know why seeing my brother with two little girls in a sandbox was a straw that broke the so-called camel's back, for her. I just know that, at that moment, I remember feeling like the world had turned itself inside out. It's the child who's supposed to cry, and the mom who makes it all better, not the other way around, which is why mothers will move heaven and earth to hold it together in front of their own kids.

Even then I knew that if Jacob was the one who made her cry, I was the one who had to stop it.

Of course I know where they are; my mother has called me from the courthouse. But that doesn't keep me from being unable to concentrate on Civitas or Geo until they come home.

I wonder if my teachers will accept that as an excuse: *Sorry I didn't get my homework done: my brother was being arraigned.*

Sure, my geometry teacher will say. *Like I haven't heard* that *one a thousand times.*

The minute I hear the door open, I run into the mudroom to find out what happened. My mother walks in, alone, and sits down on the bench where we usually dump our school backpacks.

"Where's Jacob?" I ask, and very slowly she looks up at me.

"In jail," she whispers. "Oh, my God, he's in jail." She bends at the waist until she is doubled over.

"Mom?" I touch her shoulder, but she doesn't move. It scares me to death, and it's eerily familiar.

It takes me a second to place it— the way she's staring off into space, the way she won't respond: this is how Jacob looked last week, when we couldn't get him to come back to us.

"Come on, Mom." I slip an arm around her waist and lift her. She feels like a bag of bones. I guide her upstairs, wondering why the hell Jacob is in jail. Aren't you supposed to be guaranteed the right to a speedy trial? Could it have been *that* speedy? If only I'd done my Civitas homework, maybe I'd understand what had happened, but this much I know: I am not about to ask my mother.

I sit her down on the bed and then I kneel and take off her shoes. "Just lie down," I suggest, which seems like something she'd say if the tables were turned. "I'll get you a cup of tea, okay?"

In the kitchen I set the kettle to boil and have a tsunami of déjà vu: the last time I did this—boil a kettle, take out a tea bag, and hook its paper tag over the edge of a mug—I was in Jess Ogilvy's house. It's really just a matter of luck that Jacob's the one sitting in jail right now, and I'm here. It could easily have been the other way around.

Part of me is relieved about that, which makes me feel like total crap.

I wonder what the detective said to Jacob. Why my mother brought him down there in the first place. Maybe that's why she's so messed up now: not grief but guilt. That much, I understand. If I'd gone to the cops and told them I had seen Jess alive and naked earlier that day, would it have made matters worse for Jacob, or better?

I don't really know how my mother takes her tea, so I put in milk and sugar and carry it upstairs. She is sitting up now, the pillows piled behind her. When she sees me, she tears up. "My boy," she says, as I sit down beside her. She cups her hand around my cheek. "My beautiful boy."

She might be talking about me, and she might be talking about Jacob. I decide it doesn't really matter.

"Mom," I ask. "What's going on?"

"Jacob has to stay in jail . . . for two weeks. Then they'll take him to court again to see if he's competent to stand trial."

Okay, I may not be a rocket scientist, but sticking someone who may not be able to handle a trial in jail doesn't seem like the best way to see if they're able to handle a trial. I mean, if you can't handle a trial, how the hell could you handle jail?

"But . . . he hasn't done anything wrong," I say, and I look carefully at my mother, to see if she knows more than I do.

If she does, she's not showing it. "That doesn't seem to matter."

Today in Civitas we talked about the cornerstone of our country's legal system: that you're innocent until proven guilty. Locking someone up in jail while you try to figure out what to do next doesn't seem like you're giving him the benefit of the doubt. It sounds like you're already assuming he's screwed, so he might as well get comfortable in his future living quarters.

My mother tells me how Jacob got suckered into talking to the detective. How she ran to find him a lawyer. How Jacob was arrested in front of her. How he decked the bailiffs when they tried to grab his arms.

I don't understand why this lawyer wasn't able to get Jacob released and back home. I read enough Grisham novels to know that happens all the time, especially for people who don't have a previous record.

"So what happens now?" I ask.

I don't just mean for Jacob, either. I mean for us. All those years I wished Jacob didn't exist, and now that he's not in the house, it's like there's an elephant in the room. How am I supposed to make a can of soup for dinner, knowing that my brother is in a cell somewhere? How am I supposed to get up in the morning, go to school, pretend that this is life as usual?

"Oliver—that's the lawyer—says that people get unarrested all the time. The police get some new evidence, and they let the original suspect go."

She is holding on to this like it's a lucky charm, a rabbit's foot, an amulet. Jacob will be unarrested, and we can all go back to the way we were. Never mind that the way we were wasn't that terrific, or that *unarrested* doesn't mean the slate is wiped entirely clear so you forget what happened. Imagine spending twenty years in prison for a crime you never committed before you're acquitted thanks to DNA evidence. Sure, you're free now, but you don't get back those twenty years. You don't ever stop being "that guy who used to be in prison."

Because I don't know how to say this to her—and I'm *sure* she wouldn't want to hear it, anyway—I reach for the remote control on her nightstand and turn on the TV that's sitting on the dresser across the room. The news is on, the weatherman predicting a storm sometime next week. "Thanks, Norm," the anchorwoman says. "Breaking news in the case of the murder of Jessica Ogilvy . . . Police have arrested eighteen-year-old Jacob Hunt of Townsend, Vermont, in connection with the crime."

Beside me, my mother freezes. Jacob's school photo fills the screen. In it, he is wearing a striped blue shirt and, as usual, not staring at the camera. "Jacob is a senior at Townsend Regional High School and was tutored by the victim."

Holy shit.

"We'll have more on this story as it develops," the anchor promises.

My mother lifts the remote control. I figure she is going to turn off the television, but instead, she hurls it at the screen. The remote breaks apart, and the TV screen cracks. She rolls onto her side.

"I'll get the broom," I say.

In the middle of the night, I hear noises in the kitchen. I creep downstairs to find my mother, rummaging through a drawer to find the phone book. Her hair is loose, her feet are bare, and there's a toothpaste stain on her shirt. "Why isn't it listed under 'Government,'" she mutters.

"What are you doing?"

"I have to call the jail," she says. "He doesn't like it when it's dark. I could bring him a night-light. I want them to know that I can bring him a night-light, if that helps."

"Mom," I say.

She picks up the telephone.

"Mom . . . you need to go to bed."

"No," she corrects. "I need to call the jail—"

"It's three in the morning. They're asleep." I look at her. "Jacob's asleep."

She turns her face to mine. "Do you really think so?"

"Yeah," I say, but the word has to squeeze itself out around the knot in my throat. "Yeah, I do."

Here are the things I am afraid of:

That the subject Jacob loves the most has stopped being an interest and has started to become an obsession.

That this is why he's in jail in the first place.

That when he was last with Jess, something made him feel scared, or cornered, which is what makes him snap.

That you can love someone and hate him at the same time.

That age has nothing to do with who is the older brother.

If you think having a brother who's got Asperger's makes me a pariah, imagine having one who's in jail. The next day I am in school—yes, more on that later—and everywhere I go, I hear the whispers.

I heard he cut off her finger with a knife and kept it.

I heard he hit her with a baseball bat.

I always thought he was creepy.

The reason I'm taking up space in my classes today—and believe me, that's all I'm doing, since my brain is too busy blocking the gossip I over-hear—is that my mother thought it was the best plan. "I have to go to the jail," she said, which I had figured would happen. "You can't stay home for two weeks. You have to go back sometime."

I knew she was right, but didn't she also realize that people were going to ask about Jacob? Make assumptions? And not just the kids. Teachers would come up to me full of fake sympathy when what they really wanted was some dirt they could take back to the teachers' lounge. The whole thing made me feel sick to my stomach.

"What am I supposed to say if some-one asks?"

My mother hesitated. "Tell them your brother's attorney said you can't talk about it."

"Is that true?"

"I have no idea."

I took a deep breath. I was going to come clean, to tell her about break-ing into Jess's house. "Mom, I have to talk to you about something . . ."

"Can I take a rain check?" she said. "I want to be there when the doors open at nine. There's plenty of cereal for breakfast, and you can take the bus."

Now, I'm sitting in biology next to Elise Howath, who is a pretty good lab partner even if she's a girl, when she slips a note to me.

I'm really sorry to hear about your brother.

I want to thank her, for being nice. For being the first person to give a shit about Jacob instead of crucifying him like the media and the stupid court already have for what he's done.

What he's done.

I grab my backpack and run out of class, even though Mr. Jennison is still yammering away, and he doesn't even comment (which tells me, more than anything, that this is not my life but a parallel universe). I keep walking down the hall without a hall pass, and no one stops me. Not when I cruise past the principal's office and the guidance department. Not when I bust through the double doors near the gym into the blinding light of afternoon and start walking.

Apparently in the public schools, if you have a relative arrested for murder, the administration and teachers pretend you are invisible.

Which, to be honest, isn't really all that different from the way I was treated before.

I wish I had my skateboard with me. Then I could move faster, maybe outdistance the facts that keep circling in my head:

I saw Jess Ogilvy alive and well. Shortly after that, Jacob went to her house.

Now she's dead.

I've seen my brother put a chair through a wall and smash a window with his hand. I've been in his way, sometimes, when he has a meltdown. I've got the scars to prove it.

You do the math.

My brother is a murderer. I test the words under my breath and immediately feel a pain in my chest. You can't say it the way you'd say *My brother is six feet tall* or *My brother likes scrambled eggs,* even if they are all accurate facts. But the Jacob I knew a week ago is no different than the Jacob I saw this morning. So does that mean I was too stupid to notice some major flaw in my brother? Or that anyone—even Jacob—might suddenly turn into a person you never imagined?

I sure as hell qualify.

All my life I've thought I have nothing in common with my brother—and it turns out we are both criminals.

But you didn't kill anyone.

The voice echoes in my head, an excuse. For all I know, Jacob's got his reasons, too.

That makes me run faster. But I could be a goddamned bullet and still not manage to outstrip the sad fact that I'm no better than those assholes at school: I have already assumed my brother is guilty.

Behind the school, if you go far enough, you hit a pond. It's a community hot spot in the winter—on weekends someone lights a bonfire and brings marshmallows to roast; and a few enterprising hockey dads sweep the ice with wide shovels so that pickup games can break out all across its surface. I step onto the ice, even though I don't have skates with me.

It's not crowded on a weekday. A few moms with toddlers, pushing milk crates as they learn to skate. An old man in those black figure skates that always make me think of Holland, or the Olympics. He's doing figure eights. I dump my backpack on the edge of the snow and shuffle my feet little by little, until I am standing dead center.

Every year there's a competition in Townsend to see when the ice will fully melt. They stick a pole in the ice that's attached to some kind of digital clock, and when the ice melts enough for the pole to tilt, it trips a switch and records that moment in time. People put money down on which day and hour the ice will melt, and the person with the closest guess gets the jackpot. Last year, I think it was about $4,500.

What if the moment the ice melted was right now?

What if I went under?

Would those kids skating around hear the splash? Would the old man come to my rescue?

My English teacher says a rhetorical question is one that's asked even though an answer isn't expected: *Is the Pope Catholic?* Or *Does a bear crap in the woods?*

I think it's a question that has an answer you don't really want to hear.

Does this dress make me look fat?

Are you really that stupid?

If the ice melts and no one sees me go under, did I ever really exist?

If I were the one in jail, would Jacob believe the worst of me?

Just like that, I sit down in the middle of the pond, on the ice. It's cold through my jeans. I picture myself freezing from the inside out. They will find me and I'll be a sculpture, a statue.

"Hey, kid, you okay?" The old man has skated over to me. "You need some help?"

Like I said: an answer you don't really want to hear.

I didn't sleep much last night, but when I did, I dreamed. I dreamed that I was breaking Jacob out of jail. I did it by reading through all his *CrimeBusters* notebooks and copying the behavior of cat burglars. As soon as I rounded the corner of the prison where Jacob was being kept in a cell, he was ready. *Jacob*, I said, *you have to do exactly what I tell you to do*, and he did, which is how I knew it was a dream. He was quiet, and he followed my lead, and he didn't ask any questions. We tiptoed past the guard booth, and we both hopped into a giant trash bin, covering ourselves with paper and garbage. The custodian finally came and wheeled us right through the buzzers and the locked gate, and just as he was about to dump the giant trash bin into the Dumpster outside, I yelled, *Now!* and Jacob and I jumped out and started running. We ran for hours, until the only things following us were falling stars, and then we finally stopped in a field of tall grass and laid down on our backs on the ground.

I didn't do it, Jacob told me.

I believe you, I said, and it was really true.

On that day when Jacob was supposed to make a friend for homework, those two little girls he met in the sandbox had to leave. They ran off without saying good-bye, leaving my thirteen-year-old brother alone and digging in the sand.

I was afraid to look at my mother again. So instead, I walked to the sandbox and sat down on the edge. My knees came up to my chin; I was too big for the space—it was crazy to see my brother squeezed into it.

I picked up a rock and started to paw through the sand with it. "What are we looking for?" I asked.

"Allosaurus," Jacob replied.

"How are we going to know when we find it?"

Jacob's face lit up. "Well, its vertebrae and skull won't be as heavy as those of other dinosaurs. That's what the name means, translated: *different lizard.*"

I imagined any kid Jacob's age watching him play paleontologist in a sandbox and wondered if he'd *ever* have a friend.

"Theo," he suddenly whispered, "you know we're not *really* going to find allosaurus in here."

"Um, *yeah.*" I laughed. "But if we did, that would be some story, wouldn't it?"

"The news vans would come," Jacob said.

"Screw the news, we'd be on *Oprah,*" I told him. "Two kids who find a dinosaur skeleton in a sandbox. We might even wind up on the Wheaties box."

"The fabulous Hunt brothers." Jacob grinned. "That's what they'd call us."

"The fabulous Hunt brothers," I repeated, and I watched Jacob dig to the bottom with his shovel. I wondered how long it would be before I outgrew him.

Jacob

I don't really understand what's happening.

At first I thought maybe this was protocol, like the way that my mother was wheeled out of the hospital after she gave birth to Theo, even though she could easily have walked and carried him in her arms. Maybe it was a liability issue, which is why the bailiffs had to get me out of the courtroom (this time they were a little more hesitant to *touch* me). I assumed they would lead me to the front of the building, or maybe to a loading dock where defendants could be picked up and taken home.

Instead, I was stuffed into the back of a

police car and driven two hours and thirty-eight minutes to jail.

I do *not* want to be in jail.

The officers who drop me off are not the same ones who take me into the jail. This new one wears a different colored uniform and asks me the same questions that Detective Matson asked me at the police station. There are fluorescent lights on the ceiling, like they have at Walmart. I don't enjoy going to Walmart for this very reason—the lights spit and hiss sometimes due to their transformers, and I worry that the ceiling will collapse on me. Even now, I cannot speak without glancing up at the ceiling every few moments. "I'd like to call my mother now," I say to the officer.

"Well, I'd like a winning lottery ticket, but something tells me neither of us is going to get what we want."

"I can't stay here," I tell him.

He's still typing on his computer. "I don't remember asking for your opinion."

Is this man particularly thickheaded? Or is he trying to annoy me? "I'm a student," I explain, the same way I might explain mass spectrometry to someone who doesn't have a clue about trace evidence analysis. "I have to be at school by seven forty-seven in the morning, or else I won't have time to get to my locker before class."

"Consider yourself on winter break," the officer says.

"Winter break isn't until February fifteenth."

He punches a button on the keyboard. "All right. Stand up," he says, so I do. "What's in your pockets?"

I glance down at my jacket. "My hands."

"So you're a wiseass," the officer says. "Empty them, come on."

Confused, I hold my palms up in front of me. There's nothing in them.

"Your pockets."

I pull out a stick of gum, a green pebble, a piece of sea glass, a strip of photographs of my mother and me, and my wallet. He takes them all. "Hey—"

"The money will be logged in to your account," he says. I watch him write notes on a piece of paper, and then he opens my wallet and takes out my money and my picture of Dr. Henry Lee. He starts to count the money, and by accident, he drops the pile. When he gathers it back up, it's out of order.

Sweat breaks out on my forehead. "The money," I say.

"I didn't take any, if that's what you're worried about."

I see a twenty rubbing up against a dollar bill, and the five-dollar bill is backward, with President Lincoln facedown.

In my wallet, I make sure that everything is in order from the smallest denomination to the biggest, and everything faces up. I have never taken cash out of my mother's wallet without her permission, but sometimes when she is unaware I sneak into her purse and organize her money for her. I just don't like the thought of all that chaos; the coin pocket is already haphazard enough.

"You okay?" the officer says, and I realize he is staring at me.

"Could you ..." I can barely speak, my throat has gotten so tight. "Could you just put the bills in order?"

"What the hell?"

With my hand curled to my chest, I point a single finger at the stack of bills. "Please," I whisper. "The ones go on top."

If at least the money looks the way it is supposed to, that's something that hasn't changed.

"I don't believe this," the officer mutters, but he does it, and once that twenty is resting safely at the bottom of the pile, I let out the breath I've been holding.

"Thanks," I say, even though I noticed at least two of the bills are still upside down.

Jacob, I tell myself, *you can do this. It doesn't matter if you are in another bed tonight instead of your own. It doesn't matter if they do not let you brush your teeth. In the grand scheme of things, the world will not stop spinning.* (That is a sentence my mother likes to use when I get nervous about a change in routine.)

Meanwhile the officer leads me to another room, one not much bigger than a closet. "Strip," he says, and he folds his arms.

"Strip what?" I answer.

"All of it. Underwear, too." When I realize he wants me to take off my clothes, I am so surprised that my jaw drops.

"I'm not changing in front of you," I say, incredulous. I won't even change for gym class in the locker room. I have a doctor's note from Dr. Moon saying that I do not have to, that I can participate in class while wearing my normal clothes.

"Again," the officer says, "I didn't *ask* you."

On television I've seen inmates wearing jumpsuits, although I never really gave much thought to what happened to their clothes. But what I am remembering now is bad. Very Bad, with capital letters. On television, the jumpsuits are always orange. Sometimes it is enough to make me change the channel.

I can feel my pulse accelerate at the thought of all that orange, touching my skin. Of the other inmates, wearing the same color. We would be like an ocean of hazard warnings, a sea of danger.

"If you don't take off your clothes," the officer says, "I will do it for you."

I turn my back to him and peel off my coat. I pull my shirt over my head. My skin is white, like a fish belly, and I don't have rippling stomach muscles like the Abercrombie & Fitch guys; this embarrasses me. I unzip my jeans and pull down my underwear and then remember my socks. Then I crouch into a ball and carefully organize my clothes so that the olive khaki pants are on the bottom, then the green shirt, finally the green boxers and socks.

The officer takes the clothes and starts shaking them out. "Hands out at your sides," he says, and I close my eyes and do what he says, even when he makes me turn around and bend down and I can feel his fingers moving me apart. A soft cloth sack hits my chest. "Get dressed again."

Inside it is clothing but not my own. Instead, there are three pairs of socks, three pairs of underwear, three T-shirts, thermal pants, a thermal top, three pairs of dark blue pants and matching shirts, rubber flip-flops, a jacket, a hat, gloves, a towel.

This is a huge relief. I won't be wearing orange after all.

I have been to one sleepover in my life. It was at the home of a boy named Marshall, who has since moved to San Francisco. Marshall had a lazy eye and was, like me, often the butt of classmates' jokes in second grade. Our mothers were the ones who organized the sleepover, after mine learned that Marshall could spell the names of most dinosaurs from the Cretaceous period as well. My mother and I talked for two whole weeks about what would happen if I woke up in the middle of the night and wanted to come home (I'd call). What would happen if Marshall's mother served something for break-fast that I didn't like (I would say *No thank you*). We talked about how Marshall might not have his clothes organized in his closet the way I do and how he had a dog and dogs sometimes drop hair on the floor without intending to.

The night of the sleepover my mother dropped me off after dinner. Marshall asked if I wanted to watch *Jurassic Park,* and I said yes. But when I started telling him during the video what was anachronistic and what was downright fictionalized, he got angry and told me to shut up and I went to play with his dog instead.

The dog was a Yorkshire terrier with a pink bow in its hair even though it happened to be male. It had a very small pink tongue, and it licked my hand, which I thought I would like but which I wanted to wash off immediately.

That night when we went to sleep Marshall's mother put a rolled blanket between us to divide up his full-size bed. She kissed him on the forehead and then she kissed me, which was strange because she was not my mother. Marshall told me that in the morning if we got up early we could watch TV before his mother got up and caught us. Then he fell asleep, but I didn't. I was awake when the dog came into the room and burrowed underneath the covers, scratching me with its tiny black toenails. And I was still awake when Marshall wet the bed in his sleep, too.

I got up and called my mother. It was 4:24 A.M.

When she arrived, she knocked on the door, and Marshall's mother answered it in her bathrobe. My mother thanked her on my behalf. "I guess Jacob's an early riser," she said. "*Very* early." She tried to laugh a little, but it sounded like a brick falling.

When we got into the car, she said, "I'm sorry."

Even though I didn't meet her gaze, I could feel her looking at me. "Don't ever do that to me again," I answered.

I have to fill out a form for visitors. I can't imagine who might want to come, so I write down my mother's name and my brother's name and our address, and their birth dates. I add Jess's name, too, although I know she can't visit, obviously, but I bet she would have wanted to.

Then a nurse examines me, taking my temperature and checking my pulse, just like at the doctor's office. When she asks me if I'm on any medication, I tell her yes, but she gets angry when I don't know the names of the supplements, when I can only tell her the colors, or the fact that it comes in a syringe.

Finally, I am taken to the place where I will be staying. The officer walks me down a hallway until we reach a booth. Inside, another officer pushes a button, and the metal door in front of us slides open. I am given another laundry bag, this one with two sheets and two blankets and a pillowcase.

The cells are on the left side of a hallway that has a metal grate instead of a floor. Each cell has two beds, a sink, a toilet, and a television inside it. Each cell also has two men inside. They look like the same people you would see on the street, except of course they have all done something bad.

Well, maybe not. After all, *I'm* here, too.

"You'll stay here for a week while you're evaluated," the officer says. "Based on your behavior, you might be moved to the minimum-security population." He nods at one cell, which, unlike the others, has a smaller window. "That's the shower," the officer says.

How am I supposed to make sure I shower first when there are so many other people around?

How am I going to brush my teeth when I don't have my toothbrush with me?

How will I take my shot in the morning, and my supplements?

As I think about these details, I feel myself starting to lose control.

It's not like a tsunami, although I'm sure that's what it looks like to someone on the outside. It's more like a packet of mail that's wrapped tight several times with a rubber band. When it snaps, the band stays in place—out of habit, or out of muscle memory, I don't know—and then one tiny move of the packet and it begins to unravel. Before you know it, there is nothing holding that packet of letters together.

My hand starts moving a little, my fingers playing a beat on my thigh.

Jess is dead and I am in jail and I missed *CrimeBusters* today and my right eye has a tic now that I can't stop.

We stop walking when we reach the cell at the end of the hallway. "Home sweet home," the officer says. He unlocks the door to the cell and waits for me to move inside.

The minute he locks the door again, I grab the bars. I can hear the lights buzzing overhead.

Butch Cassidy and the Sundance Kid didn't go to jail; instead they jumped off a cliff. *"Kid, the next time I say 'Let's go someplace like Bolivia,'"* I mutter, *"let's* go *someplace like Bolivia."*

My head hurts, and out of the corners of my eyes, I am seeing red. I shut them, but the sounds are still there and my hands feel too big for my body and my skin is getting tighter. I picture it stretching so hard that it splits.

"Don't worry," a voice says. "You'll get used to it."

I spin around and hold my hands clutched in front of my chest, the way I used to walk sometimes when I wasn't concentrating on looking like everyone else. I'd assumed the officer had put me in a special cell for people who have to be in jail but shouldn't really be. I had not realized that I, like everyone else, would have a roommate.

He is wearing all his blue clothes plus his jacket and hat, pulled down to his eyebrows. "What's your name?"

I stare at his face without looking him in the eye. He has a mole on his left cheek, and I have never liked people with moles. *"I am Spartacus."*

"No shit? Then I hope you're in here for killing your parents." He gets up from the bunk and walks behind me. "How about I call you Bitch instead?" My hands grip the bars more tightly. "Let's get some things straight, so that you and me, we get along. I get the bottom bunk. I get to go out to the exercise yard before you do. I pick the TV channel. You don't fuck with me, and I won't fuck with you."

There is a common behavior in dogs that are put together in close quarters. One will snap at the other until the beta dog knows that the alpha dog is to be obeyed.

I am not a dog. Neither is this man. He is shorter than I am. The mole on his cheek is raised, and shaped like a beehive.

If Dr. Moon were here she'd ask, *What's the number?*

Sixteen. On a scale of one to ten, ten being the highest, my anxiety level is a sixteen. Which is the worst number, because it's (a) even, (b) has an even square root, and (c) its even square root has an even square root.

If my mother were here, she'd start singing "I Shot the Sheriff." I stick my fingers in my ears so I cannot hear him and I close my eyes so I cannot see him and I start to repeat the chorus without any breaks between the words, just a ribbon of sound that I can imagine circling me like a force field.

Suddenly he grabs my shoulder. "Hey," he says, and I start to scream.

His hat has fallen off so that I can see he is a redhead, and everyone knows that people with red hair don't really have red hair, they have orange hair. And worse, his hair is long. It falls all around his face and his shoulders, and if he leans any closer it might land on me.

The sounds that I make are high and piercing, louder than the voices of everyone who is telling me to *shut the fuck up,* louder than the officer who tells me he'll write me up if I do not stop. But I can't, because by now, the sound is oozing out of all my pores and even when I press my lips together my body is screaming. I grab the bars of the cell door—*contusions are caused by blood vessels that are broken as the result of the blow*—and smack my head against them—*cerebral contusion associated with subdural hematoma in the front lobe is associated with mortality*—and again—*each red blood cell is one-third hemoglobin*—and then just as I predicted my skin cannot contain what's happening inside me and it splits and the blood runs down my face and into my eyes and mouth.

I hear:

Get this fucking nutcase out of my house.

And

If he's got AIDS I'm gonna sue this state for everything it's got.

My blood tastes like pennies, like copper, like iron—*Blood makes up seven percent of the total body weight—*

"On the count of three," I hear. Two people grab my arms and I am moving, but my feet don't feel like they belong to me and it's too yellow under the lights and there is metal in my mouth and metal on my wrists and then I don't see or hear or taste anything at all.

I think I might be dead.

I make this deduction from the following facts:

1. The room that I am in is monochromatic—floor, walls, ceiling all the color of pale flesh.

2. The room is soft. When I walk, it feels like walking on a tongue. When I lean against the walls, they lean against me, too. I cannot reach the ceiling, but it stands to reason it is

the same. There's one door, without any windows, or a knob.

3. There is no noise except for my breathing.

4. There is no furniture. Just a mat, which is flesh-colored, too, and soft.

5. There is a grate in the middle of the floor, but when I look down inside it, I cannot see anything. Maybe that's the tunnel that leads back to earth.

Then again, there are other factors that lead me to believe that I might not actually be dead after all.

1. If I were dead, why would I be breathing?

2. Shouldn't there be other dead people around?

3. Dead people don't have fierce headaches, do they?

4. Heaven probably does not have a door, knob notwithstanding.

I touch my hand to my scalp and find a bandage shaped like a butterfly. There is blood on my shirt that has dried brown and stiff.

My eyes are swollen, and there are tiny cuts on my hands.

I walk around the grate, giving it a wide berth. Then I lie down on the mat with my arms crossed over my chest.

This is what my grandfather looked like, in his coffin.

This is not how Jess looked.

Maybe she's what is inside that grate. Maybe she is on the other side of that door. Would she be happy to see me? Or angry? Would I look at her and be able to tell the difference?

I wish I could cry, like other humans do.

Emma

Jacob's medicines and supplements fill two full gallon-size Ziploc bags. Some are prescription—antianxiety meds given by Dr. Murano, for example—and others, like the glutathione, I get online for him. I am waiting outside the visitors' entrance of the jail, holding these, when the door is unlocked.

My mother used to tell me how, when she was a little girl, her appendix burst. That was back in the day before parents were allowed to stay with their children during hospitalizations, and so my grandmother would arrive four hours before visiting hours began and would stand at the front of a roped-off queue that my mother could see from her hospital bed. My grandmother would just stand there, smiling and waving, until they let her in.

If Jacob knows I'm waiting for him, if he knows that I will see him every day at nine o'clock—well, that's a routine he can cling to.

I would have expected there to be more people waiting with me for the front door to open, but maybe for the rest of the mothers who have come to jail to visit their sons, this is old hat. Maybe they are used to the routine. There is only one other person waiting with me, a man dressed in a suit and carrying a briefcase. He must be a lawyer. He stamps his feet. "Cold out," he says, smiling tightly.

I smile back. "It is." He must be a defense attorney, coming in here to see his client. "Do you, um, know how this works?"

"Oh, first time?" he says. "It's a piece of cake. You go in, give up your license, and go through the metal detectors. Kind of like checking in for a flight."

"Except you don't go anywhere," I muse.

He glances at me and laughs. "That's for damn sure."

A correctional officer appears on the other

side of the glass door and turns the lock. "Hey, Joe," the lawyer says, and the officer grunts a greeting. "You see the Bruins last night?"

"Yeah. Answer me this. How come the Patriots and the Sox can win championships but the Bs are still skating like crap?"

I follow them to a control booth, where the officer steps inside and the lawyer hands over his driver's license. The lawyer scribbles something on a clipboard and hands his keys to the officer. Then he walks through a metal detector, heading down a hall where I lose sight of him.

"Can I help you, ma'am?" the officer asks.

"Yes. I'm here to visit my son. Jacob Hunt."

"Hunt." He scans a list. "Oh, Hunt. Right. He just came in last night."

"Yes."

"Well, you're not approved yet."

"For what?"

"Visitation. You'll probably be clear by Saturday—that's when visiting hours are, anyway."

"Saturday?" I repeat. "You expect me to wait till *Saturday*?"

"Sorry, ma'am. Until you're cleared, I can't help you."

"My son is autistic. He needs to see me.

When his routine gets changed, he can get incredibly upset. Even violent."

"Guess it's a good thing he's behind bars, then," the officer says.

"But he needs his medication . . ." I lift the two Ziploc bags and set them on the lip of the counter.

"Our medical staff can administer prescription meds," the officer says. "I can get you a form to fill out for that."

"There are dietary supplements, too. And he can't eat glutens, or caseins—"

"Have his doctor contact the warden's office."

Jacob's diet and supplements, however, weren't mandated by a doctor—they were just tips, like a hundred others, that mothers of autistic kids had learned over the years and had passed down to others in the same boat, as *something that might work.* "When Jacob breaks the diet, his behavior gets much worse . . ."

"Maybe we should put all our inmates on it, then," the officer says. "Look, I'm sorry, but if we don't get a doctor's note, we don't pass it along to the inmate."

Was it my fault that the medical community couldn't endorse treatments that autistic parents swore by? That money for autism research was spread so thin that even though many physicians would agree these supplements helped Jacob to focus or to take the edge off his hypersensitivity, they couldn't scientifically tell you why? If I'd waited for doctors and scientists to tell me conclusively how to help my son, he would still be locked in his own little world like he was when he was three, unresponsive and isolated.

Not unlike, I realize, a jail cell.

Tears fill my eyes. "I don't know what to do."

I must look like I'm about to fall apart, because the officer's voice gets softer. "Your son have a lawyer?" he asks.

I nod.

"Might be a good place to start," he suggests.

From Auntie Em's column:

What I Know Now That I Wish I'd Known Before I Had Kids

1. If you stick a piece of bread in a VCR, it will not come out intact.

2. Garbage bags don't work as parachutes.

3. *Childproofing* is a relative term.

4. A tantrum is like a magnet: eyes cannot help but lock onto you and your child when it happens.

5. Legos are not absorbed by the digestive tract.

6. Snow is a food group.

7. Kids know when you are not listening to them.

8. A Brussels sprout covered in cheese is still a Brussels sprout.

9. The best place to cry is in a mother's arms.

10. You'll never be as good a mother as you want to be.

From my car, I call Oliver Bond. "They won't let me in to see Jacob," I say.

In the background I can hear a dog bark. "Okay."

"Okay? I can't see my son, and you think that's okay?"

"I meant *okay,* as in *tell me more.* Not *okay* as in . . . Just tell me what they said."

"I'm not on some approved visitors list," I

shout. "Do you think Jacob has any idea that he needs to tell the jail who can and cannot visit him?"

"Emma," the lawyer says. "Take a deep breath."

"I can't take a deep breath. Jacob does not belong in jail."

"I know. I'm sorry about that—"

"Don't be sorry," I snap. "Be *effective*. Get me in to visit my son."

He is quiet for a moment. "All right," Oliver says finally. "Let me see what I can do."

I can't say it's a surprise to find Theo at home, but I am so mentally drained that I don't have the fortitude to ask him why he is here, instead of at school. "They wouldn't let me in to see Jacob," I say.

"How come?"

Instead of answering, I just shake my head. In the buttery light of late morning, I can see the softest down on Theo's cheek and jaw. It reminds me of the first time I noticed that Jacob was growing hair underneath his armpits, and I was unnerved. It was one thing to be needed so fiercely by a child; it was another thing to have to take care of a grown man.

"Mom?" Theo says, hesitant. "Do you think he did it?"

Without thinking, I slap him hard across the face.

He falls back, reeling, his hand pressed to his cheek. Then he runs out the front door.

"Theo!" I call after him. "Theo!" But he is already halfway down the block.

I should follow him; I should apologize. I should confess that the reason I hit him wasn't what he said but because he gave voice to all the unutterable thoughts I've been thinking.

Do I believe Jacob is capable of murder?

No.

The easy answer, the knee-jerk reaction. This is my son we are talking about. The one who still asks me to tuck him in at night.

But I also remember Jacob knocking over Theo's high chair when I told him he could not have another glass of chocolate soy milk. I remember the time he hugged a hamster to death.

Mothers are supposed to be their children's biggest cheerleaders. Mothers are supposed to believe in their children, no matter what. Mothers will lie to themselves, if necessary, to do this.

I step outside and walk down the driveway, in the direction Theo ran. "Theo," I call. My voice does not sound like my own.

I have clocked 193 miles today on my car, driving to Springfield and then back home and returning again. At five-thirty I am again in the lobby of the jail visitors' entrance, with Oliver Bond standing beside me. He left a message on my cell phone instructing me to meet him here, explaining that he'd arranged a special visit for me while he sorted out long-term visiting plans.

I was so happy to hear this that I didn't even dwell on the phrase *long-term*.

At first, I hardly recognize Oliver. He isn't wearing a suit, like he was yesterday; instead, he's in jeans and a flannel shirt. This makes him seem even younger. I glance down at my own clothes—which look like something I'd wear to a staff meeting at the newspaper. What made me think I had to dress up for jail?

Oliver leads me to the booth. "Name?" the officer asks.

"Emma Hunt," I say.

He looks up. "No, the name of the person you're here to visit."

"Jacob Hunt," Oliver interjects. "We've arranged a special visit through the super-intendent's office."

The officer nods and hands me a clip-board to sign. He asks for my ID.

"Give him your keys," Oliver says. "He'll hold them while you're inside."

I pass them to the officer and then step toward the metal detector. "Aren't you coming?"

Oliver shakes his head. "I'll be waiting out here."

A second officer arrives to lead me down the hall. Instead of turning in to a room where there are tables and chairs set up, though, he leads me around the corner to a small cubicle. At first, I think it is a closet, but then I realize it's a visiting booth. A stool is pushed beneath a window that looks into a mirror image of this room. A handset is stuck to the wall. "I think there's been a mis-take," I say.

"No mistake," the officer tells me. "Non-contact visits only for inmates in protective custody."

He leaves me in the tiny chamber. Had Oliver known I wouldn't be able to see Jacob face-to-face? Had he not told me because he knew it would upset me, or had he not been given this information? And what is protective custody?

The door on the other side of the glass opens, and suddenly Jacob is there. The officer who's brought him points to the telephone on the wall, but Jacob has seen me through the glass. He presses his palms flat against it.

He has blood on his shirt and in his hair. His forehead is covered with a line of purple bruises. His knuckles are scraped raw, and he is stimming like crazy—his hand twitching at his side like a small animal, his entire body bouncing on his toes. "Oh, baby," I murmur. I point to the phone in my hand and then to the spot where he should have a receiver, too.

He doesn't pick it up. He smacks his palms against the Plexiglas that separates us.

"Pick up the phone," I cry, even though he cannot hear me. "Pick it up, Jacob!"

Instead, he closes his eyes. He sways forward and rests his cheek against the window, spreads his arms as wide as they can go.

I realize he is trying to embrace me.

I put the receiver down and step up to the

window. I mimic his position, so that we are mirrors of each other, with a glass wall between us.

Maybe this is what it is always like for Jacob, who tries to connect with people and can't ever quite manage it. Maybe the membrane between someone with Asperger's and the rest of the world is not a shifting invisible seam of electrons but, instead, a see-through partition that allows only the illusion of feeling, instead of the actual thing.

Jacob steps away from the window and sits on the stool. I pick up the phone, hoping he will follow my lead, but he isn't making eye contact. Eventually, he reaches for his receiver, and for a moment, I see some of the joy that used to spread across his face when he discovered something startling and came to share it with me. He turns the receiver over in his hands and then holds it to his ear. "I saw these on *CrimeBusters*. On the episode where the suspect turned out to be a cannibal."

"Hey, baby," I say, and I force myself to smile.

He is rocking as he sits. His free hand, the one not holding the receiver, flutters, as if he is playing an invisible piano.

"Who hurt you?"

He touches his fingers gingerly to his forehead. "Mommy? Can we go home now?"

I know precisely the last time Jacob called me that. It was after his middle school graduation, when he was fourteen. He had received a diploma. *Mommy,* he had said, running up to show me. The other kids had heard him, and they burst out laughing. *Jacob,* they teased, *your mommy's here to take you home.* Too late, he had learned that, when you're fourteen, looking cool in front of your friends trumps unadulterated enthusiasm.

"Soon," I say, but the word comes out like a question.

Jacob doesn't cry. He doesn't scream. He just lets the receiver drop from his hand, and then he puts his head down.

I automatically reach toward him, and my hand smacks into the Plexiglas.

Jacob's head lifts a few inches, and then falls. His forehead strikes the metal plate of the counter. Then he does it again.

"Jacob! Don't!" But of course, he can't hear me. His receiver dangles from its metal umbilicus, where it fell when he let go.

He keeps hitting his head, over and over. I throw open the door to the visitation booth.

The officer who brought me there is standing outside, leaning against the wall. "Help me," I cry, and he glances over my shoulder to see what Jacob is doing, then runs down the hallway to intervene.

Through the window of the visitation booth, I watch him and a second officer grab Jacob by the arms and haul him away from the window. Jacob's mouth is twisted, but I cannot tell if he is screaming or sobbing. His arms are pinned behind his back so that he can be handcuffed, and then one of the officers shoves him in the small of the back to propel him forward.

This is my son, and they are treating him like a criminal.

The officer returns a moment later, to take me back to the jail lobby. "He's going to be fine," I am told. "The nurse gave him a sedative."

When Jacob was younger and more prone to tantrums, a doctor put him on olanzapine, an antipsychotic. It got rid of his tantrums. It also got rid of his personality, period. I would find him sitting on the bedroom floor with one shoe on, the other still on the floor beside him, staring unresponsively at the wall. When he began to have seizures, we took him off the drug and never experimented with any others.

I picture Jacob lying on his back on the floor of a cell, his pupils dilated and unfocused, as he slips in and out of consciousness.

As soon as I reach the lobby, Oliver approaches with a big smile on his face. "How'd it go?" he asks.

I open my mouth and burst into tears.

I fight for Jacob's IEPs, and I wrestle him to the ground when he goes ballistic in a public place. I have carved a life out of doing what needs to be done, because you can rail to the heavens, but in the end, when you're through, you will still be ankle-deep in the same situation. I am the one who's strong, so that Jacob doesn't have to be.

"Emma," Oliver says, and I imagine he is as embarrassed as I am to find me sobbing in front of him. But to my surprise, he folds his arms around me and strokes my hair. Even more surprising . . . for a moment, I let him.

This is what you can't explain to a mother who doesn't have an autistic child: Of course I love my son. Of course I would never want a life without him. But that doesn't mean that I am not exhausted every minute of the day. That I don't worry about his future, and my lack of one. That sometimes, before I can catch myself, I imagine what my life would have been like if Jacob did not have Asperger's. That—like Atlas—I think just for once it would be nice to have someone else bear the weight of my family's world on his shoulders, instead of me.

For five seconds, Oliver Bond becomes that person.

"I'm sorry," I say, pushing away from him. "I got your shirt all wet."

"Yeah, Woolrich flannel is really delicate. I'll add the dry-cleaning bill to the retainer." He approaches the control booth and retrieves my license and keys, then leads me outside. "Now. What happened in there?" Oliver asks.

"Jacob hurt himself. He must have been smacking his head against something—his forehead is completely bruised, and there were bandages, and blood all over his scalp. He started to do it again just now in the visitation booth, and they gave him a tranquilizer. They won't give him his supplements, and I don't know what he's eating, or if he's eating at *all*, and—" I break off, meeting his gaze. "You don't have children, do you?"

He blushes. "Me? Kids? I, um . . . no."

"I watched my son slip away once, Oliver. I fought too hard to bring him back to let him go again. If Jacob *is* competent to stand trial, he won't be after two weeks of this. Please," I beg. "Can't you do anything to get him out?"

Oliver looks at me. In the cold, his breath takes shape between us. "No," he says. "But I think *you* can."

Jacob

1

1

2

3

5

8

13

And so on.

This is the Fibonacci sequence. It can be defined explicitly:

$$a(n) = \left(\frac{5+\sqrt{5}}{10}\right)\left(\frac{1+\sqrt{5}}{2}\right)^n + \left(\frac{5-\sqrt{5}}{10}\right)\left(\frac{1-\sqrt{5}}{2}\right)^n$$

It can be defined recursively, too:

$$a_0 = 1$$
$$a_1 = 1$$
$$a_n = a_{n-2} + a_{n-1}$$

This means that it is an equation based on its previous values.

I am forcing myself to think in numbers, because no one seems to understand what I say when I speak English. It is like a *Twilight Zone* episode where words suddenly have changed their meaning: I say *stop* and it keeps going; I ask to leave and they lock me up tighter. This leads me to two conclusions:

1. I am being *punk'd*. However, I don't think my mother would have let the joke go on for quite this long, which leads me to:

2. No matter what I say, no matter how clearly I say it, no one understands me. Which means I must find a better method of communication.

Numbers are universal, a language that transcends countries and time. This is a test: if someone—just one person—can understand me, then there is hope that he'll understand what happened at Jess's house, too.

You can see Fibonacci numbers in the flowering of an artichoke or the scales of a pinecone. You can use their sequence to explain how rabbits reproduce. As *n* approaches infinity, the ratio of *a*(*n*) to *a*(*n* −1) approaches *phi*, the golden ratio—1.618033989—which was used to build the Parthenon and appears in compositions by Bartók and Debussy.

I am walking, and with every step I let another number in the Fibonacci sequence come into my head. I move in smaller and smaller circles to the middle of the room, and when I get there, I start over.

1
1
2
3
5
8
13
21
34
55
89
144

An officer comes in, carrying a tray. Behind him is a nurse. "Hey, kid," he says, waving his hand in front of me. "Say something."

"One," I reply.

"Huh?"

"One."

"One what?"

"Two," I say.

"It's dinnertime," the officer tells me.

"Three."

"You gonna eat this, or throw it again?"

"Five."

"I think it's pudding tonight," the officer says, pulling the cover off the tray.

"Eight."

He inhales deeply. "Yum."

"Thirteen."

Finally, he gives up. "I told you. It's like he's on a different planet."

"Twenty-one," I say.

The nurse shrugs and lifts up a needle. "Blackjack," she says, and she plunges the syringe into my bottom while the officer holds me still.

After they are gone, I lie on the floor, and with my finger, I write the equation of the Fibonacci sequence in the air. I do this until it gets blurry, until my finger is as heavy as a brick.

The last thing I remember thinking before I disappear is that numbers make sense. You cannot say the same about people.

Oliver

The Vermont public defender's office is not called the public defender's office but rather something that sounds like it was ripped from the pages of a Dickens novel: the Office of the Defender General. However, like in all public defender's offices, the staff is overworked and underpaid. Which is why, after I send Emma Hunt off with her own homework, I head to my apartment-office to complete my own.

Thor greets me by jumping up and nailing me right in the groin. "Thanks, buddy," I wheeze, and I brush him off. He's hungry, though, so I feed him leftover pasta mixed with kibble while

I look up the information I need on the Internet and make a phone call.

Although it's 7:00 P.M.—long past office hours—a woman picks up. "Hi there," I say. "My name's Oliver Bond. I'm a new attorney in Townsend."

"We're closed now—"

"I know . . . but I'm a friend of Janice Roth, and I'm trying to track her down?"

"She doesn't work here anymore."

I know this. In fact, I also know that Janice Roth recently got married to a guy named Howard Wurtz and that they moved to Texas, where he had a job waiting with NASA. Public record searches are the best friend of the defense attorney.

"Oh, shoot—really? That's a bummer. I'm a friend of hers from law school."

"She got married," the woman says.

"Yeah, to Howard, right?"

"Did you know him?"

"No, but I know she was crazy about him," I say. "By any chance, are you a defender general, too?"

"Sadly, yes," she sighs. "You're in private practice? Believe me, you're not missing out."

"Nah, you'll get into heaven long before me."

I laugh. "Look, I have a really quick question. I'm new to practicing criminal law in Vermont, and I'm still learning the ropes."

I'm new to practicing criminal law, period, but I don't tell her that.

"Sure, what's up?"

"My client's a kid—eighteen—and he's autistic. He sort of flipped out in court during the arraignment and now he's locked up until his competency hearing. But he can't adapt to jail. He keeps trying to hurt himself. Is there any way to speed up the wheels of justice here?"

"Vermont's decidedly crappy when it comes to psychiatric care for inmates. They used to use the state hospital as a lockup for competency exams, but it lost its funding, so now Springfield gets most of the cases, since they've got the best medical care," she says. "I once had a client being held pending competency who liked to slick himself head to toe—he did it the first night with a one-pound block of butter at dinner, and with deodorant before a visit with me."

"A contact visit?"

"Yeah, the officers didn't care. I guess they thought the worst he could do was rub me down with something. Anyway, with that guy, I filed a motion to set bail," the attorney says. "That gets you back in front of the judge. Put his shrink or counselor on the stand to back up your story. But waive your client's appearance, because you don't want a repeat performance in the courtroom that will piss off the judge. Your main job is to convince the judge he's not a danger if he's not locked up, and if he's running around like a lunatic in court, that sort of messes up your case."

Motion to set bail, I write down on a pad in front of me. "Thanks," I say. "That's awesome."

"No problem. Hey, you want Janice's email?"

"Absolutely," I lie. She reads it to me, and I pretend to write it down.

When I hang up, I go to the fridge and pull out a bottle of Poland Spring. I pour half into Thor's bowl and then raise the bottle in a toast. "To Janice and Howard," I say.

"Mr. Bond," Judge Cuttings says the next day, "aren't we waiting for our competency evaluation in this case?"

"Your Honor," I reply, "I don't think we can."

The courtroom is empty, with the exception of Emma, Dr. Murano, and the prosecutor—a woman named Helen Sharp, who has very short red hair and pointed canine teeth that make me think of a vampire, or a pit bull. The judge looks at her. "Ms. Sharp? What are your feelings?"

"I don't know anything about this case, Judge," she says. "I literally got notice of this hearing this morning. The defendant is charged with murder, you ordered a competency hearing, it's the State's position that he remain locked up until then."

"With all due respect, Your Honor," I reply, "I think the court should listen to my client's mother and psychiatrist."

The judge waves me on, and with a gesture, I motion Emma to come forward to the witness stand. She has dark shadows beneath her eyes, and her hands are shaking. I watch her move them from the railing to her lap, so that the judge cannot see. "Please state your name and address," I say.

"Emma Hunt . . . 132 Birdseye Lane in Townsend."

"Is Jacob Hunt, the defendant in this case, your son?"

"Yes, he is."

"Can you tell us how old Jacob is?"

Emma clears her throat. "He turned eighteen in December."

"Where does he live?"

"With me, in Townsend."

"Is he in school?" I ask.

"He goes to Townsend Regional High School; he's a senior."

I look directly at her. "Ms. Hunt, does Jacob have any particular medical condition that makes you concerned for his safety while he's in jail?"

"Yes. Jacob's been diagnosed with Asperger's syndrome. It's high-functioning autism."

"How does Asperger's affect Jacob's behavior?"

She pauses for a moment, glancing down. "When he decides to do something, he needs to do it immediately," Emma says. "If he can't, he gets very agitated. He hardly ever shows emotion—either happy or sad—and he can't relate to the conversations of kids his own age. He takes words very, very literally—if you asked him to eat with his mouth closed, for example, he'd tell you that's impossible. He has hypersensitivity issues: bright lights, loud noises, and light touches set him off. He doesn't like being the center of attention. He needs to know exactly when something is going to happen, and if his routine gets disrupted, he becomes extremely anxious and acts in a way that makes him stand out even more: flapping his hands at his sides, or talking to himself, or

repeating movie lines over and over. When
things are really overwhelming, he'll go somewhere to hide—his closet, or under his bed—
and he'll stop speaking."

"Okay," says Judge Cuttings. "So your son is
moody, literal, and wants to do things his way
and on his own timetable. That sounds very
much like a teenager."

Emma shakes her head. "I'm not explaining
this well. It's more than just being literal, or
wanting a routine. An ordinary teenager decides
not to interact . . . for Jacob, it's not a choice."

"What sorts of changes have you seen since
your son's incarceration?" I ask.

Emma's eyes fill with tears. "He's not Jacob,"
she says. "He's hurting himself, on purpose.
He's regressing in his speech. He's started stimming again—flapping his hands, bouncing on
his toes, walking in circles. I've spent fifteen
years trying to make Jacob a part of this world
instead of allowing him to isolate himself . . .
and a single day in that jail reversed everything."
She looks at the judge. "I just want my son to
come back, before it's too late to reach him."

"Thank you," I say. "Nothing further."

Helen Sharp stands up. She is easily six feet
tall. Did I not notice that when she walked in?

"Your son . . . has he ever been incarcerated before?"

"No!" Emma answers.

"Has he ever been arrested before?"

"No."

"Are there other times you've witnessed a backslide in your son's behavior?"

"Yes," Emma says. "When plans change at the last minute. Or when he's upset and can't verbalize that."

"Then isn't it possible that his current behavior has nothing to do with incarceration, and everything to do with him feeling guilty for committing a horrific crime?"

Heat floods Emma's face. "He would never do what you've accused him of doing."

"Maybe, ma'am, but at this point your son's been charged with first-degree murder. You understand that, don't you?"

"Yes," Emma says tightly.

"And your son has been placed in protective custody, so his safety isn't at issue—"

"If his safety wasn't at issue, would he have to be in a padded cell in the first place?" Emma retorts, and I want to run up there and give her a high five.

"Nothing further," the prosecutor says.

I stand up again. "The defense calls Dr. Moon Murano."

Jacob's psychiatrist's name may sound like that of someone who grew up on a commune, but that was her parents. She must have rebelled and joined the Young Republicans, because she's turned up for court in a power suit, killer heels, and a bun so tight it is practically functioning as a face-lift. I walk her through her credentials and then ask her how she knows Jacob.

"I've been working with him for fifteen years," she says. "In conjunction with his Asperger's diagnosis."

"Tell us a little about Asperger's," I say.

"Well, the syndrome was discovered by Dr. Hans Asperger in 1944, but it wasn't known in the English-speaking world until the late 1980s, and it wasn't classified as a psychiatric disorder until 1994. Technically, it's a neurobiological disorder that affects several areas of development. Unlike some other children on the autism spectrum, kids with Asperger's are very bright and verbal and crave social acceptance . . . they just don't know how to get it. Their conversations might be one-sided; they might be focused on a very narrow topic of interest; they might use repetitive language or a monotone voice. They won't be able to read social cues or body language and therefore can't identify the feelings of people around them. Because of this, someone with Asperger's is often considered to be odd or eccentric, which leads to social isolation."

"Well, Doctor, there are a lot of folks in the world who are odd or eccentric and haven't been diagnosed with Asperger's, right?"

"Of course."

"So how *do* you diagnose it?"

"It's theory of mind: the child who chooses privacy versus the child who can't connect but wants to, desperately, and cannot put himself in the shoes of another child to better understand how to facilitate that." She glances at the judge. "Asperger's is a developmental disability, but it's a hidden one. Unlike, for example, a mentally challenged individual, a child with Asperger's might look normal and even sound fairly normal and appear incredibly competent, yet he will have crippling difficulties with communication and social interaction."

"Doctor, how often do you see Jacob?" I ask.

"I used to see him weekly when he was younger, but now we're down to once a month."

"And he's a senior in public school?"

"That's correct."

"So he doesn't have any educational delays due to his Asperger's?"

"No," Dr. Murano says. "As a matter of fact, Jacob's IQ is probably higher than yours, Mr. Bond."

"I don't doubt that," Helen Sharp murmurs.

"Does Jacob have any special accommodations at school?"

"He has an individualized education plan—an IEP—which is mandated by law for children with disabilities. Ms. Hunt and I meet with the principal and Jacob's teachers four times a year to review strategies that will help him function well at school. What's normal to certain high school students would set Jacob off into a tailspin."

"Such as?"

"Commotion in a classroom is going to be very overwhelming for Jacob. Flashing lights. Being touched. Crumpled paper. Something that's unexpected in terms of sensation—like darkness in preparation for a video or film—is hard for Jacob if he doesn't know in advance that it's going to happen," Murano says.

"So his accommodations are meant to keep him from becoming overstimulated?"

"Exactly."

"How's he doing in school this year?"

"He got all A's and one B the first semester," Dr. Murano says.

"Before he was incarcerated," I ask, "when was the last time you saw Jacob?"

"Three weeks ago, for a routine visit."

"How was Jacob doing?"

"Very, very well," the psychiatrist says. "In fact, I commented to Ms. Hunt that Jacob initiated a conversation with me, instead of the other way around."

"And this morning?"

"This morning, when I saw Jacob, I was appalled. I haven't seen him in a state like this since he was three years old. You need to understand, this is something chemical in his brain, mercury poisoning of a sort, caused by vaccinations—"

Oh crap.

"—it's only the diligent biomedical treatment regimen and Emma Hunt's commitment to her son's social interaction that's brought Jacob to the point he was prior to incarceration. You know who *really* ought to be tossed in jail? The drug companies that are getting rich off the vaccinations that triggered a wave of autism in the nineties—"

"Objection!" I yell.

"Mr. Bond," the judge says, "you can't object to your own witness."

I smile, but it's really a grimace. "Dr. Murano, thanks for your political opinion, but I don't think that's necessary right now."

"But it is. I'm seeing the same pattern: a sweet, interactive, social child has suddenly isolated himself, removing himself from stimuli, not interacting with people. We don't know enough about the autistic brain to understand what it is that brings these kids back to us, and why only some of them manage to return. But we do understand that a severely traumatic incident—like incarceration—can lead to a permanent regression."

"Do you have any reason to believe that if Jacob was released to the care of his mother, he'd be a danger to himself or others?"

"Absolutely not," Dr. Murano says. "He follows rules to the letter. In fact, that's an Asperger's trait."

"Thank you, Doctor," I finish.

Helen Sharp taps her pen on the desk in front of her. "Dr. Murano, you just referred to Jacob as a boy, didn't you?"

"Yes, I suppose I did."

"Well, he's actually eighteen years old."

"That's true."

"He's legally an adult," Helen says. "He's responsible for his actions, isn't he?"

"We all know there's a chasm between legal responsibility and emotional capacity."

"Does Jacob have a guardian?" Helen asks.

"No, he has a mother."

"Has his mother applied to be his legal guardian?"

"No," Dr. Murano says.

"Have *you* applied to be his legal guardian?"

"Jacob only turned eighteen a month ago."

The prosecutor stands up. "You said that it's very important to have Jacob adhere to a stable routine?"

"It's critical," the psychiatrist says. "Not knowing what's happening to him right now is likely what led to this breakdown."

"So Jacob needs to be able to predict his schedule, in order to feel secure?"

"That's right."

"Well, what if I were to tell you, Doctor, that in the Southern State Correctional Facility, Jacob will rise at the same time every day, will eat his meals at the same time every day, will shower at the same time every day, will go to the library at the same time every day, and so on. Why isn't that perfectly in line with what Jacob's accustomed to?"

"Because it's *not* what he's accustomed to. It is such a deviation from his ordinary daily routine, such an unplanned break, that I worry it's irrevocably affected him."

Helen smirks. "But Dr. Murano, you do understand that Jacob's been charged with the murder of his social skills counselor?"

"I understand that," she says, "and I find it very difficult to believe."

"Do you know what the evidence is against Jacob at this point?" Helen asks.

"No."

"So you're basing your assumption of his guilt or innocence on what you know of Jacob, and not on the evidence."

Dr. Murano raises a brow. "And you're basing *your* assumption on the evidence, without ever having met Jacob."

Oh, snap, I think, grinning.

"Nothing further," Helen murmurs.

Judge Cuttings watches Dr. Murano step off the witness stand. "Does the prosecution have any witnesses?"

"Your Honor, we would like a continuance, given the short notice we had—"

"If you want to make a motion to review, Ms. Sharp, that's fine, provided we get that far," the judge says. "I'll hear arguments now, counselors."

I stand up. "Judge, we want that competency hearing, and you can review the bail again after it's completed. But at this point, I have a young man who's deteriorating psychologically by the minute. I ask you to put limitations on him, on his mom, on his psychiatrist, even on me. You want him to come in here every day and check in with you? Great, I'll bring him. Jacob Hunt has a constitutional right to bail, but he also has human rights, Your Honor. If he's kept in jail much longer, I think it's going to destroy him. I'm asking—no, I'm *begging*—you to set bail in a reasonable amount and release my client until after the competency hearing."

Helen looks at me and rolls her eyes. "Judge, Jacob Hunt has been charged with the first-degree murder of a young woman he knew and supposedly liked. She was his teacher, they spent leisure time together, and the facts surrounding this crime—without getting into details—include incriminating statements the defendant made to the police and strong foren-sic evidence linking him to the crime scene. We believe this is a very, very strong case for the State. If the defendant is doing this poorly even before his bail hearing, Judge, you can imagine how much incentive he'll have to flee the jurisdiction if you let him out now. The victim's parents are already devastated by the loss of their daughter and they're terrified that this young man, who's been exhibiting violent behavior inside a jail cell and who doesn't know right from wrong, might be released. We ask that no bail be considered until after the competency hearing."

The judge looks into the gallery at Emma. "Ms. Hunt," he says. "Do you have any other children?"

"Yes, Your Honor. I have a fifteen-year-old son."

"I assume he requires attention, not to mention food and carpooling."

"Yes."

"You do understand that if the defendant were released into your custody, you'd have to be responsible for him twenty-four hours a day, and that this could significantly affect your own freedom of movement, as well as your responsibilities to your younger son?"

"I will do anything I have to do in order to get Jacob home," Emma says.

Judge Cuttings takes off his reading glasses. "Mr. Bond, I am going to release your client on certain conditions. First, his mother will have to post the family home as surety on bail. Second,

I'm going to require that the defendant be on home electronic monitoring, that he not attend school, that he stay in the house at all times, and that either his mother or another adult over the age of twenty-five be with him at all times. He is not allowed to leave the state. He'll have to sign a waiver of extradition, and he is required to see Dr. Murano and follow all her directives, including taking medication. Finally, he will comply with the competency evaluation when it is scheduled, and you will get in touch with the prosecutor to determine when and where that might take place. The prosecution does not need to file a motion; I am going to set this case down for review on the day the competency evaluation comes back."

Helen packs herself up. "Enjoy your reprieve," she tells me. "This one's a slam dunk for my side."

"Only because you're a giant," I mutter.

"I beg your pardon?"

"I said you haven't met my client."

She narrows her eyes and stalks out of the courtroom.

Behind me, Emma is locked in an embrace with Moon Murano. She looks up at me. "Thank you so much," she says, her voice breaking like waves over the syllables.

I shrug, as if I do this all the time. In reality, I've sweated through my dress shirt. "Anytime," I reply.

I lead Emma to the clerk's office to fill out paperwork and pick up the sheets that Jacob has to sign. "I'll meet you in the lobby," I say.

Although Jacob was not in court, he had to be here while we deliberated on his behalf. And now, he needs to sign the conditions of his release and the waiver of extradition.

I haven't seen him yet. In all honesty, I'm a little scared to do so. The testimony from his mother, and from Moon Murano, made him out to be a vegetable.

When I approach the holding cell, he's lying on the floor, knees curled to his chest. On his head, he's sporting a bandage. The skin around his eyes is black and blue, and his hair is matted.

Christ, if I'd had him in the courtroom, he would have gotten out of jail in ten seconds flat. "Jacob," I say quietly. "Jacob, it's me, Oliver. Your lawyer."

He doesn't move. His eyes are wide open, but they don't flicker as I come closer. I motion for the deputy to open the door of the cell and squat down beside him. "I have some papers I need you to sign," I tell him.

He whispers something, and I lean in.

"One?" I repeat. "Actually, it's several. But hey, you don't have to go back to jail, buddy. That's the good news."

For now, anyway.

Jacob wheezes. It sounds like *one, two, three, five.*

"You're counting. You're down for the count?" I stare at him. This is like playing charades with someone who has no arms and no legs.

"Ate," Jacob says, loud and clear.

He's hungry. Or was hungry?

"Jacob." My voice is firmer. "Come on already." I start to reach for him but see his whole body tense an inch before my hand makes contact.

So I back off. I sit down on the floor beside him.

"One," I say.

His eyelids blink once.

"Two."

He blinks three times.

That's when I realize that we're having a conversation. We're just not using words.

One, one, two, three. Why five, and not four?

I take my pen out of my pocket and write the numbers on my hand until I see the pattern. It's not *ate,* it's *eight.* "Eleven," I say, staring at Jacob. "Nineteen."

He rolls over. "Sign these," I say, "and I will take you to your mother." I push the papers toward him on the floor. I roll the pen in his direction.

At first Jacob doesn't move.

And then, very slowly, he does.

Jacob

Once Theo asked me if there was an antidote for Asperger's, would I take it?

I told him no.

I am not sure how much of me is wrapped up in the part that's Asperger's. What if I lost some of my intelligence, for example, or my sarcasm? What if I could be afraid of ghosts on Halloween *instead* of the color of the pumpkins? The problem is that I do not remember who I was without Asperger's, so who knows what would remain? I liken it to a peanut butter and jelly sandwich that you peel apart. You can't really get rid of the peanut butter without taking some of the jelly as well, can you?

I can see my mother. It's like the sun when you're underwater, and brave enough to open your eyes. She's unfocused and slightly runny and too bright to see clearly. I am that far below the surface.

I have a sore throat from screaming so loud; I have bruises that reach to the bone. The few times I fell asleep, I woke up crying. All I wanted was someone who understood what I had done, and why. Someone who gave a damn as much as I did.

When they gave me that injection at the jail, I dreamed that my heart had been cut out of my chest. The doctors and the correctional officers passed it around in a game of Hot Potato and then tried to sew it back into place, but it only made me look like the Frankenstein monster. *See,* they all exclaimed, *you can't even tell,* and since that was a lie, I could trust nothing they said anymore.

I would not take the jelly without the peanut butter, but sometimes, I wonder why I could not have been lunch meat, which everyone prefers.

There used to be a theory that autistic brains didn't work right because of the gaps between the neurons, the lack of connectivity. Now there's a new theory that autistic brains work too well, that there is so much going on in my head at once I have to work overtime to filter it out, and sometimes the ordinary world becomes the baby tossed out with the bathwater.

Oliver—who says he is my lawyer—spoke to me in the language of nature. That's all I've ever wanted: to be as organic as the whorl of seeds in a sunflower or the spiral of a shell. When you have to try so hard to be normal, that means you're not.

My mother walks forward. She's crying, but there's a smile on her face. For God's sake, is it any wonder I can't ever understand what you people are feeling?

Usually, when I go where I go, it's a room with no doors and no windows. But in jail, that *was* the world, and so I had to go somewhere else. It was a metal capsule, sunk to the bottom of the sea. If anyone tried to come for me, with a knife or a chisel or a crust of hope, the ocean would sense the change and the metal would implode.

The problem was the same rules applied to me, trying to get out.

My mother is five steps away. Four. Three.

When I was very small, I watched a Christian television program on a Sunday morning geared to kids. It was about a special-needs boy playing hide-and-seek with some other children in a junkyard. The other kids forgot about him, and a day later, the police found him suffocated in an old refrigerator. I did not get a religious message out of that, like the Golden Rule or eternal salvation. I got: *Do not hide in old refrigerators.*

This time, when I went where I went, I thought I'd gone too far. There was no more pain and nothing mattered, sure. But no one would find me, and they'd eventually stop looking.

Now, though, my head is starting to hurt again, and my shoulders ache. I can smell my mother: vanilla and freesia and the shampoo she uses that comes in a green bottle. I can feel the heat of her, like asphalt in the summer, the minute before she wraps her arms around me. "Jacob," she says. My name rises on the roller coaster of a sob. My knees give with relief, with the knowledge that I have not faded away after all.

CASE 6: BITE ME

You probably know who Ted Bundy is—a notorious serial killer who was linked to the murder of thirty-six victims, although many experts believe that number is closer to one hundred. He would approach a woman in a public place, gain trust by feigning injury or impersonating an authority figure, and then abduct her. Once the victim was in his car, he'd hit her in the skull with a crowbar. He strangled all but one of his victims. Many bodies were driven miles away from where they disappeared. While on death row, Bundy admitted that he decapitated over a dozen of his victims and kept their heads for a while. He visited the bodies and applied makeup to the corpses or engaged in sexual acts. He kept souvenirs: photos, women's clothing. To this day, many of his victims remain unknown.

It is widely believed that the expert testimony by Dr. Richard Souviron, a forensic dentist, was what secured Bundy's conviction and eventual execution. Bite marks were found on the buttocks of the victim Lisa Levy. The first was a complete bite mark. The second was rotated so that there were two impressions of the lower teeth. This gave authorities more places to compare dental records against the mark, which increased the odds of a match.

The analysis of the bite marks was possible only because a particularly savvy crime scene investigator who was taking pictures at the scene included a ruler in the photo of the bite mark, in order to show scale. Without this photograph, Bundy might have been acquitted. The bite mark had degraded past identifiable by the time the case was presented in court, so the only useful evidence of its original size and shape was that photograph.

6

Rich

"Care to do the honors?" Basil asks me.

We are crowded into Jessica Ogilvy's bathroom—me and the pair of CSIs who have been combing the house for evidence. Marcy's taped up the windows with black paper and is standing ready with her camera. Basil has mixed the Luminol to spray all over the tub, the floor, the walls. I flip the light switch and plunge us into darkness.

Basil sprays the solution, and suddenly the bathroom lights up like a Christmas tree, the grout between the tiles glowing a bright, fluorescent blue.

"Hot damn," Marcy murmurs. "I love it when we're right."

Luminol glows when it meets the correct catalyst—in this case, the iron in hemoglobin. Jacob Hunt might have been smart enough to clean up the mess he'd left behind after murdering Jess Ogilvy, but there were still traces of blood that would go far toward convincing a jury of his guilt.

"Nice work," I say, as Marcy takes a furious run of photographs. Assuming the blood matches the victim's, this latest piece of the puzzle helps me map out the crime. "Jacob Hunt comes for his appointment with the victim," I muse, thinking aloud. "They argue, maybe knocking over the CD rack and the mail and a few stools, and he corners her—right here, apparently—beating her up and eventually striking a blow that kills her." As the Luminol loses its glow, I flip on the lights. "He cleans up the bathroom, and then he cleans up the victim, dressing her and dragging her to the culvert."

I glance down at the floor. In full light, you can't see the chemical, and you can't see the blood at all. "But Jacob's a CSI buff," I say.

Basil grins. "I read this article in *Esquire* about how women find us sexier than firemen—"

"Not all women," Marcy qualifies.

"And so," I continue, ignoring them, "he comes back to the scene of the crime and decides to cover his tracks. The thing is, he's smart—he wants to pin this on Mark Maguire. So he thinks to himself, *If Mark did this, how would he try to cover it up?* As a kidnapping. So he puts on Mark Maguire's boots and stomps around outside, and then cuts the screens in the windows. He cleans up the CDs and the mail and the overturned stools. But he also knows Mark would be sharp enough to want to throw investigators off the trail a little, so he types up the note for the mailman and packs a bag full of the victim's clothes and takes it with him—both hints that Jess left of her own accord."

"You're losing me," Marcy says.

"Jacob Hunt doctored his crime scene to look like it had been committed by some-one else—someone who would doctor a crime scene to hide his involvement. It's fucking brilliant." I sigh.

"So what are you thinking?" Basil asks. "Lovers' quarrel?"

I shake my head. "I don't know." Yet.

Marcy shrugs. "Too bad perps never seem inclined to talk."

"Good thing victims do," I say.

Wayne Nussbaum is up to his elbows in the chest cavity of a dead man from Swanton when I snap on a mask and booties and enter the room. "I can't hang around anymore," I say. For the past forty-five minutes I've been cooling my heels in Wayne's office.

"Neither can he," Wayne replies, and I notice the ligature marks around the guy's neck. "Look, it's not like I could have predicted a murder-suicide would throw me off schedule." He lifts a gleaming red organ in his palm, his eyes dancing. "Come on, Detective. Have a heart."

I don't crack a smile. "That the kind of stuff you learn at clown college?"

"Yeah. It comes after Pie Throwing 101." He turns to his diener, a young woman who assists him during autopsies. Her name is

Lila, and she once tried to hit on me by inviting me to a rave in South Burlington. Instead of flattering me, it just made me feel really old.

"Lila," he says, "give me ten minutes."

He strips off his gloves and jacket and booties as soon as we're out of the sterile atmosphere and walks beside me down the hall to his office. He shuffles files on his desk until I see one with Jess Ogilvy's name on the tab. "I don't know what else I can tell you that my report didn't already spell out, crystal clear," Wayne says, sitting down. "The cause of death was a subdural hematoma, due to a basilar skull fracture. He popped her so hard he drove her skull into her brain and killed her."

I knew that. But it wasn't really why Jess Ogilvy had died. *That* was because she'd said something to Jacob Hunt that had set him off. Or maybe she had refused to say something to him—such as *I feel the same way about you.*

It would be simple enough to assume that a boy who fell for his tutor—and was rebuffed—might lash out at her.

Wayne skims through his report. "The lacerations on her back—drag marks—were made postmortem. I'd assume they occurred when the body was moved. There were bruises, however, that were made premortem. The facial ones, of course. And a few on her upper arms and throat."

"No semen?"

Wayne shook his head. "Nada."

"Could he have worn a condom?"

"Highly unlikely," the medical examiner says. "We didn't get any pubic hairs or any other physical evidence concurrent with rape."

"But her underwear was on backward."

"Yeah, but that only proves that your perp hasn't shopped for lingerie—not that he's a rapist."

"Those bruises," I say. "Can you tell how old they are?"

"Within a day or so," Wayne replies. "There's not really a reliable technique to determine the age of a bruise beyond color and immunohistochemical methods. Bottom line is, people heal at different rates, so although I could look at two bruises and say one occurred a week before the other, I can't look at two bruises and say one occurred at nine A.M. and the other occurred at noon."

"So conceivably, the choke marks around her throat—and the fingerprint bruises on her arms—those could have happened minutes before she died?"

"Or hours." Wayne tosses the folder to a pile on the side of his desk. "He could have threatened her and then come back to beat her to death."

"Or it could have been two different people at two different times." My gaze meets his.

"Then Jessica Ogilvy truly did have the shittiest day on record," the coroner says. "I suppose you could charge the boyfriend with assault. It seems like an unnecessary complication, though, if your perp already confessed to moving the body."

"Yeah. I know." I just didn't understand why that bothered me so much. "Can I ask you something?"

"Sure."

"Why did you stop being a clown?"

"It wasn't fun anymore. Kids screaming

in my face, barfing their birthday cake in my lap . . ." Wayne shrugs. "My clients here are much more predictable."

"I guess."

The coroner looks at me for a long moment. "You know the hardest case I ever did? Motor vehicle accident. Woman rolls her SUV on the highway, and her baby pops right out of the car seat and suffers severe spinal injuries and dies. They brought the whole car seat into the morgue. I had to put that dead baby back into the seat and show how the mother didn't buckle it the right way, which is why the kid fell out." Wayne stands up. "Sometimes you have to keep reminding yourself that you're in this for the victim."

I nod. And wonder why that label makes me think not of Jess Ogilvy but of Jacob Hunt.

The boy who answers the door at the Hunt household looks nothing like his brother, but the minute I show my badge, the color drains from his face. "I'm Detective Matson," I say. "Is your mother home?"

"I, uh . . . I plead the Fifth," the kid says.

"That's great," I tell him. "But it wasn't a particularly probing question."

"Who's at the door?" I hear, and then Emma Hunt steps into my line of sight. The minute she recognizes me, her eyes narrow. "Did you come to check up on me? Well, I'm here, with the boys, just like the judge ordered. Close the door, Theo. And *you*," she says, "can talk to our lawyer."

I manage to wedge my foot in the door just before it closes. "I have a search warrant." I hold up the piece of paper that will allow me to comb through Jacob's bedroom and take away what might constitute evidence.

She takes the paper out of my hand, scans it, and then lets the door swing open again. Without speaking, she turns on her heel. I follow her into the house, pausing when she picks up the phone in the kitchen and calls her baby-faced lawyer. "Yes, he's here now," she says, cupping her hand around the receiver. "He gave the paper to me."

She hangs up a moment later. "Apparently I don't have a choice."

"I could have told you that," I say cheerfully, but she turns away and walks upstairs.

I keep a few steps behind until she opens a door. "Jacob? Baby?" I stand in the hallway and let her talk softly to her son. I hear words like *required* and *legal,* and then she reappears with Jacob at her side.

It takes me by surprise. The kid's whole face is black and blue; a butterfly bandage disappears into his hairline. "Jacob," I say. "How are you doing?"

"How does it *look* like he's doing?" Emma snaps.

I'd been told by Helen Sharp that Jacob was released into his mother's custody pending the competency hearing. She had said that, apparently, Jacob couldn't handle jail well. We had laughed about it. Who *can* handle jail well?

My job, as a detective, is to go behind the scenes and see what strings are controlling the puppets. Sometimes that means collecting evidence, or swearing out arrest warrants, or getting background information, or conducting interrogations. But it usually also means I miss what is going on onstage. It was one thing to arrest Jacob and send him off to his arraignment; it is another thing entirely to see this boy in front of me again in this condition.

He doesn't look like the kid I interviewed a week ago. No wonder his mother wants my head.

She takes Jacob's hand to lead him down the hallway, but we are all stopped by the thin, reedy sound of the boy's voice. "Wait," Jacob whispers.

Emma turns, her face lighting up. "Jacob? Did you say something?"

I get the sense that, if he *has* been saying anything, it's not a lot. He nods, his mouth working for a moment before another syllable is forced out. "I want . . ."

"What do you want, baby? I'll get it for you."

"I want to watch."

Emma faces me, her eyebrows raised in a question.

"Not possible," I tell her flatly. "He can stay in the house, but he can't be anywhere near the room."

"Can I speak to you for a moment?" she asks evenly, and she walks into Jacob's bedroom, leaving him in the hallway. "Do you have any idea what kind of hell it is to watch your child become completely un-responsive?"

"No, but—"

"Well, this is the *second* time for me. I haven't even been able to get him out of his bed," she says. "And as I recall, the last thing you said to me was that I should trust you. I did, and you stabbed me in the back and arrested my son, after I of-fered him up to you on a silver platter. From where I'm standing, my son wouldn't be hanging on by a thread if it weren't for you. So if watching you load up your god-damn boxes with his possessions is what brings him back to the world of the living, then I would hope for the sake of common decency you'd simply let him."

By the time she finishes, her eyes are glittering and her cheeks are flushed. I open my mouth, about to talk about search and seizure cases and the Supreme Court, but then change my mind. "Jacob?" I stick my head out the door. "Come on in."

He sits down on the bed, and Emma leans against the doorjamb with her arms crossed. "I'm, uh, just going to take a look around," I say.

Jacob Hunt is a wicked neat freak. One

weekend with Sasha and I'm forever finding tiny socks wedged into the couch or cereal underfoot in the kitchen or books left strewn across the living room floor. But something tells me this isn't the case with Jacob. His bed is made with military precision. His closet is so organized it looks like an advertisement. I'd assume he has a full-blown case of OCD, except for the fact that there are exceptions to the rule: his math notebook, lying open, is a disaster—loose-leaf pages haphazardly stuffed, papers falling out, handwriting so messy it looks like modern art. The same goes for a bulletin board on one wall, which is overstuffed with papers and pictures and photographs overlapping each other. Dirty dishes and mugs litter his desk.

Directly across from the desk is a small table with an overturned fish tank that has been kitted out like a fuming chamber. Jacob sees me looking at it. "What do you get prints off?" I ask.

"Don't answer that, Jacob," Emma interjects.

"Toothbrushes," he replies. "Mugs. I once got a great partial off a manila folder with magnetic powder."

His mother and I both stare at him—
Emma because he's probably said more
in the last second than in the past three
days; and I because there are CSIs who
don't even know that technique for getting prints off a porous surface.

I pick up the trash bin beside the desk
and begin to leaf through it. There are several drafts of an English essay. There's a
gum wrapper. What's extraordinary about
the contents is not *what* they are but
how they are: instead of being balled up
or crumpled, each piece of garbage has
been folded into crisp eighths. Even the
tiny gum wrapper. The trash is stacked,
like laundry.

The first item I take is Jacob's police
scanner—now I know how he managed
to get to the crime scene for the hypothermic guy. Jacob's hand begins to flap a
little harder. "That . . . that's mine."

Emma puts her hand on his shoulder.
"Remember what I said?"

I quickly procure the items that are
in the fuming chamber: a mug, a mirror,
the tank itself. I look under Jacob's bed,
but there is only a pair of slippers and two

plastic bins—one filled with back issues of the *Journal of Forensic Sciences*, the other filled with Legos. From his bookshelf I take the complete DVD series of *CrimeBusters*, and then I see the composition notebooks. He told me he has more than a hundred, and he wasn't lying. I pull the first one down.

"You can't have those," Jacob cries.

"I'm sorry, Jacob." *Episode 74*, I read. *Silent Witness, 12/4/08.*

Two teenagers out for a joyride run over a deaf man, who turns out to be already dead.

This is followed by a list of evidence. *Solved*, it reads, *0:36.*

Emma has her head bent close to Jacob's now. She's murmuring, but I cannot hear the words. Turning my back to them, I flip through the entries. Some are repeats of episodes; Jacob seems to have written about each of them when they aired, even if he'd seen the show before. Some of them have the disclaimer that Jacob could not solve the crime before the TV detectives did.

There are kidnappings. Stabbings. Cult

ritual murders. One episode catches my eye: *Joffrey puts on her boyfriend's boots and leaves prints in the mud behind the house to mislead investigators.*

Stuck between the pages is a pink index card, and as I scan it I realize this is a note Jacob has written to himself:

> **I am miserable. I can't stand it anymore.**
> **The people who supposedly care don't.**
> **I get my hopes up and everyone eventually lets me down. I finally know what's wrong with me: all of you. All of you who think I'm just an autistic kid, so who really cares? Well, I hate you. I hate all of you. I hate how I cry at night because of you. But you are just people. JUST PEOPLE.**
> **So why do you make me feel so small?**

Was this written a week ago, a month, a year? Was it in response to bullying in school? To a teacher's criticism? To something Jess Ogilvy said?

It could point to motive. I quickly close the journal and stick the notebook into the box. You can't see that index card anymore, but I know it's there, and it feels too private, too raw to be considered simply evidence. All of a sudden I am flooded by the image of Jacob Hunt huddled in this room after a whole day of trying unsuccessfully to blend in with the hundreds of kids in his school. Who, out of all of us, hasn't felt marginalized at some point? Who hasn't felt like they don't belong?

Who hasn't tried . . . and failed?

I had been the fat kid, the one who was stuck in the soccer goal during gym class and cast as a rock in the school play. I'd been called Doughboy, Lardass, Earthquake Boy, you name it. In eighth grade, after a graduation ceremony, a kid had come up to me. *I never knew your real name was Rich,* he'd said.

When my dad got laid off and we had to move to Vermont for his new job, I spent the summer reinventing myself. I ran—a half mile the first day, and then a whole one, and gradually more. I ate only green things. I did five hundred sit-ups every morning before I even brushed my teeth. By the time I got to my new school, I was a totally different guy, and I never looked back.

Jacob Hunt can't exercise himself into a new personality. He can't move to another school district and start over. He'll always be the kid with Asperger's.

Unless, instead, he makes himself the kid who killed Jess Ogilvy.

"I'm all done here," I say, stacking the boxes. "I just need you to sign the receipt for the property so you can eventually get it back."

"And when might that be?"

"When the DA's done with it." I turn to say good-bye to Jacob, but he's staring at the empty spot where his fuming chamber was located.

Emma walks me downstairs. "You're wasting your time," she says. "My son isn't a murderer."

I push the inventory receipt toward her, silent.

"If I were Jess's parents, I'd want to know the police were actively trying to find the person who killed my child instead of basing their entire case on the ridiculous notion that an autistic boy with no criminal history—a boy who loved Jess—killed her."

She signs the receipt I give her and then opens the front door. "Are you even listening?" she says, her voice rising. "You've got the wrong person."

There have been times—albeit very rarely—that I wished this were the case. When I snapped handcuffs on an abused wife who'd gone after her husband with a knife, for example. Or when I arrested a guy who'd broken into a grocery store to steal formula for his baby because he couldn't afford it. But just like then, I can't contradict the evidence that's in front of me now. I may feel bad for someone who's committed a crime, but that doesn't mean he hasn't committed it.

I pick up the boxes and, at the last moment, turn back. "I'm sorry," I say. "For what it's worth . . . I'm really sorry."

Her eyes flash. "You're *sorry*? For what, exactly? Lying to me? Lying to Jacob? Throwing him into jail without giving any thought to his special needs—"

"Technically, the judge did that—"

"How *dare* you," Emma shouts. "How dare you come in here as if you're on our side, and then turn around and do this to my son!"

"There are no sides," I yell back at her. "There's just a girl, who died alone and scared and who was found a week later frozen solid. Well, I've got a girl, too. What if it had been her?" By now my face is flushed. I am inches away from Emma. "I didn't do this to your son," I say, more softly. "I did this *for* my daughter."

The last thing I see is Emma Hunt's jaw drop. She doesn't speak to me as I heft the boxes more firmly in my arms and walk down her driveway, but then, it's never the differences between people that surprise us. It's the things that, against all odds, we have in common.

Jacob

My mother and I are riding in the car to the office of the state psychiatrist, who happens to work out of a hospital. I am nervous about this because I don't like hospitals. I have been in them twice: once when I fell out of a tree and broke my arm, and once when Theo got hurt after I knocked over his high chair. What I remember about hospitals is that they smell white and stale, the lights are too bright, and every time I've been in one I've either been in pain or been ashamed or maybe both.

This makes my fingers start to flutter on my leg, and I stare at them as if they are disconnected from my body. For the past three days,

I've been doing better. I'm taking all my supplements again and my shots, and it hasn't felt quite as much as if I'm constantly swimming in a bubble of water that makes it harder to understand what people say or to focus on them.

Believe me, 1 know it's not normal to flap my hands or walk in circles or repeat words over and over, but sometimes it's the easiest way to make myself feel better. It's like a steam engine, really: Fluttering my hands in front of my face or against my leg is my exhaust valve, and maybe it looks weird, but then again, just compare it to the folks who turn to alcohol or porn to alleviate pressures.

1 haven't been out of the house since 1 left the jail. Even school is off-limits now, so my mother has found textbooks and is home-schooling both Theo and me. It's sort of nice, actually, not having to stress out about the next time 1 will be accosted by another student and will have to interact; or if a teacher will say something 1 don't understand; or if I'll need to use my COP pass and look like a total loser in front of my peers. 1 wonder why we never thought of this before: learning without socialization. It's every Aspie's dream.

Every now and then, my mother looks at me in the rearview mirror. "You remember what's going to happen, right?" she asks. "Dr. Cohn is going to ask you questions. All you have to do is tell the truth."

Here's the other reason I'm nervous: the last time I went off to answer questions without my mother, I wound up in jail.

"Jacob," my mother says, "you're stimming."

I slap my free hand over the one that's fluttering.

When we get to the hospital, I walk with my head ducked down so that I do not have to see sick people. I have not vomited since I was six years old; the very thought of it makes me sweat. Once when Theo got the flu, I had to take my sleeping bag and quilt and stay in the garage because I was afraid I'd catch it. What if coming here for a stupid competency interview turns out to be much worse than anyone anticipates?

"I don't understand why he couldn't come to us," I mutter.

"Because he's not on our side," my mother says.

The way competency works is this:

1. The State of Vermont hires a psychiatrist who will interview me and tell the judge everything the DA wants to hear.

2. My lawyer will counter this with Dr. Moon, my own psychiatrist, who will tell the judge everything Oliver Bond wants to hear.

Frankly, I don't see the point, since we all know this is how it's going to shake out, anyway.

Dr. Martin Cohn's office is not as nice as Dr. Moon's. Dr. Moon decorates in shades of blue, which have been proven to enhance relaxation. Dr. Martin Cohn decorates in industrial gray. His secretary's desk looks like the one my math teacher uses. "Can I help you?" she asks.

My mother steps forward. "Jacob Hunt is here to see Dr. Cohn."

"You can go right in." She points to another doorway.

Dr. Moon has that, too. You go into her office through one door and exit through the other, so that no one who's waiting will see you. I know it's supposed to be about privacy, but if you ask me, it's like the psychiatrists themselves are buying into that stupid belief that therapy is something to hide.

I put my hand on the doorknob and take a deep breath. *This time you're coming back,* I promise myself.

* * *

A joke:

A guy is flying in a hot-air balloon and he's lost. He lowers himself over a cornfield and calls out to a woman. "Can you tell me where I am and where I'm headed?"

"Sure," this woman says. "You are at 41 degrees, 2 minutes, and 14 seconds north, 144 degrees, 4 minutes, 19 seconds east; you're at an altitude of 762 meters above sea level, and right now you're hovering, but you were on a vector of 234 degrees at 12 meters per second."

"Amazing! Thanks! By the way, do you have Asperger's syndrome?"

"I do!" the woman replies. "How did you know?"

"Because everything you said is true, it's much more detail than I need, and you told me in a way that's of no use to me at all."

The woman frowns. "Huh. Are you a psychiatrist?"

"I am," the man says. "But how the heck could you tell?"

"You don't know where you are. You don't know where you're headed. You got where you are by blowing hot air. You put labels on people after asking a few questions, and you're in exactly the same spot you were in five minutes ago, but now, somehow, it's my fault!"

Dr. Martin Cohn is smaller than I am and has a beard. He wears glasses without rims, and as soon as I come into the room, he walks toward me. "Hello," he says. "I'm Dr. Cohn. Take a seat."

The chairs are metal frames with pleather cushions. One is orange, and that's totally not happening. The other is gray and has a sunken circle in the middle, as if the cushion has simply given out.

When I was younger and I was asked to take a seat, I'd lift it up. Now I know that it means I am supposed to sit down. There are many statements that do not mean what they say: *Mark my words. Hang around. Just a second. Get off my back.*

The psychiatrist takes out a pen from his pocket. He sits down, too, and puts his yellow pad on his lap. "What's your name?"

"Jacob Thomas Hunt," I say.

"How old are you, Jacob?"

"Eighteen."

"Do you know why you're here?"

"Don't *you?*"

He writes something down on his paper. "Do you know that you've been charged with a crime?"

"Yes. Thirteen VSA, section 2301. *Murder committed by means of poison, or by lying in wait, or by willful, deliberate and premeditated killing, or committed in perpetrating or attempting to perpetrate arson, sexual assault, aggravated sexual assault, robbery or burglary, shall be murder in the first degree. All other kinds of murder shall be murder in the second degree.*"

I would have thought reciting the entire statute would impress Dr. Cohn, but he doesn't register any emotion.

Maybe he's got Asperger's, too.

"Do you understand whether that's a major or minor charge, Jacob?"

"It's a felony that carries a minimum sentence of thirty-five years to life in prison."

Dr. Cohn looks up over his glasses. "What about probation?" he asks. "Do you know what that is?"

"It's when you have to check in with a court officer for a certain amount of time," I say. "You have to follow rules and give reports, you have to have a job, you have to live somewhere where they know your address, you have to stay out of trouble, you have to not drink alcohol . . ."

"Right," Dr. Cohn says. "Tell me, Jacob, what should your lawyer focus on in order to defend you?"

I shrug. "My innocence."

"Do you understand what a plea of guilty or not guilty means?"

"Yes. *Guilty* means that you admit you committed the crime and that you need to be punished for it. *Not guilty* means you don't admit you committed the crime and you don't think you should be punished for it . . . but it's not the same as being innocent, because in our legal system you get found guilty or not guilty. You don't get found innocent, even if you are, like me."

Dr. Cohn stares at me. "What's a plea bargain?"

"When the prosecutor talks to the lawyer and they agree on a sentence, and then they both go before the judge to see if the judge will accept that, too. It means you don't have to have a trial, because you've admitted to the crime by taking the plea."

These are all easy questions, because the end of every *CrimeBusters* episode is a trial, where the evidence is relayed to a judge and jury. If I'd known the questions were going to be this simple, I wouldn't have been so nervous. Instead, I'd been expecting Dr. Cohn to ask me about Jess. About what happened that afternoon.

And of course I couldn't tell him, which would mean I'd have to lie, and that would be breaking the rules.

"What's an insanity plea?" Dr. Cohn asks.

"When you claim you're not guilty because you were dissociated from reality at the time you committed the crime and can't be held legally responsible for your actions. Like Edward Norton in *Primal Fear*."

"Great flick," the psychiatrist says. "Jacob, if your lawyer thinks you shouldn't testify, would you agree to that?"

"Why wouldn't I want to testify? I'm going to tell the truth."

"When can you speak out in the courtroom?"

"I can't. My lawyer told me not to talk to anyone."

"What do you think your chances are of being found not guilty?"

"One hundred percent," I say, "since I didn't do it."

"Do you know how strong the case is against you?"

"Obviously not, since I haven't seen the discovery—"

"You know what discovery is?" Dr. Cohn asks, surprised.

I roll my eyes. "Pursuant to Rule Sixteen of the Vermont Rules of Discovery, Rules of Procedure for the Superior Court, the Prosecution is required to turn over all the evidence they have in the case, including the photographs, documents, statements, physical examinations, and any other material that they intend to use at the trial, and if they don't turn it over, then I'm allowed to go free."

"Do you understand the difference between the defense, the prosecution, the judge, the jury, the witnesses . . . ?"

I nod. "The defense is my team—my lawyer and the witnesses and me, because we're defending me against the crime the prosecution's charged me with. The judge is the man or woman who has authority over everyone in the courtroom. He runs the trial and listens to the evidence and makes decisions about the law, and the judge I met a few days ago wasn't very nice and sent me to jail." I take a breath. "The jury is a group of twelve that listens to the facts and hears the evidence and the arguments of the lawyers and then goes into a room where no one can hear them or see them and they decide the outcome of the case." As an afterthought I add, "The jury is supposed to be twelve peers, but technically that would mean every single person on the jury should have Asperger's syndrome, because then they'd *really* understand me."

Dr. Cohn makes another note. "Do you have confidence in your lawyer, Jacob?"

"No," I say. "The first time I met him I wound up in jail for three days."

"Do you agree with how he's handling the case?"

"Obviously not. He needs to tell them the truth so that the charges will be dismissed."

"That's not how it works," Dr. Cohn says.

"It worked that way in *My Cousin Vinny*," I tell him. "When Joe Pesci tells the court that the car isn't the same as the one the witness identified because it had different tires. And it worked that way on *CrimeBusters,* episode eighty-eight. Do you want me to tell you about it?"

"No, that's okay," Dr. Cohn says. "Jacob, what would you do if a witness told a lie on the stand?"

I feel my fingers start to flutter, so I clamp my other hand down on top of them. "How would I know?" I say. "Only the liar knows that he's lying."

Oliver

On paper, Jacob Hunt not only looks competent to stand trial but looks like a damn prelaw student, one who is probably more qualified to defend himself than I am.

Only the liar knows that he's lying.

It's the third time I've read Jacob's answers to Dr. Cohn, the state shrink, and the third time that statement has jumped out at me. Is Jacob Hunt brilliant, with a photographic memory that I could have used back in law school? Or is he just snowing his mother . . . and everyone else?

Either way, during my last pass through the report, I realized that I didn't have a snowball's chance in hell of challenging his competency—especially in a place like Vermont. No, if anyone's feeling incompetent right now, it's me—because I have to tell Emma that I'm not even going to fight the State on this one.

I drive to the Hunts'—since Emma and Jacob are basically under house arrest, I can't very well ask them to meet me at my office. Thor's riding in my lap, half tucked beneath the steering wheel.

I pull into the driveway and cut the ignition but don't make a move to get out of the car. "If she goes haywire," I tell the dog, "I'm counting on you to defend me."

Because it's cold today—just above zero degrees—I carry Thor inside my coat and head to the front door. Emma answers before I can even knock. "Hi," she says. "It's good to see you." She even smiles a little, which makes her soft around all the edges. "Frankly, when you're stuck in the house, even a visit from the electric company meter reader is a highlight of the day."

"And here I thought you were starting to like me." Thor pops his head between the buttons of my coat. "Would it be okay to bring him in? It's really cold in the car."

She eyes the dog warily. "Is it going to pee on my carpet?"

"Only if you keep looking at him like that."

I set Thor on the floor of the mudroom and watch him trot away. "I don't like dog hair," Emma murmurs.

"Then aren't you lucky you weren't born a spaniel?" I take off my coat and fold it over my arm. "I got the competency results back."

"And?" In one heartbeat, Emma is focused, intense.

"Jacob's competent to stand trial."

She shakes her head, as if she hasn't quite heard me right. "You saw what happened during the arraignment!"

"Yes, but that's not the legal definition of competency, and according to the state psychiatrist—"

"I don't care about the state psychiatrist. Of course they're going to find someone who says what the DA wants. Aren't you at least going to fight back?"

"You don't understand," I tell her. "In Vermont you could be Charlie Manson and you'd still be found competent to stand trial." I sit down on one of the benches in the mudroom. "You ever hear of a guy named John Bean?"

"No."

"In 1993, he tied his mother up and built a funeral pyre for her with furniture he'd chopped into pieces. He threw bleach in her eyes, but his mother was able to escape. At his first appearance before a court, Bean told the judge he was the reincarnation of Jesus Christ. The judge said that his statements were bizarre and indicated an inability to comprehend what was happening. When he was charged with kidnapping for the same event, he refused counsel. He wanted to plead guilty, but the court wouldn't accept that, so he was given a public defender. Bean told an evaluator that he believed he was the father of the public defender's children and that she was the author of a comic strip and was a cross between Janet Reno and Janet Jackson. Through the next eight years of representation, he never discussed his case with his attorney—who raised the competency issue with the court—"

"I don't see what this has—"

"I'm not done," I say. "The defense shrink said Bean reported having computer chips inside him that were letting him be programmed. The state psychiatrist found him psychotic. During the trial, Bean tore the radiator out of the wall, threw the court television, and got hold of one of the officers' guns. He told his attorney that he was seeing serpents coming out of people's heads in the courtroom, and that angels were controlling the witness. He was convicted, and before sentencing, he told the court that in Riverside Park they put a memorial stone in the name of the Freddie Mercury Foundation, after Freddie Mercury had killed a Catholic priest. After that, he said Tony Curtis said he would be Bean's father, and he used the greater power of Simon the Pig—the same power that had created the Nazi government—to bring him into his house and feed him human flesh. Oh, and a cat talked to him subliminally."

Emma stares at me. "None of this has anything to do with Jacob."

"It does," I say, "because in the State of Vermont, in spite of everything I just told you, John Bean was found competent to stand trial. *That's* legal precedent."

Emma sinks down onto the bench beside me. "Oh," she says, her voice small. "So what do we do now?"

"I, uh, think we need to plead insanity."

Her head snaps up. "What? What are you talking about? Jacob's not insane—"

"You just told me he wasn't competent to stand trial, and now you're telling me he's too competent to use an insanity defense. You can't have it both ways!" I argue. "We can look at the discovery when it comes in . . . But from what you've told me, there's a pretty strong case against Jacob, including a confession. I really believe it's the best way to keep him out of jail."

Emma paces the mudroom. A shaft of sunlight falls across her hair and her cheek, and suddenly I remember an art history course I took in college: in Michelangelo's *Pietà*, Raphael's *Madonna and Child*, da Vinci's *Madonna of the Rocks*, Mary was never seen smiling. Was it because she knew what was coming down the pike?

"If the insanity defense works," Emma asks, "does he get to come home?"

"It depends. The judge has the right to put him in a secure treatment facility until he's sure Jacob won't hurt anyone again."

"What do you mean, 'secure treatment facility'? You're talking about a mental hospital?"

"Pretty much," I admit.

"So my son can either go to jail or be put in a mental hospital? What about the third option?"

"What third option?"

"He's free to go," Emma says. "He's acquitted."

I open my mouth to tell her that's a huge gamble, to say that she'd have a better chance of teaching Thor to knit, but instead, I take a deep breath. "Why don't we go ask Jacob?"

"No way," Emma replies.

"Unfortunately, that's not your choice." I stand up and walk into the kitchen. Jacob is picking through a bowl of blueberries and giving the smaller ones to Thor.

"Did you know he likes fruit?" Jacob asks.

"He'll eat anything that's not nailed down," I say. "We have to talk about your case, dude."

"Dude?" Emma's come into the room and is standing behind me, arms folded.

I ignore her and approach Jacob. "You passed the competency test."

"I did?" he says, beaming. "Did I do really well?"

Emma steps forward. "You did *great,* baby."

"We need to start thinking about your defense," I say.

Jacob puts down the bowl of blueberries. "I have some cool ideas. There was this time on *CrimeBusters* when—"

"This isn't a TV show, Jacob," I say. "This is really important. This is your *life.*"

He sits down at the kitchen table and lifts Thor onto his lap. "Did you know that the guy who invented Velcro got the idea from taking his dog for a walk in the Alps? When the burrs caught on its fur, he thought about how something with hooks could catch onto anything with a loop."

I sit down across from him. "Do you know what an affirmative defense is?"

He nods and spits back the legal definition: "It's a reason for finding the defendant not guilty, such as self-defense, defense of another person, or not guilty by reason of insanity. The defendant has to raise it a certain amount of time before a trial, usually in writing."

"What I've been thinking, Jacob, is that your best odds at this trial involve an affirmative defense."

His face lights up. "Right! Of course! Defense of another person—"

"Who were you defending?" I interrupt.

Jacob looks down at Thor and plays with the tags on his collar. *"Surely you can't be serious,"* he says. *"I am serious . . . and don't call me Shirley."*

"Do you really think you're in a position to be making jokes right now?"

"It's from *Airplane!*" Jacob says.

"Well, it's not funny. The State has a really

good case against you, Jacob, which is why I think we need to use an insanity defense."

Jacob's head snaps up. "I'm not crazy!"

"That's not what it means."

"I know what it means," he says. "It means that a person isn't responsible for criminal conduct if, as a result of mental disease or defect, he lacked the capacity to understand right from wrong at the moment the act was committed." He stands up, knocking Thor to the floor. "I don't have a mental disease or defect. I have a quirk. Right, Mom?"

I glance at Emma. "You have *got* to be kidding me."

She hikes her chin up a notch. "We've always said that Asperger's isn't a disability . . . just a *different* ability."

"Great," I say. "Well, Jacob, either I run the insanity defense or you can take that quirk of yours right back to prison."

"No, actually, in the State of Vermont, you can't run an insanity defense if I tell you that you can't," Jacob answers. "It's all in the Vermont Supreme Court case of State versus Bean, one-seventy-one Vermont Reports two-ninety, seven-sixty-two Atlantic Reporter second twelve fifty-nine, two thousand."

"Jesus Christ, you *know* that case?"

"Don't *you*?" He raises his brows. "Why can't you just tell them the truth?"

"Fine, Jacob. What's the truth?"

No sooner have I asked than I realize my mistake. Any lawyer knows to be careful what you ask when representing a criminal defendant, since anything he says might incriminate himself. If he gets on the stand later and denies what he told you earlier, you're left in a quandary and have to either withdraw from representation (which would prejudice him) or tell the court that he's not being truthful (which would prejudice him even more). Instead of asking *what happened,* you dance around the truth and the facts. You ask the client how he'd answer certain questions.

Or in other words, I just royally screwed up. Now that I've asked him for the truth, I can't let him get up on the stand and incriminate himself.

So I stop him from answering.

"Wait, I don't want to hear it," I say.

"What do you mean you don't want to hear it! You're supposed to be my *lawyer*!"

"The reason we can't tell the court the truth is that facts speak a lot louder in a courtroom."

"You can't handle the truth," Jacob yells. "I'm not guilty. And I'm *definitely* not insane!"

I scoop up Thor and stalk into the mudroom, Emma following. "He's right," she says. "Why do you have to plead insanity? If Jacob's not guilty, shouldn't the judge get to hear that?"

I spin around so quickly she falls back. "I want you to think about something. Say you're on the jury for this case, and you've just listened to a long list of facts that tie Jacob to the murder of Jess Ogilvy. Then you get to watch Jacob on the stand explaining his version of the truth. Which story would *you* believe?"

She swallows, silent, because this point (at least) she cannot argue: Emma knows very well what Jacob looks like and sounds like to other people, even when Jacob doesn't know it himself. "Look," I tell her, "Jacob has to accept that this insanity defense is the best chance we've got."

"How are you going to convince him?"

"I'm not," I say. "*You* are."

Rich

The teachers at Townsend Regional High School all know Jacob Hunt, even if they haven't had him in class. This is partly due to his current infamy, but I get the sense that, even before he was arrested for murder, he was the kind of kid everyone could spot in the halls—because he stuck out like a sore thumb. After interviewing staff for several hours, and hearing how Jacob used to sit by himself during lunch and how he'd move from class to class wearing bulky headphones to block out the noise (and the rude comments of classmates), there is a part of me wondering how Jacob managed to wait eighteen years to commit murder.

What I've learned is that Jacob twisted his schoolwork around his passion for CSI. In English class, when he had to read a biography and give an oral report, he chose Edmond Locard. In math, his independent research project involved Herb Macdonald's angled impact of the point of origin of blood spatter.

His guidance counselor, Frances Grenville, is a thin, pale woman whose features resemble a garment that's been washed so often its original color has faded. "Jacob would do anything to fit in," she says, as I sit in her office, thumbing through Hunt's file. "Quite often, that would make him the butt of jokes. In a way, he was doomed if he tried to fit in, and doomed if he didn't." She shifts uncomfortably. "I used to worry he'd bring a gun into school one day, you know, to get even. Like that boy over in Sterling, New Hampshire, a few years back."

"Did Jacob ever do that? Get even, I mean."

"Oh, no. Honestly, he's the sweetest child. Sometimes he'd come here during free periods and do his homework in the outer office. He fixed my computer when it crashed, once, and even recovered the file I'd been working on. Most of the teachers love him."

"And the rest?"

"Well, some are better with special needs kids than others, but you didn't hear it from me. A student like Jacob can be challenging, to say the least. There's some deadwood in this school, if you know what I mean, and when you get a kid like Jacob who challenges a lesson plan you've been too lazy to adapt for the past twenty years—and when it turns out he's *right*—well, that doesn't always sit well." She shrugs. "But you can ask the staff. On the whole, Jacob interacted much more fluidly with them than with his peers. He wasn't caught up in the usual high school adolescent drama—instead, he wanted to talk about politics, or scientific breakthroughs, or whether *Eugene Onegin* was really Pushkin's tour de force. In many ways, having Jacob around was like talking to another teacher." She hesitates. "No, actually, it was like talking to the kind of enlightened scholar that teachers *wish* they could grow up to be—before bills and

car payments and orthodontist appoint-
ments get in the way."

"If Jacob wanted so badly to fit in with
students, what was he doing in the teachers' room?" I ask.

She shakes her head. "I suppose there's
only so many times you can take being rebuffed before you need some validation,"
Mrs. Grenville says.

"What do you know about his connection to Jessica Ogilvy?"

"He enjoyed spending time with her. He
referred to her as his friend."

I glance up. "How about as his girlfriend?"

"Not that I know of."

"Did Jacob ever have a girlfriend in
school?"

"I don't think so. He took a girl to prom
last year, but he talked more about Jess,
who'd encouraged him to do it, than about
his actual date."

"Who else did Jacob hang around
with?" I ask.

Mrs. Grenville frowns. "Here's the thing,"
she says. "If you asked Jacob for a list of
his friends, he'd probably be able to give
you that list. But if you asked those same

kids for their lists, Jacob wouldn't be on them. His Asperger's leads him to mistake proximity for emotional connection. So, for example, Jacob would say he's friendly with the girl he's paired with as a lab partner in physics, even though that might not be a reciprocal feeling."

"So he wasn't considered a discipline problem?"

Mrs. Grenville purses her lips. "No."

I place the open school file on her desk and point to a note inside it. "Then why was Jacob Hunt suspended for assault last year?"

Mimi Scheck is the kind of girl I drooled over in high school, in spite of the fact that she wasn't aware we even inhabited the same building for four years. She has long black hair and a body made for worship, artfully showcased in clothes that reveal just an inch of skin above the waistline of her jeans when she reaches up or bends down. She also looks so nervous that she'd bolt, if not for the fact that Mrs. Grenville just closed the door of her office.

"Hi, Mimi," I say, smiling. "How are you doing today?"

She looks from me to the guidance counselor, her lips pressed tight. Then she melts into the couch, anguished. "I swear, I didn't know about the vodka until I got to Esme's."

"Well. That's interesting . . . but it's not why I asked to speak to you today."

"It's not?" Mimi whispers. "Oh, crap."

"I wanted to ask you about Jacob Hunt."

Her face goes beet red. "I don't really know him very well."

"You were involved in an incident last year that led to his suspension, right?"

"It was all just a big joke," she says, rolling her eyes. "I mean, how was I supposed to know he couldn't even take a joke?"

"What happened?"

She sinks down farther on Mrs. Grenville's couch. "He was always hanging around. It was creepy, you know? I mean, I'd be, like, talking to my friends and he'd be standing there eavesdropping. And then I got a forty on a math quiz because Mr. LaBlanc is the biggest jerk ever and I got really mad and asked to be excused to go to the bathroom. But I never went to the bathroom, I just went around the corner and started crying because if I failed math again my parents were going to take away my phone *and* make me give up my Facebook account—and Jacob walked up to me. I guess he'd left class for one of his weirdo breaks or something, and he was headed back. He didn't say anything, he just kept staring at me, and I told him to get lost. So he said he would stay with me because that's what friends do, and I said that if he really wanted to be my friend, he'd go into math class and tell Mr. LaBlanc to go fuck himself." Mimi hesitated. "So he did."

I glance at the guidance counselor. "And that's why he was suspended?"

"No. He got detention for that."

"And then?" I ask.

Mimi's gaze slides away. "The next day a bunch of us were hanging out in the commons when Jacob showed up. I guess I sort of ignored him. I mean, it's not like I was actively being *mean* to him or anything. And he just went crazy and came after me."

"He hit you?"

She shakes her head. "He grabbed me and threw me up against a locker.

He could have killed me, you know, if a teacher hadn't stopped him."

"Can you show me how he grabbed you?"

Mimi looks at Mrs. Grenville, who nods, encouraging her. We both stand up, and Mimi takes a step forward until she has backed me against the wall. She has to reach up because I am taller than she is, and then gingerly, she wraps her right hand around my throat. "Like this," she says. "I had bruises for a week."

The same bruises, I realize, that Jess Ogilvy had revealed at her autopsy.

Emma

As if I need any further reminder after Oliver Bond's visit that my life is not and never will be what it was, my editor calls. "I was hoping you could come in this afternoon," Tanya says. "There's something we need to discuss."

"I can't."

"Tomorrow morning?"

"Tanya," I say, "Jacob's under house arrest. I'm not allowed to leave."

"Well, that's sort of why I wanted to meet . . . We think that it might be best for everyone right now if you took a leave of absence from your column."

"Best for everyone?" I repeat. "How is losing my job best for me?"

"It's temporary, Emma. Just until this . . . blows over. Surely you understand," Tanya explains. "We can't really endorse advice from—"

"From a writer whose son was accused of murder?" I finish for her. "I write *anonymously.* No one knows about me, much less Jacob."

"For how long? We're in the news business. Someone's going to dig this up, and then we'll be the ones who look like idiots."

"By all means," I say hotly. "We wouldn't want you to look like idiots."

"We're not cutting you off. Bob's agreed to keep you at half salary plus benefits if you do freelance editing of the Sunday section for us in return."

"Is this the part where I'm supposed to fall to my knees in gratitude?" I ask.

She is quiet for a moment. "For what it's worth, Emma," Tanya says, "you're the last person in the world who deserves this. You've already got your cross to bear."

"Jacob," I say, "is not a cross to bear. He's my son." My hand is shaking where it holds the phone. "Go edit your own fucking Sunday section," I tell her, and I hang up.

A tiny cry escapes as I realize the magnitude of what I've just done. I'm a single parent; I hardly make any money as is; I can't work outside the home right now—how am I going to afford to live without a job? I could call my old boss from the textbook company and beg for freelance assignments, but it's been twenty years since I worked there. I could scrape by on whatever savings we've got, until this is over.

And when will that be?

I admit that I've taken our legal system for granted. I assumed that the innocent prevail, that the guilty get their due. But as it turns out, it isn't as simple as saying you're not guilty if you're not guilty. As Oliver Bond has pointed out, the jury has to be convinced. And connecting with strangers is Jacob's weakest link.

I keep waiting to wake up. To have someone surprise me with the hidden camera and tell me this is all a big joke: that *of course* Jacob is free to go, that *of course* there has been some mistake. But no one surprises me, and I wake up every morning and nothing has changed.

The worst thing that could happen would be if Jacob goes to prison again, because they don't understand him there. On the other hand, if he's hospitalized, he'll be with doctors. Oliver said that he'd be kept in a secure treatment facility until the judge could be sure that he wouldn't hurt anyone again. Which means that he'd have a chance, however slight, of getting out one day.

I pull myself up the stairs heavily, as if my feet have been cast in lead. At Jacob's door, I knock. He is sitting on his bed, *Flowers for Algernon* folded on his chest. "I finished," he says.

As part of our new home-schooling protocol, I have to make sure he keeps up with the school curriculum, and this novel was the first assignment for his English class. "And?"

"It was stupid."

"I always thought it was sad."

"It's stupid," Jacob reiterates, "because he never should have had the experiment done."

I sit down beside him. In the narrative, Charlie Gordon, a retarded man, undergoes a surgical procedure that triples his IQ, only to have the experiment ultimately fail and leave him with subnormal intelligence again. "Why not? He got to see what he was missing."

"But if he never had that procedure, he would never *know* he was missing it."

When Jacob says things like this—truths so raw most of us won't even admit them in silence, much less speak them out loud—he seems more lucid than anyone else I know. I do not believe my son is insane. And I do not believe that his Asperger's is a disability, either. If Jacob didn't have Asperger's, he wouldn't be the same boy I love so fiercely: the one who watches *Casablanca* with me and can recite all of Bogey's dialogue; the one who remembers the grocery list in his head when I've inadvertently left it sitting on the counter; the one who never ignores me if I ask him to get my wallet out of my handbag or run upstairs to get a ream of paper for the printer. Would I have rather had a kid who doesn't struggle so hard, who could make his way in the world with less resistance? No, because that child wouldn't have been Jacob. The crises may be what stick in my mind when it comes to him, but the in-between moments are the ones I would not have missed for the world.

Still, I know why Charlie Gordon had the

procedure done. And I know why I am about to have a conversation with Jacob that makes my heart feel like it's turned to ash. It's because, whenever possible, humans err on the side of hope.

"I have to talk to you about what Oliver said," I begin.

Jacob sits up. "I'm not crazy. I'm not letting him say that about me."

"Just hear me out—"

"It's not the truth," Jacob says. "And you always have to tell the truth. House rules."

"You're right. But sometimes, it's okay to tell a little lie, if it gets you to the truth in the long run."

He blinks. "Saying I'm insane isn't a little lie."

I look at him. "I know you didn't kill Jess. I believe you. But you have to get twelve strangers on a jury to believe you. How are you going to do that?"

"I'm going to tell them the truth."

"Okay. Pretend we're in court, then, and tell it to me."

His eyes flicker across my face and then fix on the window behind me. *"The first rule of Fight Club is don't talk about Fight Club."*

"That's exactly what I mean. You can't use

movie quotes in a courtroom to say what happened . . . But you *can* use a lawyer." I grasp his arms. "I want you to promise me that you'll let Oliver say whatever he has to in order for you to win this case."

He jerks his chin down. *"One martini, please,"* he mutters. *"Shaken, not stirred."*

"I'm going to take that as a yes," I say.

Theo

If a school day is seven hours long, six of those are eaten up by blocks of time that are full of nothing but crap: teachers yelling at kids who misbehave, gossip as you walk to your locker, recap of a math concept you understood the first time it was explained. What being home-schooled has taught me, more than anything, is what a waste of a life high school is.

When it's just me and Jacob, sitting at the kitchen table, I can blow through my work in about an hour's time if I leave the reading stuff for before I fall asleep. It helps that my mother second-guesses the curriculum a lot. ("We're skipping this part. If imaginary numbers were meant to be learned, they would have made themselves real," or "For God's sake, how many times have you studied the Puritans now, since first grade? A hundred? Let's just move on to the Reformation.") At any rate, I *like* being home-schooled. By definition, you're an outcast, so you don't have to worry about sounding stupid if you give the wrong answer or if that hot girl from your English class is checking you out when you go up to the whiteboard to write your equation for the math homework. I mean, we don't even *have* a whiteboard here.

Since Jacob works on different stuff than I do, he's buried in his work on one end of the table and I'm at the other. I finish before him, but then again, I did even when we worked on regular homework before. He may be freaking brilliant, but sometimes whatever's cooking in his brain doesn't quite translate onto the page. I guess it's a little like being the world's fastest bullet train but your wheels don't fit the rails.

As soon as I finish my French homework (*Que fait ton frère? Il va à la prison!*), I close my textbook. My mom looks up from her cup of coffee. Usually, she's typing away at her computer, but she hasn't even been able to focus on that today. "Done," I announce.

She stretches out her lips, and I know it's supposed to be a smile. "Great."

"You need me to do anything?" I ask.

"Turning back time would be nice."

"I was thinking more along the lines of the grocery store," I suggest. "We have, like, nothing to eat here."

It's true, and she knows it. She isn't allowed to leave the house as long as Jacob's stuck here, and that means we're on a slow road to starvation unless I do something about it. "You can't drive," she says.

"I've got my skateboard."

She arches a brow. "Theo, you cannot skateboard with groceries."

"Why not? I'll use those green bags I

can loop over my arms, and I won't buy anything heavy."

It doesn't take her very long to be convinced, but then we hit another snafu—she has only ten bucks in her wallet, and I can't very well pretend to be Emma Hunt when I hand over her credit card. "Hey, Jacob," I say, "we need to borrow some money."

He doesn't look up from his history book. "Do I look like a bank?"

"Are you kidding me?" My brother has, I swear, every dollar he's ever been given for a birthday, Christmas, you name it. I have only seen him spend money once, on a thirty-five-cent pack of gum.

"Don't," my mother says quietly. "Let's not get him upset." Instead, she rummages in her wallet and pulls out her ATM card. "Stop off at the bank in the shopping center, and take out some cash. My PIN is 4550."

"Really?" I say, beaming. "You just gave me your PIN?"

"Yes, so don't make me regret it."

I grab the card and head out of the

kitchen. "So, is it your computer pass-word, too?"

"Soy milk," she says. "And gluten-free bread, and no-salt ham. And anything else you want."

I make the executive decision to not take my skateboard and instead walk to the bank. It's only two miles into town anyway. I keep my head ducked and tell myself it's because of the wind, but really it's because I don't want to run into anyone I know. I pass cross-country skiers on the golf course and a pair of joggers. When I get to the bank, I realize that it's after hours and I don't know how to get into the little lobby where the ATM is located. Instead, I walk around to the back of the building, where there is a drive-up machine. I stand behind a Honda and wait my turn.

ENTER AMOUNT, the screen reads. I type in $200, and then I hesitate and cancel the transaction. Instead of doing a withdrawal, I look up the account bal-ances.

Could we really have only $3,356 in

our savings account? I try to remember whether my mother gets statements from more banks than just this one. If there's a safe in our house where she keeps money.

I know that the Townsend Inn hires fifteen-year-olds as busboys for the restaurant. And I am pretty sure that, if I can get a lift into Burlington, I could work at the McDonald's. Clearly, if someone needs to be employed, it's me—since my mother can't leave the house right now, and since Jacob has proven himself pathologically incapable of holding down a job.

He's had three. The first was working at a pet store in town, back when he was obsessive about dogs. He got fired for telling his boss that she was stupid to keep the dog food in the back of the store, since the bags were so heavy. The second job he had was bagging groceries at a food co-op, where the cashiers kept telling him to "get his ducks in a row" as the items came down the conveyor belt and then got mad because he wouldn't listen, when in reality Jacob probably just didn't understand. The third job was selling concessions at a snack bar during the summer at the town pool. I guess that worked out fine for the first hour or so, but when lunch-time came and there were six kids shouting to him for sno-cones and hot dogs and nachos all at once, he took off his apron and just walked out.

A car drives up behind me, which makes me feel like a moron. I shuffle my feet and punch the Withdrawal button, and then enter $200 on the keypad. When the money comes out of the mouth of the machine, I stuff it into my pocket. And then I hear my name being called.

"Theo? Theo Hunt, is that you?"

I feel guilty, as if I've been caught in the act of doing something I shouldn't be. But it's not, like, illegal to *walk* up to a drive-up ATM, is it?

The door of the car behind me opens, and out steps my biology teacher, Mr. Jennison. "How are you doing?" he asks.

I remember how once, when my mother was getting on Jacob's back because he refused to make small talk at a distant cousin's wedding, he said that he would have asked Aunt Marie how she was doing if he really truly cared . . . but he didn't, so pretending he did would be a big lie.

There are times when Jacob's world makes a lot more sense to me than the one the rest of us live in. Why *do* we ask people how they're doing when we don't give a crap about the answer? Is Mr. Jennison asking me that question because he's worried about me, or because it's something to say to fill up the air between us?

"I'm okay," I say, because old habits die hard. If I were like Jacob, I would have answered directly: *I can't sleep at night. And sometimes, when I run too fast, I can't breathe.* But in reality, someone who asks you how you're doing doesn't want to hear the truth. He wants the pat answer, the expected response, so that he can go on his merry way.

"You need a lift? It's freezing out here."

There are some teachers I have really liked, and others I've really disliked, but Mr. Jennison doesn't fall into either category. He's nondescript, from his thinning hair to his lectures; the kind of teacher whose name I'll probably forget by the time I go to college. I'm pretty sure that—until recently—he could say the same about me: I was an average student in his class who didn't excel or fail enough to leave an impression. Until, of course, all this happened.

Now I'm the boy at the center of six degrees of separation: *Oh yeah, my aunt was Theo's third-grade teacher. Or I sat behind him at a school assembly once.* I am the kid whose name they will toss out at cocktail parties years from now: *That autistic murderer kid? I was in his brother's class at Townsend High.*

"My mom's double-parked across the street," I mumble, realizing too late that, if our car was indeed in town, it would most likely be at this drive-through ATM right now. "Thanks anyway," I say, and I leave in such a hurry that I almost forget to take the transaction receipt.

I jog all the way to the grocery store, as if I'm expecting Mr. Jennison to tail me in his car and call me a liar to my face. Only once do I think about taking the $200 and hopping on a bus and leaving for good. I imagine sitting in the backseat next to a pretty girl who shares her trail mix with me, or an old lady who's knitting a cap for her new-born grandson, who asks me where I'm headed.

I imagine telling her that I'm going to visit my big brother at college. That we're really close and that I miss him when he's away at school.

I imagine how cool it would be if small talk wasn't lies.

When I'm getting ready to go to sleep that night, my toothbrush goes missing. Furious—this isn't the first time this has happened, believe me—I stalk down the hall to my brother's room. Jacob's got an audiotape of Abbott and Costello's "Who's on First" routine playing on an old tape deck. "What the hell did you do with my toothbrush this time?" I ask.

"I didn't touch your stupid tooth-brush."

But I don't believe him. I glance at the old fish tank he uses for a fuming chamber, but it's not there—it was seized as evidence.

Abbott's and Costello's voices are so faint, I can barely make out the words. "Can you even hear that?" I say.

"It's loud enough."

I remember once, at Christmas, when my mom got Jacob a watch. She had to return it because the ticking noise drove him crazy.

"I'm not crazy," Jacob says, and for a second I wonder if I've spoken out loud.

"I never said you were!"

"Yes, you did," Jacob says.

He's probably right. His memory's like a steel trap. "Considering all the shit you steal from my room for your fuming chamber and your crime scenes, I think we can call it even."

What's the guy's name on first base?
No. What is on second.
I'm not asking you who's on second.

Who's on first.
I don't know.
He's on third, we're not talking
about him.

Okay, so I know some people find that comedy routine hilarious, but I've never been one of them. Probably the reason Jacob likes it so much is that it makes perfect sense to him, since the names are taken literally.

"Maybe it got thrown out," Jacob says, and at first I think it's Costello's line, until I realize that he's talking about my toothbrush.

"Did you do it?" I ask.

Jacob stares at me. It always gives me a jolt when that happens, because he spends so much time *not* looking me in the eye. "Did you?" he replies.

Suddenly I'm not sure what we're talking about, but I don't think it's oral hygiene. Before I can respond, my mother sticks her head in the doorway. "Which one of you does this belong to?" she asks, holding up my toothbrush. "It was in my bathroom."

I grab it from her. On the cassette

deck, Abbott and Costello are arguing over the canned laugh track.

**Now that's the first thing you've
said right.
I don't even know what I'm talking
about!**

"I told you so," Jacob says.

Jacob

When I was little, I convinced my brother that I had superpowers. Why else would I be able to hear what our mother was doing upstairs when we were downstairs? Why not say that the reason fluorescent bulbs made me dizzy was that I was so sensitive to light? When I missed a question Theo asked me, I told him it was because I could hear so many conversations and background noises at once, that sometimes it was hard for me to focus on just one sound at a time.

For a while, it worked. And then my brother figured out I wasn't gifted with extrasensory perception. I was just strange.

Having Asperger's is like having the volume of life at full blast all the time. It's like a permanent hangover (although I admit I have only been drunk once, when I tried Grey Goose straight to see the effect it would have on me and was dismayed to learn that, rather than giggling, like everyone on television who's drunk, I only felt more displaced and disoriented, and the world only got more fuzzy and indistinct). All those little autistic kids you see smacking their heads against walls? They're not doing it because they're mental. They're doing it because the rest of the world is so loud it actually hurts, and they're trying to make it all go away.

It's not just sight and sound that are ratcheted up, either. My skin is so sensitive that I can tell you whether my shirt is cotton or polyester just by its temperature against my back. I have to cut all the labels out of my clothes so they don't rub because they feel like coarse sandpaper. If someone touches me when I am not expecting it, I scream—not out of fear but because it sometimes feels like my nerve endings are on the outside rather than the inside.

And it's not just my body that's hypersensitive: my mind is usually in overdrive.

I've always thought it strange when someone describes me as robotic or flat, because if anything, I'm always panicked about *something.* I don't like to interact with people if I can't predict how they are going to respond. I never wonder what I look like from someone else's point of view; I would never even have *thought* to consider that if my mother had not brought it to my attention.

If I give a compliment, it's not because it's the right thing to say, it's because it's true. Even routine language doesn't come easily to me. If you say *thank you,* I have to rummage around in my database brain for *you're welcome.* I can't chat about the weather just for the sake of filling up silence. The whole time I'm thinking, *This is so fake.* If you're wrong about something, I will correct you—not because I want to make you feel bad (in fact, I am not thinking of you at all) but because facts are very important to me, more important than people are.

Nobody ever asks Superman if X-ray vision is a drag; if it gets old looking into brick buildings and seeing guys beat their wives or lonely women getting wasted or losers surfing porn sites. Nobody ever asks Spider-Man if he gets vertigo. If their superpowers are anything like mine, it's no wonder they're always putting themselves in harm's way. They're probably hoping for a quick death.

Rich

Mama Spatakopoulous will not talk to me until I agree to eat a little something, which is how I wind up with a full plate of spaghetti and meatballs as I ask her questions about Jess Ogilvy. "Do you remember this girl?" I ask, showing her a photo of Jess.

"Yes, poor thing, I saw on the news what happened."

"I understand that she came here a few days before she was killed?"

The woman nods. "With her boyfriend, and that other one."

"You mean Jacob Hunt?" I show her a picture of Jacob, too.

"That's him." She shrugs.

"Do you have any security cameras in here?"

"No. Why? Is the neighborhood dangerous?"

"I just thought I might be able to see the interaction that afternoon," I say.

"Oh, I can tell you that," Mama Spatakopoulous says. "It was a big fight."

"What happened?"

"The girl, she got very upset. She was crying, and eventually she ran out. She stuck the Hunt kid with the bill and a whole pizza."

"Do you know why she was upset?" I ask. "What they were fighting about?"

"Well," the woman says, "I couldn't hear everything, but it seemed like he was jealous."

"Ms. Spatakopoulous." I lean forward. "This is very important: did you hear anything Jacob said in particular that was threatening to Jess? Or see him physically attack her in any way?"

Her eyes widen. "Oh, it wasn't Jacob

who was jealous," she says. "It was the other one. The boyfriend."

When I intercept Mark Maguire, he is leaving the student center with two of his buddies. "How was lunch, Mark?" I ask, stepping away from the lamppost against which I've been leaning. "Did you order pizza? Was it as good as Mama Spatakopoulous's?"

"You've got to be kidding," he says. "I'm not talking to you."

"I'd think as a grieving boyfriend you'd want to do just that."

"You know what I want to do? Sue the shit out of you for what you did to me!"

"I let you go," I say, shrugging. "People get unarrested all the time." I fall into step beside him. "I just had a really interesting chat with the pizza lady. She seems to remember you and Jess fighting when you were there."

Mark starts walking, and I fall into step beside him. "So what? So we fought. I already told you that."

"What was that fight about?"

"Jacob Hunt. Jess thought he was some helpless moron, and the whole time he was using that act to get her interested in him."

"Interested how?"

"He *wanted* her," Mark says. "He played pathetic so that she'd be in the palm of his hand. At the restaurant, he had the nerve to ask her out. In front of me, like I wasn't even there. All I did was put Hunt in his place—and remind him that his mommy was buying him Jess's company."

"How did she react?"

"She got pissed." He stops in his tracks and faces me. "Look, maybe I'm not the most sensitive guy . . ."

"Gee, I didn't notice."

Mark glares at me. "I'm trying to make a point here. I said and did things I'm not proud of. I'm jealous; I wanted to be number one on Jess's list. Maybe I crossed the line a few times, trying to make sure of that. But I never would have hurt her, never. The reason I started the fight at the pizza place in the first place was to protect her. She trusted everyone; she only saw the good in people. I could read right through Hunt's bullshit, even if Jess couldn't."

"What do you mean?"

He folds his arms. "My freshman year roommate still played with Pokémon cards. He never showered, and he pretty much lived in the computer lab. I probably said less than ten sentences to him all year. He was fucking brilliant—graduated early and went to go design missile systems for the Pentagon or something. He probably had Asperger's, too, but no one ever slapped a label on him other than *nerd*. All I'm saying is that there's a difference between being mentally retarded and being socially retarded. One's a handicap. The other's just a Get Out of Jail Free card."

"I think current psychiatry might trump you, Mark. There's a difference between being socially awkward and being clinically diagnosed with Asperger's."

"Yeah." He meets my gaze. "That's what Jess used to say, and now she's dead."

Oliver

When I step into the kitchen at the Hunts' house for the second day in a row, Emma is cooking something at the stove while Jacob sits at the kitchen table. I look from his face, bent toward the table over a gruesome collection of crime scene photography, to his mother's. "Go ahead," Emma says.

"The Americans with Disabilities Act prohibits discrimination by the State or local government, including in the courts," Jacob recites, in his monotone. "In order to be protected by the Americans with Disabilities Act, you have to have a disability or have a relationship with someone with a disability. A person with a disability is defined as a person with a physical or mental impairment that substantially limits one or more major life activities . . . like communication . . . or is a person who is perceived by others as having such an impairment."

He flips a page; now the pictures are of bodies in a morgue. Who the hell publishes this kind of book?

"Dr. Moon and my mother say I have quirks, but other people, like my teachers and the kids at school and that judge, might assume I have a disability," Jacob adds.

I shake my head. "I don't really understand."

"There's a logical and valid legal reason for you to speak for me," Jacob says. "You may use the insanity defense, if you think it will work best during the trial." He stands up, tucking the book under his arm. "But for the record, I personally subscribe to the belief that normal is just a setting on the dryer."

I nod, considering this. "What movie is that from?"

Jacob rolls his eyes. "Not everything's from a movie," he says, and he walks off.

"Wow." I walk toward Emma. "I don't know how you did that, but thank you."

"Don't underestimate me," she answers, and

with a spatula, she flips the fish that is being sautéed in a pan.

"Was that the only reason you asked me to come over?"

"I thought that was what you wanted," Emma says.

"It was. Until I smelled what you were cooking." I grin. "I'll knock ten bucks off my retainer if you feed me lunch."

"Don't you have a built-in cafeteria downstairs from your office?"

"A guy gets sick of red sauce every now and then," I say. "Come on. Surely you could use a little grown-up conversation after being cooped up in the house."

Emma makes a pretense of looking around the kitchen. "Sure . . . where's the other grown-up?"

"I'm ten years older than Jacob," I remind her. "So what are we eating?"

"Sea bass with garlic."

I sit down at one of the counter stools and watch her carry a pot of boiling something to the sink and dump it in a colander. The steam curls the hair around her face. "One of my favorites," I say. "I'm so glad you invited me."

"Fine," she sighs. "Stay already."

"All right, but only if you can contain your enthusiasm for my company."

She shakes her head. "Make yourself useful and set the table."

There's an intimacy to being in someone else's kitchen that makes me homesick—not for my apartment over the pizza place but for my childhood home. I grew up as the youngest of a big family in Buffalo; sometimes even now I miss the sound of chaos. "My mom used to cook fish on Fridays," I say as I open and close drawers, trying to find the silverware.

"Are you Catholic?"

"No—Norwegian. Fish is a Scandinavian aphrodisiac."

Emma's cheeks flush. "Did it work?"

"My parents had five kids," I say, and I gesture at the sea bass. "Foreplay on a platter."

"I guess I could go along with the metaphor," Emma murmurs. "My ex's cooking could be considered contraception."

"Would it be rude to ask how long you've been a single parent?"

"Yes," Emma says. "But the short answer is, since Jacob's diagnosis." She takes some milk out of the refrigerator and pours it into a pan, then begins to whip the contents with a hand mixer. "He's not involved with Jacob or Theo, except for the monthly child support."

"Well, you should be proud of doing it all on your own."

"Yeah, I'm proud. I have a son accused of murder. What mother wouldn't think of herself as a huge success after that?"

I look up at her. "Accused," I repeat. "Not convicted."

For a long moment she looks at me, as if she is afraid to believe there could be someone else who believes Jacob might not be guilty. Then she begins to make up individual plates. "Jacob, Theo!" she yells, and the boys file into the kitchen.

Jacob takes his and immediately returns to the living room and the television. Theo thunders down the stairs, takes one look at me sitting at the table, and frowns. "Shouldn't he be buying *us* lunch?" he asks.

"It's lovely to see you, too," I answer.

He looks at me. "Whatever."

As he shuffles back upstairs with his meal, Emma fixes plates for the two of us. "Usually we all sit down to dinner together," she says, "but sometimes it's nice to have a break from each other, too."

"I imagine that's hard when you're all under house arrest."

"It's pretty sad when the high point of my day is walking to the end of the driveway to get the mail." Leaning down, she sets a plate in front of me.

There's a block of white fish, creamy white mashed potatoes, and a tiny hill of white rice.

"Meringues for dessert?" I guess.

"Angel food cake."

I poke at the food with my fork.

She frowns. "Is the fish undercooked?"

"No, no—it's great. I've just, um, never seen anyone color-coordinate a meal before."

"Oh, it's February first," she says, as if that explains everything. "The first of every month is a White Food Day. I've been doing it so long I forget it's not normal."

I taste the potatoes; they're out of this world. "What do you do on the thirty-first? Burn everything to a black crisp?"

"Don't give Jacob any ideas," Emma says. "Would you like some milk?"

She pours me a glass, and I reach for it. "I don't get it. Why does the color of his food matter?"

"Why does the texture of velvet send him into a panic? Why can't he stand the hum of an espresso machine? There are a million questions I don't have answers for," Emma replies, "so the easiest thing to do is just roll with the punches and keep him from having a meltdown."

"Like he did in court," I say. "And jail."

"Exactly. So Monday's food is green, Tuesday's is red, Wednesday's is yellow . . . you get the idea."

I think for a moment. "Don't take this the wrong way, but it seems like sometimes Jacob's more adult than you or me—and other times, he gets totally overwhelmed."

"That's him. I truly think he's smarter than anyone I've ever met, but he's also more inflexible. And he takes every little thing that happens to heart, because he's the center of his universe."

"And yours," I point out. "He's the center of your universe, too."

She ducks her head. "I guess."

Maybe my Scandinavian parents knew what they were doing, because maybe it's the fish and maybe it's the way she looks in that moment—surprised, and a little flustered—but to my shock I realize I'd like to kiss her. However, I can't because she's my client's mother, and because she would probably knock me flat on my ass.

"I assume you have a plan of attack," she says.

My eyes widen—is she thinking the same thing about me? I tamp down an image of me pinning her to the table.

"The quicker the better," Emma says, and my pulse triples. She glances over her shoulder to the living room, where Jacob is slowly shoveling rice into his mouth. "I just want this whole nightmare to be over."

And with those words, I come crashing back to my sad little reality. I clear my throat, totally professional. "The most damaging discovery is the confession Jacob made. We need to try to get rid of it."

"I thought I was going to be able to sit with Jacob in the interrogation room. If I'd been there, it would never have gotten this far, I just know it. They had to be asking him questions he didn't understand, or firing them at him too fast."

"We have a transcript. The questions were pretty straightforward, I think. Did you tell Matson that Jacob had Asperger's before they started talking?"

"Yes, when he came to interview Jacob the first time."

"First time?"

Emma nods. "He was going through Jess's appointment book, and Jacob's social skills lesson was on it, so the detective asked him a few questions."

"Were you there to help translate?"

"Right here at the kitchen table," Emma says. "Matson acted like he completely understood Jacob's issues. That's why, when he told me to bring Jacob to the station, I assumed it was going to be the same sort of interview and that I could be part of it."

"That's good, actually," I tell her. "We can probably file a motion to suppress."

"What's that?"

Before I can answer, Jacob comes into the kitchen with his empty plate. He sets it in the sink and then pours himself a glass of Coca-Cola. "Under the Fifth Amendment of the U.S. Constitution, you have a right to remain silent, unless you waive that right, and in certain circumstances if the police don't read you your Miranda rights or properly ask you to waive them, anything you say can be used against you. A defense attorney can file a motion to suppress in order to prevent that evidence from coming before the jury." Then he walks back to the living room.

"That's just plain wrong," I mutter.

"It is?"

"Yeah," I say. "How come *he* gets to drink Coke on White Food Day?"

It takes a moment, and then, for the very first time, I hear the music of Emma Hunt's laugh.

Emma

I did not expect to feed Jacob's lawyer lunch.

I didn't expect to enjoy his company so much, either. But when he makes a joke about White Food Day—which is, let's face it, as ridiculous as everyone in the fairy tale pretending the emperor is beautifully clothed instead of stark naked—I can't help myself. I start to giggle. And before I know it, I am laughing so hard I cannot catch my breath.

Because when you get right down to it, it's funny when I ask my son, *How did you sleep?* And he answers: *On my stomach.*

It's funny when I tell Jacob I'll be there in

a minute and he starts counting down from sixty.

It's funny that Jacob used to grab my collar every time I came home, his interpretation of "catch you later."

It's funny when he begs for a forensics textbook on Amazon.com and I ask him to give me a ballpark figure and he says, *Second base.*

And it's funny when I move heaven and earth to give Jacob white food on the first of the month and he breezily pours himself a glass of Coke.

It's true what they say about Asperger's affecting the whole family. I've been doing this for so long, I forgot to consider what an outsider would think of our pale rice and fish, our long-standing routines—just like Jacob has no capacity to put himself in the shoes of someone else he encounters. And, as Jacob has learned one rebuff at a time, what looks pitiful from one angle looks absolutely hilarious from another.

"Life's not fair," I tell Oliver.

"That's the reason there are defense attorneys," he replies. "And Jacob's right about the legal jargon, by the way. I'm going to file a motion to suppress because the police were on notice that they weren't dealing with someone mentally able to truly understand his Miranda rights—"

"I know my Miranda rights!" Jacob yells from the other room. "You have the right to remain silent! Anything you say can and will be used against you in a court of law—"

"I've got it, Jacob, I'm good," Oliver calls back. He stands up and puts his plate on the counter. "Thanks for lunch. I'll let you know what happens with the hearing."

I walk him to the door and watch him unlock his car. Instead of getting into it, though, he reaches into the backseat and then walks toward me again, his face sober. "There's just one more thing," Oliver says. He reaches for my hand and presses a miniature-size Milky Way into it. "Just in case you want to sneak it in before Brown Thursday," he whispers, and for the second time that day, he leaves me smiling.

CASE 7: BLOOD IS THICKER THAN WATER

Ernest Brendel's sister didn't believe her brother's friend, who came to tell her, one fall day in 1991, that Ernest had been kidnapped—along with his wife, Alice, and young daughter, Emily—as part of a mafia scheme. But Christopher Hightower insisted that they needed ransom money, and as proof, he took her outside to Ernest's Toyota, the car he'd driven there. He pointed to the backseat, which was soaked through with blood. There was more blood in the trunk. Eventually, police would match that blood evidence to Ernest Brendel. But they'd also prove that Hightower—not the mafia—was to blame for Brendel's death.

To most people, Chris Hightower was a commodities broker with ties to his Rhode Island community. He taught Sunday school and worked with at-risk kids. But one fall day in 1991, he went on a murder rampage, killing his friend Ernest Brendel and Brendel's family. Facing financial trouble and estranged from his wife, Hightower purchased a crossbow and drove to Brendel's house. He hid in the garage and fired an arrow into Brendel's chest when the man arrived back home. While trying to escape, Brendel was shot twice more. He managed to crawl into the second car in the garage, a Toyota, where Hightower smashed his skull with a crowbar.

Hightower then picked Emily up from an after-school program at the YMCA by offering Brendel's license as proof that he was a family friend who could be trusted to take the girl home. When Alice Brendel arrived home that night, she and Emily were drugged with sleeping pills. It was the last time anyone from the Brendel family was seen alive.

The next day Hightower bought a brush, a hose, some muriatic acid, and a fifty-pound bag of lime. He scrubbed the garage with muriatic acid to clean up the blood. He cleaned the car with baking soda and washed away more blood.

Six weeks later a woman walking a dog stumbled over two shallow graves. One housed the remains of Ernest Brendel. The second held Alice Brendel—found with a scarf wrapped around her neck—and Emily, who was believed to have been buried alive. In the grave was an empty bag of lime. In the Toyota that Hightower had been driving, police found the torn corner of that bag of lime, as well as the Home Depot receipt for the lime and the muriatic acid.

Hightower was convicted and is serving three life sentences. With friends like that, who needs enemies?

7

Theo

I've done the math: eventually, I'm going to be the one who has to take care of my brother.

Don't get me wrong. I'm not such a colossal ass that I'm going to totally ignore Jacob when we're grown up and when (I can't even imagine this) Mom isn't around. What sort of pisses me off, though, is the silent assumption that, when Mom is unable to pick up after Jacob's messes anymore, three guesses who'll have to take over.

Once, I read this news story on the Internet about a woman in England whose son was retarded—big-time retarded, not disabled the way Jacob is disabled but, like, unable to brush his own teeth or remember to go to the bathroom when the urge strikes. (Let me just say here that if Jacob wakes up one day and needs an adult diaper, I don't care if I'm the last person on earth—I'm not changing it.) Anyway, this woman, she had emphysema and she was slowly dying, and it got to a point where she could barely sit up in a wheelchair all day, much less help her son out. Then there was a photo of her with her son, and although I was expecting a kid my age, Ronnie was easily in his fifties. He had a chin full of thick stubble and a potbelly poking out from his Power Rangers T-shirt, and he was giving his mother this big, gummy smile while he hugged her in her wheelchair, where she sat with tubes running into her nose.

I couldn't take my eyes off Ronnie. It was like I suddenly realized that one day, when I was married with a houseful of rug rats and doing the corporate thing, Jacob might still be watching his stupid *CrimeBusters* episodes and eating yellow foods on Wednesdays. My mom and Dr. Moon, Jacob's shrink, always talked about this abstractly, as evidence of why they thought vaccines had something to do with autism, and why autism was a relatively new phenomenon (*"If it's really been around forever, where are all the autistic kids who've grown up and become adults? Because believe me, even if they'd been diagnosed as something else we'd know who they are."*) But until that very second I hadn't made the connection that, one day, Jacob would be one of those adults with autism. Sure, he might be lucky enough to hold down a job like all those Aspies in Silicon Valley, but when he had a meltdown and started destroying his cubicle at said job, we all know who they'd call first.

Ronnie clearly never had grown up and never would, and that was why his mother was being featured in this newspaper, the *Guardian*: she had placed an ad asking for a family that would take in Ronnie and treat him like their own when she was dead. He was a sweet boy, she said, even if he still wet the bed.

Good freaking luck, I had thought. Who takes on someone else's crap willingly? I wondered what kind of people would respond to Ronnie's mom. Mother Teresa types, maybe. Or those families that you always see in the back pages of *People* magazine who foster-parent twenty special needs kids and somehow manage to shape them into a family. Or, worse, maybe some lonely old perv who figured a fellow like Ronnie wouldn't realize if he was copping a feel every now and then. Ronnie's mom said a group home wasn't an option, since he'd never been in one and couldn't adapt to one at this point. All she wanted was someone who might love him the way she did.

Anyway, the article got me thinking about Jacob. He could handle a group home, maybe, if he were still allowed to shower first in the morning.

But if I tossed him into one (and don't ask me how you even go about getting a spot), what would that say about me? That I was too selfish to be my brother's keeper, that I didn't love him.

Well, still, a little voice in my head said, *you never signed on for this.*

Then I realized: Neither did my mother, but it didn't make her love Jacob any less.

So here's the deal: I know that, down the road, Jacob will be my responsibility. When I find a girl I want to marry, I'm going to have to propose with this contingency—that Jacob and me, we're a package deal. When I least expect it, I might have to make excuses for him, or talk him down from his freak-out session, like my mom does now.

(I am not saying this out loud, but there is a part of me that's been thinking if Jacob is convicted of murder—if he's imprisoned for life—well, mine gets a little bit easier.)

I hate myself for even thinking that, but I'm not going to lie to you.

And I guess it doesn't matter if it's guilt that gets me to take care of Jacob in the future, or love, because I'll do it.

It just would have been nice to be asked, you know?

Oliver

Mama Spatakopoulous is standing at my office-apartment door with the day's offering. "We had a little extra rigatoni," she says. "And you're working so hard, you look skinnier every day."

I laugh and take the container out of her hands. It smells incredible, and Thor starts jumping around my ankles to make sure I don't forget to give him his cut of the bounty. "Thanks, Mrs. S.," I say, and as she turns to leave, I call her back. "Hey—what food do you know that's yellow?" I've been thinking about how Emma feeds Jacob, according to his color scheme. Hell, I've been thinking about Emma, period.

"You mean like a scrambled egg?"

I snap my fingers. "Right," I say. "Omelets, with Swiss cheese."

She frowns. "You want me to make you an omelet?"

"Hell no, I'm sticking to the rigatoni." Before I can explain the rest, my office phone starts to ring. Excusing myself, I hurry back inside and pick it up. "Oliver Bond's office," I say.

"Note to self," Helen Sharp replies. "That line's a little more effective when you hire someone else to deliver it."

"My, uh, secretary just stepped out to use the restroom."

She snorts. "Yeah, and I'm Miss America."

"Congratulations," I say, my voice dripping with sarcasm. "What's your talent? Juggling the heads of defense attorneys?"

She ignores me. "I'm calling about the suppression hearing. You subpoenaed Rich Matson?"

"The detective? Well . . . yeah." Who *else* was I supposed to subpoena, after all, in a motion that would try to suppress Jacob's confession at the police station?

"You don't have to subpoena him. I have to have Matson there, and I go first."

"What do you mean you go first? It's my motion."

"I know, but this is one of those weird cases where, even though it's your motion, the State has the burden of proof, and we have to put on all the evidence to prove the confession is good."

For practically every other motion, it's the other way around—if I want a ruling, I have to work my ass off to prove why I deserve it. How on earth was I supposed to know the exception to this rule?

I'm glad Helen's not in the room with me, because my face is bright red. "Well, *jeez,*" I say, feigning nonchalance. "I know that. I was just seeing if you were on your toes."

"While I have you on the phone, Oliver, I have to tell you. I don't think you can play this case both ways."

"What do you mean?"

"You can't claim your client's insane *and* that he didn't understand his Miranda rights. He recited them from memory, for God's sake."

"Where's the conflict?" I ask. "Who the hell memorizes Miranda verbatim?" Thor starts to bite my ankles, and I spill a little rigatoni into his dog dish. "Look, Helen. Jacob couldn't do three days in jail. He certainly can't do thirty-five years. I'm going to negotiate this case any way I can to make sure he doesn't get locked up again." I hesitate. "I don't suppose you would consider letting Jacob just live with his mom? You know, put him on probation for the long haul?"

"Sure. Let me get right back to you on that, after my lunch with the Easter Bunny, the Tooth Fairy, and Santa," Helen says. "This is *murder,* or have you forgotten that? You may have a client with autism, but I've got a dead body, and grieving parents, and that trumps *everything.* Maybe you can toss the special needs label around to get funding in schools or special accommodations, but it doesn't preclude guilt. See you in court, Oliver."

I slam down the phone and look down to find Thor lying on his side in a happy pasta coma. When the phone rings again, I grab it. "What?" I demand. "Was there some other legal procedure I've managed to screw up? Did you want to tell me you're going to tattle to the judge?"

"No," Emma says hesitantly. "But what legal procedure did you screw up?"

"Oh, I'm sorry. I thought you were . . . someone else."

"Apparently." There is a beat of silence. "Is everything okay with Jacob's case?"

"Couldn't be better," I tell her. "The prosecution's even doing my homework for me." I want to change the topic as quickly as possible, so I ask after Jacob. "How are things in the Hunt household today?"

"Well, that's sort of why I'm calling. Do you think you could do me a favor?"

A dozen favors run through my mind, most of which would greatly benefit me and my current lack of a love life. "What is it?"

"I need someone to stay with Jacob while I run out to do an errand."

"What errand?"

"That's sort of personal." She draws in her breath. "Please?"

There has to be some neighbor or relative better suited to the task than I am. But then again, maybe Emma doesn't have anyone else she can ask. From what I've seen these past few days, that's one hell of a lonely household. Still, I can't resist asking, "Why me?"

"The judge said someone over twenty-five."

I grin. "So all of a sudden I *am* old enough for you?"

"Forget I even asked," Emma snaps.

"I'll be there in fifteen minutes," I say.

Emma

Asking for help doesn't come easily to me, so you'd better believe that, if I actually do make a request, I've exhausted all other options. Which is why I don't feel great about making myself even more beholden to Oliver Bond by asking him to stay with Jacob while I run out of the house for this appointment. Even worse is scheduling the appointment, which feels like the physical manifestation of conceding defeat.

The bank is quiet on a Wednesday. There are a few retirees meticulously filling out deposit slips, and one of the tellers is talking to another about why Cabo is a better vacation destination than Cancún. I stand in the center of the bank, eyeing the banner advertising twelve-month CDs and a small table filled with logo paraphernalia—a stadium blanket, a mug, an umbrella—that can be mine if I open a new checking account.

"Can I help you?" a woman asks.

"I have an appointment," I say. "To see Abigail LeGris?"

"You can take a seat," she says, and she points to a bank of chairs outside a cubicle. "I'll let her know you're here."

I've never been rich, and I've never needed to be. Somehow, the boys and I have cobbled along on my writing and editing income, and the checks that Henry faithfully sends each month. We don't need much. We live in a modest house; we don't go out on the town very often or take vacations. I shop at Marshalls and a local thrift store that has recently become trendy for teenagers. The bulk of my expenses involve Jacob—his supplements and his therapies, which aren't covered by insurance. I think I got so used to making those accommodations fiscally that I stopped seeing them as accommodations and instead view them as the norm. But that said, sometimes I have lain awake at night and wondered what would happen if, God forbid, there was a car accident and we had medical bills that skyrocketed. If some remarkable therapy became available to Jacob that required a payout we could not afford.

In my laundry list of contingencies, I never thought to include the legal fees incurred when your son is accused of murder.

A woman with dyed jet-black hair and a suit that's wearing her instead of the other way around steps out of the cubicle. She has a very tiny nose stud and doesn't look much older than twenty. Maybe this is what happens to snowboard chicks whose knees get arthritic, to Goth girls whose eyeliner aggravates dry-eye syndrome—they are forced to grow up like the rest of us. "I'm Abby LeGris," she says.

When she shakes my hand, her collared shirt gaps a little, and I can see the edge of a Celtic tattoo on her neck.

She leads me into her cubicle and gestures for me to take a seat. "So," she says. "How can I help you today?"

"I was hoping to talk about a second mortgage. I, well, I need a little extra cash." As I say the words, I'm wondering if she can ask me what I'll use that cash for. If it's illegal to lie to a bank about that sort of thing.

"So basically you're looking for a line of credit," Abigail says. "That means you only pay us back for the portion you use."

Well, that sounds reasonable.

"How long have you lived in your home?" she asks.

"Nineteen years."

"Do you know how much you owe currently on your mortgage?"

"Not exactly," I say. "But we got the loan here."

"Let's look you up," Abigail says, and she asks me to spell my name so that she can find me on her computer system. "Your home's worth $300,000, and your first mortgage was for $220,000. Does that sound right?"

I can't remember. All I can see is the night Henry and I danced through the house that was ours, our bare feet echoing on the wood floor.

"The way it works, banks lend a portion of the equity of a home, around eighty percent. So that's $240,000. Then we subtract the amount of the first mortgage loan and . . ." She looks up from her calculator. "You're talking about a $20,000 line of credit."

I stare at her. "That's all?"

"In today's market, it's important for the client to have a vested interest in the house. Makes them less likely to default on the loan." She smiles at me. "Why don't we fill in some of the other blanks here," Abigail says. "Starting with your employer?"

I've read statistics that say references aren't checked more than fifty percent of the time, but surely a bank must fall in the other half. And once they call Tanya and realize I've quit, they'll be wondering how I'm going to pay *one* mortgage, much less *two*. Saying I am picking up the slack with self-employment won't help, either. I've been a freelance editor long enough to know that, for institutions like banks and future employers, *self-employed* translates to "nearly jobless but scraping by."

"I'm currently unemployed," I say softly.

Abigail leans back in her chair. "Well," she says. "Do you have other sources of income? Rental property? Dividends?"

"Child support," I manage.

"I'm going to be totally honest with you," she says. "It's not likely you'll get a loan without another source of income."

I cannot even look at her. "I really, really need the money."

"There are other credit sources," Abigail says. "Car title loans, loan predators, credit cards—but the interest will kill you in the long run. You're better off asking someone close to you. Is there a family member who might be able to help?"

But my parents are both gone, and it is a family member I'm *trying* to help. I'm the one—I'm always the one—who takes care of Jacob when things are falling apart.

"I wish there was something I could do," Abigail says. "Maybe once you get another job . . ."

I mumble my thanks and leave her cubicle while she is still speaking. In the parking lot, I sit in my car for a moment. My breath hangs in the cold air, like thought balloons of all the things I wish I could explain to Abigail LeGris. "I wish there was something I could do, too," I say out loud.

It isn't fair to Jacob or to Oliver, but I don't go right home. Instead, I drive past the elementary school. It's been a long time since I've had reason to go there—after all, my boys are grown now—but in the winter, they flood a front field into an ice rink, and kids bring their skates. During recess, little girls spin in circles on the ice; boys chase hockey pucks from one end to the other.

I pull over across the street, where I can watch. The kids who are playing outside are tiny—I'd say first or second graders—and it seems impossible that Jacob was ever that small. When he'd been a student here, his aide had taken him onto the ice rink with a pair of borrowed skates and had Jacob push two stack milk crates around. It was the way most toddlers learned to skate, and they'd quickly graduate to the tripod method, where a hockey stick provided a third leg for balance, before feeling confident enough to glide off without any props. But Jacob, he never did get past those milk crates. In skating—as with most physical things—he was clumsy. I remember coming to watch him, and seeing his feet splay out from beneath him, so that he'd land in a heap on the ice. *If it wasn't slippery, I wouldn't keep falling,* he said to me, apple-cheeked and breathless after recess, as if having something to blame made all the difference.

A sharp rap at my window makes me

jump. I roll it down to find a police officer standing there. "Ma'am," he says, "can I help you?"

"I was just . . . I had something in my eye," I lie.

"Well, if you're all right now, I have to ask you to move along. This is a bus zone; you can't stay here."

I glance at the kids on the ice again. They look like molecules colliding. "No," I say softly. "I can't."

When I get back home and open the door, I hear the sound of someone being beaten to a pulp. *Unhh. Ow. Ooof.* And then, to my horror, Jacob's laughter.

"Jacob?" I call, but there's no answer. Still wearing my coat, I rush into the house toward the sounds of the fight.

Jacob stands—perfectly unharmed—in front of the television in the living room. He's holding what looks like a white remote control. Oliver stands beside him, holding a matching remote control. Theo is sprawled behind them on the couch. "You so suck at this," he says. "Both of you."

"Hello?" I take a step into the room, but their eyes are all glued to the television. On the screen, two 3-D cartoon figures are boxing. I watch as Jacob moves his remote control, and the figure on the screen swings his right arm and knocks down the other character.

"Ha!" Jacob exclaims. "I knocked you out."

"Not yet," Oliver says, and he swings his arm without looking first, hitting me.

"Ouch," I say, rubbing my shoulder.

"Oh, jeez, sorry," Oliver says, lowering his remote control. "I didn't see you there."

"Obviously."

"Mom," Jacob says, his face animated in a way I haven't seen in weeks, "this is the coolest thing. You can golf and play tennis and bowl—"

"And assault people," I say.

"Technically, it's boxing," Oliver interjects.

"And where did this come from?"

"Oh, I brought it over. I mean, everyone likes playing the Wii."

I stare at him. "So you didn't think there was anything wrong with bringing a violent video game system into my house without asking my permission first?"

Oliver shrugs. "Would you have said yes?"

"No!"

"I rest my case." He grins. "Besides, we're not playing Call of Duty, Emma. We're just boxing. It's a *sport*."

"An *Olympic* sport," Jacob adds.

Oliver tosses his remote to Theo. "Take over for me," he instructs, and he walks me into the kitchen. "So how was your errand?"

"It was . . ." I start to answer but become distracted by the state of the kitchen. I missed it when I first ran through, trying to find the source of the moans and groans I was hearing, but now I see that pots and pans are crammed into the sink, and nearly every mixing bowl we own is stacked on the counter. A pan still sits on the range. "What happened here?"

"I'm going to clean up," Oliver promises. "I just got distracted playing with Theo and Jake."

"Jacob," I correct automatically. "He doesn't like nicknames."

"He didn't seem to mind when I called him that," Oliver says. He crosses in front of me to the oven and punches buttons to turn it off before grabbing a rainbow pot holder that Theo made me once for Christmas when he was small. "Have a seat. I saved you some lunch."

I sink into a chair—not because he told me to but because I honestly cannot remember the last time someone cooked for me, instead of the other way around. He transfers the warmed food to a plate he removes from the refrigerator. When Oliver leans forward to set it in front of me, I can smell his shampoo—like fresh-cut grass and pine trees.

There is an omelet with Swiss cheese. Pineapple. Corn bread. And on a separate plate, yellow cake.

I look up at him. "What is this?"

"It's from one of your mixes," he says. "Gluten-free. But the icing Jake and I made from scratch."

"I wasn't talking about the cake."

Oliver sits down at the kitchen table and reaches across to snag a piece of pineapple off the plate. "It's Yellow Wednesday, right?" he says, matter-of-fact. "Now eat it, before the omelet gets cold."

I take a bite, and then another. I eat the whole block of corn bread before I realize how hungry I am. Oliver watches me, grinning, and then bounces up just like his avatar did on the television screen after Jacob decked him. He opens the refrigerator. "Lemonade?" he asks.

I set down my fork. "Oliver, listen."

"You don't have to thank me," he answers. "Really. This was way more fun for me than reading discovery."

"There's something I have to tell you." I wait for him to sit down again. "I don't know how I'm going to pay you."

"Don't worry. My babysitting fees are pretty cheap."

"I'm not talking about that."

He looks away from me. "We'll figure something out."

"How?" I demand.

"I don't know. Let's just get through the trial and then we can sort it out—"

"*No.*" My voice falls like an ax. "I don't want your charity."

"Good, because I can't afford to give it," Oliver says. "Maybe you can do some paralegal work for me or editing or something."

"I don't know anything about law."

"That makes two of us," he replies, and then he grins. *"Kidding."*

"I'm serious. I'm not going to let you try this case if we can't work out some kind of payment schedule."

"There *is* one thing you could help me out with," Oliver admits. He looks like a cat that's devoured the whole carton of half-and-half. Like a guy waiting under the covers, watching a woman undress.

Where the hell did *that* thought come from?

Suddenly, my cheeks are burning. "I hope you aren't about to suggest that we—"

"Play a game of virtual tennis?" Oliver interrupts, and he holds up a small electronic game cartridge he's taken from his pocket. He widens his eyes, all innocence. "What did you *think* I was going to say?"

"Just so you know," I say, grabbing the cartridge out of his hand, "I have a wicked serve."

Oliver

At the police station, Jacob admitted that chipping Jess Ogilvy's tooth was an accident. That he moved her body and set up a crime scene around it.

Any juror who hears that is going to make the very simple and logical leap that he's confessed to murder. After all, it's not like dead bodies are lying around all over the place to feed the passions of autistic kids who are obsessed with criminology.

Which is why my best hope of keeping Jacob out of prison for life is to strike that entire police interview before it can be admitted as evidence. In order to do this, we have to have a suppression hearing, which means that—once again—Emma and Jacob and I have to face the judge.

The only problem is that the *last* time I had Jacob in a courtroom, things didn't exactly go swimmingly.

This is why I'm wound tight as a spring beside my client as we watch Helen Sharp lead the detective through a direct examination. "When did you first become involved with this case?" she asks.

"On the morning of Wednesday, January thirteenth, I received information that there was a missing person from Jess Ogilvy's boyfriend, Mark Maguire. I investigated, and on January eighteenth, after an extensive search, Ms. Ogilvy's body was found in a culvert. She had died of internal bleeding as the result of a head trauma, had multiple contusions and abrasions, and was wrapped in the defendant's quilt."

Jacob furiously writes something down on the pad I've placed in front of him and tips it toward me. *He's wrong.*

I take the pad from him, suddenly hopeful. An oversight like this bit of mistaken evidence would be just the kind of detail Jacob might have neglected to mention to anyone. *It wasn't your quilt?*

It's not technically internal bleeding, he scrawls. *It's blood pooling between the dura that covers the brain and the arachnoid, which is the middle layer of the meninges.*

I roll my eyes. *Thanks, Dr. Hunt,* I write.

Jacob frowns. *I'm not a doctor,* he scribbles.

"Let's back up a minute," Helen says. "Did you speak to the defendant before finding Ms. Ogilvy's body?"

"Yes. As we went through the victim's calendar, I interviewed everyone who'd come in contact with her on the day she was last seen, and the ones who were supposed to meet with her. Jacob Hunt was due to have a tutoring session with Ms. Ogilvy at 2:35 P.M. on the afternoon of her disappearance. I met with him to inquire whether or not that meeting had taken place."

"Where did you meet?"

"At the defendant's home."

"Who was present when you got to the house that day?" Helen asks.

"Jacob Hunt and his mother. I believe his younger brother was upstairs."

"Had you ever met Jacob before this day?"

"Once," the detective says. "He showed up at a crime scene I was working several days earlier."

"Did you think he might be a suspect?"

"No. Other officers had seen him on-site before, too. He liked to show up and offer unsolicited advice about crime scene analysis." He shrugs. "I figured he was just a kid who wanted to play cop."

"When you first met with Jacob, did anyone tell you he had Asperger's syndrome?"

"Yes," Matson says. "His mother. She said Jacob had a very hard time communicating and that a lot of his behaviors which might look like guilty behavior to an outside observer were actually the symptoms of his autism."

"Did she ever tell you that you couldn't speak with her son?"

"No," Matson says.

"Did the defendant tell you that he didn't want to speak with you?"

"No."

"Did he give you any indication on that first day you met that he didn't understand what you were saying, or who you were?"

"He knew exactly who I was," Matson replies. "He wanted to talk about forensics."

"What did you discuss during that initial meeting?"

"I asked him if he'd seen Jess for his

appointment, and he said no. He also told me that he knew Jess's boyfriend, Mark. That was pretty much it. I left my card with his mother and said that she should give a call if anything else came up, or if Jacob remembered something."

"How long did this conversation last?"

"I don't know; all together five minutes maybe?" Matson says.

The prosecutor nods. "When did you next learn that Jacob Hunt knew something more about this case?"

"His mother called and said Jacob had some new information about Jess Ogilvy. Apparently he'd forgotten to tell us that, when he was at her house, waiting for her, he tidied up some things and alphabetized the CDs. The victim's boyfriend had mentioned that the CDs had been reorganized, and that made me want to talk to Jacob some more."

"Did Jacob's mother tell you he wouldn't understand you if you asked him questions?"

"She said that he might have trouble understanding questions that were phrased a certain way."

"During that second conversation, did Jacob say he didn't want to talk to you, or that he didn't understand your questions?"

"No."

"Did the defendant's mother have to translate for him, or tell you to rephrase your questions?"

"No."

"And how long did this second conversation last?"

"Ten minutes, tops."

"Did you have another conversation with Jacob Hunt?" Helen asks.

"Yes, the afternoon after we discovered Jess Ogilvy's body in the culvert."

"Where did that conversation with the defendant take place?"

"The police station."

"Why did Jacob come in to speak to you again?"

"His mother called me," Matson says. "She was very upset because she believed her son had something to do with the murder of Jess Ogilvy."

Suddenly Jacob stands up and faces the gallery, so that he can see Emma. "You thought that?" he asks, his hands balled into fists at his sides.

Emma looks like she's been hit in the stomach. She looks at me for help, but before I can do or say anything, the judge smacks his gavel. "Mr. Bond, control your client."

Jacob starts flapping his left hand. "I need a sensory break!"

Immediately, I nod. "Your Honor, we need a recess."

"Fine. Take five minutes," the judge says, and he leaves the bench.

The minute he's gone, Emma steps over the bar. "Jacob, listen to me."

But Jacob's not listening; he's emitting a high-pitched hum that has Helen Sharp covering her ears. "Jacob," Emma repeats, and she puts her hands on either side of his face, forcing him to face her. He closes his eyes.

"I shot the sheriff," Emma sings, *"but I didn't shoot the deputy. I shot the sheriff, but I did not shoot the deputy. Reflexes got the better of me . . . and what is to be must be."*

The bailiff standing in the room shoots her a dirty glance, but the tension melts out of Jacob's shoulders. *"Every day the bucket a-go a well,"* he sings, in his flat monotone. *"One day the bottom a-go drop out."*

"That's it, baby," Emma murmurs.

Helen is watching every move, her mouth slightly agape. "Gee," she says, "my kid only knows the words to 'Candy Man.'"

"Hell of a song to be singing when you're on trial for murder," the bailiff mutters.

"Do not listen to him," Emma says. "You listen to me. I believe you. I believe you didn't do it."

Interestingly, she doesn't look Jacob in the eye when she says this. Now, he'd never have noticed—since he's not looking her in the eye, either. But by Emma's own reasoning with the detective, if you assume that someone who doesn't look you in the eye is either lying or on the autism spectrum—and Emma isn't on the autism spectrum—what does that imply?

Before I can interpret this any further, the judge comes back, and Helen and Rich Matson take their places again. "Your only job here is to stay cool," I whisper to Jacob, as I lead him back to the defense table. And then I watch him take a piece of paper, fold it into an accordion pleat, and begin to fan himself.

"How did Jacob get to the police station?" Helen asks.

"His mother brought him down."

Jacob fans a little faster.

"Was he placed under arrest?"

"No," the detective says.

"Was he brought in a cruiser?"

"No."

"Did a police officer accompany his mother to the police department?"

"No. She brought her son in voluntarily."

"What did you say when you saw him there?"

"I asked if he could help me with some cases."

"What was his response?"

"He was extremely excited and very willing to go with me," Matson says.

"Did he indicate that he wanted to have his mother in the room, or that he wasn't comfortable without her?"

"To the contrary—he said he wanted to help me."

"Where did the interview take place?"

"In my office. I started to ask him about the crime scene he'd crashed a week earlier, which involved a man who died of hypothermia. Then I told him I'd really like to pick his brain about Jess Ogilvy's case, but that it was a little trickier, since it was still an open investigation. I said he'd have to waive his rights to not discuss it, and Jacob quoted me Miranda. I read along as he recited it verbatim, and then I asked him to read over it and initial it and sign at the bottom so that I knew he understood, and hadn't just memorized some random words."

"Was he able to answer your questions intelligibly?" Helen asks.

"Yes."

Helen offers the Miranda form into evidence. "No further questions, Your Honor," she says.

I stand up and button my suit jacket. "Detective, the very first time you met with Jacob, his mother was there, right?"

"Yes."

"Did she stay the entire time?"

"Yes, she did."

"Great," I say. "How about the second time you met with Jacob? Was his mother there?"

"Yes."

"In fact, she's the one who brought him to the station at your request, correct?"

"That's right."

"But when she asked you if she could stay with him, you refused?"

"Well, yeah," Matson says. "Since her son is eighteen."

"Yes, but you were also aware that Jacob is on the autism spectrum, isn't that true?"

"It is, but nothing he'd said previously had led me to believe he couldn't be interrogated."

"Still, his mother told you he had a hard time with questions. That he got confused under pressure, and that he couldn't really understand subtleties of language," I say.

"She explained something about Asperger's syndrome, but I didn't pay a lot of attention to it. He seemed perfectly capable to me. He knew every legal term imaginable, for God's sake, and he was more than happy to talk."

"Detective, when you told Jacob what happens during an autopsy, didn't he quote *Silence of the Lambs* to you?"

Matson shifts in his chair. "Yes."

"Does that indicate that he really understood what he was doing?"

"I figured he was trying to be funny."

"It's not the first time Jacob's used a movie quote to answer one of your questions, is it?"

"I can't recall."

"Let me help you, then," I say, grateful to Jacob for his verbatim memory of the conversation. "When you asked him if Jess and her boyfriend, Mark, fought, he said *'Hasta la vista, baby,'* didn't he?"

"That sounds about right."

"And he quoted a third movie line to you at one point during your interrogation, didn't he, Detective?"

"Yes."

"When was that?"

"I asked him why he'd done it."

"And he said?"

"Love means never having to say you're sorry."

"The only crime Jacob Hunt committed," I argue, "is quoting from a movie as sappy as *Love Story.*"

"Objection," Helen says. "Are we doing closings now? Because nobody sent me the memo."

"Sustained," the judge answers. "Mr. Bond, save the editorial commentary for yourself."

I turn back to Matson. "How did that third interview, at the station, end?"

"Abruptly," the detective replies.

"In fact Ms. Hunt arrived with me, saying that her son wanted a lawyer, didn't she?"

"That's right."

"And once she made that announcement, what did Jacob say?"

"That he wanted a lawyer," Matson answers. "Which is when I stopped questioning him."

"Nothing further," I say, and I sit down beside Jacob again.

Freddie Soto is a former cop whose oldest son is profoundly autistic. After working for the state police in North Carolina for years, he went back to school and got his master's in psychology. Now, he specializes in teaching law enforcement professionals about autism. He's written articles for the *FBI Law Enforcement Bulletin* and for *Sheriff* magazine. He was a consultant for ABC

News on a *20/20* special about autism and the law and false confession. He helped develop the state of North Carolina's 2001 curriculum about why law enforcement needs to recognize autism, a curriculum now in use in police departments around the globe.

His fee for expert testimony is $15,000 plus first-class plane fare, which I didn't have. But we started talking on the phone, and when he heard that I had been a farrier, he divulged that he had partial ownership of a racehorse that wound up with flat feet. The horse meant everything to his son, so he had fought to keep the animal from being euthanized. When I suggested pads to keep the soles from bruising and wedges on the hooves with integral frog supports and a soft packing material underneath to realign the hoof pasterns by reducing the weight on the heels without crushing the horns and deforming the heels, he said he'd testify for free if I agreed to fly down to North Carolina and take a look at his horse when the trial was through.

"Can you tell us, Mr. Soto, would someone with Asperger's syndrome have the same difficulties dealing with law enforcement personnel as someone who is autistic?" I ask.

"Naturally, since Asperger's is on the autism spectrum. For example, a person with Asperger's might be nonverbal. He might have a hard time interpreting body language, like a command presence or a defensive pose. He may have a meltdown if confronted by flashing lights or sirens. His lack of eye contact may lead an officer to believe he's not listening. He may appear stubborn or angry. Instead of answering a question asked by an officer, he might repeat what the officer has said. He'll have trouble seeing from someone else's point of view. And he will tell the truth—relentlessly."

"Have you ever met Jacob, Mr. Soto?"

"I have not."

"Have you had a chance to review his medical records from Dr. Murano?"

"Yes, fifteen years' worth," he says.

"What in those medical records fits the possible indicators for Asperger's?"

"From what I understand," Soto replies, "Jacob is a very bright young man who has trouble making eye contact, doesn't communicate very well, speaks in movie quotes from time to time, exhibits stimulatory behavior, such as flapping his hands, and sings certain songs repetitively as a means of self-calming. He also can't break down complex questions, has trouble judging personal space and interpreting body language, and is supremely honest."

"Mr. Soto," I ask, "have you also had a chance to read the police reports and the transcript of Jacob's recorded statement with Detective Matson?"

"Yes."

"In your opinion, did Jacob understand his Miranda rights at the time they were given?"

"Objection," Helen says. "Your Honor, Miranda is intended to prevent violations of an individual's Fifth Amendment rights purposefully by the police; however, there's nothing that requires the police to know all the inner workings of any particular individual defendant's developmental abilities. The test under a motion to suppress is whether the police officer fulfilled his obligation, and that shouldn't be flipped around to ask whether Jacob Hunt has some unknown disorder that the officer should have identified."

There is a tug on the bottom of my suit jacket, and Jacob passes me a note:

"Your Honor," I say, and I read exactly what Jacob's written: *"The test under Miranda is whether a defendant knowingly and voluntarily has waived his right to silence."*

"Overruled," the judge says, and I glance at Jacob, who grins.

"It's highly doubtful that Jacob truly understood Miranda, given the way Detective Matson behaved. There are things a law enforcement agency can do to make sure autistic people understand their rights in that sort of situation, and those measures were not implemented," Soto replies.

"Such as?"

"When I go to police departments and work with the officers, I recommend talking in very short, direct phrases and allowing for delayed responses to questions. I tell them to avoid figurative expressions, like *Are you pulling my leg?* Or *You think that's bright?* I suggest that they avoid threatening language and behavior, that they wait for a response or eye contact, and that they don't assume a lack thereof is evidence of disrespect or guilt. I tell them to avoid touching the individual and to be aware of a possible sensitivity to lights, sounds, or even K-9 units."

"Just to be clear, Mr. Soto, were any of those protocols followed, in your opinion?"

"No."

"Thanks," I say, and I sit down beside Jacob as Helen rises to cross-examine my witness. I am excited—no, I am *beyond* excited. I have just knocked it out of the park. I mean, honestly, what are the odds of finding an expert like this, in a field no one has even heard of, who can win your motion for you?

"What stimuli inside Detective Matson's office would have set Jacob off?" Helen asks.

"I don't know. I wasn't there."

"So you don't know if there were loud noises or bright lights, do you?"

"No, but I have yet to find a police department that's a warm and welcoming space," Soto says.

"So in your opinion, Mr. Soto, in order to effectively interrogate someone who has Asperger's syndrome, you have to take them down to Starbucks and buy them a vanilla latte?"

"Obviously not. I'm just saying that measures could have been taken to make Jacob more comfortable, and by being more comfortable, he might have been more aware of what was going on at the time instead of being suggestible enough to do or say whatever it took to get out of there as quickly as possible. A kid with Asperger's is particularly prone to making a false confession if he thinks it's what the authority figure wants to hear."

Oh, I want to hug Freddie Soto. I want to make his racehorse run again.

"For example," he adds, "when Jacob said,

Are we done now? Because I really have to go, that's a classic response to agitation. Someone who knew about Asperger's might have recognized that and backed off. Instead, according to the transcript, Detective Matson hammered Jacob with a series of questions that further confused him."

"So it's your expectation that police officers need to know what each individual defendant's triggers are in order to effectively interrogate them?"

"It sure wouldn't hurt."

"You do understand, Mr. Soto, that when Detective Matson asked Jacob if he knew his Miranda rights, Jacob actually recited them verbatim rather than waiting for the detective to read them aloud?"

"Absolutely," Soto replies. "But Jacob could probably also recite to you the entire script of *The Godfather: Part II.* That doesn't mean he has any real understanding of or emotional attachment to that particular film."

Beside me, I see Jacob open his mouth to object, and immediately, I grab his forearm where it rests on the table. Startled, he turns to me, and I shake my head, hard.

"But how do you know he *doesn't* understand his Miranda rights?" Helen asks. "You yourself said he's very bright. And he told the detective he understood them, didn't he?"

"Yes," Soto admits.

"And by your own testimony, didn't you also say Jacob is supremely honest?"

My brilliant witness, my stellar find, opens and closes his mouth without answering.

"Nothing further," Helen says.

I am about to tell the judge that the defense rests when, instead, something else entirely pops out of my mouth. "Mr. Soto," I ask, getting to my feet, "would you agree that there is a difference between a true understanding of the law and a photographic memory of the law?"

"Yes. That's exactly the difference between someone with Asperger's and someone who truly understands Miranda rights."

"Thank you, Mr. Soto, you can step down," I say, and I turn back to the judge. "I'd like to call Jacob Hunt to the stand."

Nobody is happy with me.

During the recess I asked for before Jacob's testimony, I told him that all he had to do was answer a few questions. That it was okay to speak out loud when I asked questions, or if the judge or Helen Sharp asked questions, but that he shouldn't say anything other than the answers to those questions.

In the meantime, Emma danced around us in circles, as if she was trying to find the best spot to sink her knife into me. "You can't put Jacob on the stand," she argued. "That's going to traumatize him. What if he breaks down? How's that going to look?"

"That," I said, "would be the best that could possibly happen."

That shut her up pretty quickly.

Now, Jacob is visibly nervous. He's rocking on the chair in the witness stand, and his head is bent at some strange angle. "Can you tell us your name?" I ask.

Jacob nods.

"Jacob, you have to speak out loud. The stenographer's writing down your words, and she has to be able to hear you. Can you tell me your name?"

"Yes," he says. "I can."

I sigh. "What is your name?"

"Jacob Hunt."

"How old are you?"

"Eighteen."

"Jacob, do you know what the Miranda warning says?"

"Yes."

"Can you tell me?"

"You have the right to remain silent. Anything you say can and will be used against you in a court of law. You have the right to speak to an attorney, and to have an attorney present during any questioning. If you cannot afford a lawyer, one will be provided for you at government expense."

"Now, Jacob," I ask, "do you know what that means?"

"Objection," Helen argues as Jacob starts to hit his fist against the side of the witness box.

"I'll withdraw the question," I say. "Jacob, can you tell me what the Second Amendment to the Constitution says?"

"A well regulated Militia, being necessary to the security of a free State, the right of the people to keep and bear Arms shall not be infringed," Jacob recites.

Atta boy, I think. "What does that mean, Jacob?"

He hesitates. *"You'll shoot your eye out, kid!"*

The judge frowns. "Isn't that from *A Christmas Story*?"

"Yes," Jacob replies.

"Jacob, you don't know what the Second Amendment really means, do you?"

"Yes, I do: *A well regulated Militia, being necessary to the security of a free State, the right of the people to keep and bear Arms shall not be infringed.*"

I look at the judge. "Your Honor, nothing further."

Helen is already on the prowl. I watch Jacob shrink back in his seat. "Did you know Detective Matson wanted to talk to you about what happened to Jess?"

"Yes."

"Were you willing to talk to him about that?"

"Yes."

"Can you tell me what it means to waive your rights?"

I hold my breath as Jacob hesitates. And then slowly, beautifully, the right fist he's been banging against the wooden railing unfurls and is raised over his head, moving back and forth like a metronome.

Emma

I was furious when Oliver pulled this stunt. Wasn't he the one who'd said putting Jacob on the witness stand would only be detrimental to the trial? Even if it was a judge here, not a jury of twelve, Jacob was bound to suffer. Thrusting him into a situation certain to make him have a meltdown simply for the sake of being able to say to the judge, *See, I told you so,* seemed cruel and pointless, the equivalent of jumping off a building in order to command attention, which you'd be too dead to enjoy in the aftermath. But Jacob rose to the occasion—granted, with stims and tics. He didn't freak out, not even when that Dragon Lady of a prosecutor started in on him. I have never been so proud of him.

"I've listened to all the evidence," Judge Cuttings says. "I've observed the defendant, and I do not believe that he voluntarily waived his Miranda rights. I also believe that Detective Matson was on notice that this defendant has a developmental disorder and yet did nothing to address that disability. I'm going to grant the motion to suppress the defendant's statement at the police station."

Once the judge leaves, Oliver turns around and gives me a high five as Helen Sharp begins to pack up her briefcase. "I'm sure you'll be in touch," Helen says to Oliver.

"So what does it mean?" I ask.

"She's going to have to make her case without Jacob's confession. Which means that the prosecutor's job just got a lot harder."

"So it's good."

"It's *very* good," Oliver says. "Jacob, you were perfect up there."

"Can we go?" Jacob asks. "I'm starving."

"Sure." Jacob stands up and starts walking down the aisle. "Thanks," I say to Oliver, and I fall into place beside my son. I am halfway up the aisle when I turn around.

Oliver is whistling to himself, pulling on his overcoat. "If you want to join us for lunch tomorrow . . . Fridays are blue," I tell him.

He looks up at me. "Blue? That's a tough one. Once you get past the blueberries and yogurt and blue Jell-O, what's left?"

"Blue corn chips. Blue potatoes. Blue Popsicles. Bluefish."

"That's not technically blue," Oliver points out.

"True," I reply, "but it's still allowed."

"Blue Gatorade's always been my favorite," he says.

On the way home, Jacob reads the newspaper out loud from his spot in the backseat. "They're building a new bank downtown, but it's going to eliminate forty parking spaces," he tells me. "A guy was taken to Fletcher Allen after he crashed his motorcycle into a snow fence." He flips the page. "What's today?"

"Thursday."

His voice races with excitement. "Tomorrow at three o'clock Dr. Henry Lee is going to be speaking at the University of New Hampshire, and the public is welcome!"

"Why is that name familiar?"

"Mom," Jacob says, "he's only the most famous forensic scientist ever. He's worked on thousands of cases, like the suicide of Vince Foster and JonBenét Ramsey's murder and the O. J. Simpson trial. There's a phone number here for information." He starts rummaging in my purse for my cell phone.

"What are you doing?"

"Calling for tickets."

I glance at him in the rearview mirror. "Jacob. We cannot go see Dr. Lee. You aren't allowed to leave your house, much less the state."

"I left the house today."

"That's different. You went to court."

"You don't understand. This is *Henry Lee*. This is a once-in-a-lifetime opportunity. I'm not asking to go out to a movie. There's got to be something Oliver can do to get a furlough or something for the day."

"I don't think so, babe."

"So you're not even going to try? You're just going to assume that the answer's no?"

"That's right," I tell him, "since the alternative to having you under house arrest is being thrown back in jail. And I am a hundred percent sure that the warden would

not have given you a day pass to see Henry
Lee speak, either."

"I bet he *would,* if you told him who
Henry Lee was."

"This isn't up for discussion, Jacob," I say.

"*You* left the house yesterday . . ."

"That's completely different."

"Why? The judge said you had to watch
over me at all times."

"Me, or another adult—"

"See, he already made exceptions for *you*—"

"Because I wasn't the one who—" Realizing what I am about to say, I snap my mouth
shut.

"Who what?" Jacob's voice is tight. "Who
killed someone?"

I turn in to our driveway. "I didn't say
that, Jacob."

He stares out the window. "You didn't
have to."

Before I can stop him, he jumps out of
the car while I'm still pulling to a stop. He
runs past Theo, who stands at the front door
with his arms crossed. A strange car is
parked in the driveway, with a man behind
the wheel.

"I tried to get him to leave," Theo says,
"but he said he would wait for you." With that

information, he goes back into the house and leaves me face-to-face with a small, balding man with a goatee shaved in the shape of a W. "Ms. Hunt?" he says. "I'm Farley McDuff, the founder of Neurodiversity Nation. Maybe you've heard of us?"

"I'm afraid I haven't . . ."

"It's a blog for people who believe that atypical neurological development is a matter of simple human difference and, as such, should be celebrated instead of cured."

"Look, this isn't a very good time right now—"

"There's no time like the present, Ms. Hunt, for those in the autism community to stand up for the respect they deserve. Instead of having neurotypicals try to destroy diversity, we believe in a new world where neurological plurality is accepted."

"Neurotypical," I repeat.

"Another word for what's colloquially called 'normal,'" he says. "Like you." He smiles at me, but he cannot hold my gaze for more than a heartbeat. He thrusts a pamphlet into my hand.

MAJORITISM—An unrecognized condition.

Majoritism is an incapacitating developmental condition which affects 99% of the population in areas of mental function, including self-awareness, attention, emotional capacity, and sensory development. The effects begin at birth and cannot be cured. Luckily, the number of those afflicted by majoritism is decreasing, as a better understanding of autism emerges.

"You've got to be kidding me," I say. I step around him, intent on getting inside my house.

"Why is it so delusional to think that a person who feels someone else's grief or pain isn't hampered by that excess of emotion? Or that imitating others in order to fit in to the crowd is more acceptable than doing what interests you at any given moment? Why isn't it considered rude to look a total stranger in the eye when you first meet him, or to invade his personal space by shaking hands? Couldn't it be considered a flaw to veer off topic based on a comment someone else makes instead of sticking to your original subject? Or to be oblivious when something in your environment changes—like a piece of clothing that gets moved from a drawer to a closet?"

That makes me think of Jacob. "I really have to go—"

"Ms. Hunt, we think that we can help your son."

I hesitate. "Really?"

"Do you know who Darius McCollum is?"

"No."

"He's a man from Queens, New York, who has a passion for anything transit-related. He wasn't much older than Jacob the first time he took over the E train headed from the World Trade Center to Herald Square. He's taken city buses out for a spin. He tripped the emergency brakes on an N train and impersonated a transit worker in uniform in order to fix it himself. He's posed as a railroad safety consultant. He's been convicted more than nineteen times. He also has Asperger's."

A shiver goes down my spine that has nothing to do with the cold. "Why are you telling me this?"

"Do you know of John Odgren? At age sixteen he stabbed a student to death at a suburban high school in Sudbury, Massachusetts. He'd previously had knives and a fake handgun confiscated at school but didn't have a history of violent behavior. He has Asperger's, and a special interest in weapons. But as a result of the stabbing, the link between Asperger's and violence was raised— when in fact medical experts say there's no known link between Asperger's and violence, and in fact kids diagnosed with the disorder are far more likely to be teased as victims than to be perpetrators themselves." He takes a step forward. "We can help you. We can rally the autistic community to spread the word. Imagine all the mothers who'll stand behind you, once they realize their own autistic children might be targeted by neurotypicals once again—not just to be 'fixed' this time around but possibly to be charged with murder over what might otherwise be a misunderstanding."

I want to say that Jacob is innocent, but— God help me—I can't make the words come out of my mouth. I don't want my son to be the poster child for *anything*. I just want my life to go back to the way it used to be. "Mr. McDuff, please get off my property, or I'll call the police."

"How convenient that they'd already know the quickest route here," he says, but he moves back toward his car. He hesitates at the door, a small, sad smile twitching at the corner of his mouth. "It's a neurotypical world, Ms. Hunt. We're just taking up space in it."

I find Jacob at his computer. "Tickets are thirty-five dollars each," he says, without turning to face me.

"Have you ever heard of a group called Neurodiversity Nation?"

"No. Why?"

I shake my head and sit down on his bed. "Never mind."

"According to MapQuest, it will take three hours and eighteen minutes to get there."

"To get where?" I ask.

"UNH? Remember? Dr. Henry Lee?" He pivots in his chair.

"You can't go, Jacob. Period. I'm very sorry, but I'm sure Dr. Lee will be speaking again sometime in the future."

Will you be in prison then?

The thought jumps into my head like a cricket onto a picnic blanket, and it is equally unwelcome. I walk toward his desk and stare down at him. "I need to ask you something," I say quietly. "I need to ask you, because

I haven't, and I need to hear your voice saying the answer. Jess is dead, Jacob. Did you kill her?"

His face collapses around a frown. "I did *not*."

The breath I have not realized I am holding rushes out of me. I throw my arms around Jacob, who stiffens in the sudden embrace. "Thank you," I whisper. "Thank you for that."

Jacob doesn't lie to me. He can't. He tries, but it is so blatantly obvious that all I have to do is give a beat of silence before he caves in and admits the truth.

"You do realize that keeping me locked up in this house for weeks or months could be considered criminal behavior. That good parents do not treat their children like caged animals."

"And you do realize that even if we had Oliver go before the judge to ask for an exception, Dr. Lee's speech would be over before the judge scheduled the hearing?" I point out. "I'm sure it will be recorded. We can listen to the podcast."

"That's not the same!" Jacob yells.

The cords of his neck stand out in relief; he is dangerously close to losing control again. I moderate my voice so that it spreads like a balm. "Take a deep breath. Your Asperger's is showing."

"I hate you," Jacob says. "This has nothing to do with my Asperger's. It's about being made a slave in my own household." He shoves me aside, heading for the hallway.

I use every ounce of strength I can to hold him back. I know better, but sometimes, when Jacob is being particularly supercilious, I can't help but argue back. "You walk out that door, and you'll be in jail before morning. And this time, I swear, I won't try to get you out," I tell him. "I may be six inches shorter than you and fifty pounds lighter, but I am still your mother, and no means no."

He struggles against the restraint of my arms for a few seconds, and then all the fight goes out of him. Almost too easily, he sinks onto his bed and puts a pillow over his head.

Without another word, I back out of Jacob's bedroom and close the door behind me. I lean against the wall for a moment, sagging under the weight of the relief his admission has brought me. I had been telling myself that the reason I hadn't directly asked Jacob earlier if he had murdered Jess was that I was afraid he'd be disappointed in me for even believing it was a possibility. But the real reason I'd waited so long was that I was afraid to hear his answer. How many times, after all, had I asked Jacob a question only to hope for a white lie?

Do I have too many wrinkles?

I just baked these—it's a new recipe. What do you think?

I know you're angry, but you don't really *wish your brother had never been born, do you?*

Even today on the witness stand, the expert Oliver had found said Aspie kids don't lie.

Then again.

Jacob told me Jess didn't talk to him that Tuesday he was supposed to meet with her, but he didn't tell me she was dead.

Jacob told me that he'd been to Jess's house, but he neglected to mention that he'd found it in a state of disarray.

And he never mentioned taking his rainbow quilt anywhere.

Technically, he had told me the truth. And at the same time, he had lied by omission.

"Mom?" Theo yells. "I think I set the toaster on fire . . ."

I hurry downstairs. By the time I am extricating the charred bagel with two knives, I've convinced myself that everything Jacob *hasn't* told me has been an oversight, a typical Aspie side effect of having so much information that some of it gets lost or forgotten.

I have convinced myself that this could not have been deliberate.

Jacob

The term *stir-crazy* comes from the early 1900s. *Stir* was slang for *prison,* based on the Gypsy word *stariben. Stir-crazy* was actually a play on an older expression, *stir-bugs,* which described a prisoner who became mentally unstable due to being locked up too long.

You can attribute my next actions to the fact that 1 was stir-crazy, or to the correct stimulus: the fact that Dr. Henry Lee, my idol, was going to be 188.61 miles away from me, and 1 was not going to be able to meet him. In spite of my mother's assertions that *if* 1 went to college 1 would have to go some-where local, where 1 could live at home and benefit from her help and organization, I had long assumed that, one day, I'd apply to the University of New Haven (never mind that as a high school senior I was already over a month past deadline). I would get into the criminalist program he'd founded there, where I would be plucked from undergraduate obscurity by Dr. Lee himself, who would notice my attention to detail and my inability to be distracted by girls or frat parties or loud music emanating from dorm windows and would invite me to help him solve a real current case and consider me his protégé.

Now, of course, I had an even more pressing reason to meet him.

Imagine, Dr. Lee, I would begin. *You have set up a crime scene to point to someone else's involvement and wind up a suspect yourself.* And then together we would analyze what might have been conceived differently, to prevent it from happening the next time.

My mother and I argue about the same things over and over, such as why she refuses to treat me normally. This would be a classic example, where she is taking my desire to see Dr. Lee and twisting it into a pretzel so that it seems like an unreasonable Aspie request, instead of one grounded in reality. There are many instances where I want to do things other kids my age do:

1. Get a license and drive a car.

2. Live on my own at college.

3. Go out with my friends without her having to call their parents first and explain my quirks.
   a. It should be noted, of course, that this would apply to a time when I currently *had* friends.

4. Get a job so that I have money for the above.
   a. It should be noted that she did let me get a job, and unfortunately to date the only people who've chosen to hire me were completely unreasonable asses who couldn't see the big picture, like whether being five minutes late on a shift is truly going to cause a global catastrophe.

Instead, I watch Theo sail out the door while she waves good-bye to him. Unlike me, he will be allowed to get his driver's license sooner or later. Imagine how incredibly humiliating it will be for me to be driven around by my younger brother, the same child who used his own poop to paint a mural on the garage door once.

My mother argued that I could not have it both ways. I could not ask to be treated like an ordinary eighteen-year-old and also demand clothing with the tags cut out and refuse to drink orange juice because of its name. Maybe I did feel that I could have it both ways—be disabled sometimes and normal at other times—but then again, why *couldn't* I? Let's say that Theo sucked at growing vegetables but was really good at bowling. My mother might treat him like a slightly remedial student if she was teaching him to grow rutabagas, but when she hit the lanes with him, she'd ditch the slow voice. Not all humans have one standard, so why should I?

At any rate, whether I have simply been cooped up too long or whether I am suffering acute mental distress from my soon-to-be missed opportunity with Dr. Lee, I do the only thing that seems justifiable at the time.

I call 911 and tell them I am being abused by my mother.

Rich

It's like one of those pictures in celebrity magazines I read at the dentist's office: "What's Different?" The first shot shows Jess Ogilvy with a big smile on her face and Mark Maguire's arm draped over her shoulder. It's a photograph we took from her nightstand.

The second picture was taken by my CSI team and shows Jess with her eyes closed and ringed with bruises, her skin frozen a solid, pale blue. She is draped with a postage-stamp quilt that looks like a painter's color wheel.

Ironically, she is wearing the same sweatshirt in both photos.

There are obvious differences—the physical trauma being the biggest one. But there's something else about her I cannot put my finger on. Did she lose weight? Not really. Was it the makeup? Nah, she wasn't wearing any in either shot.

It's the hair.

Not the cut, which would be easy. It's straight in the picture of Jess and her boyfriend. In the crime scene print, though, it's curled and frizzy, a cloud around her battered face.

I pick up the photo and study it at closer range. It seems likely that curls were the default setting for her hair, given that she would have gone to the trouble to style it when out with her boyfriend. Which means that her hair got wet while the body was out in the elements . . . something easily assumed, except for the fact that she was protected from rain and snow by the concrete culvert where she was dumped.

So her hair was wet when she was killed.

And there was blood in the bathroom.

Was Jacob a Peeping Tom, too?

"Captain?"

I look up to find one of the street cops standing in front of me. "Dispatch just got a call from a kid who says he's being abused by a parent."

"Don't need a detective for that, do you?"

"No, Captain. It's just . . . the kid? He's the one you arrested for that murder."

The photo flutters out of my hand, onto the floor. "You gotta be kidding," I mutter, and I stand up and grab my coat. "I'll take care of it."

Jacob

Immediately, I realize I've made a colossal mistake.

I begin hiding things: my computer, my file cabinet. I shred papers that are sitting on my desk and tuck a stash of journals from forensics associations in the bathtub. I figure all of these things can be used against me, and they've already taken so much of what was mine.

I don't think I can be arrested *again,* but I am not entirely sure. Double jeopardy only refers to the same crime, and only after an acquittal.

I will say this for the boys in blue—they are

speedy. Less than ten minutes after my 911 call, there is a knock at the door. My mother and Theo, who are still downstairs trying to reinstall the fire alarm Theo set off with some abortive kitchen snack, are caught completely unawares.

It's stupid, I know, but I hide underneath my bed.

Rich

"What are *you* doing here?" Emma Hunt demands.

"Actually, we received a call through 911."

"I didn't call 91— Jacob!" she yells, and she turns on her heel and flies up the stairs.

I step into the house to find Theo staring at me. "We don't want to donate to the police athletic league," he says sarcastically.

"Thanks." I point up the staircase. "I'm, uh, just going to . . . go . . . ?" Without waiting for him to answer, I head toward Jacob's room.

"Abusing you?" Emma is shrieking when I reach the doorway. "You've never been abused a day in your life!"

"There's physical abuse and there's mental abuse," Jacob argues.

Emma whips her head in my direction. "I have never laid a hand on that boy. Although right now, I'm incredibly tempted."

"I have three words for you," Jacob says. "Doctor! Henry! Lee!"

"The forensic scientist?" I am completely not following.

"He's speaking at UNH tomorrow, and she says I can't go."

Emma looks at me. "Do you see what I'm dealing with?"

I purse my lips, thinking. "Let me talk to him alone for a minute."

"Seriously?" Her eyes widen. "Were you *not* in the same courtroom I was in three hours ago, when the judge told you accommodations should have been made when you questioned Jacob?"

"I'm not questioning him now," I tell her. "Not professionally, anyway."

She throws up her hands. "I don't care. Do what you want. *Both* of you."

When her last footstep fades down the

stairs, I sit down beside Jacob. "You know you're not supposed to call 911 unless you're in serious trouble."

He snorts. "So arrest me. Oh, wait, you already did."

"You ever hear of the boy who cried wolf?"

"I didn't say anything about wolves," Jacob replies. "I said I was being abused, and I am. This is the one chance I have to meet Dr. Lee and she won't even consider it. If I'm old enough to be tried as an adult, how come I'm not old enough to walk to the bus stop and travel down there on my own?"

"You're old enough. You'll just wind up with your ass in jail again. Is that what you want?" From the corner of my eye, I spy a laptop peeking out of a pillowcase. "Why is your computer under the covers?"

He pulls it free and cradles it in his arms. "I thought you'd steal it from me. Just like you took my other stuff."

"I didn't steal that, I had a warrant to seize it. And you'll get it back, one day." I glance at him. "You know, Jacob, your mother is only protecting you."

"By locking me up in here?"

"No, the judge did that. By not letting you break your bail requirements."

We are both quiet for a second, and then Jacob glances at me from the corner of his eye. "I don't understand your voice."

"What do you mean?"

"It should be angry because I made you come all the way out here. But it's not angry. And it wasn't angry when I talked to you at the police station, either. You treated me like I was just a friend of yours, but then you arrested me at the end, and people don't arrest their friends." He clasps his hands between his knees. "Frankly, people don't make sense to me."

I nod in agreement. "Frankly, people don't make sense to me, either," I say.

Theo

Why do the cops keep coming to our stupid house?

I mean, given that they've already arrested Jacob, shouldn't they let justice take its course?

Okay, I get that Jacob was the one to summon them this time. But surely a phone call would have been just as effective to get him to call off his request for help. And yet, the police—this one guy in particular—keeps showing up. He chats up my mother, and now I can hear him yapping with Jacob about maggots that land on bodies within ten minutes of death.

Tell me how, exactly, this has any bearing on the 911 call, hmm?

Here's what I think: Detective Matson isn't even here to talk to Jacob.

He's certainly not here to talk to my mother.

He's come because he knows that in order to get to Jacob's room, he has to pass mine, and that means at least two glimpses inside.

Maybe someone has reported missing the Wii game I took.

Maybe he's just waiting for me to crack, to fall at his feet and confess that I was at Jess Ogilvy's place shortly before my brother, so that he can tell that bitch prosecutor to put me on the witness stand to testify against Jacob.

For these reasons and a dozen more I haven't thought of yet, I close my door and lock it, so that when Detective Matson passes by again, I don't have to look him in the eye.

Jacob

I would not have thought it possible, but Rich Matson is not a complete and utter ass.

For example, he told me that you can tell the sex of an individual by looking at the skull, because a male skull has a square chin and a female chin is rounded. He told me that he's been to the Body Farm in Knoxville, Tennessee, where an acre of land is covered with corpses rotting in all different stages, so that forensic anthropologists can measure the effects of weather and insects on human decay. He has pictures and promised to mail me a few.

This is still not Dr. Henry Lee–worthy, but it makes a decent consolation prize.

I learn that he has a daughter who, like Jess, faints at the sight of blood. When I tell him that Jess used to do this, too, his face twists, as if he's smelled something awful.

After a while I promise him not to call the police on my mother again, unless she is causing me dire bodily harm. And he convinces me that an apology to her might go a long way right now.

When I walk him downstairs, my mother is pacing in the kitchen. "Jacob has something to tell you," he announces.

"Detective Matson is going to send me photographs of decomposing bodies," I say.

"Not that. The other thing."

I push my lips out and then suck them in. I do it twice, as if I'm melting the words in my mouth. "I shouldn't have called the cops. Asperger's impulsiveness."

My mother's face freezes, and so does the detective's. Only after I've said it do I realize that they're probably assuming Jess's death was Asperger's impulsiveness, too.

Or in other words, talking about my Asperger's impulsiveness was a bit too impulsive.

"I think we're all set here," the detective says. "You two have a nice evening."

My mother touches his sleeve. "Thank you."

He looks at her as if he is about to tell her something important, but instead he says, "You have nothing to thank me for."

When he leaves, a lick of cold air from outside wraps around my ankles.

"Would you like me to make you something to eat?" my mother asks. "You never had lunch."

"No thanks. I'm going to lie down," I announce, although I really just want to be alone. I've learned that when someone invites you to do something and you really don't want to, they don't particularly want to hear the truth.

Her eyes fly to my face. "Are you sick?"

"I'm fine," I tell her. "Really."

I can feel her staring at me as I walk up the stairs.

I don't plan to lie down, but I do. And I guess I fall asleep, because all of a sudden Dr. Henry Lee is there. We are crouched down on either side of Jess's body. He examines the tooth in her pocket, the abrasions on her lower back. He looks up the cavities of her nostrils.

Oh yes, he says, crystal clear. *I understand.* I can see why you had to do what you did.

CASE 8: ONE IN SIX BILLION

In the 1980s and '90s, over fifty women in the Seattle-Tacoma, Washington, area were murdered. Most of the victims were prostitutes or teen runaways, and most of the bodies were dumped in or near the Green River. Dubbed the Green River Killer, the murderer was unknown until science managed to catch up to crime.

In the early 1980s, while performing autopsies on the victims, pathologists and medical technologists were able to recover small amounts of DNA in semen left behind by the killer. These were retained as evidence, but then-current scientific techniques proved worthless, since there wasn't enough material for testing.

Gary Ridgway, who was arrested in 1982 on a prostitution charge, was a suspect in the Green River killings, but there wasn't any evidence to formally link him to the crimes. In 1984, he passed a polygraph test. In 1987, while searching his home, the King County Sheriff's department took a saliva sample from Ridgway.

By March 2001, improvements in DNA typing technology had identified the source of the semen on the victims' bodies. In September 2001, the lab received results: they were able to get a comparative match between the DNA in that semen and the DNA in Ridgway's saliva. A warrant was issued for his arrest.

The DNA results linked Ridgway to three of the four women listed as victims in his indictment. Sperm samples taken from one of these victims, Carol Ann Christensen, were so conclusive that not more than one person in the world, excluding identical twins, would exhibit that particular DNA profile. Ridgway was charged with three more murders after microscopic paint evidence found with the bodies matched paint at his workplace. In return for confessing to more of the Green River murders, Ridgway was spared the death penalty and is currently serving forty-eight life sentences with no possibility of parole.

8

Oliver

A month later I am sprawled on the couch in the Hunts' living room, caught in a weird déjà vu: I am scanning the discovery that's been sent to me, which includes Jacob's journals on *Crime-Busters,* while he sits on the floor in front of me watching on TV the very same episode I'm reading about. "Want me to tell you how it ends?" I ask.

"I already know." Not that that's kept him from writing down yet another journal entry, this one in a brand-new composition-style notebook.

Episode 49: Sex, Lies, and iMovie
Situation: After a suicide note is spliced

into the credits of a feature at a film festival, a B-movie director is found dead in
the back of a car—but the team suspects
foul play.

Evidence:

Trailer from festival

Cuttings from editing studio—who is the
blonde and is she really dead or just acting?

Hard drive of director's computer

Director's collection of rare butterflies—
red herring, entomology not involved

Acid in pipes

Solved: By ME! 0:24.

"You figured it out in twenty minutes?"

"Yeah."

"The butler did it," I say.

"No, actually, it's the plumber," Jacob corrects. So much for making a joke.

We've gotten into a routine: instead of stay-ing at my office during the day, I do my trial preparation here at the Hunts'. That way, I can watch Jacob if Emma needs to run out, and I have my client available to answer any ques-tions I've got. Thor likes it, because he spends most of the day curled up in Jacob's lap. Jacob likes it, because I bring the Wii with me. Theo likes it because if I bring guacamole on Green Monday for his brother, I slip a personal-size nongreen sausage pizza into the fridge for him.

I don't really know if Emma likes it.

Theo walks past us in the living room to a file cabinet in the back. "You still doing your homework?" Jacob asks.

There's not really any malice in his tone—it's flat, like everything else Jacob says—but Theo flips him the bird. Usually Theo's the one to finish his work first, but today, he seems to be dragging.

I wait for Jacob to tell him to go fuck himself, but instead, he just fixes his glassy gaze on the television again.

"Hey," I say, approaching Theo.

He startles and takes the piece of paper he's scanning and stuffs it into his jeans pocket. "Stop sneaking up on me."

"What are you doing in here anyway? Isn't this your mother's file cabinet?"

"Isn't this none of your business?" Theo says.

"No. But Jacob is. And you should apologize."

"I should also have five servings of vegetables a day, but *that* rarely happens," he replies, and he heads back into the kitchen to finish his homework.

I know Jacob well enough by now to pick up on the cues that flag his emotions. The fact that he's rocking back and forth slightly means whatever Theo just said rattled him more than he's letting on. "If you tell your mother he does that shit to you," I say, "I can bet you it will stop."

"You don't tell on your brother—you take care of him. He's the only one you've got," Jacob recites. "It's a rule."

If I could only make the jury see how Jacob lives from one decree to another; if I could make the connection between a kid who won't even break one of his mother's rules much less the law governing our country; if I could somehow prove that his Asperger's makes it virtually impossible for him to cross that line between right and wrong—well, I could win his case.

"Hey, after lunch I want to talk to you about what's going to happen later this week when we—"

"Shh," Jacob says. "The commercial's over."

I flip the page and see an entry that doesn't have an episode number.

I start reading, and my jaw drops. "Oh, shit," I say out loud.

A month ago, after the suppression hearing, I'd called Helen Sharp. "I think you need to give up," I told her. "You can't prove the case. We're willing to take probation for five years."

"I can win this without his police department confession," she said. "I've got all the statements that were made at the house before Jacob was in custody; I have the forensic evidence at the scene and eyewitness evidence that goes to motive. I've got his history of violence, and I've got the defendant's journals."

At the time, I'd shrugged it off. Jacob's journals were formulaic, and every other piece of evidence she listed was something I could excuse away on cross.

"We're going forward," Helen had said, and I'd thought, *Good freaking luck.*

Here's what the journal says:

> **At Her House. 1/12/10.**
> **Situation: Girl missing.**
> **Evidence:**
> **Clothes in pile on bed**
> **Toothbrush missing, lip gloss missing**
> **Victim's purse and coat remain**
> **Cell phone missing . . . cut screen . . .**
> **boot prints outside match up with boyfriend's footwear.**

"Jesus Christ, Jacob," I explode, so loud that Emma comes running in from the laundry room. "You wrote about Jess in your *CrimeBusters* journals?"

He doesn't respond, so I stand and turn off the TV.

"What do you mean?" Emma says.

I pass her the photocopy of the notebook. "What were you *thinking*?" I demand.

Jacob shrugs. "It was a crime scene," he says simply.

"Do you have any idea what Helen Sharp is going to do with this?"

"No, and I don't care," Emma replies. "I want to know what *you're* going to do about it." She folds her arms and moves a step closer to Jacob.

"I don't know, to be honest. Because after all the work we did to get the police station statement thrown out, this brings it all back in."

Jacob repeats what I said, and then repeats it again: *Brings it all back. Brings it all back.* The first time I heard him do it, I thought he was mimicking me. Now I know it's echolalia; Emma explained it to me as just the repetition of sounds. Sometimes Jacob does that by reciting movie quotes, and sometimes it's an immediate parroting of something he's heard.

I just hope no one hears him doing it in court, or they'll assume he's a wiseass.

"Bring it all back," Jacob says again. "Bring *what* all back?"

"Something that's going to make the jury assume you're guilty."

"But it's a crime scene," Jacob says again. "I just wrote down the evidence like usual."

"It's not a fictional crime scene," I point out.

"Why not?" he asks. "I'm the one who created it."

"Oh my God," Emma chokes. "They're going to think he's a monster."

I want to put my hand on her arm and tell her I will be able to keep that from happening, but I cannot make that kind of promise. Even having been with Jacob for the past month, like I have, there are still things he does that strike me as utterly chilling—like now, when his mother is hysterical and he turns away without registering any remorse and cranks up the volume on his TV show. Juries, which are supposed to be about reason, are actually always about the heart. A juror who watches Jacob stare blankly through the graphic testimony about Jess Ogilvy's death will deliberate his fate with that image etched in her mind, and it cannot help but sway her decision.

I cannot change Jacob, which means I have to change the system. This is why I've filed a motion, and why we're going to court tomorrow, although I haven't yet broken the news to Emma yet.

"I need to tell you both something," I say, as Emma's watch begins to beep.

"Hold on," she says, "I'm timing Theo on a math quiz." She faces the kitchen. "Theo? Put your pencil down. Jacob, lower that volume. Theo? Did you hear me?"

When there's no answer, Emma walks into the kitchen. She calls out again, and then I hear her footsteps overhead, in Theo's room. A moment later, she is back in the living room, her voice wild. "He never did his math quiz. And his coat and sneakers and backpack are missing," she says. "Theo's gone."

Theo

Let me just say that I think it's pretty insane that a kid who's fifteen, like me, can fly across the country without a parent. The hardest part was getting the ticket, which turned out to not be very hard at all. It was no secret that my mother keeps an emergency credit card buried in her file cabinet, and honestly, didn't this count as an emergency? All I had to do was dig it out, get the number off the front and the PIN code on the back, and book my ticket on Orbitz.com.

I had a passport, too (we'd driven

up to Canada once on a vacation that lasted approximately six hours, after Jacob refused to sleep in the motel room because it had an orange carpet), which was stored one file folder away from the emergency credit card. And getting to the airport was a piece of cake; it took two hitched rides, and that was that.

I wish I could tell you I had a plan, but I didn't. All I knew was that, directly or indirectly, this was my fault. I hadn't killed Jess Ogilvy, but I'd seen her the day she died, and I hadn't told the police or my mother or anyone else—and now Jacob was going to be tried for murder. In my mind, it was like a chain reaction. If I hadn't been breaking into houses at the time, if I hadn't been in Jess's, if I had never locked eyes with her—maybe that missing link would have broken the string of events that happened afterward. It was no great secret that my mother was totally freaking out about where the money would be coming from for Jacob's trial; I figured that if I was ever going to remove my karmic debt, I might as well start by finding the solution to that problem.

Hence: this visit to my father.

On the plane, I am sitting between a businessman who's trying to sleep and a woman who looks like a grandmother—she's got short white hair and a light purple sweatshirt with a cat on it. The businessman is shifting in his seat because he's got a kid behind him who keeps kicking it.

"Jesus H. Christ," he says.

I've always wondered why people say that. Why the *H*? I mean, what if his middle name was Stanley?

"I'm stuck on the last one," the grandma says.

I pull my iPod earphone free. "Sorry?"

"No, that doesn't fit." She is hunched over a crossword puzzle in the back of the *US Airways* magazine. It had been filled out halfway. I hate that; doesn't the jerk who is sitting in the seat on the previous flight think someone else might want to try it on his own? "The clue is *Regretted*. And it's four letters."

Theo, I think.

Suddenly the businessman comes

out of his seat and twists around. "Madam," he says to the kid's mom, "is there any chance you could keep your brat from being so incredibly rude?"

"That's it," the grandma says. "Rude!"

I watch her write it in pencil. "I, uh, think it's spelled differently," I suggest. "R-U-E-D."

"Right," she says, erasing it to make the correction. "I admit to being a horrendous speller." She smiles at me. "Now, what's bringing you out to sunny California?"

"I'm visiting someone."

"Me, too. Someone I've never met—my first grandbaby."

"Wow," I say. "You must be pretty stoked."

"If that's a good thing, then yes, I guess I am. My name's Edith."

"I'm Paul."

Okay, I don't know where the lie came from. I shouldn't have been surprised—after all, I'd hidden my involvement in this whole nightmare for over a month now, and I was getting really good at pretending I wasn't the same person I was back then. But once I made up the name, the rest kept coming. I was on school break. I was an only child. My parents were divorced (Ha! *Not* a lie!), and I was going to see my dad. We were planning on taking a college tour of Stanford.

At home, we don't talk about my father. In world studies class we learned about indigenous cultures who no longer speak the names of the dead—well, we no longer say the name of the person who quit when the going got tough. I don't really know the details of my parents' split, except that I was still a baby when it happened, and so of course there's a piece of me that thinks I must have been the straw that broke the camel's back. But I do know that he tries to pay off his guilt by sending my mom a child support check every month. And I also know that he has replaced Jacob and me with two little girls who look like china dolls and who probably have never broken into a house or stimmed a day in their short lives. I know this because he sends us a Christmas card every year, which I throw out if I get to the mail before my mother does.

"Do you have brothers or sisters?" Edith asks.

I take a sip of the 7-Up I bought for three bucks. "Nope," I say. "Only child."

"Stop it," the businessman says, and for one awful moment I think he's going to tell this woman who I really am. Then he turns around in his seat. "For the love of God," he says to the little kid's mom.

"So, Paul," Edith says, "what do you want to study at Stanford?"

I am fifteen, I have no idea what I want to do with my life. Except fix the mess I've made of it.

Instead of answering, I point down at her crossword puzzle. "Quito," I say. "That's the answer to forty-two across."

She gets all excited and reads aloud the next clue. I think about how happy she'll be if we finish this cross-word puzzle. She'll get off the plane and tell her son-in-law, or whoever is picking her up, about the nice young man she met. About how helpful I was. How proud my parents must be of me.

Jacob

My brother is not as smart as I am.

I am not saying this to be mean; I'm just stating a fact. For example, he has to study all his vocabulary words if he wants to do well on a test; I can look at the page and it's stuck in my head for easy retrieval after that first glance. He would leave the room if two adults started discussing adult things, like current events; I would just pull up a chair and join the conversation. He doesn't care about storing information away like a squirrel would save nuts for the winter; it's only interesting to Theo if it has current real-life applications.

However, I am not nearly as intuitive as my brother. This is why when I begin to let some of that stored information bleed free—like for example how Steve Jobs and Steve Wozniak released the Apple 1 computer on April Fool's Day 1976—and the person I am speaking with begins to go glassy-eyed and make excuses, I will keep talking, although Theo would easily read the clues and shut up.

Being a detective is all about intuition. Being a good crime scene investigator, however, requires great thoroughness and intelligence. Which is why, while my mother is rendered immobile by her panic over Theo's disappearance and Oliver is doing stupid things like patting her shoulder, I go to Theo's bedroom and get on his computer.

I am very good with computers. I once took my guidance counselor's laptop apart and put it back together, motherboard and all. I could probably configure your wireless network in my sleep. Here is the other reason I like computers: when you are talking to someone online, you don't have to read expressions on faces or interpret tones of voice. What you see is what you get, and that means I don't have to try so hard when I interact. There are chat rooms and message boards for Aspies like me, but I don't frequent them. One of the house rules in the family is to not go to websites my mother has not vetted. When I asked her why, she made me sit down with her and watch a television show about sexual predators. I tried to explain that the website I wanted to chat on wasn't quite the same thing—that it was only a bunch of people like me trying to connect without all the bullshit that's part of face-to-face meetings—but she wouldn't take no for an answer. *You don't know what these people are like, Jacob,* she said to me. In fact, I did. It was the people in the real world I didn't understand.

It takes only a few clicks to delve into his cache—even though he thinks he's emptied it, nothing is ever really gone on a computer—and to see where he was last surfing the Net. Orbitz.com, flights to San Jose.

When I bring downstairs the printout of the webpage that has his ticket information on it, Oliver is trying to convince my mother to call the police. "I can't," she says. "They won't want to help me."

"They don't get to pick and choose their cases—"

"Mom," I interrupt.

"Jacob, not now," Oliver says.

"But—"

My mother looks at me and starts crying. I watch one tear make an S-curve down her cheek. "I want to talk to you," I say.

"I'm getting the phone," Oliver says. "I'm dialing 911."

"I know where Theo is," I tell them.

My mother blinks. "You what?"

"It was on his computer." I hand her the printed page.

"Oh my God," my mother says, holding her hand up to her mouth. "He's going to Henry's."

"Who's Henry?" Oliver asks.

"My father," I answer. "He walked out on us."

Oliver takes a step backward and rubs his chin.

"He's connecting in Chicago," I add. "His plane leaves in fifteen minutes."

"You can't catch him before he takes off," Oliver says. "Does Henry know? About Jacob?"

"Of course he knows about me. He sends checks every year for my birthday and Christmas."

"I meant does Henry know about the murder charge?"

My mother looks down at the fault line between the cushions of the couch. "I don't know.

He might have read about it in the papers, but I didn't talk to him about it," she admits. "I didn't know how to tell him."

Oliver holds out the phone. "Now's the time to figure that out," he says.

I don't like to think of Theo on a plane; I don't like planes. I understand Bernoulli's principle, but for the love of God, no matter how physical forces are being exerted on the wings for lift, the hardware weighs a million pounds. For all intents and purposes, it should fall out of the sky.

My mother takes the phone and starts to dial a long-distance number. It sounds like the notes of a game show theme song, but I can't remember which one.

"Christ," Oliver says. He looks at me.

I don't know how I'm supposed to respond. *"We'll always have Paris,"* I say.

When Theo was eight, he became convinced that there was a monster living underneath the house. He knew this because he could hear its breath every night when the radiators in his room hissed awake. I was eleven and very into dinosaurs at the time, and as thrilling as it was for me to assume that there might be a sauropod rooting around under the foundations of our house, I knew this was not likely:

1. Our house was built in 1973.

2. To build it, there would have been an excavation.

3. The probability of the world's sole long-lost dinosaur surviving the excavation and residing beneath my basement floor would be pretty slim.

4. Even if it had survived, what the hell would it be eating?

"Grass clippings," Theo said, when I told him all this. "Duh."

One of the reasons I like having Asperger's is that I *don't* have an active imagination. To many—teachers and guidance counselors and shrinks included—this is a great detriment. To me, it's a blessing. Logical thinking keeps you from wasting time worrying, or hoping. It prevents disappointment. Imagination, on the other hand, only gets you hyped up over things that will never realistically happen.

Like running into a hadrosaur on your way to the bathroom at 3:00 A.M.

Theo spent two weeks freaking out in the middle of the night when he heard the hiss from heating registers in his room. My mother tried everything—from warm milk before bedtime to an illustrated diagram of the heating system of the house to an unnecessary dose of children's Benadryl at night to knock Theo out—but like clockwork, he'd start screaming in the middle of the night and would run out of his room and wake both of us.

It was getting old, frankly, which is why I did what I did.

After my mother tucked me in, I stayed up with a flashlight hidden under my pillow and read until I knew she had gone to bed, too. Then I took my pillow and blankets and sleeping bag and camped outside Theo's bedroom door. That night, when he woke up screaming and tried to run to my mother's room to wake her up, too, he tripped over me.

He blinked for a second, trying to figure out if he was dreaming. "Go back to bed," I said. "There's no stupid dinosaur."

I could tell he didn't believe me, so I added, "And if there *is,* he'll kill me first before he gets to you."

This actually worked. Theo crawled back into bed, and we both fell asleep again. My mother was the one who found me sprawled on the floor the next morning.

She panicked. Assuming I'd had some kind of seizure, she started shaking me. "Stop, Mom," I finally said. "I'm fine!"

"What are you doing out here?"

"I *was* sleeping . . ."

"In the hallway?"

"Not the hallway," I corrected. "In front of Theo's room."

"Oh, Jacob. You were trying to make him feel safe, weren't you?" She threw her arms around me and held me so tight I thought I just *might* have a seizure after all. "I knew it," she babbled. "I knew it! All those books; all those idiot doctors who said kids with Asperger's have no theory of mind and can't empathize . . . You *do* love your brother. You wanted to protect him."

I let her embrace me, because it seemed to be what she wanted to do. Behind Theo's door, I could hear him starting to stir.

What my mother had said was not technically inaccurate. What those doctors and books all say about how Aspies like me cannot feel anything on behalf of others—that's total bullshit. We understand when someone else is in pain; it just affects us differently than it affects other humans. I see it as the next step of evolution: I cannot take away your sadness, so why should I acknowledge it?

In addition, I hadn't slept in front of Theo's door because I wanted to protect him. I'd slept in front of his door because I was exhausted after a week of midnight crying, and I only wanted to get a good night's rest. I was looking out for my own best interests.

You could say, actually, that this was the impetus behind what happened with Jess, too.

Oliver

Emma wants to call US Airways and make them stop the plane from departing, but the entire system is automated. When we finally do reach a human employee, he's in Charlotte, North Carolina, and has no way of contacting the Burlington gate. "Here's the thing," I tell her. "You can beat him there by flying direct to San Francisco. It's almost the same distance to Palo Alto from the San Jose airport." She looks over my shoulder at the computer screen, which has the flight I've found. "With the layover in Chicago that Theo's going to make, you'll still get in an hour before he does."

She leans forward, and I can smell the

shampoo in her hair. Her eyes flicker over the flight information, hopeful—and then land on the bottom, and the price. "$1,080? That's ridiculous!"

"Same-day fares aren't cheap."

"Well, that's not in my budget," Emma says.

I click on the button to purchase the ticket. "It's in mine," I lie.

"What are you *doing*! You can't pay for that—"

"Too late." I shrug. The truth is, financially, I'm a little shaky now. I have one client, and she can't afford to pay me, and worse, I'm okay with that. Surely I missed the Bloodsucking Your Client class in law school, since all evidence points to me being the poster boy for Financially Ruined Defense Attorneys. But at the same time, I'm thinking that I can sell my saddle—I have a beautiful English one that's in storage below the pizza place. No use having it when I don't have a horse anyway.

"I'll add it to the bill," I say, but we both know I probably won't.

Emma closes her eyes for a moment. "I don't know what to say."

"Then just be quiet."

"You shouldn't have to get involved in this mess."

"Lucky for you the only other thing I had to do today was organize my sock drawer," I joke, but she's not laughing.

"I'm sorry," Emma replies. "It's just . . . I don't have anyone else."

Very slowly, very deliberately, so that she will not startle or pull away, I thread my fingers through hers and squeeze her hand. "You have me," I say.

If I were a better man, I wouldn't have eavesdropped on Emma's conversation with her ex-husband. *Henry,* she said. *It's Emma.*

No, actually, I can't really call back later. It's about Theo.

He's fine. I mean, I think he's fine. He's run away from home.

Well, of course I know that. He's on his way to your place.

Yes, California. Unless you've moved lately.

No, I'm sorry. That wasn't an insult . . .

I don't know why. He just took off.

He used my credit card. Look, can we just talk about this when I get there?

Oh. Did I forget to mention that?

If all goes well, I'll land before Theo.

Meeting us at the airport would be great. We're both on US Airways.

Then there is a hesitation.

Jacob? she replies. *No, he won't be joining me.*

It is decided that I will camp out for the night to be the over-twenty-five-year-old adult watching Jacob while Emma hauls Theo's ass back across the country. At first, after she leaves, it seems like a piece of cake—we can play the Wii. We can watch TV. And, thank God, it's Brown Thursday, which is relatively easy: I can cook Jacob a burger for dinner. It isn't until an hour after she leaves that I remember my hearing tomorrow— the one I had not yet told Emma about, the one I will have to take Jacob to by myself.

"Jacob," I say, while he is engrossed in a television show about how Milky Way bars are made. "I have to talk to you for a second."

He doesn't respond. His eyes don't even flicker from the screen, so I step in front of it and turn it off.

"I just want to have a little chat." When Jacob doesn't answer, I keep speaking. "Your trial starts in a month, you know."

"A month and six days."

"Right. Well, I've been thinking about how . . . hard it might be for you to be in court all day long, and I figured we need to do something about it."

"Oh," Jacob says, shaking his head. "I can't be in court all day. I have schoolwork to do. And I have to be home by four-thirty so that I can watch *CrimeBusters.*"

"I don't think you get it. It's not your call. You go to court when the judge says you go to court, and you get to come home when he's ready to let you go."

Jacob chews on this information. "That's not going to work for me."

"Which is why you and I are going back to court tomorrow."

"But my mother's not here."

"I know that, Jacob. I didn't plan for her to be away. But the fact of the matter is, the whole reason we're going is something *you* said to me."

"Me?"

"Yes. Do you remember what you told me when you decided I could run an insanity defense?"

Jacob nods. "That the Americans with Disabilities Act prohibits discrimination by the state or local governments, including the courts," he says, "and that some people consider autism to be a disability, even if I don't happen to be one of them."

"Right. But if you *do* consider Asperger's syndrome to be a developmental disability, then under the ADA you're also entitled to provisions in court that will make the experience easier for you." I let a slow smile loose, like a card that's been played close to the chest. "Tomorrow, we're going to make sure you get them."

Emma

From Auntie Em's column archives:

> **Dear Auntie Em,**
> Recently I have been dreaming about my ex. Should I consider this a sign from a higher power and call him to say hi?
>
> **Sleepless in Strafford**

> **Dear Sleepless,**
> Yes, but I wouldn't tell him you are calling because he's starring in your dreams. Unless he happens to say, "Gosh, it's so

strange that you called today, because I
dreamed about you last night."
                                                    Auntie Em

I asked Henry out on our first date, because
he didn't seem to be picking up on hints
that I was his for the taking. We saw the
movie *Ghost* and went out to dinner afterward, where Henry told me that, scientifically, ghosts could simply not exist. "It's
basic physics and math," he said. "Patrick
Swayze couldn't walk through walls *and* tag
along behind Demi Moore. If ghosts can
follow someone, that means their feet apply
force to the floor. If they go through walls,
though, they don't have any substance. They
could either be material or be unmaterial,
but they can't be both at the same time. It
violates Newton's rule."

He was wearing a T-shirt that said FULL
FRONTAL NERDITY, and his corn silk hair
kept falling into his eyes. "But don't you
wish it could be true?" I asked him. "Don't
you wish love was so strong it could come
back to haunt you?"

I told him the story of my mother, who
one night had woken up at 3:14 A.M. with a
mouth full of violet petals and the scent of

roses so thick in the air that she could not breathe. An hour later she was roused by a phone call: her own mother, a florist by trade, had died of a heart attack at 3:14 A.M. "Science can't answer everything," I told Henry. "It doesn't explain love."

"Actually it does," he told me. "There have been all kinds of studies done. People are more attracted to people with symmetrical features, for example. And symmetrical men smell better to women. Also, people who have similar genetic traits are attracted to each other. It probably has something to do with evolution."

I burst out laughing. "That is *awful,*" I said. "That is the most unromantic thing I've ever heard."

"I don't think so . . ."

"Oh, really. Say something that will sweep me off my feet," I demanded.

Henry looked at me for a long moment, until I could feel my head growing lighter and dizzier. "I think you might be perfectly symmetrical," he said.

On our second date, Henry took me to Boston. We had dinner at the Parker House, and then he hired a hansom cab to take us around the Boston Common. It was late November, and frost crouched in the bare branches of the trees; when we settled into the back of the carriage, the driver handed us a heavy wool blanket to put over our laps. The horse was spirited, stamping its feet and snorting.

Henry was telling me riddles. "The ratio of an igloo's circumference to its diameter?"

"I give up."

"Eskimo *pi*," he said. "How about half of a large intestine?"

"I don't know . . ."

"A semicolon."

"That's not a math or science joke," I said.

"I'm a Renaissance Guy." Henry laughed. "Eight nickels?"

I shook my head.

"Two paradigms," he said.

The puns weren't, by definition, funny. But on Henry's lips, they were. Lips that were curved at the ends and that always seemed a little embarrassed to smile, lips that had kissed me good night on our first date with a surprising amount of force and intensity.

I was staring at his lips when the horse dropped dead.

Technically, it wasn't dead. It had slipped

on a patch of black ice, and its front legs had buckled. I had heard one snap.

We rolled in slow motion out of the hansom cab, Henry twisting so that he would cushion my fall. "You all right?" he asked, and he helped me to my feet. He held the rough blanket around me while the police came, and then animal control. "Don't watch," Henry whispered, and he turned my face away when the officer pulled out a pistol.

I tried to focus on the words on Henry's T-shirt, where his coat was gaping open: DOES THIS PROTON MAKE MY MASS LOOK FAT? But the sound was like the world cracking in half, and the last thing I remember was wondering who wore a T-shirt in the winter, and if that meant his skin was always warm, and if I would ever get to lie against it.

I woke up in an unfamiliar bed. The walls were cream-colored, and there was a dresser made of dark wood with a television on it. It was very clean and . . . corporate. *You fainted,* I told myself. "The horse," I said out loud.

"Um," a voice said quietly. "He's in that big carousel in the sky?"

I rolled over to find Henry pressed against

the far wall, still wearing his coat. "You don't believe in heaven," I murmured.

"No, but I figured you would. Are you . . . are you okay?"

I nodded gingerly, testing. "What's wrong? Don't women swoon around you all the time?"

He grinned. "It *was* a little Victorian of you."

"Where are we?"

"I got a room at the Parker House. I thought you might need to lie down for a while." His cheeks bloomed a bright red. "I, um, don't want you to get the wrong idea, though."

I came up on an elbow. "You don't?"

"Well . . . n-not unless you want me to," he stammered.

"Well, *that's* a little Gothic," I said. "Henry, can I ask you something?"

"Okay."

"What are you doing all the way over there?"

I held out my hand and felt the mattress give under his weight as Henry crawled onto it. I felt his mouth come down against mine, and I realized that this relationship would not be what I'd imagined it to be: me, playing teacher to the shy young computer science geek. I should have known from watching Henry work at the office: programmers moved slowly and deliberately, and then waited to see the reaction. And if they did not succeed the first time, they would try over and over again, until they broke through that fifth dimension and got it right.

Later, when I was wearing Henry's T-shirt and his arms were wrapped around me, when we had turned on the television and were watching a show on primates in the Congo with the volume muted, when he had fed me chicken nuggets from the kids' room service menu, I thought how clever I'd been to see past what other people saw in Henry. The silly T-shirts, the Star Wars canteen in which he stored his coffee, the way he could barely look a woman in the eye—beneath that exterior was a man who touched me as if I were made of glass, who focused with such intensity on me that sometimes I had to remind him to breathe when we were making love. I never imagined at the time that Henry wouldn't be able to love anything other than me—not even a baby he'd made. I never imagined that all that passion between us would pool beneath the tangled threads of

Jacob's genetic code, waiting for just the perfect storm to dig in its roots, to burst and blossom into autism.

Henry is waiting for me when I get off my plane. I walk toward him, stopping an awkward foot away. I lean forward to embrace him just as he turns away toward the arrivals monitor, which means I close my arms around nothing but air. "He should be landing in twenty minutes," Henry says.

"Good," I reply. "That's good." I look at him. "I'm really sorry about this."

Henry stares down the empty corridor past the security barrier. "You going to tell me what's going on, Emma?"

For five minutes, I tell him about Jess Ogilvy, about the murder charge. I tell him I'm sure Theo's escape had something to do with all of this. When I'm finished, I listen to the call for a passenger about to miss his plane and then muster the courage to meet Henry's gaze. "Jacob's on trial for *murder*?" he says, his voice shaky. "And you didn't *mention* it?"

"What would you have done?" I challenge. "Fly back to Vermont to be our white knight? Somehow I doubt that, Henry."

"And when this hits the papers out here? How am I supposed to explain to my seven- and four-year-old that their half brother is a murderer?"

I reel back as if he's slapped me. "I'm going to pretend you didn't just say that," I murmur. "And if you knew your son at all, if you had ever actually spent time with Jacob instead of just sending a check every month to ease your conscience, you'd know that he's innocent."

A muscle tics in Henry's jaw. "Do you remember what happened on our fifth anniversary?"

That time of my life, when we were trying every intervention and therapy possible to get Jacob to connect with the world again, is a dark blur.

"We were out at a movie—the first time we'd been alone in months. And suddenly this strange man walks down the aisle and crouches down and starts talking to you, and a minute later you walk out with him. I sat there thinking, *Who the hell is this guy and where is my wife going with him?* And I followed you into the lobby. Turned out that he was the father of our babysitter—and an EMT. Livvie had called him in a panic because

Theo was bleeding like crazy. He went to the house, put a butterfly bandage on Theo, and came and got us."

I stare at Henry. "I don't remember any of this."

"Theo wound up getting ten stitches in his eyebrow," Henry says. "Because Jacob had gotten angry and knocked over his high chair when Livvie had her back turned."

Now it is coming back to me—the panic we came home to with Jacob in total meltdown mode and Theo hysterically crying, a knot the size of his tiny fist rising over his left eye. Henry making the hospital run while I was left behind to calm Jacob. I wonder how it is possible to put something so far out of one's mind, to rewrite history. "I can't believe I forgot that," I say softly.

Henry glances away from me. "You were always good at seeing what you wanted to see," he answers.

And then suddenly, we both notice our son.

"What the hell?" Theo says.

I fold my arms. "My thoughts exactly," I reply.

It is a strange thing to be in an airport and to not be celebrating a reunion or a departure.

It is even stranger to sit in the backseat of Henry's car and listen to him making small talk with Theo as if Theo isn't smart enough to know that, at some point, a colossal bomb is going to drop.

When Theo went into the restroom at the airport, Henry came up with a plan. "Let me talk to him," Henry said.

"He won't listen to you."

"Well, he ran away from *you*," Henry pointed out.

The freeways here are white as bone and clean. There's no cracking from frost heaves, like in Vermont. Shiny and happy and new. No wonder Henry likes it. "Theo," I say, "what were you *thinking*?"

He twists in his seat. "I wanted to talk to Dad."

In the rearview mirror, Henry meets my gaze. *I told you so.*

"Haven't you ever heard of a phone?"

But before he can answer, Henry pulls into a driveway. His house has Spanish tiles on its roof and a plastic, child-size princess castle on the front lawn. That makes my chest tighten.

Meg, Henry's new wife, bursts out the front door. "Oh, thank goodness," she says, clasping her hands together when she sees Theo in the front seat. She is a tiny blonde with überwhite teeth and a shiny ponytail. Henry approaches her, leaving me to wrestle my own bag out of the trunk. Standing beside each other, with their blue eyes and golden hair, they look like a poster for the quintessential Aryan family. "Theo," Henry says, all fatherly, too little too late, "let's go into the library and talk a little."

I want to hate Meg, but I can't. She immediately surprises me by linking her arm through mine and leading me into the house. "You must have been worried sick," she says. "I know I would have been."

She offers me coffee and a slice of lemon–poppy seed cake while Theo and Henry vanish deeper into the house. I wonder if the cake was just lying around, if she is the sort of mother who makes sure there is a homemade baked good at all times on the kitchen counter, or if she'd popped it in the oven after Henry told her I was coming. I'm not quite sure which image upsets me more.

Her daughters (well, Henry's, too) dart across the living room threshold to get a peek at me. They are sprites, little tow-headed fairies. One of them wears a pink sequined tutu. "Girls," Meg says. "Come on in here and meet Ms. Hunt."

"Emma," I say automatically. I wonder what these little girls make of a stranger who has the same last name they do. I wonder if Henry has ever explained me to them.

"This is Isabella," Meg says, lightly touching the taller girl on the crown of her head. "And this is Grace."

"Hello," they chime, and Grace pops her thumb in her mouth.

"Hi," I answer, and then I don't know what to say.

Did Henry feel there was some balance to his second life, having two girls instead of two boys? Grace tugs on her mother's shirt and whispers in her ear. "She wants to show you what she does in ballet," Meg says apologetically.

"Oh, I love ballet," I say.

Grace puts her arms in the air and touches her fingertips together. She begins to turn in a circle, wobbling only a little. I clap for her.

Jacob used to spin. It was one of his stims, when he was little. He'd go faster and faster until he crashed into something, usually a vase or another breakable item.

I already know it's not true by looking at her, but if little Grace turned out to be autistic, would Henry run away again?

As if I've conjured him, Henry ducks into the room. "You were right," he says to me. "He won't talk without you there." Whatever small satisfaction this gives me vanishes as Grace sees her father. She stops spinning and hurls herself at him with the force of a tropical storm. He lifts her into his arms and then tousles Isabella's hair. There is an ease to Henry that I have not seen in him before, a quiet confidence that this is where he belongs. I can see it etched on his face, in the tiny lines that now fan out from his eyes, lines that were not there when I loved him.

Meg takes Grace on her hip and grasps Isabella's hand. "Let's give Daddy a chance to talk to his friends," she says.

Friends. I loved him; I created children with him, and this is what we have been demoted to.

I follow Henry down a corridor to the room where Theo is waiting. "Your family," I say. "They're perfect." But what I'm really saying is, *Why didn't I deserve this with you?*

Oliver

"Well, Mr. Bond," the judge says. "Here you are again."

"Like a bad penny," I reply, smiling.

Jacob and I are in court again, this time without Emma. She had called late last night and left a message saying that she and Theo would be flying home today. I hoped to have good news for her when she arrived; God knows she would need some by then.

The judge glances over the half-moons of his glasses. "We've got a motion before the court for accommodations during the trial of Jacob Hunt. What are you looking for, Counselor?"

Sympathy for a client who is incapable of

showing any himself . . . but I can't admit that. After Jacob's last outburst in court, I thought about asking the judge to let him watch the proceedings from a separate room, but I need him in full view of the jury in order to make my defense work. If I'm playing the disability card, they have to be able to see Asperger's manifesting itself in its full glory. "First, Your Honor," I say, "Jacob needs sensory breaks. You've seen how he can get agitated by courtroom procedure—he has to be able to get up and leave the courtroom when he feels the need to do so. Second, he would like to have his mother sitting at the defense table beside him. Third, due to Jacob's sensitivity to stimuli, we ask that Your Honor not use his gavel during the proceedings, and that the lights be turned down in the courtroom. Fourth, the prosecution needs to ask questions in a very direct and literal manner—"

"For God's sake," Helen Sharp sighs.

I glance at her but keep talking. "Fifth, we request that the length of the day in court be abbreviated."

The judge shakes his head. "Ms. Sharp, I'm quite sure you have objections to those requests?"

"Yes, Your Honor. I don't have a problem with

numbers one, three, and five, but the others are absolutely prejudicial."

"Mr. Bond," the judge says, "why are you asking for your client's mother to sit at counsel table?"

"Well, Your Honor, you've seen Jacob's outbursts. Emma Hunt serves as a coping mechanism for him. I think that, given the stress of a court experience, having his mother beside him would be beneficial to all involved."

"And yet, Ms. Hunt is not with us today," the judge points out. "But the defendant seems to be faring well."

"Ms. Hunt wanted to be here, but there has been a . . . family emergency," I say. "And in terms of stress, there's a huge difference between coming to court for a motion and coming for a full-blown murder trial."

"Ms. Sharp," the judge asks, "what is the basis for your objection to having the defendant's mother sit at counsel table?"

"It's twofold, Your Honor. There's a concern about how to explain to the jury the defendant's mother's presence there. She's testifying as a witness, so she will clearly be identified as the defendant's mother, and as the court well knows, it is not good protocol to allow anyone other than the attorney and clients to sit at counsel table. Giving her the elevated position at table awards her more importance in the eyes of the jury, and it becomes an unexplained incident that negatively impacts the State. Moreover, we've heard all too often that the defendant's mother interprets for him. She intervenes at his school with teachers, with strangers, with police officers. She's the one who burst into the station and told the detective she had to be present at the interrogation. Judge, what's to prevent her from writing an entire script for Jacob and passing it to him or whispering in his ear during the course of the trial to coach him into saying or doing something inappropriate and prejudicial?"

I stare at her for a moment. She's *really* good.

"Mr. Bond? How do you respond?" the judge asks.

"Judge, Jacob's mother's presence at counsel table is the equivalent of having a Seeing Eye dog for a defendant who's blind. The jury will understand if told that it's not just an animal in the courtroom—it's a necessity, an accommodation being made for the defendant because of his disability. Jacob's mother, and her proximity to him during the trial, can be explained the same way," I say. "What you're ruling on today, Judge, is what accommodations need to be made to ensure that my client has a fair trial. That right, and those accommodations, are assured to him pursuant to the Americans with Disabilities Act and, even more important, pursuant to the Fifth, Sixth, and Seventh Amendments of the United States Constitution. Does this mean giving Jacob some minor concessions that other defendants don't get in court? Yes, because those other defendants don't have to deal with the crippling inability to communicate effectively and to interact with other people like Jacob does. For them, a trial is not a gigantic mountain standing between them and freedom, without even having the most basic tools with which they can begin climbing."

I glance surreptitiously at the judge and make the snap decision to tone it down a little. "So how do we explain Jacob's mother's position to the jury? Easy. We say that the judge has given her a right to sit at counsel table. We say that this isn't usual practice, but in this case she has a right to sit there. As for her role in the trial, Your Honor, I will have her agree not to speak to Jacob but instead to communicate with him via writing, and those notes can be turned in to the court at the close of the day or during each recess, so that Ms. Sharp gets to see exactly what dialogue is going on between them."

The judge removes his glasses and rubs the bridge of his nose. "This is an unusual case, with unusual circumstances. I've certainly had a good number of defendants come in front of me who had a hard time communicating . . . But in this case, we have a young man facing very serious charges and possible incarceration for the rest of his life, and we know he has a diagnosed inability to communicate the way the rest of us do . . . so it would be an oversight to expect him to behave in a courtroom the way the rest of us would." He looks at Jacob, who—I imagine—is still not meeting his gaze. "What a fair trial looks like for this defendant may well be different from what it looks like for others, but that's the nature of America—we make room for everyone, and that's what we're going to do for Mr. Hunt." He looks down at the motion before him. "All right. I'm going to allow for the sensory breaks. We will ask the bailiff to set up a special room at the back of the courtroom, and anytime the defendant feels the need to leave, he is to pass a note to you, Mr. Bond. Is that satisfactory?"

"Yes," I say.

"Then, Counselor, you may approach and

ask me to call for a recess. You will explain to your client that he may not leave the court-room until the recess has been called and he's been excused by the court."

"Got it, Your Honor," I reply.

"As for your third request, I will not use my gavel for the duration of this trial. However, I'm not going to turn down the lights. It's a security hazard for the bailiffs. Hopefully, having sensory breaks will help compensate, and I have no objection to the defendant turning out the lights in the break room in the rear of the court."

Jacob tugs on my coat. "Can I wear sunglasses?"

"No," I say curtly.

"Third, I'll shorten the court sessions. We will break the trial into three forty-five-minute sessions in the morning, two in the afternoon, with fifteen-minute breaks in between. We will adjourn at four P.M. every day. I assume that will be satisfactory, Mr. Bond?"

"Yes, Your Honor."

"I agree to allow the defendant's mother to sit at counsel table; however, they can only communicate in writing, and those notes must be turned in to the court at every break. Finally, in regard to your request for the prosecution's questioning to be direct and simple," the judge says, "that I will deny. You can ask whatever short, literal questions you like, Mr. Bond, but the defendant has no constitutional right to direct how the State chooses to present its case." He sticks my motion back inside a folder. "I trust that's all satisfactory, Mr. Bond?"

"Of course," I say, but inside, I'm doing handsprings. Because all of these little quirks and concessions are greater than the sum of their parts: the jury cannot help but see that Jacob's different from your average defendant, from the rest of us.

And should be judged accordingly.

Theo

I wake up sneezing.

When I open my eyes, I'm in a pink room and there are feathers tickling my nose. I jackknife upright in the narrow little bed and remember where I am—one of the girls' rooms. There are mobiles with glittery stars and piles of stuffed animals and a pink camouflage rug.

I sneeze again, and that's when I realize I'm wearing a pink feather boa.

"What the fuck," I say, unspooling it from my neck, and then I hear giggling. I lean over the side of the bed and find my father's younger kid—I think her name is Grace—hiding under the bed.

"You said a bad word," she tells me.

"What are you doing here?"

"What are *you* doing here?" she asks. "This is *my* room."

I flop back down on the mattress. Between the time my flight arrived and the Talk, I probably got all of four hours of sleep. No wonder I feel like shit.

She slips out from underneath the bed and sits down beside me. She's really little—I'm not good with kid ages, though. She has purple nail polish on her toes, and she's wearing a plastic tiara.

"How come you're not in school?"

"Because it's Friday, silly," Grace says, although this doesn't make any sense to me. "You have really big feet. They're bigger than Leon."

I'm wondering who Leon is, but then she takes a stuffed pig and holds it up against the bare sole of my foot.

My watch is on the nightstand, next to a book about a mouse too shy to tell anyone her name. I read it last night before I went to bed. It's only 6:42 A.M., but we are leaving early. We've got a plane to catch.

"Are you my brother?" Grace asks.

I look at her. I try really hard, but I can't see a single feature we have in common. And that's really weird, because my mom has always told me I remind her of my dad. (For the record, now that I've seen for myself, it's not true. I'm just blond, that's all, and everyone else in my household has dark hair.) "I guess you could say that," I tell her.

"Then how come you don't live here?"

I look around at the princess poster on the wall, the china tea set on a table in the corner. "I don't know," I say, when the real answer is *Because you have another brother, too.*

This is what happened last night:

I got off the plane and found my parents—both of them—waiting for me outside airport security. "What the hell?" I blurted out.

"My thoughts exactly, Theo," my mother said curtly. And then, before she could tear me a new one, my father said we were going to his house to discuss this.

He made stupid conversation for the twenty-minute drive, while I felt my mother's eyes boring holes into the back of my skull. When we reached his home, I got a glimpse of a really pretty woman who had to be his wife before he led me into the library.

It was very modern, and totally unlike our house. There were windows that made up one entire wall, and the couch was black leather and full of right angles. It looked like the kind of room you see in magazines at doctors' offices, and not anywhere you'd want to live. Our couch was made of some red, stain-proof fabric, and yet there was a stain on the arm from where I spilled grape juice once. The zippers on two of the pillows were broken. But when you wanted to flop down and watch TV, it fit you perfectly.

"So," my father said, gesturing to a seat. "This is a little awkward."

"Yeah."

"I mean, I don't really have much of a right to tell you that running away was a stupid thing to do. And that you scared your mother to death. And I'm not going to tell you that she's out for blood—"

"You don't *have* to tell me that."

He clasps his hands between his knees. "Anyway, I've been thinking about it, and I'm not going to tell you any of those things." He looks at me. "I figured you came all the way out here so that I would *listen.*"

I hesitate. He seems so familiar to me, but that's crazy—given that I talk to him twice a year, on Christmas and my birthday. And yet, maybe that's what being related to someone does for you. Maybe it lets you pick up where you left off, even if that was fifteen years ago.

I want to tell him why I'm there—the story of Jacob's arrest, the truth behind my own breaking and entering, the phone message I never gave my mother from the bank, denying her the second mortgage loan—but all the words jam in my throat. I choke on the sentences until I cannot breathe, until tears spring to my eyes, and what comes out finally is none of these things.

"Why didn't I matter?" I say.

This is not what I wanted. I wanted him to see me as the responsible young man I've become, trying to save my family, and I wanted him to shake his head and think, *I sure fucked up. I should have stayed with him, gotten to know him. He turned out so well.* Instead, I'm a blubbering mess, with my nose running and my hair in my eyes and I'm so tired; I'm suddenly so freaking tired.

When you expect something, you're sure to be disappointed. I learned that a long time ago. But if this had been my mother sitting next to me, her arms would have wrapped around me in an instant. She would have rubbed my back and told me to relax, and I would have let myself melt against her until I felt better.

My father cleared his throat, and didn't touch me at all.

"I'm, uh, not very good at this kind of thing," he said. He shifted, and I wiped my eyes, thinking he was trying to reach out to me, but instead he took his wallet out of his back pocket. "Here," he says, holding out a few twenties. "Why don't you take this?"

I look at him, and before I know it, a laugh has snorted its way out of me. My brother is about to be tried for murder, my mother wants my head on a silver platter, my future's so dim I might as well be buried in a coal mine—and my father can't even pat me on the back and tell me I'm going to be okay. Instead, he thinks sixty bucks is going to make everything better.

"I'm sorry," I say, laughing in earnest now. "I'm really sorry."

It strikes me that I'm not the one who should be saying that.

I don't know what I was thinking, coming out here. There are no silver bullets in life, there's just the long, messy climb out of the pit you've dug yourself.

"I think maybe you should go get Mom," I say.

I'm sure my father thinks I'm crazy, laughing my ass off like this when a minute before I was sobbing. And as he gets up—relieved to get the hell away from me, I'm sure—I realize why my father seems familiar. It's not because we have anything in common, much less share a genetic code. It's because, with his obvious discomfort and the way he won't look at me now and the fact that he doesn't want physical contact, he reminds me so much of my brother.

I don't speak to my mom the whole time my father is driving us to the airport. I don't say a word when my father gives her a check, and she looks at the number written on it, and cannot speak. "Just take it," he says. "I wish . . . I wish I could be there for him."

He doesn't mean it. What he really wishes is that he was *capable* of being there for Jacob, but my mother seems to understand this, and whatever money he's given her helps, too. She gives him a quick good-bye hug.

Me, I hold out my hand. I don't make the same mistake twice.

We don't talk in the departure lounge, or as we're boarding, or during takeoff. It isn't until the pilot gets on the loudspeaker to mumble about our cruising altitude that I turn to my mother and tell her I'm sorry.

She is flipping through an in-flight magazine. "I know," she says.

"Really sorry."

"I'm sure."

"Like, about stealing your credit card number. And all of that."

"Which is why you're paying me back for these tickets—return trips, too—even if it takes you till you're fifty-six," she says.

The flight attendant walks by, asking if anyone would like to purchase a beverage. My mother holds up her hand. "What do you want?" she asks me, and I say tomato juice. "And I'll have a gin and tonic," she tells the flight attendant.

"Really?" I am impressed. I didn't know my mother drank gin.

She sighs. "Desperate times call for desperate measures, Theo." Then she looks up at me, her brow wrinkled in thought. "When was the last time you and I were alone like this?"

"Um," I say. "Never?"

"Huh," my mother says, considering this.

The flight attendant returns with our drinks. "Here you go," she chirps. "You two getting off in L.A. or continuing on to Hawaii?"

"I wish," my mother says, and when she twists the bottle top of the gin, it makes a sighing sound.

"Don't we all?" The flight attendant laughs, and she moves down the aisle.

The page my mother has stopped at in her magazine is a tourism spread of Hawaii, actually, or at least something equally tropical. "Maybe we should just stay on the plane and go there," I say.

She laughs. "Squatters' rights. Sorry, sir, we're not vacating seats Fifteen A and B."

"By dinnertime, we could be sitting on a beach."

"Getting tan," my mother muses.

"Drinking piña coladas," I suggest.

My mother raises a brow. "Virgin for you."

There is a pause, as we both imagine a life that will never be ours.

"Maybe," I say after another moment, "we should bring Jacob along. He loves coconut."

This will never happen. My brother won't get on a plane; he'd have the Mother of all Meltdowns before that happened. And you can't exactly row a boat to Hawaii. Not to mention the fact that we are categorically broke. But still.

My mother lays her head on my shoulder. It feels weird, like I'm the one taking care of her, instead of the other way around. Already, though, I'm taller than her, and still growing. "Let's do that," my mother agrees, as if we have a prayer.

Jacob

I have a joke:

> *Two muffins are in an oven.*
> *One muffin says, "Wow, it's really hot in*
> *here."*
> *The other one jumps and says, "Yikes! A*
> *talking muffin."*

This is funny because

1. Muffins don't talk.

2. I am sane enough to know that. In spite of what my mother and Oliver and practically

every psychiatrist in Vermont seem to think,
I have never struck up a conversation with a
muffin in my entire life.

3. That would just be plain corny.

4. You got that joke, too, right?

My mother said that she would be talking to
Dr. Newcomb for a half hour, yet it has been
forty-two minutes and she still has not come
back into the waiting room.

We are here because Oliver said we have to
be. Even though he managed to get all those
concessions at court for me, and even though
all of those help him prove his insanity defense to the jury (although don't ask me how—
insanity is not equivalent to disability, or even
quirkiness), apparently we also have to meet
with a shrink he's found whose job it will be
to tell the jury that they should let me go because I have Asperger's.

Finally, when it has been sixteen minutes longer than my mother said it would
be—when I have started to sweat a little
and my mouth has gone dry, because I'm
thinking maybe my mother forgot about
me and I will be stuck in this little waiting
room forever—Dr. Newcomb opens the door.

"Jacob?" she says, smiling. "Why don't you come in?"

She is a very tall woman with an even taller tower of hair and skin as smooth and rich as dark chocolate. Her teeth gleam like headlights, and I find myself staring at them. My mother is nowhere in the room. I feel a hum rise in my throat.

"Where's my mom?" I ask. "She said she'd be back in a half hour, and now it's forty-seven minutes."

"We took a little longer than I expected. Your mom went out the back way and is waiting for you just outside," Dr. Newcomb says, as if she can read my mind. "Now, Jacob, I've had a lovely talk with your mom. And Dr. Murano." She sits down and offers me the seat across from her. It's upholstered in zebra stripes, which I don't really like. Patterns in general make me uneasy. Every time I look at a zebra, I can't figure out whether it's black with white stripes or white with black stripes, and that frustrates me.

"It's my job to examine you," Dr. Newcomb says. "I have to give a report back to the court, so what you say here isn't confidential. Do you understand what that means?"

"Intended to be kept secret," I say, rattling

off the definition and frowning. "But you're a doctor?"

"Yes. A psychiatrist, just like Dr. Murano."

"Then what I tell you is privileged," I say. "There's doctor-patient confidentiality."

"No, this is a special circumstance where I'm going to tell people what you say, because of the court case."

This whole procedure is starting to sound even worse—not only do I have to speak to a psychiatrist I don't know, but she plans to blab about the session. "Then I'd rather talk to Dr. Moon. She doesn't tell anyone my secrets."

"I'm afraid that's not an option," Dr. Newcomb says, and then she looks at me. "Do you have secrets?"

"Everyone has secrets."

"Does having secrets sometimes make you feel bad?"

I sit very upright on the chair, so that my back doesn't have to touch the crazy zigzagged fabric. "Sometimes, I guess."

She crosses her legs. They are really long, like a giraffe's. Giraffes and zebras. And I am the elephant, who cannot forget.

"Do you understand that what you did, Jacob, was wrong in the eyes of the law?"

"The law doesn't have eyes," I tell her. "It

has courts and judges and witnesses and juries, but no eyes." I wonder where Oliver dug *this* one up. I mean, *honestly.*

"Do you understand that what you did was wrong?"

I shake my head. "I did the right thing."

"Why was it right?"

"I was following the rules."

"What rules?"

I could tell her more, but she is going to tell other people, and that means that I will not be the only one who gets into trouble. But I know she wants me to explain; I can tell by the way she leans forward. I shrink back in the chair. It means touching the zebra print, but it's the lesser of two evils.

"*I see dead people.*" Dr. Newcomb just stares at me. "It's from *The Sixth Sense,*" I tell her.

"Yes, I know," she says, and she tilts her head. "Do you believe in God, Jacob?"

"We don't go to church. My mom says religion is the root of all evil."

"I didn't ask what your mom thinks about religion. I asked what *you* think about it."

"I *don't* think about it."

"Those rules you mentioned," Dr. Newcomb says.

Didn't we get off this topic?

"Do you know that there's a rule against killing people?"

"Yes."

"Well," Dr. Newcomb asks, "do you think it would be wrong to kill somebody?"

Of course I do. But I can't say that. I can't say it because to admit to this rule would break another one. I stand up and start walking, bouncing up and down on my toes because sometimes it helps me jog the rest of my brain and body into sync.

But I don't answer.

Dr. Newcomb isn't giving up, though. "When you were at Jess's house on the day she died, did you understand that it's wrong to kill somebody?"

"I'm not bad," I quote. *"I'm just drawn that way."*

"I really need you to answer the question, Jacob. On the day that you were at Jess's house, did you feel like you were doing something wrong?"

"No," I say immediately. "I was following the rules."

"Why did you move Jess's body?" she asks.

"I was setting up a crime scene."

"Why did you clean up the evidence at the house?"

"Because we're supposed to clean up our messes."

Dr. Newcomb writes something down. "You had a fight with Jess during your tutoring session a couple of days before she died, right?"

"Yes."

"What did she say to you that day?"

"'Just get lost.'"

"But you went to her house on Tuesday afternoon anyway?"

I nod. "Yes. We had an appointment."

"Jess was obviously upset with you. Why did you go back?"

"People are always saying things that aren't true." I shrug. "Like when Theo tells me to *get a grip.* It doesn't mean *hold something,* it means *calm down.* I assumed Jess was doing the same kind of thing."

"What were your reactions to the victim's responses?"

I shake my head. "I don't know what you're talking about."

"When you got to Jess's house, did you yell at her?"

At one point I had leaned right down into her face and screamed at her to wake up.

"Yes," I say. "But she didn't answer me."

"Do you understand that Jess is never coming back?"

Of course I understand that. I could probably tell Dr. Newcomb a thing or two about body decomposition. "Yeah."

"Do you think Jess was scared that day?"

"I don't know."

"How do you think you would have felt, if you were the victim?"

For a moment, I consider this. "Dead," I say.

Oliver

Three weeks before we go to trial, we start jury selection. You would think that, with autism being diagnosed at the rate it currently is, finding a jury of Jacob's peers—or at least parents who have children on the spectrum—would not be as difficult as it is. But the only two jurors with autistic children who are in our initial pool are the ones Helen uses her peremptory strikes against to get them removed.

In between my stints in court, I receive the reports from Dr. Newcomb and Dr. Cohn, the two psychiatrists who've met with Jacob. Unsurprisingly, Dr. Cohn has found Jacob quite sane—the State's shrink would declare a *toaster* sane—and Dr. Newcomb has said that Jacob was legally insane at the time the crime was committed.

Even so, Newcomb's report isn't going to be that much help. In it, Jacob comes off sounding like an automaton. The truth is, jurors might want to be fair, but their gut instinct about a defendant has a great deal to do with the verdict rendered. Which means that I'd better stack the odds to make Jacob look as sympathetic as possible, since I have no intention of letting him actually testify. With his flat affect, his darting eyes, his nervous tics—well, that would just be a disaster.

A week before the trial begins, I turn my attention to getting Jacob ready for court. When I reach the Hunt household, Thor bolts out of the car and runs to the porch, his tail wagging. He's gotten pretty attached to Theo, to the point where I sometimes wonder if I ought to just leave him curled up on the kid's bed overnight, since he seems to have taken up residence there anyway. And God knows Theo needs the company—in the wake of his cross-country journey, he's been grounded until he's thirty—although I keep telling him that I can probably find a reason to appeal.

I knock, but no one answers the door. I've

gotten used to letting myself inside, though, so I walk in and watch Thor trot upstairs. "Hello," I call out, and Emma steps forward with a smile.

"You're just in time," she says.

"For what?"

"Jacob got a hundred on a math test, and as a reward I'm letting him set up a crime scene."

"*That's* macabre."

"Just another day in my life," she says.

"Ready!" Jacob calls from upstairs.

I follow Emma, but instead of heading to Jacob's room, we continue on to the bathroom. When she pushes open the door, I gag, my hand pressed against my mouth.

"What . . . what is this?" I manage.

There is blood everywhere. It's like I've stepped into the lair of a serial killer. One long line of blood arcs horizontally across the white shell of the shower wall. Facing that, on the mirror, are a series of drops in various elongated shapes.

Even more strange, Emma doesn't seem to be the least bit upset that the walls of the shower and the mirror and sink are completely drenched with blood. She takes one look at my face and starts laughing. "Relax, Oliver," she says. "It's just corn syrup."

She reaches over to the mirror, dabs her finger to the mess, and holds it up to my lips.

I can't resist the urge to taste her. And yeah, it *is* corn syrup, with red dye, I'm guessing.

"Way to contaminate a crime scene, Mom," Jacob mutters. "So you remember that the tail of the bloodstain usually points in the direction the blood was traveling . . ."

All of a sudden I can see Jess Ogilvy standing in the shower, and Jacob across from her, standing right where Emma is.

"I'll give you a hint," Jacob tells Emma. "The victim was right here." He points to the bath mat between the shower stall and the mirror over the sink.

I can easily picture Jacob with a bleach solution, wiping down the mirror and the tub at Jess Ogilvy's place.

"Why the bathroom?" I ask. "What made you choose to set your crime scene here, Jacob?"

Those words are all it takes to make Emma understand why I'm so shaken. "Oh, God," she says, turning. "I didn't think . . . I didn't realize . . ."

"Blood spatter's messy," Jacob says, confounded. "I thought my mom would be less likely to yell at me if I did it in the bathroom."

A line from Dr. Newcomb's report jumps out at me: *I was following the rules.*

"Clean it up," I announce, and I walk out.

"New rules," I say, when the three of us are sitting at the kitchen table. "First and foremost: No more crime scene staging."

"Why not?" Jacob demands.

"You tell me, Jake. You're on trial for homicide. You think it's smart to create a fake murder a week before your trial? You don't know what neighbors are peeking through your curtains—"

"(A) Our neighbors are too far to see through the windows and (B) that crime scene upstairs was nothing like what was at Jess's house. This one showed the arterial bleed in the shower and also the cast-off pattern of blood flung from the knife that killed the victim behind her, on the mirror. At Jess's—"

"I don't want to hear it," I interrupt, covering my ears.

Every time I think I have a chance to save Jacob's ass, he does something like this. Unfortunately, I waver between thinking that behavior like what I've just witnessed proves my case (how could he *not* be considered insane?) and thinking that it's chillingly off-putting to a jury. After all, Jacob's not talking to imaginary giant rabbits, he's pretending to kill someone. That looks pretty fucking deliberate to me. That looks like practice so that, in reality, he might get it perfect.

"Rule number two: you need to do exactly what I tell you in court."

"I've been to court, like, ten times now," Jacob says. "I think I can figure it out."

Emma shakes her head. "Listen to him," she says quietly. "Right now, Oliver's the boss."

"I'm going to give you a stack of Post-its every time we walk into that courtroom," I tell him. "If you need a break, you hand me a note."

"What kind of note?" Jacob says.

"Any note. But you only do it if you need a break. I'm also going to give you a pad and a pen, and I want you to write stuff down—just like you would if you were watching *Crime-Busters.*"

"But there's nothing interesting going on in that courtroom—"

"Jacob," I tell him flatly, "your life is being decided in there. Rule number three: you can't talk to anyone. Not even your mother. And you," I say, turning to Emma, "cannot tell him how he's supposed to feel, or react, or what he should look like or how he should act. Everything you two pass back and forth is going to be read by the prosecution and the judge. I don't even want you two discussing the weather, because they're going to interpret it, and if you do anything suspicious, you're going to be kicked off that counsel table. You want to write *Breathe,* that's fine. Or *It's okay, don't worry.* But that's as specific as I want you to get."

Emma touches Jacob's arm. "You understand?"

"Yes," he says. "Can I go now? Do you have any idea how hard it is to get corn syrup off a wall once it dries?"

I completely ignore him. "Rule number four: you will wear a button-down shirt and a tie, and I don't want to hear that you haven't got the money for it because this isn't negotiable, Emma—"

"No buttons," Jacob announces, in a tone that brooks no argument.

"Why not?"

"Because they feel weird on my chest."

"All right," I say. "How about a turtleneck?"

"Can't I wear my lucky green sweatshirt?" Jacob asks. "I wore it when I took my SATs, and I got 800 on the math section."

"Why don't we go up to your closet and find something?" Emma suggests, and we all trudge upstairs again, this time to Jacob's room. I studiously avoid looking into the bathroom as we pass.

Although the police still have his fuming chamber as evidence, Jacob has configured a new one, an overturned planter. It's not transparent, like his fish tank, but it must be getting the job done, because I can smell the glue. Emma throws open the closet door.

If I hadn't seen it with my own eyes, I would never have believed it. Chromatically ordered, Jacob's clothes hang side by side, not quite touching. There are jeans and chinos in the blue area; and a rainbow of long- and short-sleeved tees. And yes, in its correct sequence, the lucky green sweatshirt. It looks like a Gay Pride shrine in there.

There is a fine line between looking insane in court and looking disrespectful. I take a deep breath, wondering how to explain this to a client who cannot think beyond the feeling of a placket of buttons on his skin. "Jacob," I say, "you have to wear a shirt with a collar. And you have to wear a tie. I'm sorry, but none of this will work."

"What does the way I look have to do with you telling the jury the truth?"

"Because they still see you," I answer. "So you need to make a good first impression."

He turns away. "They're not going to like me anyway. Nobody ever does."

He doesn't say this in a way that suggests he feels sorry for himself. More like he's just telling me a fact, relating the way the world works.

After Jacob leaves to clean up his mess, I remember that Emma's in the room with me. "The bathroom. I . . . I don't know what to say." She sinks down onto Jacob's bed. "He does this all the time—sets up scenes for me to solve. It's what makes him happy."

"Well, there's a big difference between using a bottle of corn syrup to get your jollies and using a human being. I don't need the jury to be wondering how far a leap there is from one to the other."

"Are you nervous?" she asks, turning to face me.

I nod. I probably shouldn't be admitting this to her, but I can't help it.

"Can I ask you something?"

"Sure," I say. "Anything."

"Do you believe he killed Jess?"

"I already told you that doesn't matter to a jury—we're utilizing the defense most likely to—"

"I'm not asking you as Jacob's lawyer," Emma interrupts. "I'm asking you as my friend."

I draw in my breath. "I don't know. If he did, I don't believe it was intentional."

She folds her arms. "I just keep thinking that if we could get the police to reopen the case, to look harder at Jess's boyfriend—"

"The police," I say, "think they've found their murderer, based on the evidence. If they didn't, we wouldn't be going to court on Wednesday. The prosecutor thinks she's got enough proof to make a jury see things her way. But Emma, I'm going to do everything I can to keep that from happening."

"I have a confession to make," Emma says. "When we saw Dr. Newcomb? I was supposed to meet with her for a half hour. I told Jacob that I'd be thirty minutes. And then I very intentionally kept talking for another fifteen. I wanted Jacob to get rattled, because I was late. I wanted him stimming by the time he met with her, so that she'd be able to write about all that behavior in the court report." Emma's eyes are dark and hollow. "What kind of mother does that?"

I look at her. "One who's trying to save her son from going to prison."

Emma shivers. She walks to the window, rubbing her arms, even though it is downright hot in the room. "I'll find him a collared shirt," she promises. "But *you'll* have to get it on him."

CASE 9: PAJAMA GAME

Early in the morning on February 17, 1970, the officers at Fort Bragg, North Carolina, responded to a call from Army Doctor Jeffrey MacDonald. They arrived to find his pregnant wife, Colette, and two young daughters dead from multiple stab wounds. Colette had been stabbed thirty-seven times with a knife and an ice pick, and MacDonald's torn pajama top was draped on top of her. On the headboard of the bed, in blood, was the word PIG. MacDonald himself was found with minor wounds, beside his wife. He said he'd been hurt by three males and a woman in a white hat who chanted, "Acid is groovy, kill the pigs." When the men attacked him, MacDonald said that he pulled his pajama top over his head and used it to block the jabs of the ice pick. Eventually, he said, he was knocked unconscious.

The Army didn't believe MacDonald. The living room, for example, didn't show signs of a struggle, except for an overturned table and plant. Fibers from the torn pajama top were not found in the room where it was torn but rather in the bedrooms of his daughters. They theorized that MacDonald killed his wife and daughters and tried to cover up the murders by using articles about the Manson Family in a magazine that was found in the living room. The Army dropped the case because of the poor quality of the investigative techniques, and MacDonald was honorably discharged.

In 1979 MacDonald was tried in a civilian court. A forensic scientist testified that the doctor's pajama top, which he said had been used to block his attackers, had forty-eight clean, cylindrical holes that were too tidy for a violent attack—to make a hole that shape, the top would have had to be immobile, something that was very unlikely if MacDonald was defending himself from someone trying to stab him. The scientist also showed how, by folding the top a certain way, those forty-eight holes could have been created by twenty-one jabs—the exact number of times Colette Mac-Donald had been stabbed with an ice pick. The holes lined up with the pattern of her wounds, indicating that the pajama top had been placed on her before she was stabbed and not used in self-defense by MacDonald. He was sentenced to life in prison for three murders and still maintains that he is innocent.

9

Theo

It isn't the first time I've wrestled my brother into a coat and tie. "Jesus, Jacob, cut it out before you give me a black eye," I mutter, holding his hands pinned over his head and straddling his body, which twists like a fish that's suddenly found itself on a dock. My mother is working her hardest to make a knot in his tie, but Jacob's thrashing so much that it's practically a noose.

"Do you really need to button it?" I yell, but I doubt she can hear me. Jacob's got us beat in sheer decibels. I bet the neighbors can hear him, and I wonder what they think. Probably that we're sticking pins in his eyeballs.

My mother manages to fasten one of the tiny buttons on the oxford shirt collar before Jacob bites her hand. She makes a little squeak and jerks her fingers away from his neck, leaving one of the buttons still unfastened. "That's good enough," she says, just as Oliver arrives to pick us all up for the first day of the trial.

"I knocked," he says, but obviously we wouldn't have heard him downstairs.

"You're early," my mother answers. She is still wearing a bathrobe.

"Well, let's see the finished product," Oliver says, and my mom and I both step away from Jacob.

Oliver looks at him for one long moment. "What the hell is this?" he asks.

Okay, I'll admit, Jacob's not going to win any fashion awards, but he's in a coat and tie, which were the criteria. He is wearing a polyester suit the color of an egg yolk that my mother found at a thrift store. A pale yellow shirt, with a stretchy golden knit tie.

"He looks like a *pimp,*" Oliver says.

My mother presses her lips together. "It's Yellow Wednesday."

"I don't care if it's polka-dot Sunday," Oliver says. "And neither does anyone on that jury. That's the kind of suit Elton John wears to a gig, Emma, not what a defendant wears to trial."

"It was a compromise," my mother insists.

Oliver runs a hand down his face. "Didn't we talk about a blue blazer?"

"Fridays are blue days," Jacob says. "I'm wearing one then."

"And coincidentally you are also wearing it today," Oliver replies. He glances at me. "I want you to help me, while your mother goes and gets dressed."

"But—"

"Emma, I don't have time to fight with you right now," Oliver tells her.

My mother is planning to wear a very simple dark gray skirt with a blue sweater. I was here when Oliver went through her entire closet channeling his inner Heidi Klum and picked out what he said would be "dark and conservative."

Angry, my mother huffs out of Jacob's room. I fold my arms. "I just got him into those clothes. No way I'm getting him out of them."

Oliver shrugs. "Jacob, take that off."

"*Gladly*," Jacob explodes, and he rips the clothes off his own body in seconds flat.

Oliver tackles him. "Get the pinstriped shirt and the blazer and the red tie," he orders, squinting into Jacob's open closet. The second I do, Jacob takes one look at the clothing—styles he hates, *plus* they're the wrong color—and lets out a bloodcurdling scream.

"Holy shit," Oliver murmurs.

I reach for Jacob's hands and pin them over his head again. "You ain't seen nothing yet," I say.

The last time I had to dress my brother in a coat and tie we were headed to my grandfather's funeral. My mother was not herself that day, which is maybe why Jacob didn't put up as big a fight about the clothes as he did today. Neither of us owned a coat and tie, so my mother had borrowed them from a neighbor's husband. We were younger then, and a man's jacket fit neither of us. We sat on the side of the viewing room where the coffin was with our clothes swimming on us, as if we'd been bigger before our grief hit.

In reality, I didn't know my grandfather very well. He'd been in a nursing home since my grandmother died, and my mom dragged us to visit him twice a year. It smelled like pee, and I used to get totally creeped out by the old people in their wheelchairs, whose skin seemed stretched too shiny and tight over bony knuckles and knees. The one good memory I had of my grandfather involved sitting on his lap when I was really little and having him pull a quarter out of my ear. His breath smelled like whiskey, and his white hair, when I touched it, was stiff as a Brillo pad.

But still, he was dead, and I thought

I should feel something . . . because if I didn't, that meant I was no better than Jacob.

My mother had, for the most part, left us to our own devices while she accepted the condolences of people whose names she didn't even know. I sat next to Jacob, who was staring straight ahead at the casket. It was black and propped up on fancy saw-horses that were covered with red velvet drapes. "Jacob," I whispered. "What do you think happens after?"

"After what?"

"After, you know. You die. Do you think you still get to go to heaven even if you never went to church?" I thought about this for a moment. "Do you think that you recognize people in heaven, or is it like moving to a new school and starting over?"

Jacob looked at me. "After you die, you decompose. Calliphoridae arrive on a body within minutes of death. The blowflies lay eggs in open wounds or natural orifices even before death, and their larvae hatch out in twenty-four hours. So even though maggots can't live underground, the pupal cases might be buried alive with the corpse and do their work from inside the coffin."

My jaw dropped.

"What?" Jacob challenged. "Did you really think embalming lasted forever?"

After that, I didn't ask him any more questions.

Once Jacob has been forced into his new formal wear, I leave Oliver to deal with the fallout and go to my mother's bedroom. She doesn't answer when I knock, so I push the door open a little bit and peek inside. "In here," she calls from her closet.

"Mom," I say, and I sit down on her bed.

"Is Jacob dressed?" She pokes her head around the doorframe.

"Pretty much." I pick at a thread on her quilt.

In all the years we have lived here, my mother has slept on the left side of the bed. You'd think by now she would have branched out and taken over the whole damn thing, but no. It's like she's still waiting for someone to crawl into the other side.

"Mom," I repeat. "I have to talk to you."

"Sure, baby. Shoot," she says. And then, "Where the hell are my black heels?"

"It's kind of important. It's about Jacob."

She steps out of the closet and sits down beside me on the bed. "Oh, Theo," she sighs. "I'm scared, too."

"It's not that—"

"We're going to do this the way we've done everything when it comes to Jacob," she promises. "Together."

She gives me a tight squeeze, which only makes me feel more miserable, because I know I'm not going to say what I want to say to her, what I *need* to say.

"How do I look?" she asks, drawing away from me.

For the first time, I notice what she's wearing. Not the conservative skirt and blue sweater and pearls that Oliver picked out for her but instead, a totally out-of-season bright yellow sundress. She grins at me. "It's Yellow Wednesday," she says.

Jacob

The first job from which I was fired was a pet store. I will not give the name of the chain, because I'm not sure if that's printable, and I have enough legal trouble to last me a lifetime right now. However, I will say—objectively—that I was the best employee they had and that, in spite of this, they still dismissed me.

Even though when someone bought a corgi puppy, I offered facts along with Puppy Chow. (It's related to the dachshund! Its name is Welsh and means dwarf dog!)

Even though I didn't steal from the cash register, like one of my coworkers.

Even though I didn't tell on that coworker.

Even though I wasn't rude to customers and never bitched when it was my turn to clean the public restrooms.

What my boss (Alan, who was nineteen and an extremely viable candidate for Proactiv) told me was that customers had complained because of my appearance.

No, I did not have snot running down my face. I wasn't drooling. I didn't wear my pants halfway to my knees, like the coworker I referenced above. All I did, ladies and gentlemen of the jury, was refuse to wear the store uniform. It was a blue button-down shirt. I wore it on Fridays, but honestly, it was bad enough I had to deal with buttons—was I supposed to put up with wearing colors on their off days, too?

No one had complained, by the way. And it was easy to spot me as an employee because, even when I wasn't wearing the uniform, I still wore a tag as big as a newborn's head that read, HELLO MY NAME IS JACOB, CAN I HELP YOU?

The real reason I was fired was that, after several weeks of making excuses to Alan about why my uniform did not appear on my body unless I happened to be scheduled to work on a Friday, I finally told him that I was autistic and that 1 had a thing about clothing colors, not to mention buttons. So in spite of the fact that the puppies genuinely loved me, and that 1 sold more of them than any other person working here; in spite of the fact that even at the moment 1 was fired one of the employees was texting her boyfriend instead of ringing up a customer and another one was flirting with Steve in Amphibians—in spite of all these things, 1 was made a scapegoat because of my disability.

Yeah, I'm playing the Asperger's card.

All 1 know is that before 1 told Alan 1 had AS he was willing to make excuses along with me, and afterward, he just wanted me gone.

This is the story of my life.

We ride to the courthouse in Oliver's car. My mother is in the front seat, and Theo and 1 are in the back. 1 spend most of the trip looking at the things 1 took for granted, sights 1 hadn't seen while 1 was cooped up under house arrest: the Colony diner, with its busted neon sign, advertising EAT AT THE COLON. The picture window of the pet store where 1 used to work, with a Gordian knot of puppies on view. The movie theater where 1 lost my first tooth and the cross on the side of the road where a teenager once died en route to school during an ice storm. The Restwood Bible Church billboard that reads, FREE COFFEE! ETERNAL LIFE! MEMBERSHIP HAS ITS PRIVILEGES!

"Okay," Oliver says, after he pulls into a parking spot and turns off the ignition. "Here we go."

I open my door and step out of the car, and suddenly there are a thousand sounds hitting me like arrows and so much light that everything goes white. I can't hold my hands up to my eyes and my ears at the same time, and somewhere in between the screaming I can hear my name and my mother's voice and Oliver's. They multiply before my eyes, microphones like cancer cells, and they are coming closer.

Oliver: Shit—I should have thought of this . . .

Mom: Jacob, close your eyes, baby. Can you hear me? Theo? Have you got ahold of him?

And then there is a hand on my arm, but who can say if it belongs to my brother or to one of the strangers, the ones who want to cut my veins lengthwise and bleed me dry, the ones with headlight eyes and cavern mouths who want a piece of me to stick into their pockets and take away, until there's nothing left.

I do what any ordinary person would do when faced with a horde of wild animals gnashing their teeth and wielding micro-phones: I run.

It feels fantastic.

Keep in mind I have been in a cage that's twenty by forty feet, two stories high. I may not be as fast as I'd like to be, because I am wearing dress shoes and also I am a natural klutz, but I manage to get far enough away to not hear their voices anymore. I can't hear anything, really, but the wind whistling in my ears and my breathing.

And then suddenly I'm knocked off my feet.

"Fuck it," Oliver wheezes. "I'm getting too old for this."

I can barely speak because he's lying flat on my back. "You're . . . twenty-eight . . . ," I grunt.

He rolls off me, and for a moment we are both sprawled on the pavement underneath a sign at a gas station. UNLEADED $2.69.

"I'm sorry," Oliver says after a moment. "I should have seen that coming."

I push up on my elbows to look at him.

"There are a lot of people who want to see what happens with your case," he says, "and I should have prepared you."

"I don't want to go back there," I say.

"Jake, the judge is going to put you back in jail if you don't."

I run through the list of rules in my head, the ones Oliver gave me for court behavior. I wonder why he didn't give the reporters the same rules, because clearly shoving a microphone up my nostrils doesn't qualify as good etiquette. "I want a sensory break," I announce, one of the appropriate responses to Oliver when we are at the trial.

He sits up and draws his knees into his chest. A car pulls up to the gas pump a few feet away, and the guy who gets out looks at us strangely before swiping his credit card. "Then we'll ask the judge for one as soon as we get inside." He tilts his head. "What do you say, Jake? You ready to fight with me?"

I roll my toes in the bells of the dress shoes. I do it three times, because that's lucky. *"I love the smell of napalm in the morning,"* I answer.

Oliver looks away from me. "I'm nervous," he admits.

This doesn't seem like a great thing to hear

from one's attorney before going into a trial, but I like the fact that he's not lying to me. "You tell the truth," I say.

It's a compliment, but Oliver interprets it as a directive. He hesitates. "I'll tell them why you're not guilty." Then he gets up, dusting off his pants. "So what do you say?"

This phrase has always seemed to be a trick question. Most of the time it's uttered by a person when you haven't even said a damn thing, but of course, the minute you point out that you haven't said anything, you *have.*

"Do I have to go through all those people again?" I ask.

"Yeah," Oliver says, "but I've got an idea."

He leads me to the edge of the parking lot, where Theo and my mom are anxiously waiting. I want to tell Oliver something, but it fades in the face of this more immediate problem. "Close your eyes," he instructs, so I do. Then I feel him grab my right arm, and my mother grabs my left. My eyes are still closed, but I start to hear the humming of the voices, and without even realizing it, I make the same sound in the back of my throat.

"Now . . . sing!"

"I shot the sheriff . . . but I didn't shoot no deputy—" I break off. "I can still *hear* them."

So Theo starts singing. And Oliver, and my mother. All of us, a barbershop quartet but without the harmony, up the stairs of the courthouse.

It works. Probably because they are so surprised by the musical number, the Red Sea of reporters parts and we walk right up the middle.

I'm so amazed that it takes me a while to remember what was stuck like a fish bone in my throat before we walked up the steps of the courthouse.

1. I said to Oliver the verbal equation we'll call p: "You tell the truth."

2. He replied with q: "I'll tell them why you're not guilty."

3. In the logic equation of this conversation, I had made the assumption that p and q were equivalent.

4. Now I realize that's not necessarily true.

Before Jess and I started to work together, I had to go to social skills class at my school. This was largely populated by kids who, unlike me, were not particularly interested in joining the social scene. Robbie was profoundly autistic and spent most of the sessions lining crayons from end to end across the room. Jordan and Nia were developmentally disabled and spent all their time in special ed instead of being mainstreamed. Serafima was probably the most similar to me, although she had Down syndrome. She wanted to be part of the action so badly she'd crawl into the lap of a stranger and hold his face between her hands, which was cute when she was six but not so much when she was sixteen.

Lois, the teacher, had all sorts of interactive games that we had to participate in. We'd role-play and have to greet each other as if we hadn't been sitting in the same room together for the past half hour. We'd have contests to see how long we could keep eye contact. Once, she used an egg timer to show us when we should stop talking about a topic so that someone else could have a turn in the conversation, but that stopped quickly when Robbie went ballistic the first time the buzzer went off.

Every day we had to end with a circle time, where we each gave a compliment to the person next to us. Robbie always said the same thing, no matter whom he was placed beside: *I like terrapins.*

(He did, too. He knew more about them than anyone I've ever met since and probably ever will, and if not for him I'd still be confusing them with box turtles.)

Jordan and Nia always gave compliments based on appearance: *I like that you brush your hair. I like that your skirt is red.*

One day Serafima told me that she liked hearing me talk about mitochondrial DNA. I turned to her and said that I *didn't* like the fact that she was a liar, since she had just that very day used the hand signal we agreed on as a class—a peace sign raised in the air—to tell Lois that she was tired of the topic, even though I hadn't gotten to the part about how all of us in this world are related.

That was when Lois called my mother, and my mother found Jess.

I worked on compliments with Jess, too, but it was different. For one thing, I really *wanted* to give them to her. I *did* like the way her hair looked like the stringy silk you pull out of a corn husk before it goes into the boiling water, and how she drew smiley faces on the white rubber rims of her sneakers. And when 1 went on and on about forensic science, she didn't wave a peace sign in the air; instead, she'd ask more questions.

It was almost like that was her way of getting to know me—through how my mind worked. It was like a maze; you had to follow all the twists and turns in order to figure out where 1 started from, and 1 was amazed that Jess was willing to put in the time. 1 guess 1 didn't really think about the fact that my mother must have been paying her to do that, at least not until that idiot Mark Maguire said so at the pizza place. But still, it wasn't like she was sitting there counting down the minutes she had to suffer with me. You would have realized that, if you'd seen her.

My favorite session with Jess was the one where we practiced asking a girl to the dance. We were sitting at a Wendy's because it was raining—we had gotten caught in a sudden downpour. While it passed Jess decided to get a snack, although there wasn't much fast food that was gluten- and casein-free. 1 had ordered two baked potatoes and a side salad without dressing, while Jess had a cheeseburger. "You can't even have French fries?"

"Nope," 1 said. "It's all about the coating,

and the oil they're fried in. The only fast-food fries that are gluten-free are at Hooters."

Jess laughed. "Yeah, I won't be taking you there." She peered at my bare potato, my undressed salad. "You can't even have a little butter?"

"Not unless it's soy." I shrug. "You get used to it."

"So this," she said, turning the cheeseburger over in her hand, "is the kiss of death for you?"

I felt my face go bright red. I didn't know what she was talking about, but hearing her say the word *kiss* was enough to make me feel like I'd just eaten a butterfly instead of a cucumber. "It's not like an allergy."

"What would happen if you ate it?"

"I don't know. I'd get upset more easily, I guess. The diet just works, for some reason."

She looked at the bun and picked a seed off it. "Maybe I should go cold turkey, too."

"Nothing upsets you," I told her.

"Little do you know," Jess said, and then she shook her head and went back to the topic of the day. "Go ahead. Ask."

"Um," I said, looking into my potato, "so do you want to go to the dance with me?"

"No," Jess said flatly. "You've got to sell it, Jacob."

"I'm, uh, going to the dance and I thought since you might be there, too—"

"Blah blah blah," she interrupted.

I forced myself to look Jess in the eye. "I think you're the only person who gets me." I swallowed hard. "When I'm with you, the world doesn't feel like a problem I can't figure out. Please come to the dance," I said, "because you're my music."

Jess's mouth dropped open. "Oh, Jacob, yes!" she shouted, and then all of a sudden she was out of her seat and pulling me up and hugging me, and I could smell the rain in her ponytail and I didn't mind at all that she was in my space and too close. I liked it. I liked it so much that *you know what* happened and I had to push her away before she noticed or (worse) felt it hard against her.

An old couple that was sitting across from us was smiling. I have no idea what they thought we were up to, but chances are Autistic Kid with Social Skills Tutor was not high on the list. The elderly woman winked at Jess. "Looks like that's one cheeseburger you won't forget."

There's a lot about Jess I won't forget. Like

the way her fingernails were painted with sparkly purple polish that day. And how she hated barbecue sauce. How when she laughed, it wasn't a tiny, delicate thing but a sound that came from her belly.

So much time is spent with people superficially. You remember all the fun you had but nothing specific.

I'll never forget anything about her.

Oliver

When Jacob and Emma and I reach the defense table, the courtroom is already full and Helen Sharp is reviewing her notes. "The fun room's great," she says, sliding a glance toward me. "Gotta get me one of those."

By *fun room,* she means the sensory break zone, which has been erected at the rear of the courtroom. There are heavy soundproof curtains that seal it off from the gallery. Inside there are rubber balls with knobs on them and a vibrating pillow and a Lava lamp and something that reminds me of the long fabric tongues in a car wash. Emma swears all of these function as soothing devices, but if you ask me, they might just as easily have come from a fetish porn movie set.

"If you're going to ask the wizard for something, Helen," I suggest, "start with a heart."

The bailiff calls us to attention, and we stand for the arrival of Judge Cuttings. He takes one look at the four cameras in the back of the courtroom. "I'd like to remind the media they are here only by my decree—a decision that can be changed at any minute if they become intrusive in any way. And the same goes for the gallery—outbursts will not be tolerated during this trial. Counselors, please approach."

I walk toward the bench with Helen. "Given the previous experiences we've had during closed court sessions," the judge says, "I thought it might be prudent to check in with you before we begin. Mr. Bond, how is your client this morning?"

Well, he's on trial for murder, I think. *But other than that, he's doing swell.*

I have a brief flash of myself sitting on Jacob's chest so that I can button his shirt, of him sprinting down the divided highway. "Never better, Your Honor," I say.

"Are there any other problems we need to be made aware of?" the judge asks.

I shake my head, heartened by the fact that

the judge seems to truly care about Jacob's welfare.

"Good. Because a lot of people are watching this trial, and I'll be damned if I'm going to be made to look like a fool," he snaps.

So much for human charity.

"And you, Ms. Sharp? You're prepared?"

"One hundred percent, Your Honor," Helen says.

The judge nods. "Then let's begin with the prosecution's opening argument."

Emma offers me a brave smile as I sit down on Jacob's other side. She turns around to locate Theo, who is tucked in the back of the gallery, and then faces forward as Helen begins to speak.

"Four months ago, Jess Ogilvy was a bright, beautiful girl full of hopes and dreams. A graduate student at the University of Vermont, she was working toward a master's in child psychology. She balanced her studies with part-time jobs—like her recent position as caretaker for a professor's home at sixty-seven, Serendipity Way, Townsend . . . and student teaching, and tutoring special needs kids. One of her pupils was a young man with Asperger's syndrome—the same young man, Jacob Hunt, who sits before you as a defendant today. Jess helped

Jacob specifically with social skills—teaching him how to engage others in conversation, how to make friends, and how to interact in public—all tasks that were difficult for him. Jess and Jacob met twice a week, on Sundays and on Tuesdays. But on Tuesday, January twelfth, Jess Ogilvy did not tutor Jacob Hunt. Instead, that young man—the same one she had treated with kindness and compassion—murdered her in a brutal and vicious attack inside her own residence."

Behind the prosecutor's table, a woman starts weeping quietly. The mother; I don't have to turn around to see that. But Jacob does, and his face twists as he registers something familiar about her—maybe the same line of jaw her daughter had, or the color of the hair.

"Two days before her death, Jess took Jacob out for pizza on Main Street in Townsend. You'll hear evidence from Calista Spatakopoulous, the owner of the restaurant, that Jacob and Jess got into a heated argument that ended with Jess telling Jacob to 'just get lost.' You'll hear from Mark Maguire, Jess's boyfriend, that when he saw her later that night and on Monday, she was fine—but that she'd disappeared by Tuesday afternoon. You'll hear from Detective Rich Matson of the Townsend Police Department, who will

tell you how officers searched for any sign of
Jess for five days to see if she'd been abducted,
and finally tracked a GPS signal on her cell
phone to find her bruised and battered body
lying lifeless in a culvert several hundred yards
from her home. You'll hear the medical examiner testify that Jess Ogilvy had abrasions on
her back, choke marks around her neck, a
broken nose and bruises on her face, a broken
tooth . . . and that her underwear was on backward."

I scan the faces of the jurors, each of whom
is thinking, *What kind of animal would do that
to a girl?* and then glancing furtively at Jacob.

"And, ladies and gentlemen, you will get to
see the quilt that Jess Ogilvy's body was found
wrapped in. A quilt that belonged to Jacob Hunt."

Beside me, Jacob's started to shake. Emma
puts her hand on his arm, but he knocks it off.
With a finger, I push the Post-it pad I've set in
front of him a little closer. I uncap the pen I've
given him, willing him to take out his frustration in writing instead of having an outburst.

"The evidence we present will clearly show
that Jacob Hunt murdered Jess Ogilvy with
premeditation. And at the end of this trial, when
the judge instructs you to decide who's responsible, we are confident that you will find that

Jacob Hunt killed Jess Ogilvy—a vibrant young woman who considered herself his teacher, mentor, and friend—and then . . ." She walks to the prosecutor's table and rips the top piece of paper off her legal pad.

Suddenly, I realize what she's about to do.

Helen Sharp crumples the paper in one fist and lets it drop to the floor. "He threw her away like trash," she says, but by that time, Jacob's started to scream.

Emma

The minute the prosecutor reaches for the legal pad, I can finish the end of her sentence. I start to rise from my seat, but it's too late; Jacob's out of control, and the judge—who has no gavel—is pounding his fist. "Your Honor, can we have a brief recess?" Oliver yells, struggling to be heard over Jacob's shrieks. *"No . . . wire hangers . . . ever!"* Jacob screams.

"We'll take ten minutes," the judge says, and suddenly one bailiff is moving toward the jury to escort them out of the courtroom and another one is coming toward us to take us to the sensory break room. "Counsel, I want to see you at the bench."

The bailiff is taller than Jacob and is shaped like a bell, heavy in his hips. He wraps one beefy hand around Jacob's arm. "Let's go, buddy," he says, and Jacob tries to jerk away from him, and then starts thrashing. He clips the bailiff hard enough to cause him to grunt, and then suddenly Jacob goes boneless, all 185 pounds of him, and falls heavily to the floor.

The bailiff reaches down for him, but I throw myself on top of Jacob instead. "Don't touch him," I say, well aware that the jury is straining to see what's going on even as they're being shooed away, certain that every one of those cameramen has his lens trained on me.

Jacob's crying into my shoulder, making small snuffling sounds as he tries to catch his breath. "Okay, baby," I murmur into his ear. "You and I, we're going to do this together." I tug until he starts to sit up, and then I wrap my arms around him, struggling to bear the brunt of his weight as we get to our feet. The bailiff opens the gate of the bar for us and leads us down the gallery aisle to the sensory break room. As we pass, the entire courtroom falls dead silent until we are ensconced within the black curtains and all I can hear outside is the tidal swell of a murmur of sound: *What was* that? ... *Never seen anything like it ... The judge won't stand for stunts ... A ploy to get sympathy, I'll bet ...*

Jacob buries himself beneath a weighted blanket. "Mom," he says from beneath it. "She crumpled paper."

"I know."

"We have to fix the paper."

"It's not our paper. It's the prosecutor's paper. You have to let it go."

"She crumpled the paper," Jacob repeats. "We have to fix it."

I think of the woman on the jury who looked at me with abject pity on her face the moment before she was hustled out of the courtroom. *That's a good thing,* Oliver would say, but he is not me. I have never wanted to be pitied for having a child like Jacob. I've pitied other mothers, who could slip by on loving their children maybe only 80 percent of the time, or less, instead of giving it their all every minute of every day.

But I have a son who is on trial for murder.

A son who behaved the same way the afternoon of Jess Ogilvy's death as he did minutes ago when a piece of paper was torn apart.

If Jacob is a murderer, I will still love him. But I will hate the woman he's turned me into—one whom others talk about when her back is turned, one whom people feel sorry for. Because although I'd never feel that way about a mother whose child has Asperger's, I *would* feel that way about a mother whose child took the life of another mother's child.

Jacob's voice is a hammer at the back of my head. "We have to fix it," he says.

"Yes," I whisper. "We do."

Oliver

"That must be a record, Mr. Bond," Judge Cuttings drawls. "We made it a whole three minutes and twenty seconds without an outburst."

"Judge," I say, thinking on the fly, "I can't predict everything that's going to set this kid off. That's part of why you're allowing his mother to be here. But you know, with all due respect, Jacob doesn't just get ten hours of justice. He gets as much justice as he needs. That's the whole purpose of the constitutional system."

"Gee, Oliver, I don't mean to interrupt," Helen says, "but aren't you forgetting the all-American marching band and the flag that's supposed to drop from the rafters right now?"

I ignore her. "Look. I'm sorry, Your Honor. I'm sorry in advance if Jacob makes you look silly or makes me look silly or—" I glance at Helen. "Well. As I was saying, I certainly don't want my client having fits in front of the jury; it doesn't do my case any good, either."

The judge peers over his glasses. "You've got ten minutes to pull your client together," he warns. "Then we're coming back in and the prosecution will have a chance to refinish her closing."

"Well, she can't crumple the paper again," I say.

"I believe you lost that motion," Helen replies.

"She's right, Counselor. If Ms. Sharp is inclined to crumple a boatload of paper, and your client goes ballistic every time, it's to your own detriment."

"That's okay, Judge," Helen says. "I won't be doing that again. From now on, only folded paper." She bends down, picks up the little ball that sent Jacob sky-high, and tosses it in the trash can beside the stenographer's table.

I glance down at my watch—by my calculations I have four minutes and fifteen seconds to get Jacob's perfectly Zen butt into the chair beside me at the defense table. I stalk up the aisle and slip between the black curtains of the sensory break room. Jacob is hidden under a blanket, and Emma sits doubled over a vibrating pillow. "What else aren't you telling me?" I demand. "What else sets him off? Paper clips? When the clock reads a quarter to twelve? For Christ's sake, Emma, I've only got one trial to convince the jury Jacob didn't snap in a fit of rage and kill Jess Ogilvy. How am I supposed to do that when he can't even make it ten minutes without losing control?"

I'm yelling so loudly that even those stupid curtains probably can't drown me out, and I wonder if the television cameras are picking everything up with their microphones. But then Emma lifts her face, and I see how red her eyes are. "I'll try to keep him calmer."

"Aw, shit," I say, all the bluster fizzing out of me. "You're crying?"

She shakes her head. "No. I'm fine."

"Right, and I'm Clarence Thomas." I reach into my pocket and pull out a Dunkin' Donuts napkin, press it into her hand. "You don't have to lie to me. We're on the same side."

She turns away and blows her nose, then folds—folds, not crumples—the napkin and tucks it into the pocket of her yellow dress.

I pull the blanket off Jacob's head. "Time to go," I say.

For a minute I think he's coming, but then he rolls away from me. "Mom," he mutters. "Fix it."

I turn to Emma, who clears her throat. "He wants Helen Sharp to smooth out the paper first," she says.

"It's already in the trash can."

"You promised," Jacob says to Emma, his voice rising.

"Jesus," I mutter under my breath. "Fine."

I stalk down the aisle of the courtroom and fish through the trash at the stenographer's feet. She stares as if I've lost my mind, which isn't entirely impossible. "What are you doing?"

"Don't ask." The paper is underneath a candy wrapper and a copy of the *Boston Globe*. I tuck it into my jacket pocket and walk back to the sensory break room, where I remove it and smooth it out as best as I can in front of Jacob. "That's the best I can do," I tell him. "So . . . what's the best *you* can do?"

Jacob stares at the paper. *"You had me at hello,"* he says.

Jacob

I hated Mark Maguire before I even laid eyes on him. Jess had changed—instead of focusing only on me when we had our sessions, she'd answer her cell phone or fire back a text message, and every time she did, she smiled. I assumed that I was the reason for her distraction. After all, everyone else seemed to get sick of me quick enough when we were in the middle of a conversation, and it was bound to happen with Jess, although that was my greatest fear. Then one day she said she wanted to tell me a secret. "I think I'm in love," she said, and I swear to you, my heart stopped beating for a second.

"Me, too," I burst out.

CASE STUDY 1: Let me stop here for a minute and just talk about prairie voles. They are part of only a tiny fraction of the animal kingdom that practice monogamy. They mate for twenty-four hours, and then, just like that, they're together for life. However, the montane vole—which is a close relative, sharing 99 percent of the prairie vole's genetic makeup—has no interest in anything except a wham-bam-thank-you-ma'am one-night stand. How come? When prairie voles have sexual intercourse, the hormones oxytocin and vasopressin flood the brain. If the hormones are blocked, prairie voles behave more like those slutty montane voles. Even more interesting, if prairie voles get injections of those hormones but then are prevented from having sex, they still become slavishly devoted to their would-be mates. In other words: you can make a prairie vole fall in love.

The opposite, though, isn't true. You can't give a shot of hormones to a montane vole and make it lovesick. It just doesn't have the right receptors in the brain. It does, however, get a flood of dopamine to the brain when it mates, the hormonal equivalent of *Man, that feels good.* It's just missing the other two hormones, the ones that help pinpoint that ecstasy to a particular individual. Sure enough, if you genetically modify mice, removing the genes that affect oxytocin or vasopressin, they can't recognize mice they've already met.

I am a prairie vole, trapped in the body of a montane vole. If I think I've fallen in love, it's because I've considered it analytically. (Heart palpitations? Check. Lack of stress in her company? Check.) And it seems to me to be the most likely explanation for what I feel, although I could not truly tell you the difference between feelings for a romantic interest versus feelings for a close friend. Or in my case, my *only* friend.

Which is why, when Jess told me she was in love, I reciprocated.

Her eyes widened, and so did her smile. "Oh my God, Jacob," she said. "We'll have to double-date!"

That was when I realized we weren't talking about the same thing.

"I know you like having time alone for our

sessions, but it's good for you to meet people, and Mark really, truly wants to get to know you. He's a part-time ski instructor over at Stowe, and he thought maybe he could give you a free lesson."

"I don't think I'd be very good at skiing." One of the hallmarks of Asperger's is that we can barely walk and chew gum at the same time. I am forever tripping over my feet or stumbling on a curb; I could easily see myself falling off a chairlift or snowballing down a mountain.

"I'll be there to help, too," Jess promised.

And so, the following Sunday, Jess drove me to Stowe and got me fitted for rental skis and boots and a helmet. We hobbled outside and waited near the ski school sign until a black blur whizzed down the hill and sprayed us in a tsunami of powdered snow. "Hey, babe," Mark said, pulling off his helmet so that he could grab Jess and kiss her.

In one glance I could tell that Mark Maguire was everything I was not:

1. Coordinated

2. Attractive (if you're a girl, I mean)

3. Popular

4. Muscular

5. Confident

I could also tell that I was one thing Mark Maguire was not:

1. Smart

"Mark, this is my friend Jacob."

He leaned down into my face and yelled, *"Hey, dude, cool to meet you!"*

I yelled back, *"I'm not deaf!"*

He grinned at Jess. He had perfect, white teeth. "You're right. He *is* funny."

Had Jess told him I was funny? Had she meant that I made her laugh because I told good jokes or because I *was* a joke?

In that instant I hated Mark Maguire viscerally, because he'd made me doubt Jess, and up until then I had known, unequivocally, that we were friends.

"So what do you say we give the bunny hill a try?" Mark asked, and he held out a pole so that he could drag me to the rope tow. "Like this," he said, showing me how to grab on to the moving rope, and I thought I had it right but my left hand got screwed up with my right and I wound up spinning backward and collapsing on the little kid behind me. The guy running the rope tow had to shut it off while Mark hauled me to my feet again. "You okay, Jacob?" Jess asked, but Mark brushed her off.

"He's doing great," Mark said. "Relax, Jake. I teach retarded kids all the time."

"Jacob is *autistic,*" Jess corrected, and I turned around so fast that I forgot about the skis and fell down in a heap again. "I'm not retarded," I shouted, but that statement is somewhat less resonant when one cannot even untangle one's own legs.

I will say this for Mark Maguire: he taught me how to snowplow efficiently enough to make it down the bunny hill twice, solo. Then he asked Jess if she wanted to take a run up the big hill while I practiced. They left me in the company of seven-year-olds in pink snow-suits.

CASE STUDY 2: In laboratory studies, scientists have learned that, when it comes to love, a very tiny portion of the brain is actually involved. For example, friendship lights up receptors all over the cerebral cortex, but this isn't true with love, which activates parts of the brain more commonly associated with emotional responses like fear and anger. The brain of a person in love will show activity in the amygdala, which is associated with gut feelings, and in the nucleus accumbens, an area associated with rewarding stimuli that tends to be active in drug abusers. Or, to recap: the brain of a person in love doesn't look like the brain of someone overcome by deep emotion. It looks like the brain of a person who's been snorting coke.

That day at Stowe, I did two runs with the help of a kid who was learning to snowboard, then inched myself toward the main ski lift. I leaned against a rack where people could store their skis while they were in the lodge getting hot chocolate and chicken nuggets, and I waited for Jess to come back to me.

Mark Maguire is wearing a suit. He has dark circles under his eyes and I almost feel bad for him, because he must be missing Jess, too, until I remember how he hurt her.

"Can you state your name for the record?" the prosecutor asks.

"Mark Maguire."

"Where do you live, Mr. Maguire?"

"Forty-four Green Street in Burlington."

"How old are you?"

"I'm twenty-five," he says.

"And what do you do for a living?"

"I'm a grad student at UVM and a part-time ski instructor at Stowe."

"How did you know Jess Ogilvy, Mr. Maguire?"

"She'd been my girlfriend for five months."

"Where were you on Sunday, January tenth, 2010?" Helen Sharp asks.

"At Mama's Pizza in Townsend. Jess had a tutoring session with Jacob Hunt, and I liked to come along every now and then."

That is not true. He just didn't like that she was spending time with *me* and wouldn't give me up for him.

"So you know Jacob?"

"Yes."

"Do you see him in the courtroom today?"

I stare down at the table so I can't feel the serrated edges of Mark's eyes. "He's sitting over there."

"Let the record reflect that the witness has identified the defendant," the prosecutor says. "How many times, before January tenth, had you met Jacob?"

"I don't know. Maybe five or six?"

The prosecutor walks toward the witness box. "Did you get along with him?"

Mark is looking at me again, I can tell. "I didn't really pay attention to him," he says.

We are in Jess's dorm room watching a TV movie about the JonBenét Ramsey murder case, which of course was one in which Dr. Henry Lee was involved. I tell Jess what is true and what Hollywood has changed. She keeps checking her voice-mail messages, but there aren't any. I am so excited about the movie that for a while I don't realize she is crying. You're crying, I say, the obvious, and I don't get it because she didn't know JonBenét and usually people who cry at someone's death knew them very well. I'm just not very happy today, I guess, Jess says, and she stands up. When she does, she makes a sound like a dog that's been kicked. She has to stand on a chair to reach a high shelf where she keeps her extra toilet paper and Ziploc bags and Kleenex. When she grabs the box of tissues, her sweater rides up on the side and I can see them, red and purple and yellow like a tattoo, but I've watched enough CrimeBusters to know bruises when I see them.

What happened to you? I ask, and she tells me she fell down.

I've watched enough CrimeBusters *to know that's what girls always say when they don't want you to know that someone is beating them up.*

* * *

"We ordered pizza," Mark says, "the kind that Jacob can eat, without wheat in the crust. While we were waiting for it, Jacob asked Jess out. Like on a date. It was hilarious, but when I laughed at him, she got pissed off at me. I didn't have to sit around and take that, so I left."

Even worse than Mark's stare, it turns out, is my mother's.

"Did you talk to Jess at any point after that?" Helen asks.

"Yeah, on Monday. She called me and begged me to come over that night, and I did."

"What was her state of mind?"

"She thought I was mad at her—"

"Objection," Oliver says. "Speculation."

The judge nods. "Sustained."

Mark looks confused. "What was her emotional state?" Helen asks.

"She was upset."

"Did you continue to argue?"

"No," Mark says. "We kissed and made up, if you get my drift."

"So you spent the night?"

"Yes."

"What happened on Tuesday morning?"

"We were having breakfast and we started to fight again."

"About what?" Helen Sharp asks.

"I don't even remember. But I got really angry, and I . . . I sort of shoved her."

"You mean your fight became physical?"

Mark looks down at his hands. "I didn't mean to. But we were yelling and I grabbed her and pushed her against the wall. I stopped right away, said I was sorry. She told me to leave, so I did. I only had my hands on her for a minute."

My head snaps up. I grab the pen in front of me and write so hard on the legal pad that it rips through the paper. HE IS LYING, I write, and I push the pad toward Oliver.

He glances at it, and writes: ?

BRUISES ON HER NECK.

Oliver rips off the piece of paper and tucks it into his pocket. Meanwhile, Mark covers his eyes, and his voice cracks. "I called her all day long, to apologize again, and she wouldn't answer her phone. I figured she was ignoring me, and I deserved it, but by Wednesday morning I was getting worried. I went over to her place, figuring I could catch her before she went to class, but she wasn't there."

"Did you notice anything unusual?"

"The door was open. I went in, and her coat was hanging up and her purse was on the table, but she didn't answer when I called. I looked all over for her, but she was gone. There were clothes all over the bedroom, and the bed was messed up."

"What did you think?"

"At first, I figured she might have left on a trip. But she would have told me that, and she had a test that day. I called her phone, but no one answered. I called her parents and her friends, and no one had seen her; and she hadn't told anyone she was leaving. That's when I went to the police."

"What happened?"

"Detective Matson told me I couldn't file a missing person's report for thirty-six hours, but he came with me to Jess's place. I didn't get the sense he was taking me seriously, to be honest." Mark looks at the jury. "I skipped class and stayed at the house, in case she came back. But she didn't. I was sitting in the living room when I realized that someone had organized all the CDs, and I told the police that, too."

"When the police began a formal investigation," Helen Sharp asks, "were you cooperative in giving them forensic samples?"

"I gave them my boots," Mark says.

The prosecutor turns around and looks at the jury. "Mr. Maguire, how did you find out what had happened to Jess?"

He sets his jaw. "A couple of cops came to my apartment and arrested me. When Detective Matson was interrogating me, he told me Jess was . . . was dead."

"Were you released from custody shortly thereafter?"

"Yes. When they arrested Jacob Hunt."

"Mr. Maguire, did you have anything to do with Jess Ogilvy's death?"

"Absolutely not."

"Do you know how she sustained a broken nose?"

"No," Mark says tightly.

"Do you know how her tooth got knocked out?"

"No."

"Do you know how she got abrasions on her back?"

"No."

"Did you ever strike her in the face?"

"No." Mark's voice sounds like it is wrapped up in wool. He has been looking down at the floor, but when he lifts his face now, everyone can see how his eyes are wet, how he is swallowing hard. "When I left her," he says, "she looked like an angel."

As Helen Sharp finishes, Oliver stands up and buttons his suit jacket. Why do lawyers always do that? On *CrimeBusters,* the actors playing lawyers do it, too. Maybe it's so that they look professional. Or they need something to do with their hands.

"Mr. Maguire, you just testified that you were actually arrested for the murder of Jess Ogilvy."

"Yes, but they had the wrong guy."

"Still . . . for a little while, anyway, the police believed you were involved, isn't that true?"

"I suppose."

"You also testified that you grabbed Jess Ogilvy during your fight?"

"Yes."

"Where?"

"On her arms." He touches his biceps muscle. "Here."

"You choked her, too, didn't you?"

He goes beet red. "No."

"You are aware, Mr. Maguire, that the autopsy revealed bruises around Jess Ogilvy's neck, as well as on her upper arms?"

"Objection," the prosecutor says. "Hearsay."

"Sustained."

"You are aware that you're testifying here today under oath?"

"Yes . . ."

"So let me ask you again if you choked Jess Ogilvy."

"I didn't choke her!" Mark argues. "I just . . . put my hands on her neck. For a second!"

"While you were fighting?"

"Yes," Mark says.

Oliver raises his eyebrows. "Nothing further," he says, and he sits back down beside me.

Me, I duck my head, and smile.

Theo

I was nine when my mother made me
go to a therapy group for siblings of
autistic kids. There were only four of
us—two girls with faces that looked
like ground over a sinkhole, who had
a baby sister who apparently never
stopped screaming; a boy whose twin
was severely autistic; and me. We all
had to go around a circle and say
one thing we loved about our sibling,
and one thing we really hated.

The girls went first. They said they
hated the way the baby kept them

up all night, but they liked the fact that her first word had not been Mama or Dada but instead Sissy. Then I went. I said that I hated when Jacob took my stuff without asking and how it was okay for him to interrupt me to give some dinosaur fact nobody cared about but that if I interrupted him he'd get really angry and have a meltdown. I liked the way he said things, sometimes, that were hilarious—even though they weren't meant to be—like when a camp counselor told him swimming would be a piece of cake and he freaked out because he thought he'd have to eat underwater and surely would drown. Then it was the other boy's turn. But before he could speak the door burst open and his twin brother ran inside and sat down on his lap. The kid reeked—and I mean *reeked.* All of a sudden their mom poked her head into the room. "I'm so sorry," she said. "Harry doesn't like anyone but Stephen to change his diaper."

Sucks to be Stephen, I thought. But instead of getting totally embarrassed, like I would have been, or pissed off, like I also would have been, Stephen just laughed and hugged his brother. "Let's go," he said, and he held his twin's hand and led him out of the room.

We did other stuff that day with the therapist, but I wasn't concentrating. I couldn't get out of my head the image of nine-year-old Harry wearing a giant diaper, of Stephen cleaning up the messes. There was one more thing I liked about my own sibling with autism: he was potty-trained.

At our lunch break, I found myself gravitating toward Stephen. He was sitting by himself, eating apple slices from a plastic bag.

"Hey," I said, climbing into the seat next to him.

"Hey."

I opened the straw of my juice pack and poked it into the cardboard box. I stared out the window, trying to figure out what he was looking at.

"So how do you do it?" I asked, after a minute.

He didn't pretend to misunderstand. He picked an apple slice out of the bag, chewed it, swallowed. "It could have been me," he said.

Mama Spatakopoulous can't fit into the witness chair. She has to push and wedge, and finally the judge asks the bailiff to get a seat that might be more comfortable. If it were me up there, I'd want to hide under the stupid chair in embarrassment, but she seems to be perfectly happy. Maybe she thinks it's a testimonial to how good her food is.

"Mrs. Spatakopoulous, where do you work?" asks the Dragon Bitch, a.k.a. Helen Sharp.

"Call me Mama."

The prosecutor looks at the judge, who shrugs. "Mama, then. Where do you work?"

"I own Mama S's Pizzeria, on Main Street in Townsend."

"How long have you run the restaurant?"

"Fifteen years this June. Best pizza in Vermont. You come by, I'll give you a free sample."

"That's very generous of you . . .

Mama, were you working the afternoon of January tenth, 2010?"

"I work every afternoon," she says proudly.

"Did you know Jess Ogilvy?"

"Yes, she was a regular. Good girl, with a good head on her shoulders. Helped me salt the walkway once after an ice storm because she didn't want me to throw my back out."

"Did you speak to her on January tenth?"

"I waved to her when she came in, but it was a madhouse."

"Was she alone?"

"No, she came with her boyfriend, and the kid she tutored."

"Do you see that kid in the courtroom today?"

Mama S. blows my brother a kiss.

"Had you ever seen Jacob before January tenth?"

"Once or twice, he came in with his mama to get pizza. Got celiac problems, like my father, God rest his soul."

"Did you talk to Jacob Hunt that afternoon?" the prosecutor asks.

"Yes. By the time I brought the pizzas

they had ordered, he was sitting alone at the table."

"Do you know why Jacob Hunt was sitting alone?" Helen Sharp asks.

"Well, they were all fighting. The boyfriend was angry at Jacob, Jess was angry at the boyfriend for being angry at Jacob, and then the boyfriend left." She shakes her head. "Then Jess got angry at Jacob, and *she* left."

"Did you hear what they were fighting about?"

"I had eighteen take-out orders to fill; I wasn't listening. The only thing I heard was what Jess said, before she left."

"Which was what, Mama S.?"

The woman purses her lips. "She told him to get lost."

The prosecutor sits back down, and then it is Oliver's turn. I don't watch cop shows. I don't really watch anything, unless it's *CrimeBusters,* since Jacob hogs the TV. But being in court is kind of like watching a basketball game—one side scores, and then the other takes the ball back and scores, and this goes on and on. And just like basketball, I bet it all comes down to the last five minutes.

"So you really don't know what the argument was about," Oliver says.

"No." She leans forward. "Oliver, you look very handsome in your fancy suit."

He smiles, but it looks a little painful. "Thanks, Mama. So, you were in fact paying attention to your customers."

"I've got to make a living, don't I?" she says, and then she shakes her head. "You're losing weight, I think. You've been eating out too much. Constantine and I are both worried about you . . ."

"Mama, I kind of need to get through this?" he whispers.

"Oh. All right." She turns to the jury. "I didn't hear the argument."

"You were behind the counter?"

"Yes."

"Near the ovens."

"Yes."

"And there were other people work-ing around you?"

"Three, that day."

"And there was noise?"

"The phone, and the pinball, and the jukebox were all going."

"So you're not really sure what upset Jess in the first place?"

"No."

Oliver nods. "When Jacob was sitting alone, did you talk to him?"

"I tried. He wasn't big on conversation."

"Did he ever make eye contact with you?"

"No."

"Did he do anything threatening?"

Mama S. shakes her head. "No, he's a good boy. I just left him alone," she says. "It seemed to be what he wanted."

My whole life, Jacob's wanted to be part of the group. This is one of the reasons why I never brought friends home. My mother would have insisted we include Jacob, and frankly, that would have pretty much guaranteed the end of the friendship for me. (The other reason is I was embarrassed. I didn't want anyone to know what my household was like; I didn't want to have to explain Jacob's antics, because even though my mother insisted they were just quirks of his, to the rest of the free world, they looked freaking ridiculous.)

Every now and then, though, Jacob managed to infiltrate my separate life, which was even worse. It was the social equivalent of when I once built a house of cards using all fifty-two of them and Jacob thought it would be funny to poke it with his fork.

In elementary school I was a total social outcast because of Jacob, but when we got to middle school, there were people from other towns who didn't know about my brother with Asperger's. Through some miracle I managed to become friends with two guys named Tyler and Wally, who lived in South Burlington and played Ultimate Frisbee. They invited me to play after school, and when I told them sure and didn't have to even call my mom to check if it was okay, that only made me seem cooler. I didn't explain that the reason I didn't have to call was because I spent as much time away from my house as possible, that my mother was used to me not coming home until it got dark out and, half the time, probably didn't even notice I was gone.

It was, and I am not just saying this, the best day of my life. We were flinging the Frisbee around the softball field, and a few girls who had stayed after for field hockey practice came to watch in their short skirts, with the sun all caught up in their hair. I jumped extra high, showing off, and when I worked up a sweat, one of the girls let me have a drink from her water bottle. I got to put my mouth where hers had been a minute before, which was practically like kissing her, if you want to get technical.

And then Jacob showed up.

I don't know what he was doing there—apparently it had to do with some kind of testing that was being administered at my school instead of his, and he was waiting with his aide for my mother to come pick him up. But the minute he saw me and called out my name, I knew I was screwed. At first I pretended I didn't hear him, but he ran right onto the field. "Friend of yours, Hunt?" Tyler asked, and I just laughed it off. I whipped the Frisbee in his direction, extra hard.

To my surprise, Jacob—who couldn't catch a freaking *cold* if he tried—nabbed the Frisbee and started to run with it. I froze, but Tyler took off after him. "Hey, retard," he yelled at Jacob. "I'm gonna kick your ass!"

He was faster than Jacob, big surprise, and he tackled my brother to the ground. He lifted his hand to deck Jacob, but by then I was on his back, yanking him off and straddling his body as the Frisbee went spinning into the street. "You don't fucking touch him," I yelled into Tyler's face. "If anyone's going to beat up my brother, it's going to be me."

I left him in the dirt, coughing, and then took Jacob's hand and walked him to the front of the school, where I couldn't hear the girls whispering about me and my dork of a brother, where there were enough teachers milling around to keep Tyler and Wally from jumping me in revenge.

"I wanted to play," Jacob said.

"Well, they *didn't* want you to play," I told him.

He kicked at the dirt. "I wish I could be the big brother."

Technically, he was, but he wasn't talking about age. He just didn't know how to say what he meant. "You could start by not stealing someone's goddamn Frisbee," I said.

And then my mother drove up and rolled down the window. She was smiling a huge smile. "I thought I was only picking up Jacob, but look at that," she said. "You two found each other."

Oliver

I am sure that the jury isn't absorbing anything that Marcy Allston, the CSI, is saying. She's so drop-dead gorgeous that I can practically imagine the dead bodies she stumbles across sitting up and panting.

"The first time we came to the house, we dusted for fingerprints and found some on the computer and in the bathroom."

"Can you explain the process?" Helen asks.

"The skin of your fingers, the palms of your hands, and the soles of your feet aren't smooth—they are friction ridge skin, with lines that start, stop, and have certain contours or shapes. Along those lines of skin are a series of sweat pores, and if they become contaminated with sweat, blood, dirt, dust, and so on, they leave a reproduction of those lines on the object that's been touched. My job is to make that reproduction visible. Sometimes you need a magnifying glass to do it, sometimes you need a light source. Once I make the print visible, it can be photographed, and once it can be photographed I can preserve it and make a comparison against a known sample."

"Where do those known samples come from?"

"The victim, the suspects. And from AFIS, a fingerprint database for all criminals in the United States who have been processed."

"How do you make the comparison?"

"We look at specific areas and find patterns—deltas, whorls, arches, loops—and the core, the centermost part of the fingerprint. We make a visual comparison between the known fingerprint and the unknown one, looking for general shapes that match, and then we look at more specific details—ending ridges, or bifurcations where one line might split into two. If approximately ten to twelve similarities occur, a person trained in fingerprint identification will be able to determine whether the two fingerprints came from the same individual."

The prosecutor enters into evidence a chart that shows two fingerprints, side by side. Immediately, Jacob sits up a little straighter. "This fingerprint on the right was found on the kitchen counter. The one on the left is a known sample taken from Jacob Hunt during his arrest."

As she walks through the ten little red flags that show similarities between the prints, I look at Jacob. He is grinning like mad.

"Based on your comparison, did you come to a conclusion?" Helen asks.

"Yes. That this was Jacob Hunt's fingerprint in the kitchen."

"Was there anything else of note during your processing of the house?"

Marcy nods. "We found a kitchen window screen that had been cut from the outside, and the sash jimmied and broken. A screwdriver was found in the bushes below the window."

"Were there any fingerprints on the sash, or on the screwdriver?"

"No, but the temperature that day was extremely cold, which often compromises fingerprint evidence."

"Did you find anything else?"

"A boot print beneath the windowsill. We made a wax cast of the print and were able to match it to a boot on the premises."

"Do you know who that boot belonged to?"

"Mark Maguire, the victim's boyfriend," Marcy said. "We determined that these were boots he kept at the house, since he often stayed there overnight."

"Did you find anything else in the house?"

"Yes. Using a chemical called Luminol, we found significant traces of blood in the bathroom."

Jacob writes a note on the pad and gives it to me:

Bleach + Luminol = false positive for blood.

"At some point did you receive a 911 call from the victim's cell phone?" Helen asks.

"Yes. Early on January eighteenth, we responded to a culvert approximately three hundred yards from the home where Jess Ogilvy had been house-sitting, and found the victim's body."

"What was the position of the body?"

"She was propped up with her back against the cement wall, and her arms were folded in her lap. She was fully clothed."

"Was there anything else noteworthy about how the body was found?"

"Yes," Marcy replies. "The victim was wrapped in a distinctive, handmade quilt."

"Is this the quilt that you found with the victim that day?" the prosecutor asks, and she offers Marcy a bulky roll of fabric in all the colors of the rainbow, the pattern marred by dark brown areas of dried blood.

"That's the one," Marcy says, and as it is entered into evidence, I can hear Emma draw in her breath.

Helen thanks her witness, and I stand up to cross-examine. "How long have you been a CSI?"

"Four years," Marcy says.

"So not that long, then."

She raises a brow. "How long have *you* been a lawyer?"

"Have you seen a lot of dead bodies at crime scenes?"

"Fortunately, not as many as I would if I worked in Nashua or Boston," Marcy says. "But enough to know what I'm doing."

"You said that you found a fingerprint at Jess Ogilvy's house, in the kitchen, that belongs to Jacob."

"That's right."

"Can you say that the presence of that fingerprint identifies him as a murderer?"

"No. It only places him at the scene of the crime."

"Is it possible that Jacob might have left the fingerprint there at some other point?"

"Yes."

"You also found Mark Maguire's boot prints beneath a window sash that had been jimmied and cut," I say. "Is that correct?"

"Yes, we did."

"Did you find Jacob's boot prints anywhere outside?"

"No," Marcy says.

I take a deep breath. *I hope you know what you're doing,* I think silently, looking back once at Jacob. "And the blood in the bathroom—were you able to determine whether it belonged to the victim?"

"No. We tried to run a DNA test, but the results were not conclusive. There were traces of bleach in the swabs, and bleach often compromises DNA tests."

"Isn't it true, Ms. Allston, that when sprayed on bleach, Luminol also gives a positive reading?"

"Yes, sometimes."

"So the traces of blood you found might be traces of bleach instead."

"It's possible," she concedes.

"And the alleged blood in the bathroom might simply have been Jess cleaning the tile floor with Clorox?"

"Or," Marcy says, "your client cleaning blood off the tile floor with Clorox, after he murdered her."

I wince and immediately back off. "Ms. Allston, you can tell a lot about a body from the way that person is positioned at death, can't you?"

"Yes."

"Was there anything that struck you about Jess Ogilvy's body when it was found?"

Marcy hesitates. "She wasn't discarded. Someone had taken the time to sit her upright and to wrap her in a quilt, instead of dumping her."

"Someone who cared for her?"

"Objection," Helen interrupts, and like I expect, it's sustained by the judge.

"Do you know my client, Ms. Allston?"

"Actually, I do."

"How?"

"He's a crime scene junkie. He's been at a few I've been called to, and he starts giving us advice we don't particularly want or need."

"Have you ever let him help out at a crime scene?"

"Absolutely not. But it's pretty clear he's fascinated by all that stuff." She shakes her head. "Only two kinds of people show up at crime scenes: the serial killers who are checking their handiwork, and the crazies who think police work is like the television shows and want to help solve the crime."

Great. Now she's got the jury wondering which of those two categories Jacob fits. I decide to cut my losses before I completely implode. "Nothing further," I say, and Helen gets up to redirect.

"Ms. Allston, did Jacob Hunt show up at the culvert when you were processing the body?"

"No," she says. "We didn't see him at all."

Helen shrugs. "I guess this time, there was nothing for him to solve."

Jacob

If I do not become a crime scene investigator famous in my field, like Dr. Henry Lee, I am going to become a medical examiner. It is the same work, really, except that your canvas is smaller. Instead of processing an entire house or a stretch of woods to determine the story of the crime, you coax the story out of the dead person on your autopsy table.

There are many things that make dead bodies preferable to live ones:

1. They don't have facial expressions, so there's no worry about mistaking a smile for a smirk, or any of that nonsense.

2. They don't get bored if you're hogging the conversation.

3. They don't care if you stand too close or too far away.

4. They don't talk about you when you leave the room, or tell their friends how annoying you are.

You can tell, from a dead body, the sequence of events that occurred: if the abdominal gunshot wound caused the peritonitis and septicemia; if those complications were the cause of death, or if it was the respiratory distress syndrome they led to that was the final blow. You can tell if the person died in a field or was left in the trunk of a car. You can tell if a person's been shot in the head before the body was set on fire or vice versa. (When the skull is removed, you can see the blood that has started seeping as a result of the brain being boiled, a thermal injury. If you don't see that, it usually means that execution was the cause of death, not the fire. Admit it: you wanted to know.)

For all these reasons, I am very attentive when Dr. Wayne Nussbaum takes the stand to testify. I know him; I've seen him before at crime scenes. Once, I wrote him a letter and got his autograph.

He lists his credentials: Yale University Medical School followed by rotations in pathology and emergency medicine before becoming an assistant medical examiner for the State of New York and, finally, twenty years as chief medical examiner in Vermont. "Did you perform an autopsy on Jess Ogilvy?" asked Helen Sharp.

"I did. On the afternoon of January eighteenth," he said. "The body was brought to my office in the morning but had to thaw."

"What was the temperature outside when she was found?"

"Twelve degrees, which allowed for excellent preservation."

"How was she dressed?"

"She was wearing sweatpants and a T-shirt and a light jacket. She had on a bra, but her underwear was on backward. There was a tooth wrapped in toilet paper in a small front pocket of the sweatpants, and her cell phone was zipped into the pocket of her jacket."

Usually on *CrimeBusters,* when a medical examiner takes the stand, it is a five-minute testimony, tops. Helen Sharp, however, walks Dr. Nussbaum through his findings three times: once verbally, a second time with a diagram of a body while Dr. Nussbaum draws his findings in red marker; and finally with photographs he'd taken during the autopsy. Me, I'm loving every minute. I don't know about that lady on the jury, though, who looks like she is about to throw up.

"You said, Doctor, that you took samples of Jess Ogilvy's urine, heart blood, and vitreous humor from her eyes for toxicology purposes?"

"That's correct."

"What's the purpose of those exams?"

"They let us know what foreign substances are in the victim's bloodstream. In the case of the heart blood and the vitreous humor, it's at the time of death."

"What were the results?"

"Jessica Ogilvy did not have any drugs or alcohol in her system at the time of death."

"Did you take photographs of the body during the autopsy?"

"Yes," he says. "It's routine procedure."

"Did you make any notations as to unusual marks or bruises on the body?"

"Yes. The victim had bruises on her throat consistent with choking and bruises on her arms consistent with being restrained. The bruises were reddish violet and had sharp edges, which suggested that they occurred within twenty-four hours of death. In addition, the skin on her lower back had been scraped postmortem, most likely as a result of being dragged. You can see the difference in the photograph, here, between the two sorts of bruises. The postmortem one is yellowish and leathery." He pointed to another photograph, this one of Jess's face. "The victim was badly beaten. She had suffered a basal skull fracture, bruises around the eyes, and a broken nose. She was missing a front tooth."

"Were you able to tell if those injuries were pre- or postmortem?"

"The fact that bruising occurred indicates the injury was prior to death. The tooth; well, that I can't say for sure, but it did seem to be the one tucked in her pocket."

"Can you punch someone so hard in the face that they lose a tooth?"

"Yes, it's possible," Dr. Nussbaum says.

"Would someone who had been punched hard in the face present with the same sorts of injuries you found on the victim's body?"

"Yes."

"Doctor," Helen Sharp asks, "after having done the autopsy and studied the results from the toxicology labs, did you form an opinion within a reasonable degree of medical certainty about the manner of death?"

"Yes, I ruled it a homicide."

"What was the cause of Jess Ogilvy's death?"

"Blunt head trauma, which led to subdural hematoma—bleeding inside the skull, consistent with a blow or a fall."

"How long does it take to die from a subdural hematoma?"

"It can be immediate, or it can take hours. In the victim's case, it was relatively soon after injury."

"Did the bruises you found on Jess Ogilvy's neck and arms contribute to her death?"

"No."

"How about the tooth that was knocked out?"

"No."

"And there were no drugs or alcohol in her system?"

"No, there were not."

"So, Dr. Nussbaum," Helen Sharp says, "the sole cause of fatal injury to Jess Ogilvy that you found during the autopsy was a basal skull fracture that caused internal bleeding in the skull?"

"That's correct."

"Your witness," the prosecutor says, and Oliver stands up.

"All those injuries you found on Jess Ogilvy's body," he says. "You have any idea who caused them?"

"No."

"And you said that a subdural hematoma could be caused by either a blow *or* a fall."

"Correct."

"Isn't it possible, Doctor," Oliver asks, "that Jess Ogilvy tripped and fell and suffered a subdural hematoma?"

The medical examiner looks up and smiles a little.

It's one of those smiles I hate, the kind that might mean *You are so smart* but might also mean *You moron.* "It's possible Jess Ogilvy tripped and fell and suffered a subdural hematoma," Dr. Nussbaum says. "But I highly doubt that she tried to strangle herself, or knocked out her own tooth, put on her underwear backward, dragged herself three hundred yards away, and wrapped herself in a quilt in a culvert."

I laugh out loud—that's such a great line it might have been scripted for *CrimeBusters.*

My mother and Oliver both look at me, and *that* expression's easy to read. They're both one hundred percent pissed off.

"Perhaps now's a good time for a serenity break?" the judge asks.

"Sensory!" Oliver snaps. "It's a *sensory* break!"

Judge Cuttings clears his throat. "I'll take that as a yes."

In the sensory break room, I lie underneath the weighted blanket. My mother's in the bathroom; Theo has his head on the vibrating pillow. He talks through his teeth and sounds like a robot. "Tickle me, Elmo," he says.

"Jacob," Oliver says after a minute and thirty-three seconds of silence. "Your behavior in this courtroom is making me very angry."

"Well, your behavior in this courtroom is making *me* very angry," I say. "You still haven't told them the truth."

"You know it's not our turn yet. You've seen trials on television. The prosecution goes first, and then we get to undo the damage Helen Sharp's done. But Jacob, Jesus. Every time you have an outburst or you laugh at something a witness says, that adds to the damage." He looks at me. "Imagine you're a juror, and you've got a daughter about Jess's age, and then the defendant laughs out loud when the medical examiner talks about the gruesome way Jess died. What do you think that juror's saying to himself?"

"I'm not a juror," I say, "so I don't really know."

"What the medical examiner said at the end *was* pretty amusing," Theo adds.

Oliver frowns at him. "Did I *ask* you for your opinion?"

"Did Jacob ask you for *yours*?" Theo says, and then he tosses me the pillow. "Don't listen to him," Theo tells me, and he slips out of the sensory break room.

I find Oliver staring at me. "Do you miss Jess?"

"Yes. She was my friend."

"Then why don't you show it?"

"Why *should* I?" I ask, sitting up. "If *I* know I feel it, that's what counts. Don't you ever look at someone who's hysterical in public and wonder if it's because they really feel miserable or because they want others to *know* they're miserable? It kind of dilutes the emotion if you display it for the whole world to see. Makes it less pure."

"Well, that's not how the majority of people think. Most people, confronted with photographic evidence of the autopsy of someone they loved, would get upset. Maybe even cry."

"Cry? Are you kidding?" I mimic a phrase I've heard kids say at school. "I would have *killed* to be at that autopsy."

Oliver turns away. I'm pretty sure I hear him wrong.

Did you?

Rich

The running joke among those of us sequestered for the trial involves the sensory break room. If the defendant can get some special accommodation, why not the witnesses? Me, I want a Chinese food take-out room. I tell this to Helen Sharp when she comes to let me know that I'm testifying next.

"Dumplings," I say, "have been scientifically proven to enhance witness focus. And General Tso's chicken clogs the arteries just enough to increase blood flow to the brain—"

"And here all this time I thought your disability was your short—"

"Hey!"

"—attention span," Helen says. She smiles at me. "You have five minutes."

I'm only half kidding. I mean, if the court was willing to bend over backward for Jacob Hunt's Asperger's syndrome, how long will it be before this is used as a precedent by some career criminal who insists that going to jail will inflame his claustrophobia? I'm all for equality, but not when it erodes the system.

I decide to take a leak before court reconvenes and have just turned the corner toward the hallway where the restrooms are located when I smack directly into a woman who's walking in the opposite direction. "Whoa," I say, steadying her. "I'm sorry."

Emma Hunt looks up at me with those incredible eyes of hers. "I bet," she says.

In another lifetime—if I had another job, and she had a different kid—maybe we would have been talking over a bottle of wine, maybe she would be smiling at me, instead of looking like she'd just been confronted by her worst nightmare. "How are you holding up?"

"You have no right to ask me that."

She tries to push past me, but I block her with an outstretched arm. "I was just doing my job, Emma."

"I have to get back to Jacob—"

"Look, I'm sorry this happened to you, because you've already had to go through a lot. But the day Jess died, a mother lost her child."

"And now," she says, "you are going to make me lose mine."

She pushes at my arm. This time, I let her go.

It takes ten minutes for Helen to walk me through my credentials—my rank as captain, my training as detective in Townsend, the fact that I've been doing this since before Jesus was born, yada yada, all the stuff a jury wants to hear to know they are in good hands. "How did you become involved in the investigation into Jess Ogilvy's death?" Helen begins.

"Her boyfriend, Mark Maguire, came to the police station and reported her missing on January thirteenth. He hadn't seen her since the morning of the twelfth and had been unable to make contact with her. She had no planned trips, and her friends and parents did not know where she was, either. Her purse and coat were at her house, but other personal items were missing."

"Such as?"

"Her toothbrush, her cell phone." I glance at Jacob, who raises his brows expectantly. "And some clothes in a backpack," I finish, and he smiles and ducks his head, nodding.

"What did you do?"

"I went with Mr. Maguire to the house and listed the items that were missing. I also took a typed note found in the mailbox, asking for the mail to be held, and sent it to the lab for fingerprints. Then I told Mr. Maguire that we'd have to wait and see if Ms. Ogilvy returned."

"Why did you send the note to the lab?" Helen asks.

"Because it seemed strange to type a note to your mailman."

"Did you get results back from the laboratory?"

"Yes. They were inconclusive; no fingerprints were found on the paper. That led me to believe that it was possibly a note typed by someone smart enough to wear gloves when placing it. A red herring, to make us think Jess had run away on her own."

"What happened next?"

"I received a call from Mr. Maguire a day later, saying that a rack of CDs had been knocked over and then alphabetized. It didn't seem to be a clear sign of foul play—after all, this was something that Jess might have done, and in my experience, felons don't tend to be neat freaks. However, we formally opened an investigation into Ms. Ogilvy's disappearance. A CSI team was dispatched to her residence to gather evidence. I took her date book from her purse, which was found in the kitchen, and began to follow up on the meetings she had prior to her disappearance and was scheduled to have afterward."

"Did you attempt to contact Jess Ogilvy during this investigation?"

"Numerous times. We called her cell phone, but it went right into voice mail, until even that was full. With the help of the FBI, we attempted to ping her cell phone."

"What does that mean?"

"Using a GPS locator built into the device, the FBI has a software program which can find coordinates within a meter of actual physical location anywhere in the world, but in this case, the results were inconclusive. The phone has to be powered up in order for that software to work, and apparently, Jess Ogilvy's was not," I say. "We also screened the messages that came into her residence. One was from Mr. Maguire. One was from a vendor, one from the defendant's mother, and three were missed calls that originated from Jess Ogilvy's own cell phone number. Based on the time stamps of the answering machine, it suggested that Ms. Ogilvy was still alive somewhere at the time the calls were placed—or that we were being led to believe this by whoever had her cell phone."

"Detective, when did you first meet the defendant?"

"On January fifteenth."

"Had you seen him before?"

"Yes—at a crime scene a week earlier. He crashed an investigation."

"Where did you meet Mr. Hunt on January fifteenth?"

"At his house."

"Who else was present?"

"His mother."

"Did you take the defendant into custody at that time?"

"No, he wasn't a suspect. I asked him questions about his appointment with Jess. He said that he had gone to her house for the two thirty-five appointment but did not meet with her. He indicated that he walked home. He also revealed that Mark Maguire was not present when he arrived at Ms. Ogilvy's place. When I asked him whether he had ever seen Jess fight with her boyfriend, he said, '*Hasta la vista, baby.*'"

"Did you recognize that statement?"

"I believe it's attributed to the former governor of California," I say. "Before he entered politics."

"Did you ask the defendant anything else at that meeting?"

"No, I was . . . dismissed. It was four-thirty, and at four-thirty he watches a television show."

"Did you see the defendant again?"

"Yes. I received a call from Emma Hunt, his mother, indicating that Jacob had something else to tell me."

"What did Jacob say during that second conversation?"

"He presented me with Jess Ogilvy's missing backpack, and some of her clothing. He admitted that he had gone to her house and found signs of a struggle, which he cleaned up."

"Cleaned up?"

"Yes. He righted stools and picked up the mail, which had been thrown on the floor, and restacked the CDs and alphabetized them. He took the backpack, because he thought she might need it. He then proceeded to show me the backpack and the items inside."

"Did you take Jacob into custody at that time?"

"I did not."

"Did you take the clothes and backpack with you?"

"Yes. We tested them, and the results

were negative. There were no prints, no blood, no DNA."

"Then what happened?" Helen asks.

"I met the CSI team at Jess Ogilvy's home. They had found trace evidence of blood in the bathroom, and a cut screen in the kitchen window, as well as a broken window sash. They also found a boot print outside the house that seemed to match the boots worn by Mark Maguire."

"What happened after that?"

I face the jury. "Early Monday morning, January eighteenth, shortly after three A.M., Townsend Dispatch received a 911 call. All 911 calls are traced through GPS technology so responders can reach whoever is making the call. This call originated from a culvert approximately three hundred yards from the home where Jess Ogilvy was residing. I responded to the call. The victim's body—and her phone— were found there, and she was wrapped in a blanket. There's a video clip from the midday news that aired on WCAX—" I hesitate, waiting for Helen to take the tape and enter it as evidence, to pull the television monitor closer to the jury so that they can see it.

There is utter silence as the reporter's face fills the screen, her eyes watering in the cold, while crime scene investigators move along behind her. The reporter shifts her feet, and Helen freezes the image.

"Do you recognize that blanket, Detective?" she asks.

It is a multicolored quilt, definitely hand-sewn. "Yes. It was wrapped around Jess Ogilvy's body."

"Is this the same blanket?"

She holds up the quilt, with its blood-stains ruining the pattern here and there. "That's it," I say.

"What happened after that?"

"With the discovery of the body, I had several officers arrest Mark Maguire for the murder of Jess Ogilvy. I was interrogating him when I received another call."

"Did the caller identify him- or herself?"

"Yes. It was Jacob Hunt's mother, Emma."

"What was her demeanor?" Helen asks.

"She was frantic. Extremely upset."

"What did she tell you?"

The other lawyer, the one who looks like he's still in high school, objects. "That's hearsay, Your Honor," he says.

"Counsel, approach," the judge says.

Helen speaks quietly. "Judge, I would make an offer of proof that the mother called because she had just seen the news clip with that quilt on the screen and was able to link it to her son. Therefore, Your Honor, it's an excited utterance."

"The objection's overruled," the judge says, and Helen approaches me again.

"What did the defendant's mother tell you?" she repeats.

I don't want to look at Emma. I can already feel the heat of her gaze, the accusations. "She told me that the quilt belonged to her son."

"Based on the results of your conversation, what did you do?"

"I asked Ms. Hunt to bring Jacob down to the station, so that we could speak further."

"Did you place Jacob Hunt under arrest for the murder of Jess Ogilvy?"

"Yes."

"Then what happened?"

"I dismissed all charges against Mr. Maguire. I also executed a search warrant for the defendant's house."

"What did you find there?"

"We found Jacob Hunt's police scanner,

a self-constructed fuming chamber for fingerprinting, and hundreds of black-and-white composition notebooks."

"What was in those notebooks?"

"Jacob used them to record information about *CrimeBusters* episodes he watched. He'd write down the date the episode aired, and the evidence, and then whether or not he solved the crime before the television detectives did. I saw him writing in one the first time I came to his house to speak to him."

"How many did you find?"

"A hundred and sixteen."

The prosecutor enters one into evidence. "Do you recognize this, Detective Matson?"

"It's one of those notebooks. The one with the most recent entries."

"Can you turn to the fourteenth page of this notebook and tell us what you find there?"

I read aloud the subject heading.

At Her House. 1/12/10.
Situation: Girl reported missing by her
**   boyfriend.**
Evidence:

Clothes in pile on bed

Toothbrush missing, lip gloss missing

Victim's purse and coat remain

Cell phone missing

Luminol bathroom—blood detected

Knapsack taken with clothing & mailbox note—red herring for kidnapping

Cut screen—boot prints outside match up with boyfriend's footwear

Cell phone traced by 911 call to location of body in culvert

"Is there anything intriguing about this entry in particular?"

"I don't know if it's a *CrimeBusters* episode, but it's the exact crime scene we found at Jess Ogilvy's residence. It's the exact way we found Jess Ogilvy's body. And all this information is information nobody should have had," I say. "Except for the police . . . and the killer."

Oliver

I knew that Jacob was going to have trouble when those journals were presented as evidence. I wouldn't want the equivalent of my diary being read to a jury. Not that I keep a diary, or not that I would recount the evidence at a murder scene in one. So I am expecting it when he starts rocking a little bit as Helen enters the journal into evidence. I can feel the stiffening of his spine, the way he is breathing hard, the fact that he barely blinks.

When Jacob leans toward the table, I meet Emma's gaze over his head. *Now,* she mouths, and sure enough, Jacob shoves a piece of paper into my hands.

F#, it reads.

It takes me a moment to realize that he's passed me a note, just like I told him to do if he needed a sensory break.

"Your Honor," I say, standing up. "Could we take a short recess?"

"We just had a recess, Mr. Bond," Judge Cuttings says, and then he looks at Jacob, whose face is bright red. "Five minutes," he announces.

With me on one side and Emma locked on the other, we hustle Jacob up the aisle to the sensory break room. "Just hold it together for another thirty seconds," Emma soothes. "Ten more steps. Nine . . . eight . . ."

Jacob ducks inside and spins around to face us. "Oh my *God*!" he shrieks, a smile splitting his face. "Wasn't that awesome?"

I just stare at him.

"I mean, that was the whole point. They finally got it. I set up a crime scene and the cops figured the whole thing out, even the red herrings." He pokes me in the chest with his finger. "You," Jacob says, "are doing a *great* job."

Behind me, Emma bursts into tears.

I don't look at her. I can't. "I'll fix it," I say.

There is a moment when I stand up to do the cross-examination of Detective Matson that I think we might have a pissing contest instead. He takes a look at Emma—her eyes still red, her face still puffy—and narrows his gaze at me, as if her condition is my fault instead of his. And that only makes me want to sink him even more.

"The first time you met with Jacob at his house, Detective," I begin, "he quoted the movie *Terminator* to you, correct?"

"Yes."

"And the second time you met with Jacob . . . he recommended a variety of tests for you to run on the backpack?"

"Yes."

"How many?"

"Several."

I grab the legal pad that's in front of Jacob. "Did he recommend a DNA test on the straps of the backpack?"

"Yes."

"And an AP test on the underwear inside."

"I guess."

"Luminol?"

"That sounds about right."

"And what about ninhydrin on the card inside?"

"Look, I don't remember them all, but that's probably true."

"In fact, Detective," I say, "Jacob seemed to know your job better than you do."

He narrows his eyes. "He certainly knew the crime scene better than I did."

"Those composition notebooks that you found. Did you read them all?"

"Yes."

"What did the other hundred and fifteen notebooks contain?"

"Synopses," he says. "Of episodes of *CrimeBusters*."

"Do you know what *CrimeBusters* is, Detective?"

"I think you'd have to be living under a rock to *not* know," he says. "It's a police procedural television show that's probably syndicated on Mars by now."

"You ever watch it?"

He laughs. "I try not to. It's not exactly realistic."

"So the cases aren't true crime."

"No."

"Then is it fair to say that the hundred and sixteen journals you seized from Jacob's room are full of descriptions of fictional crime scenes?"

"Well, yes," Matson says, "but I don't think the one he wrote in the hundred and sixteenth journal was fictional at all."

"How do you know?" I take a few steps toward him. "In fact, Detective, there was media coverage of Jess Ogilvy's disappearance before you got hold of this notebook, wasn't there?"

"Yes."

"Her name was on the news, her parents were asking for help solving the crime?"

"Yes."

"You testified that Jacob would show up at crime scenes looking to help, correct?"

"Yes, but—"

"Did he ever offer up information that was surprising to you?"

Matson hesitates. "Yes."

"So isn't it possible, especially given that he knew this particular victim, that he wasn't using the notebook to brag about a murder . . . but rather, like he did with every *CrimeBusters* episode, using it to help solve the case?"

I turn to the jury before he can even answer. "Nothing further," I say.

Helen stands up at the prosecutor's table. "Detective Matson," she says, "can you read the notation at the bottom of the first page of the notebook?"

"It says SOLVED: ME, *twenty-four minutes.*"

"What about the notation at the bottom of the entry on page six?"

"SOLVED: THEM, **fifty-five minutes . . . Good one!**"

She walks toward Matson. "Do you have any idea what that notation indicates?"

"Jacob told me, when I first saw him writing in the journals. He marks down whether he solved the crime before the TV detectives did, and how long it took."

"Detective," Helen says, "can you read the notation at the bottom of page fourteen, the entry entitled 'At Her House' that you read for us earlier?"

He glances down at the page. "It says *SOLVED: ME.*"

"Anything else notable about that line?"

Matson looks at the jury. "It's underlined. Ten times."

Theo

At dinner, I'm the one who sees my brother stealing the knife.

I don't say anything at first. But it's perfectly clear to me, the way he pauses in the middle of his yellow rice and scrambled eggs to carve the kernels off an ear of corn—and then pushes the knife with his thumbs to the edge of the table, so that it falls into his lap.

My mother yammers on about the trial—about the coffee machine at the courthouse which only dispenses cold coffee; about what Jacob is going to wear tomorrow; about the defense, which will present its case in the morning. I don't think either of us is listening, because Jacob is trying to not move his shoulders while he wraps the knife in a napkin and I am trying to study his every move.

When he starts to get up from the table and my mother cuts him off with a sharp, forced cough, I am sure she's going to call him on his stolen cutlery. But instead, she says, "Aren't you forgetting something?"

"May I be excused?" Jacob mutters, and a minute later he's scraped his plate and heads upstairs.

"I wonder what's the matter," my mother says. "He hardly ate."

I shovel the rest of my food into my mouth and then mumble a request to be excused. I hurry upstairs, but Jacob's not in his room. The bathroom door is wide open, too. It's like he's just vanished.

I walk into my own bedroom, and all of a sudden I'm grabbed and pulled against the wall, and there's a knife at my throat.

Okay, I'm just going to say it's pretty depressing that this is *not* the first time I've found myself in this scenario with my brother. I do what I know works: I bite his wrist.

You'd think he'd see it coming, but he doesn't; the knife clatters to the floor, and I elbow him in his soft gut. He doubles over, grunting. "What the fuck are you doing?" I yell.

"Practicing."

I reach for the knife and stick it inside my desk drawer, the one I keep locked, where I've learned to keep the things I don't want Jacob to get. "Practicing murder?" I say. "You crazy motherfucker. This is why you're going to get convicted."

"I wasn't going to actually *hurt* you." Jacob sits down heavily on my bed. "There was someone looking at me funny today."

"I'd think a lot of people in that courtroom were looking at you funny."

"But this one guy followed me to the bathroom. I have to be able to protect myself."

"Right. And what do you think is

going to happen tomorrow morning when you walk into the courthouse and the metal detectors start beeping? And the stupid reporters all watch you pull a steak knife out of your sock?"

He frowns. This is one of those harebrained Aspie schemes of his, the ones he never thinks through. Like when he called the cops on my mom two months ago. To Jacob, I'm sure it seemed perfectly logical. To the rest of the free world, not so much.

"What if there's nothing wrong with me?" Jacob says. "What if the reason I act like I do and think like I do is that I'm left out all the time? If I had friends, you know, maybe I wouldn't do things that look strange to everyone else. It's like bacteria that only grows in a vacuum. Maybe there's no such thing as Asperger's. Maybe all there is is what happens to you when you don't fit in."

"Don't go telling your lawyer that. He needs Asperger's to exist big-time right now." I look at Jacob's hands. His cuticles are bitten down to the skin;

often he draws blood. My mother used to have to wrap Band-Aids around all his fingers before she sent him to school. Once, in the hallways, I heard two girls calling him the Mummy. "Hey, Jacob," I say quietly. "I'll tell you something no one else knows."

His hand flutters on his thigh. "A secret?"

"Yeah. But you can't tell Mom."

I want to tell him. I've wanted to tell someone for so long now. But maybe Jacob is right: in the absence of having space in the world, the thing that's left behind just gets bigger and more unrecognizable. It swells in my throat; it steals all the air in the room. And suddenly, I'm blubbering like a baby; I'm wiping my eyes with my sleeves and trying to pretend that my brother isn't in court; my brother isn't going to jail; that this isn't karmic payment for all the bad things I've done and all the bad thoughts I've had.

"I was there," I blurt out. "I was there the day Jess died."

Jacob doesn't look at me, and maybe that's easier. He flutters his hand a little faster and then brings it up to his throat. "I know," he says.

My eyes widen. "You do?"

"Of course I do. I saw your foot-prints." He stares just over my shoulder. "That's why I had to do it."

Oh my God. She told Jacob that I'd been spying on her naked and that she was going to go to the cops, and he shut her up. Now I'm sobbing; I can barely catch my breath. "I'm sorry."

He doesn't touch me or hug me or comfort me, the way my mom would. The way any other human would. Jacob just keeps fanning his fingers, and then he says *I'm sorry I'm sorry* like I did, an echo that's been stripped of its music, like rain on tin.

It's prosody. It's part of Asperger's. When Jacob was little, he would repeat questions I asked and throw them back at me like a baseball pitch instead of answering. My mother told me this was like his movie quotes, a verbal stim. It was Jacob's way of feeling the words in his mouth when he had nothing to say in return.

But all the same, I let myself pretend it's his robotic, monotone way of asking for *my* forgiveness, too.

Jacob

That day when we come home from court, instead of watching *CrimeBusters,* I choose a different video instead. It is a home movie of me when I was a baby, only one year old. It must be my birthday because there is a cake, and I am clapping and smiling and saying things like Mama and Dada and milk. Every time someone says my name I look up, right into the camera.

I look normal.

My parents are happy. My dad's there, and he's not even in any videos we have of Theo. My mother doesn't have the line between her eyes that she has now. Most people take home movies, after all, to capture something they want to remember, not a moment they'd rather forget.

That's not the case later on in the video. All of a sudden, instead of sticking my fingers in a cake and offering up a big gummy smile, I'm rocking in front of the washing machine, watching the clothes turn in circles. I'm lying in front of the television, but instead of watching the programming, I'm lining up Lego pieces end to end. My father isn't in the film anymore; instead there are people I don't know—a woman with frizzy yellow hair and a sweatshirt with a cat on it who gets down on the floor with me and moves my head so that I focus on a puzzle she's set down. A lady with bright blue eyes is having a conversation with me, if you can call it that:

> Lady: Jacob, are you excited about going to the circus?
>
> Me: Yes.
>
> Lady: What do you want to see at the circus?
>
> Me: (No answer)
>
> Lady: Say, At the circus, I want to see . . .
>
> Me: I want to see clowns.

Lady (gives me an M&M): I love clowns.
Are you excited about the circus?
Me: Yeah, I want to see clowns.
Lady (gives me three M&M's): Jacob,
that's great!
Me: (I stuff the M&M's into my mouth)

These are the movies my mother took as evidence, as proof that I was now a different child than the one she'd started with. I don't know what she was thinking when she recorded them. Surely she didn't want to sit and watch all this over and over, the visual equivalent of a slap in the face. Maybe she was keeping them in the hope that one day a pharmaceutical executive might arrive unexpectedly for dinner, watch the tapes, and cut her a check for damages.

As I'm watching, there's a sudden streak of silver static that makes me cover my ears, and then there's another segment of video. It's been accidentally taped over my Oscar-worthy autistic toddler film, and in it I am much older. It is only a year ago, and I am getting ready for my junior prom.

Jess took the video. She came over that afternoon while I was getting ready so that she could see the final result of our preparations.

I can hear her voice. *Jacob,* she says, *for God's sake, get closer to her. She's not going to bite you.* The video swings like an amusement park ride, and I hear Jess's voice again. *Oops, I suck at this.*

My mother has a camera and is taking a picture of me with my date. The girl's name is Amanda, and she goes to my school. She's wearing an orange dress, which is probably the reason I refuse to get closer to her, even though I usually do what Jess wants.

On television, it's like I'm watching a make-believe show and Jacob isn't me, he's a character. It's not really me who closes his eyes when my mother tries to take a picture on the front lawn. It's not really me who walks to Amanda's car and sits in the back like I always do. *Oh no,* my mother's voice says, and Jess starts laughing. *We totally forgot about that,* she says.

Suddenly the camera turns around fast, and Jess's face is fishbowl-close. *Hello, world!* she says, and she pretends to swallow the camera. She's smiling.

Then there's a line of red that moves down the television screen like a curtain, and suddenly I am only three years old again and I am stacking a green block on top of a blue block on top of a yellow block, just like the therapist has shown me. *Jacob! Good work!* she says, and she pushes a toy truck toward me as a reward. I flip it over and spin its wheels.

I want Jess to be on the screen again.

"I wish I knew how to quit you," I whisper.

Suddenly, my chest feels like it's shrinking, the way it sometimes does when I am standing with a group of kids in school and I realize I'm the only one who did not get the punch line of the joke. Or that I *am* the punch line of the joke.

I start to think maybe I've done something wrong. Really wrong.

Because I do not know how to fix it, I pick up the remote control and rewind the tape almost back to the beginning, to the time when I was no different from anyone else.

Emma

From Auntie Em's archives:

Dear Auntie Em,
How do I get a boy's attention? I am hopeless at flirting, and there are so many other girls out there who are prettier and smarter than I am. But I'm sick of never being noticed; maybe I can reinvent myself. What can I do?

Baffled in Bennington

Dear Baffled,
You don't have to be anyone except

who you already are. You just have to get a guy to take a second look. For this, there are two approaches:

1. Stop waiting: take the initiative and go talk to him. Ask him if he got the answer to number 7 on your math homework. Tell him he did a great job in the school talent show.

2. Start walking around naked.

But it's your choice.
Love,
Auntie Em

When I can't sleep, I pull a cardigan over my pajamas and sit outside on the porch steps and try to imagine the life I might have had.

Henry and I would be waiting, with Jacob, for college acceptance letters. We might pop out a bottle of champagne and let him have a glass to celebrate once he made his choice. Theo would not hole himself up in his room doing his absolute best to pretend he doesn't belong to this family. Instead, he would sit at the kitchen table, doing crosswords in the daily paper. "Three letters," he'd say, and he'd read the clue. "Hope was often found here." And we'd all guess at the answer—God? Sky? Arkansas?—but Jacob would be the one to get it right: USO.

Our boys would be listed on the honor roll quarterly. And people would stare at me when I went shopping for groceries, not because I was the mother of that autistic boy, or worse, the murderer, but because they wished they were as lucky as me.

I don't believe in self-pity. I think it's for people who have too much time on their hands. Instead of dreaming of a miracle, you learn to make your own. But the universe has a way of punishing you for your deepest, darkest secrets; and as much as I love my son—as much as Jacob has been the star around which I've orbited—I've had my share of moments when I silently imagined the person I was supposed to be, the one who got lost, somehow, in the daily business of raising an autistic child.

Be careful what you wish for.

Picture your life without Jacob, and it just may come true.

I listened to the testimony today. And yes, as Oliver has said, it's not our turn yet. But I watched the faces of the jury as they stared at Jacob, and I saw the same expression I've seen a thousand times before. That mental distancing, that subtle acknowledgment that there is *something wrong with that boy.*

Because he doesn't interact the way they do.

Because he doesn't grieve the way they do.

Because he doesn't move or speak the way they do.

I fought so hard to have Jacob mainstreamed at school—not just so that he could see the way other kids behaved but because other kids needed to see *him,* and to learn that *different* isn't synonymous with *bad.* But I cannot say, honestly, that his classmates ever learned that lesson. They gave Jacob enough rope to hang himself in social situations, and then set the blame squarely on his shoulders.

And now, after all that work to shoehorn him into an ordinary school setting, he is in a courtroom peppered with accommodations for his special needs. His only chance at acquittal hinges on his diagnosis on the spectrum. To insist that he is just like anyone else, at this moment, would be a sure prison sentence.

After years of refusing to make excuses for Jacob's Asperger's, this is the only chance he has.

And suddenly, I am running, as if my life depends on it.

It's after 2:00 A.M. and the pizza parlor is dark, the Closed sign flipped on the door, but in the tiny window above, a light is burning. I open the door to the narrow staircase that leads to the law office, climb the steps, knock.

Oliver answers, dressed in sweats and a T-shirt that has an old, faded picture of a man with furry, ursine arms. SUPPORT THE SECOND AMENDMENT, it reads. His eyes are bloodshot, and he has ink stains on his hands. "Emma," he says. "Is everything okay?"

"No," I say, pushing past him. There are take-out containers on the floor, and an empty two-liter jug of Mountain Dew lies on its side. Thor, the dog, is asleep with his chin notched over the green plastic bottle. "No, everything's not okay." I face him again, my voice catching. "It's two in the morning. I'm in my pajamas. I just ran here—"

"You *ran* here?"

"—and my son's going to prison. So no, Oliver, everything is not okay."

"Jacob's going to get acquitted—"

"Oliver," I say. "Tell me the truth."

He moves a stack of papers off the couch and sits down heavily. "You know why I'm awake at two in the morning? I'm trying to write my opening statement. Want to hear what I've got so far?" He lifts up the paper he's holding. *"Ladies and gentlemen, Jacob Hunt is . . ."* He stops.

"Is what?"

"I don't know," Oliver says. He crumples it into a ball, and I know he's thinking of Jacob's meltdown, just like I am. "I don't fucking know. *Jacob Hunt is saddled with an attorney who should have stayed a farrier,* that's what. I shouldn't have said yes to you. I shouldn't have gone to the police station. I should have given you the name of some guy who can do criminal law in his sleep, instead of pretending a novice like me might have half a chance of pulling this off."

"If this is your way of trying to make me feel better, you're doing a really lousy job," I tell him.

"I told you I suck at this."

"Well. At least now you're being honest." I sit down beside him on the couch.

"You want honest?" Oliver says. "I have

no idea if that jury is going to buy the defense. I'm scared. Of losing, of the judge laughing me out of court as a total sham."

"I'm scared all the time," I admit. "Everyone thinks I'm the mother who never gives up; that I'd drag Jacob back from the edge of hell a hundred times if I had to. But some mornings I just want to pull the covers over my head and stay in bed."

"*Most* mornings I want to do that," Oliver says, and I swallow a smile.

We are leaning against the back of the couch. The blue light from the streetlamps outside turns us both into ghosts. We aren't in this world anymore, just haunting its edges.

"You want to hear something really sad?" I whisper. "You're my best friend."

"You're right. That *is* really sad." Oliver grins.

"That's not what I meant."

"Are we still playing True Confessions?" he asks.

"Is that what we're doing?"

He reaches toward me and rubs a strand of my hair between his fingers. "I think you're beautiful," Oliver says. "Inside and out."

He leans forward the tiniest bit and breathes in, closing his eyes, before he lets the hair fall back against my cheek. I feel it inside me, as if I've been shocked.

I don't pull away.

I don't *want* to pull away.

"I . . . I don't know what to say," I stammer.

Oliver's eyes light up. *"Of all the gin joints in all the towns in all the world, she walks into mine,"* he quotes. He moves slowly, so that I know what's coming, and kisses me.

I should be with Jacob, by court order. I am already breaking rules. What's one more?

His teeth catch my lip. He tastes like sugar. "Jelly beans," he murmurs against my ear. "My biggest vice. After this."

I tangle my hands in his hair. It's thick and golden, wild. "Oliver," I gasp, as he slides his hands under my camisole. His fingers span my ribs. "I'm pretty sure you're not supposed to sleep with your clients."

"You're not my client," he says. "And I'm not nearly as attracted to Jacob." He peels back the cardigan I'm wearing; my skin burns. I cannot remember the last time someone treated me as if I were the hallowed museum piece that he had received permission to touch.

Somehow we have inched ourselves down onto the couch. My head falls to the side, along with my best intentions, when his mouth closes over my breast. I find myself staring directly into Thor's eyes. "The dog . . ."

Oliver lifts his head. "Jesus," he says, and he stands up, grabbing Thor like a football in one arm. "You've got lousy timing." He opens a closet and tosses a handful of Milk-Bones on a pillow inside, then sets Thor down and closes the door.

When he turns around again, I draw in my breath. Somehow, his T-shirt has gotten lost between the cushions. His shoulders are wide and strong, his waist tapered, his sweats riding low. He has the easy beauty of someone young enough to dismiss how lucky he is to look like that without trying.

Me, on the other hand: I'm lying on a ratty couch in a cramped room with a jealous dog in the nearby closet, with freckles and wrinkles and fifteen more pounds than I ought to have and—

"Don't," Oliver says softly, as I pull the edges of my cardigan together again. He sits down on the edge of the couch beside me. "Or I will have to kill Thor."

"Oliver, you could have any girl you want. Any girl your age."

"You know what young wine is? Grape juice. There are some things worth the wait."

"That argument would have been much more convincing coming from someone who hadn't just finished off a trough of Mountain Dew—"

He kisses me again. "Shut the hell up, Emma," he says amiably, and he puts his hands over mine where they rest on the edges of my sweater.

"It's been forever." The words are quiet, hidden against his shoulder.

"That's because," Oliver says, "you were waiting for me." He slips aside the sweater again and kisses my collarbone. "Emma. Is everything okay?" he asks, for the second time this night.

Except this time, I say yes.

I should have gotten rid of the king-size bed. There is something horribly depressing about only having to tuck in half the sheets each morning, because the other side always remains pristine. I never cross the Mason-Dixon Line of my marriage and sleep, every now and then, on Henry's side. I've left it for him, for whoever might take his place.

That turned out to be Theo, during thunderstorms, when he was afraid. Or Jacob when he was sick and I wanted to keep an eye on him. I told myself that I liked the extra space anyway. That I deserved to spread out if I wanted to, even though I have always slept curled on my side like a fiddlehead fern.

Which is why, I suppose, it feels perfect when the pink fingers of the morning stroke the sheet that Oliver's tossed over us sometime in the night, and I realize that he's curled around me: a comma, his knees tucked up behind mine and his arm tight around my waist.

I shift, but instead of letting go of me, Oliver tightens his grasp. "What time is it?" he murmurs.

"Five-thirty."

I turn in his embrace, so that I am facing him. There's stubble on his cheeks and his chin. "Oliver, listen."

His eyes squint open. "No."

"No, you're not going to listen? Or no, you're not Oliver?"

"I'm not going to listen," he replies. "It *wasn't* a mistake, and it *wasn't* just a one-time, what-the-hell night. And if you keep fighting me on this, I'll make you read the fine print on the retainer you signed, which very clearly states that the attorney's sexual services are included in the fee."

"I was going to tell you to come over for breakfast," I say drily.

Oliver blinks at me. "Oh."

"It's Thursday. Brown day. Gluten-free bagels?"

"I prefer Everything," he answers, and then he blushes. "But I guess I made that fairly obvious last night."

I used to wake up in the morning and lie in bed for thirty seconds, when whatever I had dreamed might still be possible, before I remembered that I had to get up and make whatever breakfast fit the color code and wonder whether we would survive the day without some schedule change or noise or social conundrum triggering a meltdown. I had thirty seconds when the future was something I anticipated, not feared.

I wrap my arms around Oliver's neck and kiss him. Even knowing that, in four and a half hours, this trial will start again; even knowing that I have to hurry home before Jacob realizes I am missing; even knowing that I have likely made a mess of things by doing what I've done . . . I have figured out a way to stretch those thirty seconds of bliss into one long, lovely moment.

Three letters: a place where hope was found.

Joy.

Him.

Yes.

If this happened . . . well, maybe anything can.

He puts his hands on my shoulders and gently pushes me away. "You have no idea how much it's killing me to say no," Oliver says, "but I've got an opening argument to write, and my client's mother is, well, incredibly demanding."

"No kidding," I say.

He sits up and pulls my camisole out from under his head, helps me stretch it over my head. "This isn't nearly as much fun in reverse," he points out.

We both dress, and then Oliver frees Thor from his banishment and hooks a leash onto his collar, offering to walk me partway home. We are the only people on the streets at this hour. "I feel like an idiot," I say, glancing down at my slippers and my pajama bottoms.

"You look like a college student."

I roll my eyes. "You are such a liar."

"You mean lawyer."

"Is there a difference?"

I stop walking and look up at him. "This," I say. "Not in front of Jacob."

Oliver doesn't pretend to misunderstand me. He keeps walking, tugging at Thor's leash. "All right," he says.

We part ways at the skateboarding park, and I walk quickly with my head ducked against the wind—and the view of drivers in passing cars. Every now and then, a smile bubbles up from inside me, rising to the surface. The closer I get to home, the more inappropriate that feels. As if I am cheating somehow, as if I have the audacity to be someone other than the mother I am expected to be.

By 6:15 I am turning the corner of my street, relieved. Jacob wakes up like clockwork at 6:30; he'll be none the wiser.

But as I get closer, I see that the lights are on in the house, and my heart skips a beat. I start running, panicked. What if something happened to Jacob in the middle of the night? How stupid have I been, leaving him? I hadn't scribbled a note, I hadn't taken my cell phone, and as I throw open the front door, I am nearly bent double by the weight of what might have gone wrong.

Jacob stands at the kitchen counter, already making his own brown breakfast. There are two place settings. "Mom," he blurts, excited, "you'll never guess who's here."

Before I can, though, I hear the downstairs toilet flush, and the running of the faucet, and the footsteps of the guest, who enters the kitchen with an uncomfortable smile.

"Henry?" I say.

CASE 10: WOODN'T YOU LIKE TO GET AWAY WITH MURDER?

On November 19, 1986, Helle Crafts, a Pan Am flight attendant from Connecticut, disappeared. Her husband was suspected shortly after she vanished: Richard Crafts told authorities that he hadn't left the house on November 19, but credit card records showed that he'd purchased new bedding. Shortly before his wife disappeared, he also had bought a large freezer and rented a wood chipper.

When a witness recalled seeing a wood chipper near the Housatonic River, police searched the Crafts home. Blood found on the mattress matched Helle's. A letter addressed to Helle was found near the Housatonic, and divers recovered a chain saw and cutting bar, which still had human hair and tissue in its jaws. Based on this, a more thorough evidence search was begun.

Here's what they found:

2660 hairs.

One fingernail.

One toenail.

One tooth cap.

Five droplets of blood.

(A fingernail in a U-Haul rented by Crafts chemically matched nail polish in Helle's bathroom, too, but it was thrown out of court because of the lack of a search warrant.)

From this evidence, in 1989, Crafts was found guilty of his wife's murder and sentenced to ninety-nine years in prison.

This case made Dr. Henry Lee famous. Leave it to him, a forensic hero, to secure a murder conviction . . . even without a body.

10

Emma

For just a moment, I am certain that I'm hallucinating. My ex-husband is *not* standing in my kitchen, is not coming forward to awkwardly kiss my cheek.

"What are you doing here?" I demand.

He looks at Jacob, who is pouring chocolate soy milk into a glass. "For once in my life, I wanted to do the right thing," Henry says.

I fold my arms. "Don't flatter yourself, Henry. This has less to do with Jacob than it does with your own guilt."

"Wow," he says. "Some things never change."

"What's that supposed to mean?"

"No one's allowed to be a better parent than you are. You have to be the gold standard, and if you're not, you'll cut everyone else down to make sure of it."

"That's pretty funny, coming from a man who hasn't seen his son in years."

"Three years, six months, and four days," Jacob says. I had forgotten he was still in the room. "We went out to dinner in Boston because you flew in for work. You ate beef tenderloin, and you sent it back because it was too rare at first."

Henry and I look at each other. "Jacob," I say, "why don't you go upstairs and take the first shower?"

"What about breakfast—"

"You can eat it when you come back down."

Jacob hustles upstairs, leaving me alone with Henry. "You have got to be kidding," I say, furious. "You think you can just show up here like some white knight and save the day?"

"Considering that I'm the one who cut the check for the lawyer," Henry says, "I have a right to make sure he's doing his job."

That, of course, makes me think of Oliver. And the things we did that were not job-related.

"Look," Henry says, the bluster falling from him like snow from a tree limb. "I didn't come here to make things more difficult for you, Emma. I came to help."

"You don't just get to be their father, now, because your conscience reared its ugly head. You're either a father twenty-four/seven or not at all."

"Why don't we ask the kids if they want me to stick around or leave?"

"Oh, right. That's like dangling a brand-new video game in front of them. You're a novelty, Henry."

He smiles a little. "Can't remember the last time I've been accused of *that*."

There is a commotion as Theo clatters down the stairs. "Wow, you *are* here," he says. "Weird."

"It's because of you," Henry replies. "After you came all the way to see me, I realized I couldn't sit at home and pretend this wasn't happening."

Theo snorts a laugh. "Why not? I do it all the time."

"I'm not listening to this," I say, moving around the kitchen. "We have to be in court by nine-thirty."

"I'll come," Henry said. "For moral support."

"Thank you *so* much," I say drily. "I don't know how I'd get through the day if you weren't here. Oh, wait. I've gotten through five thousand days without you here."

Theo skirts between us and opens the refrigerator. He pulls out a carton of grapefruit juice and drinks directly from it. "Gosh. What a happy little family unit we are." He glances overhead as the water in the pipes stops running. "I call the shower next," he says, and he heads back upstairs.

I sink down into a chair. "So how does this work? You sit in the courtroom and act concerned while your real family is waiting just outside the escape hatch?"

"That's not fair, Emma."

"*Nothing's* fair."

"I'm here for as long as I need to be. Meg understands that I've got a responsibility to Jacob."

"Right. A responsibility. But somehow she's neglected to invite him to sunny California to meet his stepsisters—"

"Jacob won't get on a plane, and you know it."

"So your plan is to just come step into his life and then step out of it again after the trial?"

"I don't have a plan—"

"What about afterward?"

"That's why I came." He takes a step closer. "If . . . if the worst happens, and Jacob doesn't come home . . . well, I know you'll be there for *him* to lean on," Henry says. "But I thought *you* might need someone to lean on, too."

There are a hundred comebacks running through my head—most of which ask why I would trust him now when he has a track record of abandoning me. But instead, I shake my head. "Jacob's coming home," I say.

"Emma, you have to—"

I hold up the flat of my hand, as if I can stop his words midstream. "Help yourself to breakfast. I need to get dressed."

I leave him sitting in the kitchen, and I go upstairs to my bedroom. Through the wall I can hear Theo singing in the shower. I sit down on the bed, clasp my hands between my knees.

When the boys were little, we had house rules. I'd write them on the bathroom mirror when they were in the tub so that the next time the room steamed up, they would magically appear: commandments for a toddler and his painfully literal autistic brother, laws that were not to be broken.

1. Clean up your own messes.

2. Tell the truth.

3. Brush your teeth twice a day.

4. Don't be late for school.

5. Take care of your brother; he's the only one you've got.

One night Jacob had asked me if I had to follow the rules, too, and I said yes. *But,* he pointed out, *you don't have a brother.*
Then I will take care of you, I said.
However, I didn't.
Oliver will stand up in court today, and maybe the next day and the next, and try to accomplish what I have unsuccessfully tried to do for eighteen years now: make strangers understand what it is like to be my son. Make

them feel sympathy for a child who cannot feel it himself.

When Theo's done in the bathroom, I go in. The air is still thick with heat and steam; the mirror's fogged. I can't see the tears on my face, but it's for the best. Because I may know my son, and I may believe viscerally that he is not a murderer. But the odds of a jury seeing this as clearly as I do are minimal. Because no matter what I tell Henry—or myself, for that matter—I know that Jacob isn't coming home.

Jacob

Theo is still getting dressed when I knock on his door. "What the fuck, dude?" he says, holding up a towel to his body. I close my eyes until he tells me it's okay to look, and then I walk into his room.

"I need help with my tie," I say.

I am very proud of the fact that I got dressed today without any issues. I was a little freaked out by the buttons on the shirt, which felt like hot coals on my chest, but I put on a T-shirt underneath, and now it isn't quite as painful.

Theo stands in front of me in his jeans and a sweatshirt. I wish I could wear that to the courthouse. He straightens my collar and starts to loop the ends of the tie around and around so that it will be a tie, instead of the knot I've managed to make twice. The tie is like a long, skinny knit scarf; I like it a lot more than the striped thing Oliver made me wear yesterday.

"There you go," Theo says. Then he hunches his shoulders. "So what do you think about Dad?"

"I don't think about Dad," I say.

"I mean about him being here."

"Oh," I say. "I guess it's good."

(In reality, I don't think it's either good or bad. It's not as if it's going to make much difference, after all, but it seems like normal people would have a more positive reaction to seeing a close family member, *and* he did travel 3,000 miles on a plane, so I have to give him credit for that.)

"I thought Mom was going to blow her stack."

I don't know what he means by that, but I nod and smile at him. You'd be surprised at how far that response can get you in a conversation where you are completely confused.

"Do you remember him?" Theo asks.

"He called on my birthday, and that was only three and a half months ago—"

"No," Theo interrupts. "I mean, do you remember him from back then? When he lived with us?"

I do, actually. I remember being in bed between him and my mother, and holding my hand up to his cheek while he slept. It was scratchy with incoming beard, and the texture used to intrigue me, plus I liked the sound it made when he scraped it. I remember his briefcase. He had floppy disks inside in different colors that I liked to sort by spectrum, and paper clips in a small container that I would line up on the floor of his office while he worked. Sometimes, though, when he was doing programming and got stuck or excited, he yelled, and that usually made me yell, and he would call for my mother to take me so that he could get some work done.

"He took me apple picking once," I say. "He let me ride on his shoulders and showed me how the apple pickers get the apples out of their baskets without bruising them."

For a while, I kept a list of apple facts as I learned them, because what I remembered about my father was that he at least had a passing interest in pomology, enough of one to take me out to an orchard for the day. I know, for example, that:

1. The world's top apple producers are China, the United States, Turkey, Poland, and Italy.

2. It takes about thirty-six apples to create a gallon of cider.

3. Red Delicious is the most widely grown variety in the United States.

4. It takes the energy of fifty leaves to produce a single apple.

5. The largest apple ever picked weighed three pounds.

6. Apples float because a quarter of their volume is air.

7. Apple trees are related to roses.

8. Archaeologists have found evidence of apples being eaten as early as 6500 B.C.

"That's cool," Theo says. "I don't remember anything about him at all."

I know why; it is because Theo was only a few months old when my father left. I don't remember that day, but I do remember a lot leading up to it. My mother and father often fought right in front of me. I was there, but I wasn't there—those were the days when I would find myself completely entranced by the static on the television screen or the lever of the toaster. My parents assumed that I was not paying attention, but that isn't the way it works. I could hear and see and smell and feel *everything* at once back then, which is why I had to focus so hard to pay attention to only one of the stimuli. I've always sort of pictured it like a movie: imagine a camera that can record the entire world at once—every sight, every sound. That's very impressive, but it isn't particularly useful if you want to specifically hear a conversation between two people, or see a ball coming toward you while you're standing at bat. And yet, I couldn't change the brain I'd been born with, so instead I learned how to narrow the world with makeshift blinders, until all I noticed was what I wanted to notice. That's autism, for those who've never been there themselves.

Anyway, this is also why, even though my parents might have assumed my attention was otherwise occupied, I can remember the fights they had verbatim:

Do you remember me, Emma? I live here,
too . . .

For God's sake, Henry. Are you really jealous of the time I spend with your own son?

And

I don't care how we're going to pay for
it. I'm not going to pass up a treatment for
Jacob just because—

Because what? Say it . . . You don't think
I make enough money.

Your words, not mine.

And

I want to come home from my fucking
job to my fucking house and not have ten
fucking strangers on my living room floor.
Is that so much to ask?

Those strangers are the ones who are
going to bring Jacob back to us—

Wake up, Emma. He is what he is. There's
not some miracle locked inside him waiting
to come out.

And

You've worked late every night this week.

Well, what have I got to come home to?

And

What do you mean, you're pregnant? We
said no more. We already have too much
on our plate—

I didn't exactly get pregnant by myself, you know.

You'd know. You're the one who takes the pills.

You think I tricked you? Jesus, Henry, I'm glad to know you think so highly of me. Just get out. Get out of here.

And one day he did.

Suddenly, my father knocks on Theo's door and pokes his head into the room. "Boys," he says. "How, um, how are you doing?"

Neither of us says a word.

"Jacob," he asks. "Can we talk?"

We sit down in my room, with me on the bed and my father on my desk chair. "Are you . . . okay with me being here?"

I look around. He isn't messing anything up on my desk, so I nod.

This makes him feel better, I think, because his shoulders relax. "I owe you an apology," he says. "I don't really know how to put this into words."

"That happens to me," I tell him.

He smiles a little and shakes his head. Theo looks so much like him. I've heard this all my life from my mother, but now I can also see that there's a lot of my father that reminds

me of me. Like the way he ducks his head before he starts a sentence. And how he drums
his fingers on his thighs.

"I wanted to apologize to you, Jacob," he
says. "There are some people—like your
mother—who just won't give up. I'm not one
of those people. I'm not saying it's an excuse,
only a fact. I knew enough about myself, even
back then, to understand that this wasn't a
situation I could handle."

"By *this*," I say, "you mean *me*."

He hesitates, and then he nods. "I don't
know as much about Asperger's as your mother
does," he says. "But I think maybe we've all
got something in us that keeps us from connecting to people, even when we want to."

I like the concept: that Asperger's is like a
flavoring added to a person, and although
my concentration is higher than those of others, if tested, everyone else would have traces
of this condition, too.

I make myself look my father in the eye.
"Did you know apples can rust?" I say.

"No," he says, his voice softer. "No, I did not."

In addition to the list of apple facts, I have
kept another list for my father, of questions I
might ask if the chance arose:

1. If it hadn't been for me, would you have stayed?

2. Were you ever sorry you left?

3. Do you think one day we could be friends?

4. If I promised to try harder, would you consider coming back?

It is worthwhile to note that while we were sitting in my room we discussed apples, the medical examiner's testimony of yesterday, and the article in *Wired* magazine about whether Asperger's was on the rise in Silicon Valley due to the preponderance of math-and-science genes in the geographical area. Yet I did not ask him a single one of these questions, which are still on a list in the back of my bottom-most left desk drawer.

We all ride to the courthouse together in my father's rental car. It is silver and smells like pine trees. I am sitting in my usual seat in the back behind my father, who is driving. My mother sits next to him, and Theo's beside me. As we drive I look at the spaces between the power lines on the telephone poles, which narrow at the ends and then widen in the middle, like giant canoes.

We are five minutes from the courthouse when my mother's cell phone rings. She nearly drops it before she manages to answer the call. "I'm fine," she says, but her face gets red. "We'll meet you in the parking lot."

I suppose I should be nervous, but I'm actually excited. Today is the day that Oliver gets to tell everyone the truth about what I did.

"Now, Jacob," my mother says. "You remember the rules?"

"Let Oliver do the talking," I mutter. "Pass him a note if I need a break. I'm not a moron, Mom."

"That's a matter of opinion," Theo says.

She twists around in her seat. Her pupils are large and dark, and a pulse beats in the hollow of her throat. "It's going to be harder for you today," she says quietly. "You're going to hear things said about you that might not make sense. Things that maybe you even think aren't true. But just remember, Oliver knows what he's doing."

"Is Jacob testifying?" my father asks.

My mother turns to him. "What do *you* think?"

"I was just asking, for God's sake."

"Well, you can't come in at the third act and expect me to tell you what you've missed," she snaps, and silence fills the car like sarin gas. I start to whisper the Fibonacci sequence under my breath, to make myself feel better, and Theo must feel the same way, because he says, "So . . . are we there yet?" and then laughs hysterically, as if he's told a really funny joke.

As we drive in, Oliver is leaning against his truck. It is an old pickup that, he says, is more suited to a farrier than an attorney, but it still gets him from point A to point B. We are parked in the back of the courthouse, away from the cameras and the television news vans. He glances up as we drive by, but this isn't my mother's car, so he doesn't realize it's us. It isn't until we park and step out of the rental car that Oliver sees my mother and comes forward with a big smile on his face.

And then he notices my dad.

"Oliver," my mother says, "this is my ex-husband, Henry."

"Are you kidding?" Oliver looks at my mother.

My father sticks out his hand to shake Oliver's. "Nice to meet you."

"Um. Right. Pleasure." Then he turns to me. "Oh, for the love of God . . . Emma, I can't let him go into the courtroom like this."

I look down. I'm wearing brown corduroy pants and a brown shirt, with a brown tweed blazer and the stretchy brown tie that Theo tied for me.

"It's Thursday, and he's dressed in a jacket and tie," my mother says tightly. "You might imagine that this morning I had a lot on my plate."

Oliver turns to my father. "What does he look like to you?"

"A UPS driver?" my father says.

"I was thinking *Nazi*." Oliver shakes his head. "We don't have time for you to go home and change, and you're too big to fit into my—" Suddenly he breaks off and sizes up my father with one glance. "Go trade shirts with him in the bathroom."

"But it's *white*," I say.

"Exactly. The look we're going for is not modern-day serial killer, Jake."

My father glances at my mother. "See," he says. "Aren't you glad I came?"

The first day I met Jess for social skills training I happened to be fearing for my very life.

I had been in Mrs. Wicklow's English class that year. It wasn't a particularly interesting class, and Mrs. Wicklow had the bad fortune to have a face that looked a little like a sweet potato—long and narrow, with a few sprouting hairs at the chin and an orange spray-on tan. But she always let me read aloud when we were doing plays, even if I sometimes had trouble remembering my place, and the time I forgot my notebook on the day of the open-book exam she let me take it the next day. One day, when she was out with the flu, a boy in the class named Sawyer Trigg (who had been suspended once for bringing Ny-Quil to school to sell in the cafeteria) ignored the substitute teacher and plucked bits of the spider plant off, then stuck it to his chin with gum. He jammed wadded-up paper under his shirt and started prancing through the aisles between our desks. "I'm Mrs. Witchlow," he said, and everyone laughed.

I laughed, too, but only to fit in. Because you're supposed to respect teachers, even if they're not there. So when Mrs. Wicklow came back, I told her what Sawyer had been doing, and she sent him to the principal. Later that day, he slammed me up against my locker and said, "I could fucking kill you, Hunt."

Well, I spent the rest of the day in an utter panic, because he *could* kill me, I had no doubt of that. And when Jess arrived at the school to meet me for the first time, I had a butter knife in my pocket stolen from the cafeteria—the best I could do on short notice—just in case Sawyer Trigg was lurking in the shadows of the hallways.

She told me that what I said to her was private, and that she wouldn't tell my mother about anything I wanted to keep a secret between us. I liked that—it sounded like having a best friend, at least the way it is always portrayed on television—but I was too distracted to comment. "Um, Jacob?" Jess said, when she caught me looking over my shoulder for the eighth time. "Is everything okay?"

That was when I told her everything about Mrs. Wicklow and Sawyer Trigg.

She shook her head. "He's not going to kill you."

"But he said—"

"That's his way of letting you know he's mad at you for tattling on him."

"You're not supposed to make fun of teachers—"

"You're not supposed to tell on your peers, either," Jess said. "Especially if you want them to like you. I mean, Mrs. Wicklow *has* to be nice to you; it's part of her contract. But you have to *earn* the trust of your classmates. And you just lost that." She leaned forward. "There are all kinds of rules, Jacob. Some of them are explicit, like not making fun of teachers. But others are like secrets. They're the ones you're supposed to know, even if they never get said."

That was exactly what I never seemed to understand: those unwritten rules that other people seemed to pick up as if they had a social radar device that was missing in my own brain.

"Did you laugh when Sawyer made fun of Mrs. Wicklow?"

"Yes."

"He thought you were on his side, that you were enjoying the performance. So imagine how he felt when you tattled on him."

I stared at Jess. I wasn't Sawyer, and I had been adhering to a rule; whereas he was deliberately breaking one. "I can't," I said.

A few minutes later, my mother came to pick me up. "Hello," she said, smiling at Jess. "How did it go?"

Jess looked at me, making sure she caught my eye. Then she turned to my mother. "Jacob got another boy in trouble today. Oh, and he stole a knife from the school cafeteria."

I felt my heart go to stone in my chest, and my mouth was dry as cotton. I thought this girl was going to be my friend, was going to keep my secrets. And the first thing she did was turn around and tell my mother everything that had happened today?

I was furious; I never wanted to see her again. And I felt soft and spongy in my stomach, too, as if I had just gotten off an amusement park ride, because I knew my mother was going to want to follow up on this conversation on the drive home.

Jess touched my arm to get my attention. *"That,"* she said, "is how Sawyer felt. And I will never do that to you again. Will you?"

The next day I went to school, and I waited near Sawyer's locker. "What are you doing here, prick?" he asked.

"I'm sorry," I told him, and I really, truly meant it.

Maybe it was my face, or the tone of my voice, or just the fact that I sought him out— but he stood there for a second with his locker open and then he shrugged. "Whatever," Sawyer said.

I decided that was his way of saying thanks. "Are you still thinking of killing me?"

He shook his head and laughed. "I don't think so."

I'm telling you, Jess Ogilvy was the best teacher I've ever had. And she would have understood, better than anyone, why I had to do what I did.

Oliver

What happened last night was the single most remarkable experience of my sexual history, unless you count the time I was a sophomore in college and got a letter published in *Penthouse*—the difference being, of course, that that was fictional, whereas last night really happened.

I've been thinking about it. (Okay, I've been thinking of nothing *but* it.) Once Emma and I had both admitted our biggest fears to each other, we were on equal footing. Vulnerability trumps age. When you're emotionally bare, the leap to being physically bare isn't all that far.

I woke up this morning with her hair loose over my arm and her body warm against mine and I decided that I didn't care if she had slept with me out of desperation or frustration or even distraction—I wasn't going to let her go. I had charted every inch of her last night; I wanted to return to that territory until I knew it better than anyone ever had or ever would.

Which meant I had to get her son acquitted, because otherwise, she'd never want to see me again.

To that end, I came to court this morning intending to give Jacob the best defense in the history of the State of Vermont. I was single-minded and focused and determined, until I saw her emerge from another man's car.

Her *ex's*.

He has a right to be here, I suppose—he's Jacob's father—but Emma had led me to believe that he wasn't really in the picture.

I don't like the way Henry held on to her when we were walking up the steps of the courthouse. I don't like the fact that he's bigger than I am. I don't like the fact that the one time I touched Emma's arm, as we were about to come into the courtroom, Theo saw me do it and his brows shot up to his hairline, so I had to immediately pretend it was an accidental brush of the hand.

I *really* don't like the fact that I'm preoccupied with Emma when I ought to be focused solely on her son.

As the jury files in, I take my seat beside Jacob. He looks like he's had sixty cups of coffee. He's bouncing, even though he's seated next to me at the defense table. Emma is on his right side, and I swear, I can feel the heat of her skin even with her son between us. "I don't like this," Jacob mutters.

You and me both, kid. I think. "What don't you like?"

"Her hair."

"Whose hair?"

"Hers," Jacob says, and he points to Helen Sharp without glancing at her.

Today the prosecutor is wearing her hair loose around her face. It's auburn and brushes her shoulders. It actually makes her look almost compassionate, although I know better. "Well," I say. "It could be worse."

"How?"

"It could be longer."

This makes me think of Emma last night, with her hair free and falling down her back. I'd never seen it like that, because of Jacob.

"It's a bad omen," Jacob says, and his fingers flutter on his thigh.

"There seems to be a lot of that going around," I say, and I turn to Emma. "What's Henry doing here?"

She shakes her head. "He showed up this morning when I was out for my *run*," she stresses, and doesn't meet my eye. Conversation closed.

"Make sure you tell the truth," Jacob states, and Emma and I both jerk our heads toward him. Is Jacob more intuitive than either of us gave him credit for?

"All rise," the bailiff says, and the judge strides in from his chambers.

"If the defense wishes to deliver an opening statement," Judge Cuttings says, "you may begin."

I would have preferred to give my opening statement back when Helen had given hers, so that the whole time the jury was watching Jacob's reactions during the prosecution's turn, they could have been thinking his inappropriate affect was because he has Asperger's—not because he is a sociopathic killer. But the judge didn't give me that opportunity, and so now, I just have to leave an impression that's twice as deep.

"The truth," Jacob whispers again. "You'll tell them what happened, right?"

He is talking about the jury, I realize; he is talking about Jess's murder. And there is so much riding on that one question that suddenly I have no idea how to answer Jacob without it becoming a lie. I hesitate, and then take a deep breath. *"Hello. My name is Inigo Montoya,"* I murmur to Jacob. *"You killed my father. Prepare to die."*

I know he's grinning as I stand up and face the jury. "During a trial, lawyers ask the jury to see in shades of gray. You're supposed to look at both sides of an issue. To not prejudge anything. To wait until you've heard all the evidence to make a decision. The judge has instructed you to do this, and will instruct you to do this again at the end of the trial."

I walk toward them. "But Jacob Hunt doesn't know how to do that. He can't see shades of gray. To him, the world is black or white. For example, if you ask Jacob to pitch a tent, he will toss it at you. Part of Jacob's diagnosis with Asperger's syndrome means that he won't understand the concept of a metaphor. To him, the world is a literal place." I glance over my shoulder at Jacob, who's staring down at the table. "You might have also noticed that yesterday, during this trial, Jacob didn't look the witnesses in the eye. Or that he didn't show

much emotion when the prosecution enumer-
ated the horrors of a murder scene. Or that he
might not be able to sit through testimony for
long periods of time and needs a break in that
room in the back. In fact, there may be many
moments during this trial where it seems to
you that Jacob is acting rudely, or immaturely,
or even in a manner that makes him appear
guilty. But ladies and gentlemen, Jacob cannot
help it. Those behaviors are all hallmarks of
Asperger's syndrome, a neurological disorder
on the autism spectrum with which Jacob's
been diagnosed. People with Asperger's might
have a normal or even exceptional IQ but will
also show severe deficiencies in social and
communication skills. They might be obsessed
by routine or rules, or be fixated on a certain
subject. They can't read expressions very well,
or body language. They are overly sensitive to
lights, textures, smells, and sounds.

"You are going to hear from Jacob's doctors
and his mother about his limitations, and how
they've tried hard to help Jacob overcome
them. Part of what you're going to hear is Jacob's very concrete sense of what's right and
what's wrong. In his world, rules are not just
important, they're infallible. And yet, he has no
understanding of the underlying bases of those

rules. He can't tell you how his behavior might affect another person, because it is impossible for Jacob to put himself in someone else's metaphorical shoes. He might be able to recite to you every line from *CrimeBusters* episode forty-four, but he can't tell you why the mother is upset in scene seven of the show, or how the loss of a child impacted the parents in that show. If you ask Jacob, he can't explain it. Not because he doesn't want to, and not because he's a sociopath, but because his brain simply doesn't function that way."

I walk behind the defense table and put my hand lightly on Jacob's shoulder. Immediately he flinches, just like I figured, beneath the jury's watchful eye. "If you spend some time with Jacob," I say, "you'll probably think there's something . . . different about him. Something you can't quite put your finger on. He may seem odd, or quirky . . . but you probably also won't think of him as insane. After all, he can hold a legitimate conversation with you; he knows more about certain subjects than I'll ever know; he isn't running around listening to voices in his head or setting small animals on fire. But the definition of *legal* insanity, ladies and gentlemen, is very different than what we typically think of when we think of the word *insanity.* It says that, at the moment an act was committed, the defendant—as a result of a severe mental disease or defect—was unable to appreciate the wrongfulness of his acts. What that means is that a person with a neurological disorder like Asperger's who commits a crime—a person like Jacob—can't be held responsible in the same way you or I should be held responsible. And what you will hear from the witnesses for the defense is proof that having Asperger's syndrome makes it impossible for Jacob to understand how his actions might cause harm to someone else. You will hear how having Asperger's syndrome might lead a person like Jacob to have an idiosyncratic interest that becomes overwhelming and obsessive. And you will see, ladies and gentlemen, that having Asperger's syndrome impaired Jacob's ability to understand that what he did to Jess Ogilvy was wrong."

Behind me, I hear whispering. From the corner of my eye, I see a dozen notes, stacked on my side of the defense table. Jacob is rocking back and forth, his mouth tight. After a minute he starts to write notes to Emma as well.

"No one is suggesting that Jess Ogilvy's death is anything less than a tragedy, and our sympathies must lie with her family. But don't compound that tragedy by creating a second victim."

I nod, and sit back down at the table. The notes are brief and angry:

NO.

YOU HAVE TO TELL THEM.

WHAT I DID WAS RIGHT.

I lean toward my client. "Just trust me," I say.

Theo

Yesterday, I was sitting alone in the back of the courtroom squished between a woman who was knitting a newborn baby cap and a man in a tweed jacket who kept texting on his phone during the testimony. No one knew who I was, and I liked it that way. After Jacob's first sensory break, when I went to the little curtained room and the bailiff let me slip inside, my secret identity was not so much of a secret anymore. The knitting woman, I noticed, moved to a spot on the other side of the courtroom, as if I had

some dread contagious disease instead of just a last name shared with
the defendant. The man in the tweed
coat, though, stopped texting. He kept
asking me questions: *Had Jacob ever
been violent before? Did he have the
hots for Jess Ogilvy? Did she turn him
down?* It didn't take long for me to
figure out he was some kind of reporter,
and after that, I just stood in the back
near one of the bailiffs.

Today, I'm sitting next to my father,
a guy I don't know at all.

When Oliver starts talking, my father
leans toward me. "What do you know
about this guy?"

"He likes long walks on the beach,
and he's a Scorpio," I say.

Here's what I really know. Oliver was
rubbing my mom's arm today. Not
in the oh-you're-about-to-fall-are-you-
okay way, but in a sweet-child-o'-mine
mode. What the fuck is *that* all about?
He's supposed to be saving my brother's ass, not hitting on my mother.

I know I should be relieved that my
father is here, but actually, I'm not.
I'm sitting here wondering why we are

spectators at a murder trial, instead of on the first base line at Fenway, watching the Sox play. I'm wondering how I learned to tie a tie, like I did for Jacob today, considering that my own father wasn't the one to teach it to me. I'm wondering why sharing the same DNA with a person doesn't make you automatically feel like you have something in common.

As soon as Oliver finishes his statement, I turn to my father. "I don't know how to fish," I say. "I mean, I wouldn't know how to stick a worm on a hook, or how to use a pole, or anything like that."

He just stares at me, frowning a little.

"It would have been cool if we'd fished," I say. "You know. Like in that pond behind the school."

This, of course, is just plain stupid. I was six months old when my father left us. I could barely hold myself upright, much less a fishing pole.

My father ducks his head. "I get seasick," he says. "Even just standing on a dock. Always have."

After that, we don't really talk at all.

* * *

I went to Dr. Moon once. My mother thought it would be a good idea for me to talk to a shrink about feelings I might be having, given the fact that my brother sucked up all the time and energy in our household like some giant karmic Hoover. I can't say I remember much about her, except that she smelled like incense and told me I could take off my shoes, because she herself could think better without shoes, and maybe I would, too.

On the other hand, I do still remember what we talked about. She said that, sometimes, it would be hard for me to be the younger brother, because I had to do all the stuff the older brother usually did. She told me that this might frustrate Jacob and make him mad, and that would make him act even more immature. In this she was the psychological equivalent of a weather forecast: she could tell me with precise probability what was coming, but she was completely unequipped to help me prepare for the storm.

She looks different on the witness stand than she does when she is at her office. For example, she is wearing a business suit, and her crazy long hair is tamed into a bun. Oh, and she's wearing shoes. "At first, Jacob was diagnosed with general autism spectrum disorder. Then we tweaked his diagnosis to pervasive developmental disorder. It wasn't until sixth grade that we amended his diagnosis to Asperger's syndrome, based on his inability to interpret social cues and to interact with peers in spite of his high IQ and verbal ability. For kids Jacob's age, that progression of diagnoses is very common. It doesn't mean he didn't always have Asperger's—he did—it just means that we didn't necessarily have the correct language to label it."

"Can you give a definition of Asperger's syndrome for people who aren't familiar with it, Doctor?" Oliver asks.

"It's a developmental disorder that affects the way information is processed in the brain, and it's considered to fall at the upper end of the autism spectrum. People with Asperger's are often very intelligent and very competent—in this, they differ from profoundly autistic children, who can't communicate at all—but they have crippling disabilities in the area of social interaction."

"So someone with Asperger's might be smart?"

"Someone with Asperger's might even have a genius-level IQ. However, when it comes to making small talk, he'll be completely inept. He has to be taught social interaction as if it's a foreign language, the way you or I would need to be taught Farsi."

"Lawyers sometimes have trouble finding friends," Oliver says, raising some laughter on the jury. "Does that mean we all have Asperger's?"

"No," Dr. Moon responds. "A person with Asperger's desperately wants to fit in but simply can't understand social behavior that's intuitive to the rest of us. He won't be able to read gestures or facial expressions to assess the mood of the person he's speaking to. He won't be able to interpret a nonverbal

cue, such as a yawn signifying bore-
dom when he's hogging the conversation. He won't be able to understand
what someone else is thinking or feeling; that kind of empathy is unnatural
to him. He truly is the center of his own
universe and will react based on that
principle. For example, I had a patient who caught his sister shoplifting
and ratted her out—not because he
thought he was morally responsible to
report his sister's crime but because he
didn't want to be known as the boy
whose sister had a criminal record.
Whatever a child with Asperger's does,
he does because he's thinking of how
it will affect *him,* not anyone else."

"Are there other hallmarks of the
disorder?"

"Yes. Someone with Asperger's might
have difficulty organizing and prioritiz-
ing rules and tasks. He'll tend to focus
on details instead of the big picture
and often will become obsessed for
months or years at a time by one specific subject. And he can talk about
that subject—even if it's a sophisti-
cated topic—for hours at a time. For

this reason, the disorder is sometimes referred to as the Little Professor syndrome. Children with Asperger's speak in such an adult manner they often get along better with their parents' friends than with their own peers."

"Does Jacob have that sort of obsessive focus on one subject?"

"Oh, yes. He's had several over the years—dogs, and dinosaurs, and most recently, forensic science."

"What else might we notice about a person with Asperger's syndrome?"

"He'll adhere slavishly to routine and rules. He's painfully honest. He will dislike making eye contact. He might have hypersensitivity to light or noise or touch or taste. For example, right now, Jacob is probably working very hard to block out the sound of the fluorescent lights in this courtroom, which you and I can't even hear. One moment a child with Asperger's might present as an extremely bright, if awkward, child—and the next, when his routine is disrupted, he might have a meltdown that lasts between ten minutes and several hours."

"Like a toddler's tantrum?"

"Exactly. Except it's a lot more debilitating when the child is eighteen and 180 pounds," Dr. Moon says.

I can feel my father staring at me, so I turn to him. "Does that happen a lot?" he whispers. "The tantrums?"

"You get used to it," I say, although I'm not sure this is true. In reality, you don't ever change the hurricane. You just learn how to stay out of its path.

Oliver is walking toward the jury now. "Will Jacob ever be cured of Asperger's?"

"At present," the shrink says, "there's no cure for autism. It's not something you outgrow; it's a condition you have forever."

"Dr. Murano, which of the symptoms you've related here today has Jacob manifested over the years?"

"All of them," she says.

"Even now, at age eighteen?"

"Jacob's gotten much better at rolling with the punches if a routine is disrupted. Although it's still upsetting, now he has coping mechanisms he can draw upon. Instead of having a screaming fit, like he did at age four, he'll find a song or a movie and repeat the lyrics or lines over and over."

"Doctor, this court has allowed Jacob to take sensory breaks when necessary. Can you explain what that is?"

"It's a way for Jacob to get away from the overstimulation that's upsetting him. When he feels like he's spiraling out of control, he can remove himself and go to a place that's quiet and less chaotic. In school, he has a room where he can pull himself together again, and in court, he has the same type of area. Inside are all sorts of materials that Jacob can use to calm himself down—from deep-pressure weighted blankets to a rope swing to fiber-optic lamps."

"You said that kids with Asperger's have an affinity for rules. Is that true of Jacob?"

"Yes. For example, Jacob knows that school starts at eight-twelve A.M. and because of that rule, he is on time every day. However, one week his mother told him that he would be late for school because he had a dentist appointment. He had a melt-down, put his fist through a wall in his bedroom, and could not be calmed down enough to be taken to the dentist. In Jacob's mind, he was being asked to break a rule."

"He punched in a wall? Do kids with Asperger's have a propensity for violence?" Oliver asks.

"That's a myth. In fact, a child with Asperger's is more likely to *not* misbehave than neurotypical children are, simply because he knows that's the rule. However, a child with Asperger's also has a very low fight-or-flight threshold. If he feels cornered in any way—verbally, physically, or emotionally—he might either run or strike out blindly."

"Have you ever seen Jacob do that?"

"Yes," Dr. Moon says. "At school last year he was given detention for swearing at a teacher. Apparently a young woman tricked him into behaving inappropriately by saying she'd be his friend if he did it. Afterward, he retaliated by shoving her and was suspended."

"What triggered the violent response in Jacob?"

"Being belittled, I imagine."

"Did you talk to him about the episode?" Oliver asks.

"I did."

"Did you explain why his violent response wasn't appropriate?"

"Yes."

"Do you think he understood that what he did was wrong?"

She hesitates. "Jacob's sense of right and wrong isn't based on an internalized moral code. It's based on what he has been told to do, or not to do. If you asked him whether it's right to hit someone, he would tell you no. However, he would also tell you that it's wrong to make fun of someone—and in his mind, the young woman broke that rule first. When Jacob hit her, he was not thinking of how he might hurt her, or even of how his actions would be going against a rule of behavior. He was thinking of how she'd hurt *him,* and he simply . . . reacted."

Oliver approaches the witness stand. "Dr. Murano, if I told you that Jacob had argued with Jess Ogilvy two days before she died, and that she'd told him to get lost, how would you think that had affected his behavior?"

She shakes her head. "Jess was very important to Jacob, and if they had a fight, he would have been extremely upset. In going to her house that day, he was clearly manifesting that he didn't know how to behave. He stuck to his routine rather than let the argument run its course. Most likely, Jacob's mind processed the fight like this: *Jess told me to get lost. I can't possibly get lost because I always know where I am. Therefore she didn't really mean what she said, so I will just go on as if she never said it.* Jacob would not have understood from Jess's language that she might truly not have wanted to see him. It's this inability to put himself in Jess's frame of mind that separates Jacob from his peers. Whereas another child may just be socially awkward, Jacob is dissociated entirely from empathy, and his actions and perceptions revolve around his own needs. He never stopped to imagine what Jess was feeling; all he knew was how much she was hurting *him* by arguing with him."

"Does Jacob know that it's against the law to commit murder?"

"Absolutely. With his fixation on forensic criminology, he probably could recite the legal statutes as well as you could, Mr. Bond. But for Jacob, self-preservation is the one inviolable rule, the one that trumps everything else. So just like he lost his temper with the girl at school who'd humiliated him—and truly didn't understand why that was problematic, given what she'd done to *him* first—well, I can only imagine that's what happened with Jess, too."

Suddenly Jacob stands up. "I didn't lose my temper!" he shouts, as my mother grabs his arm to make him sit down again.

Of course, the fact that he's losing his temper at this very second sort of negates what he's saying.

"Control your client, Mr. Bond," the judge warns.

When Oliver turns around, he looks

the way soldiers do in movies when they crest a hill and see a swarm of enemy forces below them—and realize that, no matter what, they don't have a prayer. "Jacob," he sighs. "Sit down."

"I need a break," Jacob yells.

Oliver looks at the judge. "Your Honor?" And then suddenly, the jury is being led out and Jacob is practically running to the sensory break room.

My father looks completely lost. "What happens now?"

"We wait fifteen minutes."

"Should I . . . Are you going to go back there with them?"

I have, every time so far. I've hung out in a corner, playing with some Koosh balls, while Jacob gets his act together. But now, I glance up at my father. "Do what you want," I say. "I'm staying here."

In my first memory, I'm really sick and I can't stop crying. Jacob is around six or seven, and he keeps asking my mother—who has been up with me all night—to get breakfast ready. It is early; the sun hasn't even come up yet.

I'm hungry, Jacob says.

I know, but I have to take care of Theo right now.

What's the matter with Theo?

His throat hurts, very bad.

There's a moment where Jacob takes this information in. *I bet if he had ice cream his throat would feel better.*

Jacob, my mother says, stunned. *You're thinking about how Theo feels?*

I don't want his throat to hurt, Jacob says.

Ice cream! Ice cream! I yell. It's not even really ice cream I'm screaming for—it's soy-based, like everything else in the freezer and fridge. But it's still something that's supposed to be a treat, not a breakfast food.

My mother gives in. *Okay. Ice cream,* she says. She puts me in my booster seat and gives me a bowl. She gives Jacob a bowl, too, and pats his head. *I'm going to have to tell Dr. Moon that you were looking out for your brother,* she says.

Jacob eats his ice cream. *Finally,* he says. *Peace and quiet.*

My mother still holds that up as an example of Jacob transcending his Asperger's to exhibit empathy for his poor, sick kid brother.

Here's what I see, now that I'm older:

Jacob got a bowl of ice cream for breakfast and didn't even have to be the one to beg for it.

Jacob got me to stop making a racket.

My brother wasn't trying to help me that day. He was trying to help himself.

Jacob

I am lying underneath the blanket that feels like a hundred hands pressing down on me, like I'm deep at the bottom of the sea and cannot see the sun or hear what's happening on the shore.

I didn't lose my temper.

I don't know why Dr. Moon would think that.

I don't know why my mother didn't stand up and object. I don't know why Oliver isn't telling the truth.

I used to have nightmares where the sun was coming too close to the earth and I was the only one who knew it, because my skin could sense a change in temperature more accurately than anyone else's. No matter what I did to try to warn people, nobody ever listened to me, and eventually trees started to burst into flame and my family was burned alive. I would wake up and see the sunrise, and I'd freak out all over again, because how could I really be sure that my nightmare had been a nightmare after all and not actually a premonition?

I think the same thing is happening now. After years of imagining I'm an alien in this world—with senses more acute than those of normal people, and with speech patterns that don't make sense to normal people, and behaviors that look odd on this planet but that, on my home planet, must be perfectly acceptable—it has actually become true. Truth is a lie and lies are the truth. The members of the jury believe what they hear, not what's right in front of their eyes. And no one is listening, no matter how loud I am screaming inside my own head.

Emma

The space beneath the blanket feels like it has a heartbeat. In the dark, I find Jacob's hand and I squeeze it. "Honey," I say, "we have to go."

He turns to me. In the blackness I can see the reflection of his eyes. "I didn't lose my temper with Jess," he mutters.

"We can talk about that later . . ."

"I didn't hurt her," Jacob says.

I stop and stare at him. I want to believe him. God, I want to believe him. But then I imagine that quilt I sewed for him, wrapped around the body of a dead girl.

"I didn't *mean* to hurt her," Jacob corrects.

Nobody looks into the face of a newborn son and imagines all the things that will go wrong in his life. Instead, you see nothing but possibility: his first smile, his first steps, his graduation, his wedding dance, his face when he is holding his own baby. With Jacob, I was constantly revising the milestones: when he willingly looks me in the eye, when he can accept a change in plans without falling apart, when he wears a shirt without meticulously cutting out the tag in the back. You don't love a child for what he does or doesn't do; you love him for who he is.

And even if he is a murderer, by design or by accident, he is still mine.

"Not connecting with his peers," Helen Sharp says. "Being the center of his own universe. Self-preservation is the one inviolable rule. Temper tantrums and anger management issues . . . Sounds to me, Dr. Murano, like Asperger's is the new *selfish*."

"No. It's not an unwillingness to consider someone else's feelings, it's an *inability* to do it."

"Yet this is a relatively new diagnosis, isn't it?"

"It first appeared in the *DSM-IV* manual

in 1994, but it wasn't new by any means. There were plenty of people with Asperger's prior to that who simply weren't labeled."

"Such as?"

"Steven Spielberg, the director. John Elder Robison, the author. Satoshi Tajiri, who created the Pokémon phenomenon. Peter Tork, of the band the Monkees. They were all diagnosed formally with Asperger's as adults."

"And they are all extremely successful, aren't they?" Helen asks.

"It seems that way."

"They've led very productive lives interacting with other people?"

"I assume so."

"Do you think any of them have trouble relating to others socially?"

"Yes, I do."

"Do you think any of them might have experienced a moment where they were picked on, or felt marginalized?"

"I don't know, Ms. Sharp."

"Really? Have you seen Peter Tork's old haircut? I'll go out on a limb and say yes, they have been teased. And yet none of these men with Asperger's is on trial for murder, are they?"

"No. Like I said, there isn't a causal link between Asperger's and violence."

"If Asperger's doesn't make someone violent, how can it be an excuse for someone like Jacob committing a horrific act of violence?"

"Objection!" Oliver says. "That's prejudicial."

"Sustained," the judge replies.

The prosecutor shrugs. "Withdrawn. Dr. Murano, how did you formalize your diagnosis of Jacob's Asperger's?"

"I had an IQ test administered, and an assessment of adaptive skills, to see how Jacob would handle certain social situations. I did interviews with Emma Hunt and with his teachers, to get a sense of Jacob's history of behavior. Asperger's doesn't show up overnight. I saw videotapes of him prior to age two, when he was still meeting developmental milestones for neurotypical children, and then the subsequent decline in behavior and interpersonal connections. And I observed him during a number of sessions, both in my office and at his school in social settings."

"There's no blood test, or any other scientific test, that can be administered to see if a child has Asperger's, is there?"

"No. It's based primarily on observation of repetitive behavior and interests, and a lack of social interaction that impairs everyday functioning, without a significant delay in language."

"So . . . it's a judgment call?"

"Yes," Dr. Murano says. "An educated one."

"If Jacob had seen another psychiatrist, isn't it possible he or she might have determined that Jacob *doesn't* have Asperger's?"

"I highly doubt it. The diagnosis most often confused with Asperger's is attention deficit/hyperactivity disorder, and when they put Aspie kids on ADHD medicine and they don't respond, it's often clear that the diagnosis needs to be revisited."

"So the criteria you used to diagnose Jacob were his inability to communicate with other people, his trouble reading social cues, his desire for routine and structure, and his fixation on certain topics?"

"Yes, that's about right," the psychiatrist says.

"Say I have a seven-year-old who is completely obsessed with Power Rangers and who has to have his cookie and milk every night before bedtime, who isn't very good about telling me what happens in school every day or sharing his toys with his younger brother. Does my seven-year-old have Asperger's?"

"Not necessarily. Let's say you have two three-year-olds in the sandbox. One says, 'Look at my truck.' The other responds, 'I have a doll.' That's parallel play, and it's normal at that age. But if you study those same two children at age eight, and one says, 'Look at my truck,' the appropriate response is something like 'That's a cool truck' or 'Can I touch it?' or some other sentence that continues the interaction with the child who made the conversational overture. However, a kid with Asperger's might still say, in response, 'I have a doll.' When the playmate walks away, the kid with Asperger's won't understand why. In his mind, he's responded to the sentence and kept the conversation going. He doesn't comprehend that what he said wasn't a valid rejoinder."

"Or," Helen Sharp says, "the kid with the doll might just be really self-centered, right?"

"With Asperger's that's often the case."

"But without Asperger's, it's occasionally the case, too. My point, Doctor, is that the diagnosis you make and the assumptions you have about Jacob are not based on anything other than your own opinion. You're not looking at a tox screen or brain waves—"

"There are a variety of psychiatric disorders where clinical observation is the only method of diagnosis, Ms. Sharp. This happens to be one of them. And any psychiatrist in this country will tell you that Asperger's syndrome is a valid disorder. It may be difficult to describe to someone else in concrete terms, but when you see it, you know what it is."

"And just to be clear. You feel that having Asperger's syndrome affected Jacob's behavior the day Jess Ogilvy was murdered."

"That's right."

"Because Jacob couldn't handle social situations well. And he wasn't empathetic. And his frustration sometimes led to anger management problems."

"That's right," Dr. Murano says.

"Which are traits you find in someone with Asperger's."

"Yes."

"What a coincidence," the prosecutor says, folding her arms. "They're also traits you find in cold-blooded killers."

Once Jacob told me that he could hear plants dying. *They scream,* he said. I thought for certain this was ridiculous until I talked to Dr. Murano about it. Kids with Asperger's, she said, have senses we can't even imagine. We filter out sounds and sights that are constantly barraging their brains, which is why sometimes it seems like they're off in their own little world. They're not, she said. They're in *our* world, but they're more engaged in it than we'll ever be.

I went home that day and I looked up plant death on the Internet. As it turned out, plants under stress emit ethylene gas, and scientists in Germany have created a device that measures the energy of those molecules as vibrations—or sound.

Now I wonder if it gets tiring, bearing witness to the last gasp of nature. If it's not only plants my son hears but the gnash of an angry ocean. A shy sunrise. A breaking heart.

Oliver

My high school guidance counselor, Mrs. Inverholl, once had me take an aptitude test to figure out my future. The number one job recommendation for my set of skills was an air traffic accident investigator, of which there are fewer than fifty in the world. The number two job was a museum curator for Chinese-American studies. The number three job was a circus clown.

I'm pretty sure *lawyer* wasn't even on the list.

Sometime after I graduated from college I heard through the grapevine that this same guidance counselor had taken an early retirement and moved to a Utopian community in Idaho, where she renamed herself Blessing and now raises alpacas.

Frances Grenville doesn't look like she's in any danger of starting a llama farm anytime soon. She is wearing a blouse buttoned to the throat, and her hands are clasped so tightly in her lap that I imagine her nails are leaving marks on the skin. "Mrs. Grenville," I say, "where are you employed?"

"At Townsend Regional High School."

"And how long have you been a guidance counselor there?"

"This is my tenth year."

"What are your responsibilities?" I ask.

"I help students with college search and selection. I write recommendations for students applying to college. And I work with students who face behavioral issues during their school career."

"Do you know Jacob?"

"I do. Because he has an IEP, I've been intimately involved in the organization of his school day, to accommodate his special needs."

"Can you explain what an IEP is?"

"An individualized education program," she says. "It's an educational plan mandated by federal law to improve educational results for children with disabilities. Each IEP is different, based on the child. For Jacob, for example, we created a list of rules to be adhered to in a school setting—because he functions well with strictures and routines."

"Have you met with Jacob for reasons other than his learning needs?"

"Yes," Mrs. Grenville says. "There have been instances where he's gotten into trouble with teachers for acting out in class."

"How so?"

"In one case, he kept telling his biology teacher that he was wrong when the teacher made certain factual statements in class." She hesitates. "Mr. Hubbard was teaching the structure of DNA. He paired adenine with adenine instead of pairing it with thymine. When Jacob told him this was incorrect, Mr. Hubbard got angry. Jacob didn't realize the teacher was angry and kept pointing out the inaccuracy. Mr. Hubbard sent him to the principal's office for being disruptive in class."

"Did he explain to you why he didn't know his teacher was angry?"

"Yes. He said that Mr. Hubbard's angry face looks a lot like other people's when they're happy."

"Does it?"

Mrs. Grenville purses her lips. "I have noticed

that Mr. Hubbard has a tendency to smirk when he gets frustrated."

"Do you happen to know if it *is* incorrect to pair adenine with adenine?"

"As it turns out, Jacob was right."

I glance back at the defense table. Jacob is smiling from ear to ear.

"Were there any other incidents when you had to help Jacob?"

"Last year, he got into trouble with a young woman. She was very upset over a poor grade and somehow communicated to Jacob that if he really wanted to be her friend, he'd tell the math teacher to go . . ." She looks down at her lap. "Fornicate with himself. Jacob was given detention for that, and later confronted the young woman and grabbed her by the throat."

"Then what happened?"

"A teacher saw him and pulled him away from the girl. Jacob was suspended for two weeks. He would have been expelled if not for his IEP and the understanding that he was provoked."

"What have you done to modify Jacob's social behavior in school?"

"He attended social skills class, but then Emma Hunt and I discussed getting a private tutor for Jacob instead. We thought he might be able to better work on specific situations that tended to upset him, so that he could deal with them more constructively."

"Did you find a tutor?"

"Yes. I contacted the university, and they put feelers out in their education department." She looks at the jury. "Jess Ogilvy was the first student to respond to the request."

"Had Jacob been meeting with her?"

"Yes, since last fall."

"Mrs. Grenville, since Jacob began his tutoring with Jess Ogilvy, have there been any incidents of him losing his temper?"

She shakes her head. "Not one," she says.

"Your witness," I say to Helen.

The prosecutor stands up. "Mr. Hubbard—the biology teacher—he was angry and Jacob didn't realize it?"

"No."

"Would you say that's a problem for Jacob? Knowing when someone's angry at him?"

"From what I know about Asperger's, yes."

"The other incident you raised involved Jacob cursing out a teacher on a dare and then attacking the girl who dared him, correct?"

"Yes."

"Had Jacob been told before to not use physical violence to solve problems?"

"Certainly," the counselor says. "He knew that was a school rule."

"But he broke that rule?" Helen asks.

"He did."

"Even though, according to your own testimony, following rules is very important to Jacob?"

"Even though," Mrs. Grenville says.

"Did he have any explanation for you as to why he broke that rule?"

Mrs. Grenville shakes her head slowly. "He said that he just snapped."

Helen considers this. "You also said, Mrs. Grenville, that since starting his tutoring sessions, Jacob hasn't lost his temper in school."

"That's correct."

"Apparently he was saving that for *after* school," Helen says. "Nothing further."

Court adjourns early that day because Judge Cuttings has a doctor's appointment. As the room empties, I gather up my files and stuff them into my briefcase. "So," I say to Emma, "I'd like to come over and talk to you about your testimony."

Out of the corner of my eye, I can see Theo and Henry making their way toward us.

"I thought we discussed this," Emma says pointedly.

We did. But I'll be damned if I'm going to go back to my office while I know Henry is under her roof.

"You can never be too ready," I tell her. "We have two cars. No sense in all of you being crammed into one. Would anyone like to ride with me?"

I am staring straight at Emma. "That's a good idea," she says. "Jacob, why don't you go?"

Which is how I wind up trailing Henry's rental car with Jacob sitting beside me in the passenger seat of the truck—and only after a small fit, because he prefers to ride in the back-seat and there isn't one. He fiddles with the radio, which is AM stations only because my truck is old enough to have been built by Moses. "You know why you can pick up AM stations better at night?" Jacob says. "Because the ion-osphere reflects radio signals better when the sun isn't radiating the heck out of the upper atmosphere."

"Thanks," I say. "I couldn't have gone to sleep tonight without knowing that."

Jacob looks at me. "Really?"

"No, I'm kidding."

He folds his arms. "Haven't you been listening to yourself in court? I don't 'get' sarcasm. I'm totally self-centered. Oh, and at any moment I might just go totally crazy."

"You're not crazy," I tell him. "I'm just trying to get the jury to see you as legally insane."

Jacob slumps in his seat. "I'm not a big fan of labels."

"What do you mean?"

"When I first got my diagnosis, my mother was relieved, because she saw it as something that would be helpful. I mean, teachers don't look at kids who are reading eight grade levels above where they should be and doing complex mathematical proofs in third grade and think they need special help, even if they *are* being teased all the time. The diagnosis helped me get an IEP, which was great, but it also changed things in a bad way." Jacob shrugs. "I guess I expected it to be like this other girl in my grade who has a port-wine stain on half her face. People go right up to her and ask about it, and she says it's a birthmark and that it doesn't hurt. End of story. No one ever asks if they can catch it like a virus, or doesn't want to play with her because of it. But you tell someone you're autistic, and half the time they talk louder to you, like you might be deaf. And the few things that I used to get credit for—like being smart, or having a really excellent memory—were all of a sudden just things that made me even more weird." He is quiet for a moment, and then he turns to me. "I'm not autistic; I *have* autism. I also have brown hair and flat feet. So I don't understand why I'm always 'the kid with Asperger's,'" Jacob says.

I keep my eyes on the road. "Because it's better than being the kid who killed Jess Ogilvy," I reply, and after that, we don't talk at all.

It figures; Henry's showed up on a day when the food is not noticeably Aspergian. Emma's made steak and baked potatoes and gravy and gluten-free brownies. If Henry notices the lack of a green vegetable—or anything on the plate that isn't brown, for that matter—he doesn't mention it.

"So, Henry," I say. "You do programming?"

He nods. "Right now I'm parsing XML for a point-and-click web app for the iPhone that'll spice up four hundred contemporary American ethnic dishes with Chinese herbs and sauces." He launches into a fifteen-minute discussion of esoteric computer programming that none of us can follow.

"Guess the apple doesn't fall far from the tree," I say.

"Actually, I work for Adobe," Henry says.

Theo and I are the only ones who find that funny. I wonder if Henry's ever been diagnosed. "And you're remarried, right?" I look at Emma when I say this.

"Yes. I've got two girls," he says, and then hurries to add, "in addition to the two boys, of course."

"Of course," I answer, and I break a brownie in half. "So when are you leaving?"

"Oliver!" Emma says.

Henry laughs. "Well, I guess that depends on how long the trial goes on." He leans back in his chair. "Emma, that was a great dinner."

Just wait till Blue Friday, I muse.

"I'd better go find myself a hotel, since I've been up for about thirty-six straight hours and I'm bound to crash and burn soon," Henry says.

"You'll stay here," Emma announces, and both Henry and I look at her, surprised. "Well, it's silly to have you stay a half hour away when we're all going to the same place tomorrow morning, isn't it? Theo, your father can sleep in your room and you can have the couch."

"What?" Theo yelps. "Why do I have to give up my room? What about Jacob?"

"Let me put it to you this way," Emma answers. "Do you want to sleep on the couch or do you want to help me when Jacob has a melt-down?"

He shoves away from the table, angry. "Where are the extra freaking pillows?"

"I don't want to put anyone out—" Henry says.

"Emma," I interrupt, "can I have a few minutes?"

"Oh, right. You wanted to go over testimony?" She turns to Jacob. "Honey, can you clear the table and load the dishwasher?"

He stands up and starts clearing as I drag Emma upstairs. "We need to go somewhere quiet," I say, and I lead her into her own bedroom.

I've never been in here. It's peaceful—all cool greens and sea blues. There's a Zen garden on the dresser with a rake and three black stones. In the sand, someone has written H-E-L-P.

"The only part I'm still nervous about is the cross-exam," Emma says, all she can manage to get out before I grab her and kiss her. It's not gentle, either. It's the physical equivalent of pouring into her all the feelings I can't put into words.

When she breaks away from me, her mouth is rosy and swollen, and that makes me take a step toward her again, but she puts her hand on my chest to hold me off. "Oh my God," she says, with a slow smile. "You're jealous."

"Well, what the hell was *that* all about? 'It's silly to have you stay a half hour away . . .'"

"It *is*. He's the boys' father, not some stranger who just came in off the street."

"So he's going to be sleeping right on the other side of this wall?"

"*Sleeping* would be the operative word in that sentence," Emma says. "He's here for Jacob. Believe me, there's no ulterior motive for Henry."

"But you used to love him."

Her eyebrows shoot up. "Do you think I've been sitting here for fifteen years pining for him? Waiting for the moment he would walk through that door again so I could hide him in a bedroom upstairs and seduce him?"

"No," I tell her. "But I wouldn't put it past *him*."

She stares at me for a moment, and then she bursts out laughing. "You haven't seen his perfect little wife and his perfect little girls. Believe me, Oliver, I'm not the great love of his life, the one he'll never forget."

"You are to me," I say.

The smile fades from her face, and then she rises up on her toes and kisses me back.

"Don't you need this?"

At the sound of Jacob's voice we jump apart, putting a few feet of space between us. He stands in the doorway, one hand still on the knob and the other one holding my legal briefcase.

"Were you just . . ." He stumbles over his words. "Are you two . . ." Without saying anything else, he throws my briefcase hard at me, so forcefully that I grunt when I catch it. He runs down the hallway into his room and slams the door.

"What did he see?" Emma asks frantically. "When did he walk in?"

Suddenly Henry is standing in the doorway, looking quizzically down the hall where Jacob's gone and then at Emma. "Everything all right up here?"

Emma faces me. "I think maybe you ought to go home," she says.

Emma

When I walk into Jacob's room, he is hunched over his desk, humming Marley and writing furiously across his green blotter:

1, 1, 2, 3, 5, 8, 13, 21, 34, 55, 89, 144, 233

I take the pencil out of his hand, and he turns in his swivel chair. *"Do I make you horny, baby?"* he says, bitter.

"No movie quotes," I tell Jacob. "Especially not *Austin Powers*. I know you're upset."

"Let me think about that. My mother is supposed to be practicing her testimony with my lawyer and instead she has her tongue halfway down his throat? Yeah, that might make me a little upset."

I tamp down the flash of anger that rises inside me. "First of all, I'm completely ready to testify. And second of all, I didn't expect to kiss him. It just happened."

"Things like that don't *just happen*," Jacob argues. "You want them to happen or you don't."

"Well, all right then, I suppose after fifteen years of being alone I don't mind being attractive to someone."

"Not *someone*," he says. "My *lawyer*."

"He's completely focused on your trial, Jacob."

"I don't care about him. I mean, if he isn't doing his job I can just fire him. But *you*," he yells. "How could you do this to me right now? You're my *mother*!"

I stand up, toe to toe with him. "One who's given up her whole life to take care of you," I say. "One who loves you so much she would trade places with you in a heartbeat. But that doesn't mean I don't deserve to be happy, too."

"Well, I hope you're really happy when I lose this trial because you were too busy being a slut."

And just like that, I slap him.

I don't know which one of us is more surprised. I have never struck Jacob in my life. He holds his palm to his cheek as the red print of my hand rises on his skin. "I'm sorry. Oh, God, Jacob, I'm sorry," I say, the words somersaulting over each other. I pull his hand down so that I can see the damage I've done. "I'll get you some ice," I say, but he is staring at me as if he's never seen me before.

So instead of leaving, I sit him down on the bed and I pull him against me the way I used to when he was little and the world became too much for him to bear. I rock, so that he doesn't have to.

Slowly, he relaxes against me. "Jacob," I tell him. "I didn't mean to hurt you." It is only after he nods that I realize I've repeated the very same words Jacob said earlier to me about Jess Ogilvy.

In all the years that Jacob has had tantrums and meltdowns and panic attacks, I have restrained him; sat on him; held him like a vise—but I have never hit him. I know the unwritten strictures: *Good parents don't spank. Reward works better than punishment.*

Yet it only took a single moment of frustration, of realizing that I couldn't simultaneously be whom he *needed* me to be and whom I *wanted* to be—for me to snap.

Is that what happened to Jacob, too?

Oliver has called four times tonight, but I didn't pick up the phone when I recognized the number on the caller ID. Maybe this is my penance; maybe I just don't know what to say.

It is just after two in the morning when my bedroom door opens a crack. I sit up immediately, expecting Jacob. But instead Henry enters. He's wearing pajama bottoms and a T-shirt that reads THERE'S NO PLACE LIKE 127.0.0.1. "I saw your light on," he says.

"Can't sleep?"

Henry shakes his head. "You?"

"No."

He gestures to the edge of the bed. "May I?"

I shift over. He sits down on my side of the bed, but I see him staring at the pillow beside me. "I know," I say. "It must seem a little weird."

"No . . . It's just that now, I sleep on the left side of the bed, like you. And I'm wondering how that happened."

I lean back against the headboard. "There are lots of things I don't have the answers for."

"I . . . don't know exactly what all the yelling was about," Henry says delicately. "But I did hear it."

"Yeah. We've had better nights."

"I owe you an apology, Emma," he says. "First of all, for showing up like this. I should have asked, at least. You've got enough on your plate without having to deal with me. I guess I was really only thinking of myself."

"Luckily, I have a lot of practice with that."

"That's the other thing I have to apologize for," Henry says. "I should have been here all the other nights there was yelling, or . . . or tantrums, or anything else that was part of raising Jacob. I probably learned more about him today in that courtroom than I've known in the eighteen years he's been alive. I should have been here to help during all the bad times."

I smile a little. "I guess that's the difference between us. I wish you'd been here for the *good* times." I look over his shoulder, into the hallway. "Jacob is sweet, and funny, and so smart he leaves me reeling sometimes. And I'm sorry you never got to know that part of him."

He reaches across the quilt and squeezes my hand. "You're a good mom, Emma," he says, and I have to look away, because that makes me think of my argument with Jacob.

Then Henry speaks again. "Did he do it?"

I turn to him slowly. "Does it matter?"

I can only remember one concrete instance when I blew up at Jacob before. It was when he was twelve and had not acknowledged the fact that it was my birthday with a card or a gift or even a hug, although I had dropped enough hints in the weeks prior. So one evening when I made dinner, I slapped it on the table in front of him with more force than usual and waited in vain—like always—for Jacob to thank me. "How about a little gratitude?" I exploded. "How about some recognition that I've done something for you?"

Confused, Jacob glanced at his plate, and then at me.

"I make your dinner. I fold your laundry. I drive you to school and back. Did you ever wonder *why* I do that?"

"Because it's your job?"

"No, it's because I love you, and when you

love someone, you do things for them with-out complaining about it."

"But you *are* complaining," he said.

That was when I realized Jacob would never understand love. He would have bought me a birthday gift if I'd told him ex-plicitly to do so, but that wouldn't really have been a gift from the heart. You can't make someone love you; it has to come from inside him, and Jacob wasn't wired that way.

I remember storming out of the kitchen and sitting on the porch for a while, under the light of the moon, which isn't really light at all, just a pale reflection of the sun.

Oliver

"Jacob," I say, as soon as I see him the next morning, "we need to talk."

I fall into step beside him as we move across the parking lot, putting enough space between us and his family to ensure privacy. "Did you know there's not really a term for a man-whore?" Jacob asks. "I mean, there's gigolo, but that suggests money was exchanged—"

"All right, look," I sigh. "I'm sorry you walked in on us. But I'm not going to apologize for liking her."

"I could fire you," Jacob says.

"You could try. But it's up to the judge, since we're in the middle of the trial."

"What if he found out about your misconduct with clients?"

"She's not my client," I say. "You are. And if anything, my feelings for your mother only make me more determined to win this case."

He hesitates. "I'm not talking to you anymore," Jacob mutters, and he increases his speed until he is nearly sprinting up the steps of the courthouse.

Ava Newcomb, the forensic shrink hired by the defense, is the linchpin of my case. If she cannot make the jury understand that some of the traits associated with Asperger's might have caused Jacob to kill Jess Ogilvy without really understanding why that was wrong, then Jacob will be convicted.

"Dr. Newcomb, what's the legal definition of insanity?"

She is tall, poised, and professional—right out of central casting. *So far,* I think, *so good.* "It states that, at the time an act was committed, the defendant was not able to know right from wrong due to a severe mental defect or illness."

"Can you give us an example of a mental defect or illness that qualifies?"

"Something that suggests psychotic breaks from reality, like schizophrenia," she says.

"Is that the only kind of mental defect that constitutes legal insanity?"

"No."

"Does Asperger's syndrome cause someone to have psychotic breaks?"

"No, but there are other symptoms of Asperger's that might prevent someone from distinguishing right from wrong at a particular moment in time."

"Such as?"

"The intense fixation on a subject that someone with Asperger's has can be overwhelming and obsessive—to the point where it impedes function in daily activities or even crosses the boundary of the law. I once had a patient who was so focused on horses that he continually was arrested for breaking into a local stable. Jacob's current special interest is forensic analysis and crime scene investigation. It was evident in my interview with him, as well as in his obsession with the television show *CrimeBusters* and the detailed journals he kept about each episode's plot."

"How might a fixation like that contribute to some of the evidence we've heard in this courtroom?" I ask.

"We have heard that Jacob was increasingly popping up at crime scenes, thanks to his police scanner," the psychiatrist says. "And Jess Ogilvy's death was part of an elaborate crime scene. The evidence was arranged to look at first glance like a kidnapping, then eventually revealed the victim. It is possible that the opportunity to create a crime scene, instead of just observing fictional ones, led Jacob to act in a way that went against rules, laws, and morality. At the time, he would only have been thinking about the fact that he was creating a real crime scene that would be solved by law enforcement officials. In this way, an Aspergian fixation on forensic analysis led Jacob to the delusional belief that, at that moment, Jess's death was a necessary part of his study of forensic science. As chilling as it seems to us, the victim becomes collateral damage during the pursuit of a greater goal."

"But didn't Jacob know that murder is illegal?"

"Absolutely. He is the poster child for following rules, for seeing things as either right or wrong with no mitigating circumstances. However, Jacob's actions wouldn't have been voluntary at that moment. He had no understanding of the nature and consequences of his actions, and he couldn't have stopped if he wanted to."

I frown slightly. "But we've also heard that

Jess Ogilvy and Jacob were extremely close. Surely that would have affected him?"

"Actually, that's another reason we can conclude that Asperger's played a role in what happened to Jess. People with Asperger's have a greatly impaired theory of mind—they can't put themselves into someone else's position to imagine what the other person might be thinking or feeling. To the layperson, it's a lack of empathy. So for example, if Jess were crying, Jacob wouldn't try to comfort her. He might know that people with tears in their eyes are usually sad, but he'd be making a cognitive judgment, not an emotional one. For someone with Asperger's, this lack of empathy is a neurobiological deficit, and it affects behavior. In Jacob's case, it would have lessened his ability to perceive the impact of his own actions on Jess."

"But still, Doctor," I say, playing devil's advocate, "there's a big difference between not handing someone a hankie when she's crying and killing her so that she can be a pawn in a crime scene setup."

"Of course there is." The psychiatrist turns to the jury. "And this is probably the hardest thing for the layperson to understand. We're always looking for motive in a crime that's as horrific as this one is. I've considered this from my discussions with Jacob and with Dr. Murano, and I think that the answer lies in the argument Jess and Jacob had the Sunday before her death.

"The calling card for Asperger's is impaired social interaction. To that end, someone with Asperger's has a very naïve and limited understanding of relationships, which might lead him to seek contact in an inappropriate way. This leads to disappointment, and even anger, if a relationship doesn't work out the way he's anticipated." She looks at Jacob. "I don't know what was said between Jacob and Jess the afternoon of her death, but I believe Jacob had a crush on his tutor. Ironically, his rigid sense of right and wrong—which you'd think would *deter* criminal behavior—might actually have backfired here. If Jess rebuffed Jacob's advances, he would have felt that she'd done something wrong to him, that *he* was the victim."

"And then what?" I ask.

"He snapped. He lashed out without realizing what he was physically doing at the time he did it."

"Nothing further," I say, and I sit down. I glance at Jacob, who is glaring at me. Emma stares straight ahead. She seems determined to not acknowledge my existence today.

Helen Sharp stands up. "There are a lot of

kids who've been diagnosed with Asperger's syndrome. So are you telling us that the world's full of ticking time bombs? That at any moment, if we look at one of those kids the wrong way, he might come after us with a carving knife?"

"No, in fact, it's the opposite. People with Asperger's aren't prone to violence. Since they don't have an active theory of mind, they aren't motivated to hurt someone; in fact, they're not thinking about that person's feelings at all. If someone with Asperger's *does* become violent, it's during the single-minded pursuit of a special interest, during a state of panic, or during a moment of complete ignorance about appropriate social interaction."

"Isn't it true, Doctor, that most defendants who claim insanity do so because of a psychotic break from reality?"

"Yes."

"But Asperger's isn't a psychotic disorder?" Helen says.

"No. It would fall more in line with personality disorders, which are characterized by perceptual and interpersonal distortions."

"In legal terms, doesn't the absence of psychotic episodes suggest that the person is personally—and criminally—responsible for his or her actions?"

The psychiatrist shifts. "Yes, but there might be a loophole for Asperger's. We can't scientifically prove that someone with Asperger's has a very different experience of subjective reality than someone who doesn't have Asperger's, and yet the extreme sensitivity to light and sound and taste and touch and texture indicate that this is the case. If that could be measured, there would be strong parallels between Asperger's and psychosis."

There is a sharp jab in my side as Jacob elbows me. He passes me a blank piece of paper.

"If that were true," Helen says, "wouldn't this suggest that someone with Asperger's has a hard time being aware of reality and his role in it?"

"Exactly. Which is why it might very well contribute to legal insanity, Ms. Sharp."

"But didn't you also say that Jacob's fixation on forensics led him to use Jess Ogilvy's death to create his own crime scene?"

"Yes."

"And wouldn't such premeditation and careful calculation suggest he knew very well what he was doing at the moment?"

Dr. Newcomb shrugs. "It's a theory," she says.

"You also mentioned a lack of empathy." Helen approaches the witness stand. "You said it's one of the features of Asperger's syndrome?"

"That's right."

"Would you consider that an emotional measure or a cognitive one?"

"Emotional."

"Is lack of empathy part of the test for legal insanity, Doctor?"

"No."

"Isn't it true that the determination for legal insanity is whether the defendant knew right from wrong at the time the act was committed?"

"Yes."

"Is that an emotional measure or a cognitive one?"

"A cognitive one."

"So lack of empathy simply means someone is cold, heartless, without remorse," Helen says. "But it doesn't necessarily mean he's unaware of the nature and consequence of his actions."

"They often go hand in hand," Dr. Newcomb says.

"Do they?" Helen asks. "A mafia hit man has no empathy when he offs his victims, but that doesn't make him legally insane, just psychopathic."

Jacob elbows me again, but I am already getting to my feet. "Objection," I say. "Is there a question buried under Ms. Sharp's grandstanding?"

"If I may," Dr. Newcomb says, turning to the judge for his permission. "Ms. Sharp seems to be trying hard to draw a parallel between someone with Asperger's and a psychopath. However, people with Asperger's don't demonstrate the superficial charm that psychopaths do, nor do they try to manipulate others. They don't have enough interpersonal skills to do it well, frankly, and that usually makes them the prey for psychopaths, rather than the predators."

"And yet," Helen qualifies, "Jacob has a history of aggression, doesn't he?"

"Not to my knowledge."

"Did he or did he not have an argument with Jess two days before her death, one that was overheard by employees of Mama S's Pizzeria?"

"Well, yes, but that wasn't a physical assault—"

"Okay, what about the fact that he was given detention last year for trying to strangle a classmate?"

A flurry of blank notes land in front of me, and again, I sweep them aside. "Just hang on," I say through my teeth to Jacob, and then I signal to the judge. "Objection—"

"I'll rephrase. Did you know that Jacob was given detention for physically assaulting a girl in his grade?"

"Yes, I remember Dr. Murano mentioning that to me. Yet it seems the trigger was the same: an interpersonal relationship that didn't quite match Jacob's intentions. He felt humiliated, and he—"

"Snapped," the prosecutor interrupts. "Right?"

"Right."

"And that's why Jess Ogilvy was killed."

"In my opinion, yes."

"Tell me this, Doctor," Helen says. "Had Jacob still snapped when he was alphabetizing the CD collection in her residence, after her death?"

"Yes."

"How about when he moved Jess's body three hundred yards to a culvert behind the house?"

"Yes."

"Had he still snapped when he sat her upright and carefully covered her with his quilt and set her hands in her lap?"

Dr. Newcomb jerks her chin the slightest bit.

"And had he still snapped days later when he went back to visit Jess's body and phoned 911 so that the police would find her?"

"Well," the psychiatrist says quietly. "I guess so."

"Then tell me, Doctor," Helen Sharp asks. "When did Jacob snap out of it?"

Emma

"They're lying," Jacob says heatedly, as soon as we are alone. "They're all lying."

I have been watching him grow more tightly wound with each passing minute of the forensic psychiatrist's cross-examination; even though Jacob passed multiple notes to Oliver, he didn't ask for a break until Helen Sharp finished going for the kill. I didn't know what would happen, to be honest—if he would refuse to let me join him for the recess, if he'd still be holding a grudge from last night's episode—but apparently, I am the lesser of the two evils at the defense table, which is why I'm granted admission to the sensory break room and Oliver is not.

"We talked about this, Jacob," I say. "Remember? How saying you're legally insane doesn't mean anything; it just gives the jury something to use to find you not guilty. It's a tool, like telling the school district you have Asperger's. That didn't change who you were . . . it only made it easier for teachers to understand your learning style."

"I don't care about the defense," Jacob argues. "I care about what those people are saying I did."

"You know how the law works. The burden of proof is on the prosecution. If Oliver can find witnesses who'll weave another scenario about what could have happened, the jury might find reasonable doubt, and then they can't convict." I reach for Jacob's hand. "It's like giving someone a book, baby, and saying there might be more than one ending."

"But I didn't want her to die, Mom. It wasn't my fault. I know it was an accident." Jacob's eyes are full of tears. "I miss her."

My breath freezes in my throat. "Oh, Jacob," I whisper. "What did you do?"

"The right thing. So why can't we tell the jury that?"

I want to block out his words, because I am about to testify, and that means I cannot lie if the prosecutor asks what Jacob's told me about Jess's death. I want to run until all I can hear is the rush of my blood, instead of his confession. "Because," I say softly, "sometimes the hardest thing to hear is the truth."

Oliver

Here's what I know:

Before we took that last sensory break, Jacob was a jittery, wild mess.

Now that we're back in session, Emma's on the witness stand, and *she's* a jittery, wild mess.

After I lead her through the basics of her identity and her relationship to Jacob, I walk up to the witness box and pretend to fumble and drop my pen. As I bend down, I whisper to her: *Just breathe.*

What the hell could have happened in the fifteen minutes they were gone?

"What do you do for a living, Ms. Hunt?"

She doesn't answer, just stares into her lap.

"Ms. Hunt?"

Emma's head jerks up. "Can you repeat the question?"

Focus, sweetheart, I think. "Your job. What do you do?"

"I used to write an advice column," she says quietly. "I was asked to take a leave of absence after Jacob's arrest."

"How did you get into that business?"

"Desperation. I was a single parent with a newborn, and a three-year-old who'd suddenly developed autistic behaviors." As she speaks, her voice gets stronger and picks up steam. "There were therapists in and out of my house all day long who were trying to keep Jacob from completely slipping away from me. I had to find work, but I couldn't leave the house."

"How did Jacob's diagnosis come about?"

"He was a perfectly healthy, happy baby," Emma says, and she looks at Jacob. For a moment she can't speak, and she shakes her head. "We gave him his shots, and within a week this very loving, interactive, verbal boy stopped being the child I knew. Suddenly he was lying on his side, spinning the wheels of his toy trucks instead of zooming them around the living room."

"What did you do?"

"Everything," Emma says. "I put Jacob through applied behavior analysis, occupational therapy, physical therapy, speech therapy. I put him on a gluten-free, casein-free diet. I gave him a regimen of vitamins and supplements that had been successful for other parents of autistic kids."

"Did it work?"

"To some extent. Jacob got to the point where he wasn't isolating himself. He could function in the world, with limitations. Eventually, his diagnosis changed from a generic autism spectrum disorder to pervasive developmental disorder to, finally, Asperger's."

"Is there a silver lining to that diagnosis?"

"Yes," Emma says. "Jacob has an amazing, dry sense of humor. He's the smartest person I know. And if I want someone to keep me company when I'm running errands or unloading the dishwasher or just taking a walk, he's quick to volunteer. He'll do anything I ask him to. And he'll also *not* do something, if I ask. I'm probably the only mother who's never had to worry about her son doing drugs or drinking underage."

"But there must be times that it's hard for you, as a parent."

"All the things I listed that make Jacob a

perfect kid—well, that's what makes him different from the *average* kid. All his life, Jacob's wanted to fit in with his peers, and all his life, I've watched him be teased or turned down. You can't imagine what it's like to force a smile when your son wins a medal at his Pee Wee T-ball team banquet for getting hit by the most pitches. You have to close your eyes when you drop him off at school and he gets out of the car, wearing a big pair of headphones to help block out the noise of the busy hallways, and then as he walks away, you see other kids teasing him behind his back."

"If I were to come to your house on a Tuesday," I say, "what would I notice?"

"The food. If it's Tuesday, all the food has to be red. Raspberries and strawberries and tomato soup. Sushi-grade tuna. Shaved rare roast beef. Beets. If it's not red, Jacob will get very agitated, and sometimes he'll go to his room and stop speaking to us. There's a color for each day of the week, for food and for clothing. In his closet, his clothes hang in rainbow order, and the different colors aren't allowed to touch."

She turns to the jury, as we've practiced. "Jacob craves routine. He gets up at six-twenty every morning—whether it's a school day or a weekend—and he knows exactly what time he has to leave for school and when he'll get back home. He never misses an episode of *Crime-Busters,* which is on the USA Network at four-thirty every day of the week. He writes notes in his journals while he's watching, even though in some cases he's seen the episode a dozen times. He always puts his toothbrush on the left side of the sink when he's done using it, and he sits behind the driver in the backseat of the car, even when he's the only other passenger."

"What happens when Jacob's routine is disrupted?"

"It's very upsetting for him," Emma says.

"Can you explain?"

"When he was little, he'd scream or throw a tantrum. Now he's more likely to withdraw. The best way I can explain it is that you'll be looking right at Jacob, and he's not with you."

"You have another son, don't you?"

"Yes. Theo is fifteen."

"Does Theo have Asperger's?"

"No."

"Are Theo's clothes arranged in rainbow order?"

She shakes her head. "Most of the time they're in a heap on his floor."

"Does he eat only red food on Tuesdays?"

"He eats anything that's not nailed down,"

Emma says, and some of the women on the jury laugh.

"Are there times that Theo doesn't feel like talking to you?"

"Absolutely. He's a very ordinary teenager."

"Is there a difference between Theo withdrawing and Jacob withdrawing?"

"Yes," Emma says. "When Theo doesn't communicate with me, it's because he doesn't want to. When Jacob doesn't communicate with me, it's because he *can't*."

"Did you take steps to help Jacob adapt better to social situations?"

"Yes," Emma says. She pauses, clears her throat. "I hired a private tutor to help him practice those skills—Jess Ogilvy."

"Did Jacob like Jess?"

Emma's eyes fill with tears. "Yes."

"How do you know?"

"He was comfortable with her, and there aren't many people he's comfortable with. She got him to do— She got him to do things that he wouldn't normally . . ." Emma breaks off and buries her face in her hands.

What the fuck?

"Ms. Hunt," I say, "thank you. Nothing fur—"

"Wait," she interrupts. "I just . . . I'm not finished."

This is news to me. I shake my head just the tiniest bit, but Emma is staring at Jacob. "I just . . . I wanted to say . . ." She turns to the jury. "Jacob told me he didn't want her to die; that it wasn't his fault—"

My eyes widen. This is unscripted territory, dangerous ground. "Objection," I blurt out. "Hearsay!"

"You can't object to your own witness," Helen says, delighted.

But I don't have to give my own witness enough rope to hang herself, either, and the rest of us as well. "Then I'm finished," I say, sitting down beside Jacob, suddenly afraid that I'm not the only one.

Jacob

She told them.

My mother told them the truth.

I look at the jury, at each of their expectant faces, because now they must know I am not the monster that all these other witnesses have made me out to be. Oliver cut my mother off before she could say the rest, but surely they understand.

"Before we begin the cross-examination, counselors," the judge says, "I'd like to make up some of the ground we lost yesterday with an early dismissal. Do either of you object to finishing out this witness's testimony before we adjourn for the day?"

That's when I look at the clock and see that it is four o'clock.

We are supposed to leave now, so I can be home in time for *CrimeBusters* at 4:30.

"Oliver," I whisper. "Say no."

"There is no way I'm leaving your mother's last words in the jury's minds all weekend long," Oliver hisses back at me. "I don't care how you deal with it, Jacob, but you're going to deal with it."

"Mr. Bond," the judge says, "would you care to let us in on your conversation?"

"My client was just letting me know the delay in adjournment is agreeable to him."

"I'm tickled pink," Judge Cuttings says, although he doesn't look tickled *or* pink. "Ms. Sharp, your witness."

The prosecutor stands up. "Ms. Hunt, where was your son on the afternoon of January twelfth?"

"He went to Jess's house for his lesson."

"What was he like when he came home?"

She hesitates. "Agitated."

"How did you know?"

"He ran up to his room and hid in the closet."

"Did he exhibit any self-destructive behaviors?"

"Yes," Emma says. "He hit his head against the wall repeatedly."

(It is interesting for me to hear this. When I have a meltdown, I don't remember the meltdown very well.)

"But you were able to calm him down, weren't you?"

"Eventually."

"What techniques did you use?" the prosecutor asks.

"I turned off the lights and put on a song that he likes."

"Was it Bob Marley's 'I Shot the Sheriff'?"

"Yes."

(It's 4:07, and I'm sweating. A lot.)

"He uses a song called 'I Shot the Sheriff' as a calming technique?" Helen Sharp asks.

"It has nothing to do with the actual song. It happened to be a melody he liked, and it would soothe him when he was having a tantrum when he was little. It just stuck."

"It certainly ties in to his obsession with violent crime, doesn't it?"

(I'm not obsessed with violent crime. I'm obsessed with solving it.)

"Jacob's not violent," my mother says.

"No? He is on trial for murder," Helen Sharp

replies, "and last year he assaulted a girl, didn't he?"

"He was provoked."

"Ms. Hunt, I have here the report of the school resource officer who was called in after that incident." She gets it stamped as evidence (now it is 4:09) and gives it to my mother. "Can you read the highlighted passage?"

My mother lifts the paper. *"A seventeen-year-old juvenile female stated that Jacob Hunt walked up to her, slammed her against the lockers, and pinned her by the throat until he was forcibly removed by a staff member."*

"Are you suggesting that's not violent behavior?" Helen Sharp asks.

Even if we leave now, we will be eleven minutes late for *CrimeBusters.*

"Jacob felt cornered," my mother says.

"I'm not asking you how Jacob felt. The only person who knows how Jacob felt is Jacob. What I'm asking you is whether you would categorize slamming a young woman up against a locker and pinning her by her neck as violent behavior."

"This *victim,*" my mother says, her voice hot, "is the same charming girl who said that if Jacob told his math teacher to go fuck himself she'd be his friend."

One of the ladies on the jury shakes her head. I wonder if it's because of what Mimi did or because my mother said *fuck.*

Once during a ratings sweep episode of *CrimeBusters* that was aired live, like a Broadway show, an extra dropped a hammer on his foot and said the f-bomb and as a result the network was fined. The censors bleeped it, but for a while it was circulating on YouTube in its full blue glory.

CrimeBusters is airing in thirteen minutes.

Oliver nudges my shoulder. "What is the matter with you? Stop it. You look crazy."

I look down. I'm slapping my hand hard against the side of my leg; I haven't even realized I am doing it. But now I'm even more confused. I thought I was *supposed* to look crazy.

"So this girl was mean to Jacob. I think we can both agree on that, right?"

"Yes."

"But that doesn't negate the fact that he was violent toward her."

"What he did was just," my mother replies.

"So, Ms. Hunt, you're saying that if a young woman says something to Jacob that isn't very nice or that hurts his feelings, he's justified in acting violent toward her?"

My mother's eyes flash, like they always do before she gets really, really, really mad. "Don't put words in my mouth. I'm saying that my son is kind and sensitive and that he wouldn't intentionally hurt a fly."

"You've heard the evidence in this case. Are you aware that Jacob argued with Jess two days before she was last seen alive?"

"That's different—"

"Were you there, Ms. Hunt?"

"No."

Right now is the last commercial for *Law & Order: SVU,* which is the show that is on the network before *CrimeBusters.* There will be four thirty-second spots and then the opening bars of music. I close my eyes and start to hum.

"You said that one of the behaviors that's indicative of Jacob's Asperger's is that he gets uncomfortable around people or cir-cumstances he doesn't know, correct?"

"Yes."

"And that he sometimes withdraws from you?"

"Yes," my mother says.

"That he has a hard time expressing his feelings to you verbally?"

"Yes."

It's the one where a child falls into a well and when Rhianna is lowered in to save the little boy, she shines a flashlight and there is a complete human skeleton there are pearls there are diamonds but the bones belong to a man it's an heiress who disappeared in the sixties and at the end you learn that she was actually a he—

"Wouldn't you agree, Ms. Hunt, that your other son, Theo, exhibits every single one of these behaviors from time to time? In fact, that *every* teenager on the planet exhibits them?"

"I wouldn't exactly—"

"Does that make Theo insane, too?"

It's 4:32 it's 4:32 it's 4:32.

"Can we please leave now?" I say, but the words are as loose as molasses and they don't sound right; and everyone is moving slowly and slurring their words, too, when I stand up to get their attention.

"Mr. Bond, control your client," I hear, and Oliver grabs my arm and yanks me off my feet.

The prosecutor's lips pull back from her teeth like a smile, but it's not a smile. "Ms. Hunt, you were the one who contacted the police when you saw Jacob's quilt on the news broadcast, isn't that true?"

"Yes," my mother whispers.

"You did it because you believed your son had killed Jess Ogilvy, didn't you?"

She shakes her head (4:34) and doesn't answer.

"Ms. Hunt, you thought your own son had committed murder, isn't that true?" the lawyer says with a voice that's a hammer.

Ms. Hunt

(4:35)

Answer the

(no)

question.

Suddenly the room goes still, like the air between the beats of a bird's wings, and I can hear everything rewinding in my head.

Control your client.

You look crazy.

The hardest thing to hear is the truth.

I stare at my mother, right into her eyes, and feel the fingernails on the chalkboard of my brain and belly. I can see the chambers of her heart, and the ruby cells of her blood, and the twisting winds of her thoughts.

Oh, Jacob, I hear, instant replay. *What did you do?*

I know what she is going to say a minute before she says it, and I can't let her do that.

Then I remember the prosecutor's words: *The only person who knows how Jacob felt is Jacob.*

"Stop," I yell as loud as I can.

"Judge," Oliver says, "I think we need to adjourn for the day—"

I get to my feet again. *"Stop!"*

My mother comes out of her seat on the witness stand. "Jacob, it's okay—"

"Your Honor, the witness has not answered the question—"

I cover my ears with my hands because they are all so loud and the words are bouncing off the walls and the floor and I stand on my chair and then on the table and finally I jump right into the middle of the space in front of the judge, where my mother is already reaching for me.

But before I can touch her I am on the floor and the bailiff has his knee in my back and the judge and jury are scrambling and suddenly there is quiet and calm and no more weight and a voice I know.

"You're okay, buddy," Detective Matson says. He reaches out a hand, and he helps me to my feet.

Once at a fair, Theo and I went into a hall of mirrors. We got separated, or maybe Theo just left me behind, but I found myself walking into walls and looking around corners that didn't really exist, and finally, I sat down on the floor and closed my eyes. That's what I want to do now, with everyone staring at me. Just like then, there's no way out that I can foresee.

"You're okay," Detective Matson repeats, and he leads the way.

Rich

Most of the time if a town cop comes into the sheriff's domain, a pissing contest ensues: they don't want me telling them how to run their outfit any more than I want them screwing up one of my crime scenes. But with Jacob on the loose in the courtroom, they probably would have welcomed the National Guard's help if it had been available, and when I hop over the bar and grab Jacob, everyone else steps away and lets me, as if I actually know what I am doing.

His head is bobbing up and down as if

he is having a conversation with himself, and one of his hands makes a weird stretching motion against his leg, but at least he isn't yelling anymore.

I walk Jacob into a holding cell. He turns away from me, shoulders pressed to the bars.

"You okay?" I ask, but he doesn't answer.

I lean against the bars from the outside of the cell, so that we are practically back-to-back. "There was a guy once who killed himself in a holding cell in Swanton," I say, as if this is ordinary conversation. "The officers booked him and left him there to sleep off a good drunk. He was standing like you, but with his arms crossed. Wearing a flannel shirt, button-down. Security camera on him the whole time. You probably can't guess how he did it."

At first, Jacob doesn't answer. Then he turns his head slightly. "He made a noose by tying the arms of the shirt around his neck," he answers. "So it looked like he was standing up against the bars on the security camera, but actually, he'd already hanged himself."

A laugh barks out of me. "Goddammit, kid. You're really good."

Jacob pivots so that he is facing me. "I shouldn't be talking to you."

"Probably not."

I stare at him. "Why did you leave the quilt? You know better than that."

He hesitates. "Of course I left the quilt. How else would anyone know that I was the one who set this all up? You still missed the tea bag."

Immediately I know he is talking about the evidence at Jess Ogilvy's house. "It was in the sink. We didn't get any prints off the mug."

"Jess was allergic to mango," Jacob says. "And me, I hate the taste."

He had been too thorough. Rather than forgetting to erase this evidence, he'd left it on purpose, as a test. I stare at Jacob, wondering what he is trying to tell me.

"But other than that," he says, smiling, "you got it right."

Oliver

Helen and I stand in front of Judge Cuttings like recalcitrant schoolchildren. "I don't ever want to see that happen again, Mr. Bond," he says. "I don't care if you have to medicate him. Either you keep your client under control for the remainder of this trial or I'm going to have him handcuffed."

"Your Honor," Helen says. "How is the State supposed to have a fair trial when we have a circus sideshow going on every fifteen minutes?"

"You know she's right, Counselor," the judge replies.

"I'm going to ask for a mistrial, Your Honor," I say.

"You can't when it's your client causing the problems, Mr. Bond. Surely you know that."

"Right," I mutter.

"If there are any motions you two want to make, think hard before you make them. Mr. Bond, I will hear you with warning before we start."

I hurry out of chambers before Helen can say anything that infuriates me even more. And then, just when I think things can't get any worse, I find Rich Matson chatting up my client. "I was just keeping him company until you got here," Matson explains.

"Yeah, I bet."

He ignores me, turning to Jacob instead. "Hey," the detective says. "Good luck."

I wait until I can't hear his footsteps anymore. "What the hell was that all about?"

"Nothing. We were talking about cases."

"Oh great. Because that was *such* a good idea the last time you two sat down for a chat." I fold my arms. "Listen, Jacob, you need to straighten out. If you don't behave, you're going to jail. Period."

"If *I* don't behave?" he says. *"Schwing!"*

"You can't possibly be old enough to remember *Wayne's World.* And regardless, I'm not the one who's the defendant. I'm totally serious, Jacob. If you pull another stunt like that, the prosecution is going to throw your ass in jail or else declare a mistrial, and that means doing this all over again."

"You promised that we'd adjourn at four o'clock."

"You're right. But in a courtroom the judge is God, and God wanted to stay late. So I don't care if we're here till four in the morning, or if Judge Cuttings announces that we're all going to get up and do the hokey pokey. You are going to park your butt in that chair next to me and not say a damn thing."

"Will you tell the jury why I did it?" Jacob asks.

"Why *did* you do it?"

I know better than to ask that. But at this point I am not thinking of perjury. I am thinking that Jacob and I need to be on the same page once and for all.

"Because I couldn't leave her," he says, as if this should be obvious.

My jaw drops. Before I can ask another question—*Did she spurn you? Did you try to kiss her, and did she struggle too much? Did you hold her too close, and suffocate her accidentally?*—a bailiff comes into the holding cell area. "They're ready for you."

I motion to the bailiff to open the cell. We are the last ones into the courtroom, with the exception of the judge and jury. Emma's eyes go straight to her son. "Is everything okay?"

But before I can fill her in, the jury files in and the judge returns. "Counsel," he says, settling himself on the bench. "Approach." Helen and I move closer. "Mr. Bond, have you spoken with your client?"

"Yes, Your Honor, and there will be no further outbursts."

"I can hardly contain myself," Judge Cuttings says. "You may continue, then."

Knowing what I know now, that insanity defense is looking stronger and stronger. I just hope the jury got that message, loud and clear. "The defense rests," I announce.

"What?" Jacob explodes behind me. "No it *doesn't*!"

I close my eyes and start to count to ten, because I'm pretty sure it's not a good idea to kill your client in front of an entire jury, and then a paper airplane sails over my shoulder. It's one of Jacob's notes, which I unfold:

I WANT TO TALK.

I turn around. "Absolutely not."

"Is there a problem, Mr. Bond?" the judge asks.

"No, Your Honor," I reply, at the same moment Jacob says "Yes."

Scrambling, I face the judge again. "We need a sensory break."

"We've been in session for ten seconds!" Helen argues.

"Do you rest, Mr. Bond?" asks Judge Cuttings. "Or is there more?"

"There's more," Jacob says. "It's my turn to talk. And if I want to take the stand, you have to let me."

"You're not taking the stand," Emma insists.

"You, Ms. Hunt, do not have leave to speak! Am I the only person here who knows we're in a court of law?" Judge Cuttings roars. "Mr. Bond, put on your final witness."

"I'd like a brief recess—"

"I bet you would. I'd like to be in Nevis instead of here, but neither one of us is going to get what we want," the judge snaps.

Shaking my head, I walk Jacob to the witness stand. I am so angry I can barely see straight. Jacob will tell the jury the truth, like he's told me, and dig his own grave. If not with the substance of what he says then with the style: no matter what's been said up to this point, no matter what's been said by the witnesses, all the jury is going to remember is this awkward boy who speaks in bursts of words and fidgets and doesn't register appropriate emotion and can't look them in the eye—all traditional expressions of guilt. It doesn't matter what Jacob says; his demeanor will convict him before he even opens his mouth.

I open the gate for him so that he can step inside. "It's your funeral," I murmur.

"No," Jacob says. "It's my trial."

I can tell the moment he realizes that this wasn't such a great idea. He's been sworn in, and he swallows hard. His eyes are wide and dart all over the courtroom.

"Tell me what happens when you get nervous, Jacob," I say.

He licks his lips. "I walk on my toes, or bounce. Sometimes I flap or talk too fast or laugh even though it's not funny."

"Are you nervous now?"

"Yes."

"Why?"

He pulls his lips back in a smile. "Because everyone's looking at me."

"Is that all?"

"Also the lights are too bright. And I don't know what you're going to say next."

Whose goddamn fault is that? I think. "Jacob, you told the court that you wanted to talk."

"Yes."

"What do you want to tell this jury?"

Jacob hesitates. "The truth," he says.

Jacob

There's blood all over the floor and she is lying in it. She doesn't answer even though I call her name. I know I need to move her so I lift her up and take her into the hallway and when I do there is even more blood that comes from her nose and her mouth. I try not to think about the fact that I am touching her body and she is naked; it isn't like in the movies where the girl is beautiful and the boy is backlit; it's just skin against skin and I am embarrassed for her because she doesn't even know she isn't wearing clothes. I don't want to get blood on the towels so I wipe her face with toilet paper and flush it.

There is underwear on the floor and a bra and sweatpants and a shirt. I put the bra on first and I know how because I watch HBO and have seen them being taken off; all I have to do is reverse it. The underwear I don't understand because there is writing on one side and I don't know if it's the front or the back, so I just put it on her any which way. Then the shirt and the sweatpants and finally socks and Ugg boots, which are the hardest because she cannot press down with her feet.

I pick her up over my shoulder—she is heavier than I thought she would be—and try to get her down the stairs. There is a turn on the landing and I trip over my feet and we both fall. I land on top of her and when I roll her over her tooth is knocked out. I know it didn't hurt her but it still makes me feel like I am going to be sick. The bruises and the broken nose for some reason weren't nearly as bad as seeing her with that missing front tooth.

I sit her up in an armchair. *Wait here,* I say, and then I laugh out loud because she can't hear me. Upstairs I mop up the blood with more toilet paper, the whole roll. It is still smeary and wet. In the laundry closet I find bleach and I pour it on the floor and use another roll of toilet paper to dry it all off.

It does cross my mind that I might get caught, and that is when I decide not just to clean up but to make a crime scene that leads in a different direction. I pack a bag of extra clothes and take her toothbrush. I type a note and stick it in the mailbox. I put on a pair of boots too big to be hers and walk around outside, cut the screen, put the kitchen knife in the dishwasher, and turn on the quick cycle. I want to be obvious, because Mark is not too smart.

I make sure to wipe away the footprints on the porch and the driveway.

Inside, I put the backpack on my shoulders and make sure I am not forgetting anything. I know I should leave the stools knocked over and the CDs scattered on the living room floor but I just can't. So I pick up the stools and the mail and then I organize the CDs the way I think she would have liked them.

I try to carry her into the woods but she gets heavier with every step so instead after a while I have to drag her. I want her to be somewhere where I know she won't have to sit in wind or rain or snow. I like the culvert because I can get to it from the highway, instead of going past her house.

I think about her even when I'm not here;

even when I know the police are all looking and I could so easily be distracted by tracking their progress or lack thereof. That's why when I come back to visit I bring my quilt. It was something I always liked and I think if she could talk she would have been really proud of me for wrapping her in it. *Good job, Jacob,* she would have said. *You're thinking of someone else for a change.*

Little did she know, that was *all* I was thinking about.

When I'm done the courtroom is so quiet I can hear the pop and hiss of the radiator and the building stretching its beams. I look at Oliver, and at my mother. I expect them to be pretty pleased, because everything should make sense now. I can't read their faces, though, or the faces of the jury. One woman is crying; and I don't know if she's sad because I was talking about Jess or because she's happy to finally know what really happened.

I'm not nervous now. If you want to know, I've got so much adrenaline in my bloodstream I could probably run to Bennington and back. I mean, *holy cow,* I have just outlined how I set up a crime scene with a dead body after successfully fooling the police into believing it was a kidnapping attempt. I have connected all the dots that the State raised as evidence in this trial. It is like the best episode of *CrimeBusters* ever, and I am the star.

"Mr. Bond?" the judge prompts.

Oliver clears his throat. He rests one hand on the railing of the witness stand, looking away from me. "All right, Jacob. You told us a lot about what you did after Jess's death. But you haven't told us about how she died."

"There isn't much to tell," I say.

Suddenly, I realize where I've seen that expression on everyone's face in this courtroom. It's the one on Mimi Scheck's face, and Mark Maguire's face, and everyone else who thinks that they have absolutely nothing in common with me.

I start to get that burning sensation in my stomach, the one that comes when I realize too late I might have done something that actually wasn't such a great idea.

And then, Oliver throws me a lifeline. "Jacob, are you sorry for killing Jess?"

I smile widely. "No," I say. "That's what I've been trying to tell you all along."

Oliver

Here's the bittersweet thing: Jacob has made himself look more insane than I ever could with a witness's testimony. Then again, he's also made himself look like a ruthless murderer.

Jacob is once again sitting at the defense table, holding his mother's hand. Emma is white as a sheet, and I can't blame her. After listening to Jacob's testimony—a detailed description in his own words of how to clean up after a mess of your own making—I find myself in the same position.

"Ladies and gentlemen," I begin, "there's been a lot of evidence produced here about how Jess Ogilvy died. We're not disputing that evidence. But if you've been paying attention at this trial, you also know that you can't judge this book by its cover. Jacob is a young man with Asperger's syndrome, a neurological disorder that precludes him from having empathy for others in the same way you or I might. When he talks about what he did with Jess's body, and at Jess's residence, he doesn't see his involvement in a horrific murder. Instead, as you've heard, he takes pride in the fact that he set up a complete crime scene, a crime scene worthy of inclusion in a journal, just like an episode of *CrimeBusters.* I'm not going to ask you to excuse him for Jess Ogilvy's death—we grieve with her parents for that loss, and do not seek to diminish the tragedy in any way. However, I am going to ask you to take the information you've been given about Jacob and his disorder, so that when you question whether he was criminally responsible at the time of Jess's death—whether he understood right from wrong in that moment the way you understand right from wrong—you will have no choice but to answer *no.*"

I walk toward the jury. "Asperger's is a tough nut to crack. You've heard a lot about it these past few days . . . and I bet you've thought, *So what?* Not being comfortable in new situations, wanting to do things the same way every day, finding it hard to make new friends—these are struggles we've all faced from time to time. Yet none of these traits impair *our* ability to make judgments, and none of *us* are on trial for murder. You might be thinking that Jacob doesn't fit your impression of a person with a diagnosable neurological disorder. He's smart, he doesn't look *crazy* in the colloquial sense of the word. So how can you be certain that Asperger's syndrome is a valid neurological disorder, and not just the latest label du jour for a kid with problems? How can you be sure Asperger's provides an explanation of his behavior at the moment a crime was committed—instead of just a fancy legal excuse?"

I smile. "Well, I offer an example from Supreme Court Justice Potter Stewart. In the fifties and sixties the Court was involved in deciding a number of obscenity cases. Since obscenity isn't protected under the First Amendment, they had to determine whether a series of pornographic films met the legal definition of obscenity, and so they'd screen them. Every week, on what was known as Obscenity Tuesday, the justices watched these films and rendered decisions. It was in *Jacobellis v. Ohio* that Justice Stewart became legendary in the legal field for saying that hard-core pornography was hard to define but that—and I quote—'I know it when I see it.'"

I turn to Jacob. "I know it when I see it," I repeat. "You haven't just listened to experts and seen medical files and seen forensic evidence—you've also watched and heard Jacob. And based on that alone, it must be clear to you that he's not just a kid with a few personality quirks. He's a kid who doesn't communicate particularly well and whose thoughts are often jumbled. He talks in a monotone and doesn't show a great deal of emotion, even when it seems warranted. Yet he was brave enough to stand up in front of you and try to defend himself against one of the most serious charges a young man like him could ever face. What he said—and how he said it—might have been upsetting to you. Shocking, even. But that's because a person with Asperger's—a person like Jacob—is not your typical witness.

"I didn't want my client to testify. I'll be honest with you. I didn't think that he could do it. When you're a witness in a trial, you have to practice saying things in a way that works to make your case. You have to present yourself in a manner that is sympathetic to the jury. And I knew Jacob could not—and would not—do that. Hell, I could barely get him to wear a tie here . . . I certainly couldn't make him express remorse, or even sadness. I couldn't tell him what he should and shouldn't say in front of you. To Jacob, that would have been lying. And to Jacob, telling the truth is a rule that has to be followed."

I look at the jurors. "What you have here is a kid who isn't working the system, because he's physically and psychologically incapable of working the system. He doesn't know how to play to your sympathies. He doesn't know what will help or hurt his chances of acquittal. He simply wanted to tell you his side of the story—so he did. And that's how you know that Jacob's not a criminal trying to squeak through a loophole. That's how you know that his Asperger's can and did and still does impair his judgment at any given moment. Because any other defendant—any *ordinary* defendant—would have known better than to tell you what Jacob did.

"You and I know, ladies and gentlemen, that the legal system in America works very well if you happen to communicate a certain way, a way Jacob *doesn't*. And yet everyone in this country is entitled to a fair trial—even people who communicate differently from the way that works best in court." I take a deep breath. "Maybe for justice to be done, then, in Jacob's case, we simply need people who are willing to listen a little more closely."

As I take my seat again, Helen stands up. "When I was a little girl I remember asking my mother why, instead of saying *toilet paper* on the wrapper, it said *bath tissue.* And you know what my mom told me? You can call it whatever you want, but all the words in the world can't dress up what it is. This isn't a case about a young man who has a hard time holding a conversation, or making friends, or eating something other than blue Jell-O on Wednesday—"

Friday, I mentally correct. Jacob reaches for his pencil and starts to write a note, but before he can, I pluck the pencil out of his hand and slip it into my coat pocket.

"It's a case about a boy who committed a cold-blooded murder and then, using his brains and his fascination with crime scenes, tried to cover his tracks. I don't contest that Jacob has Asperger's syndrome. I don't expect any of you to contest it, either. But that doesn't absolve him of responsibility for this brutal, vicious killing. You've heard from the crime scene investigators who went to the house and found traces of Jess's blood all over the bathroom floor. You've heard Jacob himself say that he washed it away with bleach and then flushed the toilet paper away. Why? Not because there's a rule about where toilet paper goes when you're done with it . . . but instead, because he didn't want anyone to know he had cleaned up that mess. He told you, ladies and gentlemen, about how he set up that entire crime scene, and how much thought he put into it. He deliberately tried to lead police down the wrong trail, to make them think Jess had been kidnapped. He slit the screen and used Mark Maguire's boots to leave footprints, to purposefully suggest that someone else was responsible for the crime. He dragged Jess's body the length of three football fields and left it outside, so that it would be harder for people to find. And when he grew tired of playing his own little game of *Crime-Busters,* he took Jess's cell phone and dialed 911. Why? Not because it was easier for him to interface with a dead body than a live one but because it was all part of Jacob Hunt's perverse plan to selfishly discard Jess Ogilvy's life in order to allow him to play forensic detective."

She faces the jury. "Mr. Bond can call this whatever he wants, but that doesn't change what it is: a young man who committed a brutal murder and who actively, over a period of days, covered it up with careful clues to mislead the police. That, ladies and gentlemen, is the MO of a calculating killer—not a kid with Asperger's syndrome."

Emma

From the archives of Auntie Em:

> **Dear Auntie Em,**
>   **What do you do if all signs point to the fact that the world as you know it is going to come to a crashing halt?**
> **Sincerely,**
> **HumptyDumptyWasPushed**

> **Dear Humpty,**
> **HELP!**
> **Love,**
> **Auntie Em**

Three days later, the jury is still deliberating.

We have settled into a routine: in the morning, Oliver brings Thor over for breakfast. Jacob takes him into the yard to throw a ball while Henry and Theo slowly animate themselves with coffee. Henry's been teaching Theo C# programming to create his own computer game, which has fascinated Theo to no end. In the afternoons, Oliver and I play Scrabble, and every now and then Jacob will call out obscure, legitimate words from the couch where he's watching *Crime-Busters*: *Qua! Za!* We don't turn on the news or read the paper, because all they talk about is Jacob.

We are not allowed to leave the house for two reasons: technically, Jacob is still under arrest, and we must be in a spot where we can get to the courthouse in twenty minutes when the jury returns. It is still strange to me to turn a corner in my own house and find Henry there—I expected him to leave by now, to come up with the excuse that one of his daughters has strep or his wife has to visit a dying aunt—but Henry insists he's here until the verdict comes back. Our conversation is full of clichés, but at least it is a conversation. *I'm making up for lost time,* he says. *Better late than never.*

We've become a family. An unorthodox one, and one cobbled together by someone else's tragedy, but after years of being the only parent in this house, I will take what I can get.

Later, while the boys are getting ready for bed, Oliver and I take Thor for a walk around the block before he goes back to his apartment over the pizza place. We talk about the horse that stepped on his ankle and broke it. We talk about how I used to want to be a writer. We talk about the trial.

We don't talk about us.

"Is it good or bad if the jury can't reach a verdict?"

"Good, I think. It probably means someone's holding out on a conviction."

"What happens next?"

"If Jacob's convicted," Oliver says, as Thor runs back and forth in front of us, lacing up the path, "he'll go to prison. I don't know if it will be the same one he was in. If he's found not guilty by reason of insanity, the judge will probably want another psychiatric evaluation."

"But then he'll come home?"

"I don't know," Oliver admits. "We'll get Ava Newcomb and Dr. Murano to put together an outpatient treatment plan, but it depends on Judge Cuttings. He could weigh the fact that Jacob committed murder and decide that he can't ignore that, and isolate him from the rest of the community."

He has told me this before, but it never seems to sink in. "In a state mental hospital," I finish. As we reach my driveway again, I stop walking, and Oliver stops, too, his hands in the pockets of his jacket. "I fought my whole life to have Jacob treated like ordinary kids in regular school, with regular programming," I say, "and now his only chance of staying out of jail means playing the Asperger's card."

"I honestly don't know what's going to happen," Oliver says. "But it's better to be prepared."

"I haven't told Jacob yet."

He looks down at his shoes. "Maybe you should."

As if we have conjured him, the door opens and Jacob stands in silhouette in his pajamas. "I'm waiting for you to say good night," he tells me.

"I'll be right there."

Jacob looks at Oliver, impatient. "Well?"

"Well what?"

"Will you just kiss her good-bye already?"

My jaw drops with surprise. Since my fight with Jacob, Oliver and I have been careful to steer clear of each other in his company. But now Oliver takes me into his arms. "I don't have to be asked twice," he says, and he presses his lips against mine.

When Jacob was little, I used to sneak into his bedroom after midnight and sit on a rocking chair next to his bed so that I could watch him sleep. There was a wonderful magic brush that painted him when he was unconscious. In his bed, I could not tell that the hand curled under the covers was the same one that had stimmed fiercely that afternoon when a girl at the park came into the sandbox where he was happily playing alone. I couldn't tell that those eyes, closed, winced when I asked him to look right at me. I couldn't watch him, easy and relaxed in his dreams, and think this was the same boy who could not remember the sequence of words to ask the lunch lady for apple juice instead of milk.

When Jacob slept, the slate was wiped clean,

and he could have been any child. Any ordinary child.

Instead, during his waking hours, he was extraordinary. And that truly was the definition for him—outside the perimeter of the norm. At some point in the English language, that word had acquired positive connotations. Why hadn't Asperger's?

You could say *I* was different. I had willingly traded my own future for Jacob's, giving up whatever fame or fortune I might have achieved in order to make sure his life was a better one. I had let every relationship slide, with the exception of the one I'd built with Jacob. I had made choices that other women would not have made. At best that made me a fierce, fighting mother; at worst, it made me single-minded. And yet, if I walked into a crowded room, people did not mystically part from me as if there was an invisible magnetic field, a polarizing reaction between my body and theirs. People did not turn to their friends and groan, *Oh, God, save me—she's heading this way.* People didn't roll their eyes behind my back when I was talking. Jacob might have acted strangely, but he'd never been cruel.

He simply didn't have the self-awareness for it.

Now, I sink down on that same chair I used to sit on years ago, and I watch Jacob sleep again. He isn't a child anymore. His face has the planes of that of an adult; his hands are strong and his shoulders sculpted. I reach out and brush his hair back from where it has fallen over his forehead. In his sleep, Jacob stirs.

I do not know what kind of life I'd have had without Jacob, but I don't want to know. If he hadn't been autistic, I could not love him any more than I already do. And even if he is convicted, I could not love him any less.

I lean down, just like I used to, and I kiss him on the forehead. It is the age-old, time-honored way for mothers to test for fever, to give a blessing, to say good night.

So why does it feel like I'm saying good-bye?

Theo

My sixteenth birthday is today, but I'm not expecting much. We're still waiting, six days later, for the jury to reach a verdict. I'm guessing, actually, that my mother won't even remember—which is why I am struck speechless when she yells *"Breakfast"* and I come downstairs with my hair still wet from my shower and there's a chocolate cake with a candle in it.

Granted, it's Brown Thursday and it's no doubt gluten-free, but beggars can't be choosers.

"Happy birthday, Theo," my mother

says, and she starts the round of singing. My dad, my brother, and Oliver all join in. I have a big, fat smile on my face. As far as I know, my father has never been to one of my birthday parties, unless you count the minute I was delivered in the hospital, and that wasn't really a party, I imagine.

Was it worth it? A little voice inside me curls like the smoke from the candle. *Was it worth all this to get a family like the ones you used to spy on?*

My mother puts her arm around my shoulders. "Make a wish, Theo," she says.

A year ago, *this* is exactly what I would have wished for. What I *did* wish for, with or without the cake. But there's something in her voice, like a string made of steel, that suggests there's a right answer here, one collective heart's desire for all of us.

Which just happens to rest in the hands of twelve jurors.

I close my eyes and blow out the candle, and everyone claps. My mother starts to cut slices from the cake and gives me the first one. "Thanks," I say.

"I hope you like it," my mother replies. "And I hope you like this."

She hands me an envelope. Inside is a note, handwritten:

Your debt is paid.

I think of my crazy trip to California to find my father, of how much money those tickets had cost, and for a second I can't talk.

"But," she says, "if you do that again, I'll kill you."

I laugh, and she wraps her arms around me from behind and kisses the top of my head.

"Hey, there's more." My father hands me an envelope, which has a cheesy "To My Son" Hallmark card inside, and forty bucks.

"You can start saving for a faster router," he says.

"That's awesome!"

Then Oliver hands me a package wrapped in Bounty paper towels. "It was this or a pizza box," he explains.

I shake it. "Is it a calzone?"

"Give me a little credit here," Oliver says.

I rip it open and find the Vermont Driver's Manual.

"After this trial's over, I thought you and I could make an appointment at the DMV and finally get that learner's permit."

I have to look down at the table, because if I don't, everyone's going to realize I'm totally about to cry. I remember how, when I was little, my mother would read us these ridiculous fairy tales where frogs turned into princes and girls woke up from comas with a single kiss. I never bought into any of that crap. But who knows? Maybe I was wrong. Maybe a person's life can change in an instant after all.

"Wait," Jacob says. Until now, he's been watching, his face bisected by a smile—and this is an improvement. At all my birthday parties growing up, the unwritten rule was that Jacob had to help me blow out the candles. It was easier to share my moment than to have him ruin the festivities with a meltdown. "I've got a present for you, too, Theo."

I don't think, in all the years that I've been alive, Jacob's ever gotten me a present. I don't think he's ever gotten *anyone* a present, unless you count the perfume I pick out at CVS for Christmas and give to my mother, after putting both my name and Jacob's on the tag. Giving gifts just isn't on my brother's radar.

"What's he got?" Oliver murmurs, as Jacob hightails it upstairs.

"I don't know," my mother answers.

A minute later, Jacob's back. He is holding a stuffed duck he used to sleep with when he was small. "Open it," he says, holding it out.

I take it and turn it over in my hands. There's no wrapping; nothing to be opened. "Um," I say, laughing a little. "How?"

Jacob turns the duck upside down and pulls on a loose thread. It unravels a little, and some of the stuffing comes out in a clump. I poke my finger into the hole and feel something smooth and hard.

"Is *that* where my Tupperware went?" my mother says when I pull it out of the chest cavity of the duck. Inside, there's something I cannot quite make out. I open the lid and find myself staring at a pink iPod Nano. Gingerly, I pick it up, knowing even before I turn it over that Jess Ogilvy's name is etched into the metal on the back.

"Where did you get that?" my mother whispers, from somewhere on the other end of the vacuum I've fallen into.

"You wanted it, didn't you?" Jacob says, still excited. "You dropped it on the way out of her house that day."

I can barely move my lips. "What are you talking about?"

"I already told you—I know you were there. I saw the tread from the bottom of your sneakers, the same ones I used here for my fake crime scene. And I knew you'd been taking other stuff from other houses—"

"What!" my mother says.

"—I saw the video games in your room." Jacob beams at me. "At Jess's, I cleaned up for you, so no one would know what you did. And it worked, Theo. No one ever found out that you killed her."

My mother gasps.

"What the hell is going on?" Oliver asks.

"I didn't kill her!" I say. "I didn't even know she lived there. I didn't think anyone was home. I was going to look around, maybe take a CD or two, but then I heard water running upstairs and I peeked in. She was naked. She was naked and she saw me. I freaked out, and she got out of the shower and she slipped. She hit her face on the edge of the sink, and that's when I ran. I was afraid she'd catch me." I can't breathe; and I'm sure that my heart's turned to clay in my chest. "She was alive when I left, in the bathroom. And then all of a sudden the news says she's dead and her body's found outside. I knew I wasn't the one who moved her out there . . . someone else had, someone who probably murdered her. I thought maybe she told Jacob about me, when he came for his lesson. And they had a fight about it. And that Jacob . . . I don't know. I don't know what I thought."

"You didn't kill Jess," my mother says.

I shake my head, numb.

My mother looks at Jacob. "And *you* didn't kill Jess."

"I just moved her body." He rolls his eyes. "I've been telling you that the whole time."

"Jacob," Oliver asks, "was Jess alive when you got to the house?"

"No! But I saw that Theo had been there, so I did what was right."

"Why didn't you call your mother, or an ambulance?" my father asks. "Why would you set up a crime scene to cover up for Theo?"

Jacob stares right at me. It hurts; it actually hurts. "House rules," he says simply. "Take care of your brother; he's the only one you've got."

"You have to do something," my mother says to Oliver. "It's new evidence. Theo can testify—"

"He might be implicated or charged with withholding—"

"You have to do something," my mother repeats.

Oliver is already reaching for his coat. "Let's go," he says.

Jacob and I are the last ones out of the kitchen. The cake is still sitting on the table, along with my other presents. It already looks like a museum exhibit, untouched. You'd never guess that, five minutes ago, we were celebrating. "Jacob?" My brother turns around. "I don't know what to say."

He awkwardly pats my shoulder. "Don't worry," Jacob replies. "That happens to me all the time."

Jacob

Today is April 15. It is the day, in 1912, that the *Titanic* sank. It's the day, in 1924, that Rand McNally published its first road atlas. It's the day, in 1947, that Jackie Robinson first played for the Brooklyn Dodgers. It is also the birthday of Leonardo da Vinci, author Henry James, the girl who plays Hermione in the Harry Potter movies, and my brother Theo.

I used to be jealous of Theo's birthday. On mine, December 21, the most impressive thing that happened was the explosion of Pan Am Flight 103 over Lockerbie, in 1988. Frank Zappa was born on my birthday, but honestly, that doesn't compare to da Vinci, does it? Plus, my birthday is on the *shortest* day of the year. I've always felt like I'd gotten shafted. Probably Frank Zappa did, too.

Today, though, I was not jealous of Theo's birthday. In fact, I couldn't wait to give him the present I'd been keeping for him.

Oliver says that, at the courthouse, Theo and I will both have a chance to talk. Apparently, it is not enough for the jury to know, as the medical examiner testified, that Jess's facial bruises were caused by a basilar skull fracture in the periorbital region, blood dissecting along fascial planes and creating the appearance of contusion. Or in other words, what looked like a girl who was beaten might very well have been a girl who simply fell down and hit her own head. Apparently, the jury—and the judge—need to hear Theo and me explain the same exact thing in different words.

I guess I'm not the only one who doesn't always understand what's been said.

My mother is driving, with Oliver in the passenger seat, and I'm in the back with Theo. My father is at our house, in case the court happens to call in the twenty minutes it takes for us to get there in person. Every time the car goes over a frost heave it makes me think of jumping on a mattress, something Theo and I used to do together when we were little. We used to believe that, if we got enough bounce going, we could reach the ceiling, but I don't think we ever did.

After all those years of Theo sticking up for me, I finally got to be the big brother. I did the right thing. I don't know why that's so difficult for these jurors to comprehend.

Theo opens his fist; inside it is the pink iPod that used to be Jess's. From his pocket, he takes out a white tangle of wires—his earbuds. He sticks them in his ears.

To all of those experts who said that because I have Asperger's I can't empathize:

So there.

People who can't empathize surely don't try to protect the people they love, even if it means having to go to court.

Suddenly Theo pulls one of the earbuds out and offers it to me. "Listen," he says, and I do. Jess's music is a piano concerto that swirls behind my eyes. I bend my head toward my brother so that the wires reach, so that, for the rest of the journey, we stay connected.

CASE 11: MY BROTHER'S KEEPER

Theo Hunt had been engaging in risky behavior. His Peeping Tom excursions had escalated into entering empty homes and taking souvenirs—electronic games and MP3 devices. On the afternoon of January 12, 2010, he entered the home of a local college professor. Unbeknownst to him, the house sitter—graduate student Jess Ogilvy—was upstairs showering. He made himself a cup of tea and then heard noises overhead and went to investigate.

It's hard to know who was more surprised—Ogilvy, who found a strange boy in her bathroom while she was stark naked, or Theo Hunt, who realized that he knew the girl in the shower, who tutored his older brother, Jacob. Ogilvy reached for a towel and exited the stall, but she stumbled, striking her head on the edge of the sink. As she struggled to her feet again, Theo Hunt ran—overturning the CD rack, several stools, and the mail on the counter during his speedy exit.

Two hours later Theo's brother, Jacob, arrived for his weekly tutoring session. A student of forensic science, he was surprised to notice a familiar footprint on the porch—the Vans sneaker tread that matched a pair belonging to his brother. Upon entering the unlocked house, Jacob found it in disarray. He called out but received no answer. Further investigation upstairs led to the discovery of Jess Ogilvy lying naked in a pool of blood.

Making the assumption that his brother was involved in her death—possibly during an altercation in the midst of a botched robbery—Jacob proceeded to alter the crime scene so that it would point away from Theo. He cleaned up and dressed the body and moved it downstairs (stumbling once on the staircase, which resulted in Ogilvy's front tooth being knocked out postmortem). Using bleach, he cleaned up the bathroom to remove blood evidence. He picked up the overturned furniture and CDs and mail and proceeded to create a crime scene that might have been interpreted by authorities at first glance as a kidnapping, and at second glance as a cover-up perpetrated by Ogilvy's stupid jerk of a boyfriend, Mark Maguire. In order to do this, Hunt had to put himself in the mind of a borderline idiot who might attempt (poorly) to make a murder scene look like a kidnapping. He packed some of Ogilvy's clothes and toiletries in a backpack but made sure that they were not clothes routinely worn by Ogilvy, which someone less astute (like Mark Maguire) would never have realized. He left a typed note—allegedly from Ogilvy herself—asking for the mail to be temporarily stopped, as if she had decided to take a trip. He then cut the screen in the kitchen with a butcher knife—a red herring for forced entry. Finally, he walked below this screen outside wearing Mark Maguire's boots, so that the police could trace this "cover-up" back to Ogilvy's boyfriend. Then Hunt carried Ogilvy's body to a culvert several hundred yards from the house and waited for investigators to piece together the information he'd left them.

Jacob Hunt neglected to realize, at the time, that he might be implicating himself in the murder. He neglected to consider that the scene he'd come across (at worst, murder at his brother's hand, and at best, a death accidentally caused by Theo) might instead be a death by natural causes: a slippery floor, a skull fracture, and a hematoma. None of this, however, really matters.

In the years afterward, Jacob's motive for restructuring the crime scene and moving the body was hotly debated. Some felt that, as there can be crimes of passion, there can be crime scenes of brotherly love. Others felt that Jacob's fixation on forensic science came into play: he wanted to experience the thrill a murderer might feel, waiting for the authorities to figure out the trail he'd left behind.

Think whatever you want. The only thing that really matters is this:

I'd do it all over again.